The Life of the World to Come

The Life of the World to Come

A Novel

Joseph Bathanti

The University of South Carolina Press

Published by the University of South Carolina Press
Columbia, South Carolina 29208

www.sc.edu/uscpress

Manufactured in the United States of America

24 23 22 21 20 19 18 17 16 15 10 9 8 7 6 5 4 3 2 1

Library of Congress Cataloging-in-Publication Data

Bathanti, Joseph.
The life of the world to come : a novel / Joseph Bathanti.
pages cm
ISBN 978-1-61117-453-3 (hardbound : alk. paper) — ISBN 978-1-61117-454-0 (ebook)
I. Title.
PS3602.A89L54 1014
813'.6—dc23
2014011488

This book was printed on recycled paper with 30 percent postconsumer waste content.

I look for the resurrection of the dead
and the life of the world to come.

THE NICENE CREED

Sometimes life takes hold of one, carries the body along,
accomplishes one's history, and yet is not real,
but leaves oneself as it were slurred over.

D. H. LAWRENCE, *Sons and Lovers*

Chapter 1

We live, Crow and I, in an attic apartment at 302½ Lark Terrace. Across the front of our duplex pants Andromeda Boulevard, a six-laned juggernaut, choked on cars, that dead-ends east in the Atlantic Ocean and west in the Great Smoky Mountains.

On the other side of Andromeda hulks Memorial Stadium, County Detox, and MacKenzie Gault Home for Unwed Mothers. From our bedroom window we look down and make out the fallow hash marks fretted across the floor of the stadium, the perimeter lights doming Detox; and, beyond, maybe a mile and a half straight down 7th Street, the downtown lights of Queen's three skyscrapers.

At odd times, a man dressed solely in the clothes of a woman, sprawls on the bench on the sidewalk below us, staring at the traffic like some maudlin jilted belle, still half-hoping her beloved will walk out of the indifferent night, sit next to her, and ask for her hand. He wears a shawl over his baggy dress, and a hat with a veil that drapes his dark heavy brow. In such raiment, he looks more than anything like a heart-broken man. As if he is a visitor, someone who has dropped from the sky. Like me. Like Crow. And like the occasional fallen angels from Gault, fey little girls impossibly enormous with child: pony tails and tattoos, a dreadful glimmer in their eyes; later with strollers, still wearing ballooned hatching smocks, aged and weighted thirty years with their lying in.

There is no terrace to our terrace, but rather a precipitous drop through beggar-lice and poison ivy to a tar alley shrouded in wild Mimosas. A little haven for all stripe of collaboration with the night. The machinations of Crow and me occasionally included, her favorite tree the Mimosa, her favorite time once the sun disappears—I there essentially to abet her whims.

Beyond the alley sprawls an abandoned little league field, the diamond given over to tares and winos; then a long row of tiny identical ramshackle white mill houses built, judging by their similarity, on the same day in the thirties when Queen couldn't have been much more than a wayfarer's respite on the way to Atlanta or even Miami.

When I arrived by accident in Queen, on the first day of 1975, I knew patently nothing of the South other than a mythic vision nurtured, I'm ashamed to say, by *Gone with the Wind:* temperate weather year-round and wild poinsettias, antebellum glory, a time-warp where feudal gentility still reigned. I had seen the movie twice before I met Crow: once at the behest of my mother, who clung to it as the final document on vanished noblesse oblige, and as she watched it sobbed into Kleenex pulled from the sleeves of her housecoat; and once to please a woman with whom I was achingly in love, who also whimpered breathtakingly throughout the movie, a woman I lost and who is, more or less, the reason I find myself in Queen.

The third time I saw *Gone with the Wind* was with Crow, entangled with her on our thrift couch; and it was in front of that epic film that I was tempted to say, God forbid, "I love you," though I wonder now if the impulse was mere reflex prompted by simpering Scarlet in the arms of Clark Gable, with whom I then egotistically identified. Crow is no southern belle, though like Scarlet she is a spitfire and a bit of a femme fatale. I am hardly Clark Gable, a man who would have never found himself in my predicament—a man who, incidentally, shaved his armpits.

Of Queen, a small, but aspiring city, in the middle of North Carolina, not far from the border of South Carolina, I knew even less than I did about the Southland. I had never heard of Queen. By happenstance alone, it ended up the place where my stolen automobile stopped when its water pump ruptured and the engine melted. I buried the license plate and owner's card and left the car, a silver hatchback Vega with *Rosechild's Pharmacy* decaled on its doors, in a culvert off I-85; then shuffled along the frigid highway like the ruffian I appeared to be until I reached the Southern 500 truck stop and thumbed a ride into Queen proper.

In the parlance of what had been my former life, I was then as I am now a lammist, a fugitive, ironically, from both the law and a minor Sicilian racketeer named Felix Costa; and I'll go so far as to say from God as well. The only item of authenticity I toted with me when I had fled Pittsburgh just two days before was my broken heart. It sits on my chest, a dagger sliced into it, a spout of fire crowning it, like those famous likenesses of Jesus in which he points to His bloody smoldering breast and stares plaintively out from the icon's gilt border. It would have been apparent the first time Crow laid eyes on me: a young man's iconographic heart superimposed on his measly jacket, a fellow who looked like he hadn't seen to himself in a bit, a troubled, fatigued, unshaven, darkly handsome mug and a busted bloody hand.

My mother had habitually instructed me to cross to the other side of the street when I encountered a shady lot like myself. Crow, however, was undaunted. If anything, my pensive seediness tithed her to me the morning I lurched into The Tea Rose, a little café in the Clarence Pfeiffer Hotel on Tyrone Street in downtown Queen, where she was working breakfast. The Pfeiffer had opened in 1913 and hadn't been tended to since. Nevertheless, it insisted doggedly on its haunted vanished past: the columned veranda, chipping mansard roof, high chandeliered ceilings, an impervious flaking grandeur—imposing and maudlin at once. Streamers and bunting, a listing glittering sign, *Happy New Year,* dangled from scrolled cornices in the lobby. Dead Mylar ballons. Champagne corks. Confetti sparkled in the funereal carpet. The Pfeiffer was hanging on—its past and present existing simultaneously—like its residents, like me, like Crow.

I had glanced up from my window table and there she stood, clutching a pot of coffee in her right hand, the other on her hip, peering down at me with discreet impatience. Wide-set, tawny eyes, oddly pale and aglow like she might shoot something out of them and I'd disappear or vaporize. Unconsciously, I lifted my bad hand and put it on the table. Her skinny black eyebrows shot up. She turned over my cup, where it lay upside down on the saucer, and poured it full of coffee.

"What happened to you?" she asked.

My first thought had been to lie, but I realized it didn't matter. "Got in a fight."

"You a fighter?"

"Uh uh."

"What you get in a fight about?"

"Girl."

"Has anybody looked at that hand?"

"Yeah. It's fine."

She looked like a little girl and a grown woman at the same time. Hair inky as a St. Joseph's missal, too crazily black to not be dyed, and chopped an inch above her shoulders. Black lipstick. Mascara, Eyeliner. But nothing on her face. Completely undoctored. Not the slightest blush nor cream nor powder. Tallish. Spare as linguine. Like the other waitresses, she wore a full striped skirt, white shirt and black necktie. On her head sat an antique hat, like the kind my old aunts and grandmother sported in ancient photos, a black velvet crescent with a brace of black feathers swooping above one eye.

Her nametag said *Crow,* her surname, which she goes by, as if this lone black bird perched on carrion that no one likes or understands; but her Christian name is Ruby Lydia. In my neighborhood Ruby Lydia would have been the brazen runaway daughter of a screaming Calabrese widow. But in the South, such appellations, wistful, anachronistic, homespun—Ruby Lydia—are not uncommon.

Crow had rust in her voice: a little creak oiled by a softening declension every time she dipped into a vowel or chipped off a final consonant. Standing next to me when I chanced to look up in my first moments of exile, that morning at The Tea Rose in Queen, she was a stark and stunning apparition. Black and white—like an Escher chess board. An exaggeration. Starved and pasty as a Diane Arbus, and an inflection that drew me to her.

"What are you staring at?" she challenged.

I had been staring. At her skin. Pale isn't the word. It was white—the white of paper. And diaphanous, almost blue, if you stared long enough. Like you could see through it.

"I'm just trying to figure out what to order."

"Have you looked at the menu?"

"No, I haven't. Sorry."

"Get the Special. Ninety-nine cents. Including the coffee. How do you like your eggs?"

"I don't care."

She smiled and walked off. Two other tables were occupied. At one, a young black man talked to himself as he sliced open a biscuit, placed his little wheel of sausage between its steaming halves, then knifed jelly onto it from little plastic packets and bit into it. He wore a tennis sweater and had open before him a big book he seemed to be arguing with. His hair was large and wooly with wisps of cotton and confetti napped into it. Snaggled teeth, nearly horizontal, jagging out of a bushy beard.

At the table next to me a grand old white-haired couple, upright and elegant, in their best clothes, the sacred mien of a man and woman who had grown very old together. The women's powdery complexion, the man's shaved jaw translucent, their tremors and ministrations as they carefully ate their breakfast and spoke in somnolent soft whispers I would learn patrician southerners spoke—a sedated perfumed hush, both grand and grandiose at once.

I gaped into the streets of Queen, beyond the Pfeiffer's wide peeling columned veranda. Barely a soul on the streets, an occasional bus barreling by. Two or three taxis and a loner in a trench coat, with his newspaper, sitting on a bench across the street. An old rococo theatre: The Blackwelder. Two Marx

Brothers: *Duck Soup* and *A Day at the Races.* Christmas decorations blew from light poles. The public trash cans flowed over with the remnants of the previous night's revelry.

New Year's day, Solemnity of Mary, Mother of God, a Holy Day of Obligation for all good Catholics. Like my mother. But she hadn't made it out of bed. By then, my absence had been confirmed. Phil Rosechild had summoned the cops to his robbed pharmacy, and reported the company car stolen. He wouldn't have yet fingered me. That wouldn't have been in his best interest. He would not have uttered my name to the police nor to his wife nor daughter, my beloved Sterling. Mentioning my name would have linked me to a motive, and the hot lamp of interrogation would have instantly turned on him.

He'd keep mum, then be aghast and saddened at the news that I hadn't come home the night before when finally my mother broke down my father and badgered him into calling the Rosechilds, beside himself when I remained gone another day and then another and the circumstantial certainty pairing my disappearance with the crime could not be disputed: that his protégé, headed for Yale Law School, the young man he hoped would marry his daughter, whom he had trusted and privileged the way he would his own son, had broken into his store, stripped the register, stole a satchel full of prescription drugs and narcotics, and sped off with the company car. He'd know just how to handle the cops. His wife and his daughter—no idea that Phil was in the caper too, neck deep, that he had set me up—were left merely befuddled and crushed.

I liked Phil. Very much. He liked me too. He'd take it all back if he could. In truth, he wouldn't harm a hair on my head. He'd carry that regret to his grave—what had happened between us. He'd say it was his fault. But he'd never tell the truth about it. What I did for him, however, my disappearance, was a *deus ex machina.* He never wanted to see me again.

I hadn't been gone even twenty-four hours, but my bed in the house where I had grown up on Saint Marie Street remained untouched. No one, other than my old pal, Dave Mazzotti, a junky, a less than reliable source, had seen me since nightfall on New Year's Eve—by my lights, a lifetime ago. I peered myopically out the restaurant window as if clicking through a View-master, each notch on the carousel a doleful tableau, yet stalled on my father trying to cajole my mother into eleven o'clock mass.

"It'll make you feel better, Sylvia. C'mon. I'll lay your clothes out for you.

"No you go, George. Light a candle for Georgie."

"We don't need any candles, Sylvia. He stayed out all night. Big deal."

"Since when does he stay out all night?"

"It's happened before, Sylvia."

"Never all night without a phone call. I have a bad feeling about this, George. He hasn't been himself lately."

"New Years's Eve, Sylvia. He's twenty-one years old—with a girlfriend."

"He's mixed up in something. You think I'm kidding?"

"He's a young man in love."

"With who? That Jew girl? I don't want to hear about it. You don't know a goddam thing about love. If something's happened to him, I'll kill myself."

My mother takes to her bed, and my father, an aging laid-off steelworker, shuffles around the house, making coffee, readying the already immaculate house. Snow continues to fall, eleven inches already coating the city. My father sits with coffee at the bare kitchen table and stares out the window. Stares south not knowing he is looking straight at me in my window in the Pfeiffer Hotel while I peer north toward him. Five hundred miles apart, we remain invisible to each other.

In a few minutes, he'll go upstairs and check on his wife, try to coax her out of bed to watch the noon news, maybe have a sandwich and a cup of coffee. She's like a little baby. He can't blame his son for staying out all night. The snow is like seconds floating down, the accumulation, almost imperceptibly, so innocently, white and silent, of time building, but simultaneously dwindling, into minutes and years. My father's gaze falls on his hand curled around the coffee cup. The hand is a gnarled artifact, something that if not attached to him he would no longer remember. He stands, washes the cup in the sink, dries it and puts it back in the cupboard. Descends the stairs into the cellar, dons hat and heavy coat, boots, gloves, grabs the snow shovel, the rock salt. After he cleans and salts the walk, he'll hack the Chrysler out of the snow and ice, fire it up and let it run for a while—out of habit, to keep the battery charged, though there's not a place in the world he aims to go on this bitter day. On the front seat, as he is slipping his key into the ignition, he will discover the envelope labeled *Mom and Dad* and the eighteen hundred dollars—no note, no explanation whatsoever—that it contains.

In five minutes Crow laid breakfast in front of me, topped my coffee, and breezed off. A plate of fried eggs, sausage and a pool of steaming white cereal that lapped against them. I launched into the eggs and sausage. I couldn't even remember when I'd eaten last. When Crow returned a minute later with orange juice and a basket of biscuits, I had eaten everything but the cereal.

"You don't know what those are, do you?" she asked.

"I guess not."

"Where you from?"

Again, my impulse was to lie, but I didn't: "Pennsylvania."

"That explains it."

"I don't think I understand."

She had been smiling at me. She had a large voluptuous mouth, big white teeth, then the ellipsoid of black lipstick ovaling it. She stood on one foot, the other crooked to her leg, akimbo, forming a triangle. Like a flamingo.

"Those are grits," she said. "It's just corn. They originated with the Indians, like most everything else. They'd take dried corn and soak it, let the kernels dry out again, then crack them into particles and cook them in water. Poor folks' food. That's where that ugly slur *cracker* comes from."

I looked up at her as if she were speaking another language. I nodded. I had heard of grits, but I'd never seen them before.

"Please don't say it looks like Cream of Wheat. Like every other arrogant Yankee who walks in here. And don't you dare reach for the sugar."

She set down the juice and biscuits, sat in the chair next to me, and slid my plate with the untouched grits in front of her. "A little butter and salt," she explained, dousing the grits with salt, then sliding in a pat of butter. "Some people like pepper too. Like this." She dusted black the white puddle, whipped it all together with a fork, then slid the plate back to me.

I took a taste. Good. I bit off half a biscuit, drank the orange juice in one gulp.

"Restaurant grits aren't very good," said Crow. "The best are homemade."

My busted right hand seized up like a claw. The fork fell from it and clattered to the table. I picked it up in my left and gouged at the grits.

"Let me give you a hand there, hungry boy." Crow took the fork from my hand, and began feeding me: the grits, then bits of biscuit she buttered.

"What's the biggest tip you've ever gotten?" I asked.

"Yankees don't know how to tip."

I smiled and closed my eyes, felt my face unfreeze, as if at that moment I only realized I had driven out of the blizzard I'd traversed to get there, and was, at least for the moment, safe and warm. Crow was a mirage, but I didn't care.

Chapter 2

My bookie, Eugene Pappa, a good-natured guy fourteen years older than me, looked like all those guys who'd grown up down on Larimer Avenue: Frank Zappa with shorter hair. He was an electrician with a wife and two children, almost seven years into a thirty year mortgage on a brick home in Stanton Heights he'd remodeled himself. Anything to do with electricity, my parents, Big George and Sylvia Dolce, called Eugene, a lifelong friend. No matter what, he'd hurry over—around the back so he didn't track up the front rooms—kiss my mother, shake hands with my father and get to work on the problem. What's more, he never failed to give them a break on the price.

My dad, a steelworker, admired Eugene. Called him a *working fool.* When Eugene was installing a new receptacle or fooling around with a hot wire, and the main switch had to be thrown for his safety, my dad held the flashlight for him and they talked about the graft among the county commissioners or how the blacks were taking over East Liberty, where we still lived. After completing a job, Eugene always sat down, visited, and had a little something: a shot and a beer, cake and coffee, sometimes a sandwich. My mom liked to send home sweets for his little ones.

My parents were unfazed by the fact that Eugene made book. They refused to moralize about such things. To them, it was merely a side job, moonlighting, another way to put bread on the table, provide a nest egg for his children.

"Who's he hurting?" my mother said. "It's not like he's a racketeer."

My dad agreed: "A lousy bet. Big deal."

God bless Eugene. Ambitious. A real go-getter. To get his electrician's license, he went to Washington Vocational for two years—every night after a full day's work. And he knew how to show respect.

All my life, I'd heard about *rackets, writing numbers, bagmen, knocking down.* Vocabulary used regularly in my home and neighborhood. Innocent diversions. Yet there had always been a decided air of secrecy about it. You had to be connected, somehow inside.

One day, when Eugene was at the house replacing the dimmer switch in the dining room, I asked to place a bet with him. Eugene looked at me for a few seconds with his characteristic wry, bemused smile, his upper teeth concealed by a big black Fu Manchu. Like: *What are you talking about?* Even though we both knew.

"Sure," he said. He'd known me all my life. I came from a good family, and was old enough to know what was what.

Wagering is a business, a science. I knew sports like I knew my catechism. I never got in over my head, and never bet anything I wasn't willing to lose. When I did lose, I took it like a man and forgot about it. Period. I was senior straight-A student at Duquesne University—the first member of my enormous extended family ever to attend college. After classes each day, I worked four or five hours delivering prescriptions for a drug store in a silver Vega with

Rosechild's Pharmacy on the doors. I planned to someday make a lot of money as a lawyer.

Like Eugene treated bookmaking, I treated betting. A second job. Mere enterprise, salting a little extra money away for law school—to help out my parents who vowed, come hell or high water, they'd pay my tuition. Later, they mused, when I got to be a big shot shyster, if I wanted to spoil them a little, then okay. For then, however, they were picking up the tab.

I bet a little baseball. Baseball wasn't like football and basketball. No point spread, but odds. Dodgers over the Braves: 17 to 10. Mets over the Pirates: 8 to 5. Tricky. Time-consuming. Games every day. I was busy: school and work year-round. For the return, baseball was too time-intensive. Never enough local press to keep you abreast of injuries, pitching rotations, how many days rest the starter had, platooning, weather conditions, winning and losing streaks. Nevertheless, I kept my hand in it. For the hell of it as much as anything else. I didn't have a girl—I still lived with my parents—and hadn't cultivated much of a social life. I simply didn't have the time for it. The kids from the neighborhood I grew up with—those who hadn't gone to college, or become some kind of deranged, reclusive artist—were in jail or junkies or dead.

Football season was what I lived for. The school and work week built toward it, and by Friday night I was literally anxious contemplating it—like a night on the town with a beautiful girl. In fact there was nothing, beautiful girls notwithstanding, that I relished more than a long weekend of gambling. I bet a few choice college games on Saturday, hit the pros hard on Sunday and then, depending on how I stood in the plus and minus columns, something at least sporting, just for fun, on Monday night. The trick was to religiously avoid the defensive bet: clawing to get back on Sunday what you lost on Saturday; and never, *never,* under any circumstances, attempting on Monday night to pry Saturday and Sunday from the tomb. The biggest sucker game on earth.

Eugene looked out for me. "Cuz, you know what you're doing? Be careful. Don't dig a grave for yourself. Your eyes are bigger than your stomach. I'd lay off that one." Or: "It's a cigar game. Bet the house." And: "Hey, you're a college boy. I'm not going to tell you what to do." It was like having a big brother in the bookie's chair. I felt charmed—like I couldn't miss. Not that I never lost. I did. But, for the most part, I faired very well and gambling made me as happy as anything I'd ever known.

During football season, early point spreads were available Wednesdays after supper. Eugene had a special telephone line he took action from in the soundproof office he built in his basement. He wrote everything down on special paper that disintegrates on contact with water; so if the cops, God forbid, raided him, everything went down the toilet. When he answered the phone, he merely said, "Yeah." I never identified myself, just asked, "What's the line?" Eugene inquired what games I was interested in betting and took it down. I often checked in every day, up until the minute before kickoff, because the point spreads tended to change if the betting got too one-sided. A team might be a ten point underdog on Wednesday, then be down to six come Saturday. I didn't believe in luck, good or bad. There was only judgment, good or bad. Do your homework, keep your head, be a man, and you'd make out fine. And I never forgot, win or lose, Tuesday was payday.

On Tuesdays, after delivering my last prescription, I visited the Pappas. Connie, Eugene's little red-haired wife, who took phone action herself sometimes when things got particularly hectic, always made a big fuss over me, going on about how proud of me my parents were, how she'd known me since I was in-arms, how smart I was—going to college and making something of myself. It was a happy house: Eugene Junior careening through the halls on his tricycle; Baby Michelle throwing her toys out of her playpen the minute I walked in, knowing I'd instantly retrieve them; open shoeboxes, filled with stacks of clean new bills that smelled like Christmas, on the living room coffee table.

If the Pappas were eating when I arrived, Connie and Eugene insisted I join them. After supper, there were always lavish desserts—napoleons, cream puffs and éclairs—that Connie baked herself. The children laughed and played. Connie told Eugene to be careful and called him *sweetheart.* He smiled when he spoke to her, kissed her whenever he entered or exited the house, sometimes when he merely left the room.

It was a picture of life I found comforting—not unlike the home in which I was raised, though my parents, while almost fawning over me, were never affectionate with each other—and there were aspects of it I hoped to someday snare: the doting wife, and happy children. But the vision stopped there. I was getting out of East Liberty—its row-houses and alleys, its blood-grouted cobblestone streets, its broken English, and rivers of Italianate sentiment and nostalgia—to make a better life elsewhere. Everyone in the neighborhood—except the Smack-wasted zombies down on Chookie's corner I used to play Little League with—desired the better life. The reason they had departed Italy in the first place.

Day by day, law school applications from universities like Yale, Georgetown, and Vanderbilt, arrived in our mailbox. Mr. Rosechild, the owner of the pharmacy, had some connections here and there, and promised to throw his weight around once I started applying. Frequently, on weekends, he scored me jobs parking cars at private parties thrown by his wealthy friends in Shadyside and Squirrel Hill. Big money to do nothing but open automobile doors the moment guests arrived at the party house, slip in and park the car, then retrieve it for them when they tipsily waltzed to the oak-lined streets and handed me scrolled fives and tens, even twenties. Sometimes I made up to five hundred dollars in one night. I loved every bit of it. The men in their tuxedos and Norman Hilton suits, the well-preserved, flirtatious women, with their discreet diamonds and shimmering dresses, who looked like Anne Bancroft and Lauren Bacall.

How handsome. How smart. They asked me my name, age, where I went to school and what I studied. "George wants to be a lawyer," they'd whisper to their razor-cut, silvery husbands who smiled and insisted on shaking my hand. On those perfect nights, promise hung in the air like expensive perfume, and every so often I dropped my hands into the green bills lining my trouser pockets. Standing at the curb, guarding my pegboard of keys that unlocked dream cars, I listened to the hired orchestra and imagined dancing under the immense striped tent by the soft light of hurricane globes, white-gloved porters instantly appearing to fill my empty champagne glass, or fetch me something exotic from the caterer's tables.

During those evenings, when the parties were at their most brilliant, I'd choose a car and cruise the city. Cadillacs and Mercedeses, Aston Martins, Citroens, once a Lambergini, a Maserati, the occasional Rolls Royce. Sunk into the leather cushions, strange music keyed to whatever frequency the rich favor, their lingering scent as secret and unfathomable as adult sex and wealth, I swung by my own neighborhood in East Liberty. Past my nodding boyhood friends on the corner, their goateed faces tucked inside dark collars, buzzed eyes registering only a long, gold car, some lucky stiff at the wheel who must have gotten over. Then past my house, the middle one in the iridescent insulbrick row on Saint Marie Street, where the living room window glowed with the gray light of the TV guttering like a votive candle in front of the sofa where my worn-out mother and father had already fallen asleep. At the curb, my father's two-door rose Rambler slouched. They were right—my ancestors. There was a better life out there.

Chapter 3

Mr. Rosechild pressed me to use the pharmacy Vega on weekends. I'd taken him up on it a few times, but this made my parents uncomfortable. They were suspicious of kindness that issued from outside the family, and ascribed to it an ulterior motive.

"Why's he so chummy with you?" asked my dad.

"Use your father's car. What do you need his car for?" my mother threw in.

My parents didn't really like Jews—which was at the heart of their suspicion. A kind of jealousy I couldn't understand. Mr. Rosechild took good care of me. Infrequently, at his invitation, I stopped by his home for a drink with him and Mrs. Rosechild after work. They lived in a townhouse in Highland Park, not many blocks from where I lived, but a distinct jump in class. It was filled with expensive, delicate burnished things kept on shelves called *etageres.* They had a fireplace and Persian rugs. Their living room was on the second floor.

They never offered beer, which is what I was used to drinking, but Manhattans, gin and tonics, vodka gimlets. I usually drank what they drank: Beefeater gin and tonic in squat heavy cut crystal tumblers with shaved ice and lime. I had never seen a fresh lime in my own home, or for that matter in any home I had ever entered. The gin went to my head, and with great deference I always refused a second drink and likewise declined their invitation to dinner. They understood, their charming smiles seemed to underscore, that I had to study, that I was going to law school, that they were somehow stewarding my unlimited future. "You're a smart boy, George," they'd say. Even the regal Beefeater on the bottle label seemed impressed with me.

One night over drinks, while Mrs. Rosechild was in the kitchen, Mr. Rosechild brought up horse racing. He told me that he had placed a few wagers over the years, that frankly he enjoyed a little sensible gambling. I said nothing. My parents only knew about my betting, though not the degree of it. My policy was to keep my mouth shut about it, even among people I trusted, like Mr. Rosechild. He confided that he wanted to start betting on football. Like everyone else in Pittsburgh, the Rosechilds were big Steelers fans, and treated every game as a social occasion: getting together with friends for parties in front of the television.

"Do you have any connections in this area?" Mr. Rosechild asked.

It was a perfectly innocent question. On one hand, I was flattered that Mr. Rosechild trusted me enough to broach the subject. Like he might a real friend or a business associate. Yet it also put me on edge. This kind of gambling was illegal. A thing among family and friends, a privilege Eugene had extended because he considered me family. With that privilege went honor and silence. The question was whether or not Mr. Rosechild, whose kindness toward me had been unlimited and motiveless, could be admitted into that privileged circle. Eugene had told me a hundred times to trust no one.

"Let me see what I can do," I replied.

At first, I did nothing; and Mr. Rosechild, a true gentleman, did not bring it up again. Meanwhile, the Steelers were giving the bookies fits. Regardless of the point spread—they might be favored by 14, 17, 24—people in Pittsburgh refused to bet against them. They bet with their hometown hearts and not their heads, a cardinal stupidity in gambling, but it paid off nevertheless. The Steelers ran roughshod over their opponents, crushing them by three or four touchdowns every Sunday. They were safe as mother's milk. Money in the bank. People who had never gambled in their lives, who didn't know a football from a clothespin, slapped money down just on general principle.

My dad, never a betting man, bet a fifty on the Steelers every week. He never even asked Eugene the line. My old Aunt Concetta, ninety-six years old and barely able to speak a word of English, except *Steelers,* called Eugene every Sunday after High Mass at Saints Peter and Paul and communicated in *Abruzzese* her wish to invest twenty dollars.

I was doing very well. Like everyone else, I bet the Steelers, a couple of hundred each week, sometimes a little more, because it was a smart bet. Period. Not a sure thing, like everyone else thought. There was no sure thing. But I spread my money around to other teams as well. Over the long haul, the Steelers would not be able to keep up their gangster level of play. The week they didn't cover the spot, everyone was going to take a huge fall. You had to know when to lay off. What the bookies banked on, what they always banked on, was their customers' greed.

Every Tuesday, when I stopped by for my envelope, Eugene complained: "I'm getting killed out there, Cuz. The line could be a hundred and these chooches still bet Steelers."

I didn't really believe Eugene ever got killed. He made it all back, and then some, with action on other games. If he got too jammed up with Steelers action, he could lay off safely what he didn't want to another bookie. Besides, he was just one of several lieutenants working for the Big Moustache, Felix

Costa. I met Felix once while picking up at Eugene's. Felix had been sitting at the dining room table drinking coffee with the Pappas. As usual Connie got up, kissed me and insisted I sit and eat.

"This is George Dolce," Eugene said to Felix, who stood and shook my hand. "George is from the old neighborhood. He's down at Duquesne. He's going to be a lawyer."

"Good for you, George," said Felix. "I think I know your old man."

I was used to seeing Felix up in Highland Park. He was an exercise fanatic, always running around the reservoir, or playing tennis. A short, muscular, tanned guy with wiry black hair sloped over his ears, a bristly trimmed moustache, and gold wire aviator glasses. He wore shorts and a tucked-in tight alligator Lacoste shirt, white socks and white tennis shoes. A gold chain, an expensive looking gold watch. Beautiful gleaming teeth. He drove a new yellow Toyota Celica with a red racing stripe. I had always wondered who he was, riding around the park talking on his car phone.

I sat at the table, not saying a word, sipping coffee and eating Connie's apricot cookies. Eugene and Felix chatted football: who was hot, who wasn't, the Steelers upcoming game with Baltimore. Felix claimed a rumor was circulating that the Steelers were actually betting on themselves that Sunday.

"You believe that?" Eugene asked.

"They wouldn't do that," Connie protested.

"It doesn't matter if it's true," said Felix. "People get wind of these things and bet the house on the Steelers. I know a guy who joined The Spa downtown where Rocky Bleier and Jack Ham work out just so he can study them the week before a game. He says he can tell if they're going to win or lose, can almost tell the score, by how hard they work out."

"That's bullshit, man."

"I know this, Eug. What I'm saying is this is a superstitious town."

"So?"

"So nothing. I gotta go. Listen, George. It was a pleasure meeting you and good luck with school. If ever you can't get hold of Eugene, call me direct."

Felix scribbled on a piece of paper, stood and handed it to me.

"Thank you," I said.

"But you don't ever say my name. We don't use names. No names. Never. I'll remember your voice. Okay? I don't give this number to just anyone. Only because Eugene vouches for you. So this number is never to be shared. End of story. Okay?"

"Yeah. Absolutely. I appreciate it very much."

"And, George, you never want to fuck with me."

"Don't pay any attention to him, Georgie," said Connie.

"Yeah. Don't pay any attention to me." Then Felix smiled and I smiled and we shook hands again.

The next day, I told a delighted Mr. Rosechild that I would be glad to place his bets through a connection I had. It seemed the right thing to do. Mr. Rosechild had always been good to me, and this was my opportunity to return the favor.

"Thank you so much, George. I would prefer, however, that this little affair remain just between you and me. It's not exactly what I'd call a secret, but it would make Mrs. Rosechild uncomfortable and I wouldn't want her to get the wrong impression. Of either of us." Then Mr. Rosechild laughed, and he and I shook hands.

Mr. Rosechild was a studious, meticulous man, careful, judicious in every aspect of his life. Down to the penny. Down to the syllable. His socks always matched his neckties. But when it came to gambling on football he was wildly impulsive. Indiscriminately he plunked down money on college teams no one had ever heard of: Wittenberg, Tulsa, Wofford, West Liberty State, Appalachian State. He bet the pros by the sound of their names, or maybe by the colors of their uniforms. If there was a line on a game, he bet it. No method, but mere guess work. He didn't know the first thing about football. The only predictable thing about him was that, like the rest of the sentimental steel town, he always bet Steelers no matter how many points they were giving away. And he always bet big on Monday night.

I counseled with him about it, tried to steer him this way or that, but Mr. Rosechild rarely listened.

"I do it for the fun, George. I don't care about the money. You worry too much about money."

But of course Mr. Rosechild was in the fortunate position of not having to worry about money.

On Tuesdays I picked up from Eugene Mr. Rosechild's winnings along with my own, or paid out whatever was owed. I never mentioned Mr. Rosechild. If Eugene suspected me of calling in someone else's bets along with my own, he never said anything. It wouldn't have concerned him. What I had with Eugene was honor and history. Trust. Eugene was merely running a business. As he had said to me so many times, "As long as my book is right come Tuesday, I don't ask questions."

Mr. Rosechild raised my hourly wage a dollar and a half; insisted I use the Vega for my own pleasure; paid me for the Saturday I couldn't work because

I had to sit for the law boards; cajoled me after closing into the back room, shelved with big stoppered jars of pills and powders, where he kept a bottle of Beefeater, limes and tonic so we could plot bet strategy for the upcoming weekend. On Wednesday afternoons, when I checked in after classes, and handed him an envelope with his winnings, he chortled like a kid and clapped me on the back.

"How I love free enterprise," he'd sing, drop ten days of antibiotics into a plastic cylinder, and hand it to me for delivery. When he had to pay out the juice to Eugene because he lost, he dipped into the packed pharmacy cash register, and spread the bills on the counter for me to scoop up. With a hand lifted prophetically in the air, he'd utter, "This too shall pass."

I began to think of Mr. Rosechild as a client. Servicing his account with Eugene, as well as advising him on his wagers, became time intensive. It cut into my studying. One weekend I decided to engage in what I regarded a business venture. Instead of turning into Eugene all of Mr. Rosechild's bets, I kept a $500 straight-up bet on the Steelers who were giving the hapless Houston Oilers thirty-five points. It was a huge chance. If the Steelers won by at least thirty-six, which could easily occur, then I, instead of Eugene, would owe Mr. Rosechild his winnings: $500. But, if the Steelers did not win by thirty-six, that half-grand—as well as the standard ten percent *juice,* fifty bucks, the bookie's commission—would end up in my pocket, not Eugene's. In essence, I set myself up as a bookie.

The Steelers were ahead 28–0 at the half. It looked like they would easily cover the spread. Franco Harris blew through the Oilers like they were cutouts. Then to the air: Bradshaw to Swann, to Stallworth. The defense chopped Houston to pieces. Like the 82nd Airborne: method, precision, ruthlessness. I was sorry I had kept the bet. Paying Mr. Rosechild $500 would drain me, and I'd have to abstain on Monday night, a thought that depressed me. The Steelers rested Franco the second half. Even so, by the end of the third quarter, it was 35–0. Then Chuck Noll pulled Bradshaw and most of the starters—which was what I had bargained for all along. The Oilers finally scored, then the Steelers added a field goal. The game ended 38–7. The Steelers failed to cover the spread and I had nailed Mr. Rosechild for $500, plus the additional $50.

Mr. Rosechild wanted the Vikings by six over the St. Louis Cardinals on Monday night. For another $500. In the back room of the pharmacy, with the Beefeater looking over our shoulders, I had many times lectured Mr. Rosechild on the foolhardiness of trying to get it all back on Monday night. You had to know when to stay on the canvas.

"How about just half of that, Mr. Rosechild? I hate to see you get stung."

"Just give me the five hundred on Minnesota, George. You are very nice, but I can take the hit if need be."

I felt badly about the $550 I'd already made at Mr. Rosechild's expense. It seemed dishonest. And I especially didn't want to see him drop another $550 on Monday night. I liked Mr. Rosechild very much. But what was I supposed to do? He, not I, had initiated our arrangement. What was the difference whether I pocketed the bread or Eugene or Felix or whoever the hell got it? I had been prepared to pay up if Rosechild had hit on the Oilers game. Besides, the guy was loaded. It wasn't like he was scraping to get by. Five hundred dollars, along with the juice, was nothing to him. My dad had to bust his ass for every nickel he earned. Plus, Mr. Rosechild bet like a jerk. He wanted to be a big shot, but he didn't know shit about the game. A little caprice to amuse himself was all it was to him. Because he already had the life I craved—not just for myself, but for my parents too. In fact, the case could be made that Mr. Rosechild was using me.

I'm in business, I told myself. Pure and simple. In the end, I kept Mr. Rosechild's Monday night bet, rather than calling it into Eugene. Since I was already into Rosechild for five-fifty, the worst I could do—say the Vikings won and I had to cough up the five hundred—was make fifty bucks. It was a smart move. There wasn't a thing wrong with what I was doing.

Fran Tarkenton was brilliant for the Vikings, but St. Louis quarterback Jim Hart was better. The Cards staged a comeback capped by a 53 yard Jim Bakken field goal with three seconds left. St. Louis won 23–21. With the juice, Mr. Rosechild was out $1100, counting the Steelers game, and it all came to me.

On Tuesday, after work, before my visit to Eugene's, I felt decided regret as I collected Mr. Rosechild's debt. In his white smock, standing behind the counter, looking over his black-rimmed tiny reading glasses clamped at the tip of his long nose, the pharmacist looked bewildered.

"George, George, George," he muttered dolefully. "My eyes were bigger than my stomach." He removed one by one from the register eleven hundred dollar bills swelled with portraits of thrifty Benjamin Franklin and handed them to me. He wagged a finger in my face, and said, "It's only paper." Then he smiled. I looked down at the money and was relieved.

"I'll see you tomorrow, Mr. Rosechild."

"Take the Vega, George. Should a prince like you have to walk?"

"It's a nice night."

"At your age, they're all nice nights."

And they were nice nights. I ate supper with my parents, who marveled at what a good son they had brought into the world. "Thank God," they'd say to each other after I bent to kiss each of them and excused myself to my room to study. A handsome boy with real respect, straight A's in college, a job and a savings account. "He'll make something of himself. Not like that scum down on the corner."

In my room, before opening my school books, I studied the spreadsheets for that week's games and pondered my moves. Little by little, I was banking money. If I kept my head, remained intelligent—not emotional—about risk, and stayed within my means like a good businessman, I'd be able to save enough for law school. Realistically, my parents would never be in a position to help me. The tuition at Duquesne, even though I lived at home and had a job, was already a strain on them.

The next week a chastened Mr. Rosechild went light on his betting. I kept a few of his bets, including a hundred dollar stab at the Steelers, who were giving up twenty-one to the Rams. The rest I laid off to Eugene, including my own wagers.

The Steelers killed the Rams by thirty-six points. Paying off Mr. Rosechild with one of those Ben Franklins he had owned just a week before made me feel benevolent, somehow exonerated of shady dealings. Mr. Rosechild had had to pay me, and now I was paying him. Free enterprise among consenting adults.

Chapter 4

In early October, on my dad's way home from work, two drunken kids ran a stop sign and broadsided the Rambler. Even though they rammed him on the driver's side, he came out of it without a scratch. But the car was demolished. My parents could never afford anything but a used car, so naturally they carried only liability. No collision. The kids who hit him didn't have insurance. It cost my dad fifty bucks to have a tow truck drag what was left of the Rambler to the junkyard.

My dad was a millwright at the Edgar Thomson Steel Works, all the way out in Braddock. He had to have a car. While my mom and dad fretted over what to do about replacing the Rambler, my dad left the house at five o'clock every morning and took three buses to the mill. My mother, who had crippling arthritis, and sometimes needed a cane to walk, threatened to get a job.

At a five-and-ten, A & P, one of the bakeries, anywhere. She wasn't too good to work, she declared. They had to have a car, but where were they going to get the money? They had paid every cent of my college since I started, but it wasn't cheap. Duquesne was a private school. Catholic. They didn't want me anywhere else. The tuition was figured into their budget, but there wasn't a dollar extra.

"I can take the bus," my dad assured my mom. "You can't stand being on your feet all day. You can hardly walk."

She slumped into a vinyl chair at the kitchen table and cried.

Life without a car proved impossible. Some nights my dad didn't get home until eight o'clock. Because of her legs, my mom couldn't get up and down the bus steps to go to the market, get her hair done and go to Mass; and she refused to use the cane outside of the house. I told them I had enough in savings to buy them a car, or pitch in with them to get another. But they wouldn't hear of it. For another week they suffered. My dad cursed and my mom cried in front of the TV with hot water bottles on her knees, the house reeking of Bengay.

One night I pulled up in front of our house with a long, forest-green two-door Chrysler Newport with a black vinyl top. It was a '68, but it looked like new. Only 73,000 miles. Twenty-nine hundred dollars cash for it at Perry Cervone's lot, where our family had always bought cars and Christmas trees. I wasn't so sure that Perry, another businessman, *a real operator,* as my mom termed him, had cut me quite the deal he claimed he had. But I didn't care, even though the nearly three grand bashed a big dent in my savings. It was a dependable, good-looking car that would ease my parents' hardship.

My mother wept over the car and, for a moment, my dad, for fear he might break down too, said nothing. It was a beautiful car. I was the best son. God love me. But their hearts were broken that I had dipped into my own pockets to do for them. "God bless you," my mother cried and threw herself at me. One thing, however, and my parents were adamant about this: they refused to look on the automobile as a gift. The money I had bought it with was a loan. Just a loan. Which they would return with interest, I could be sure. In the meantime, they would continue to pay my tuition. This was a matter of honor.

I had already made up my mind that I'd never accept the first nickel of repayment from my parents. They had selflessly taken care of me all my life. The car was a small thing. Even so, I began to worry about money.

The next week, I decided again to keep a few of Mr. Rosechild's bets—with an added twist. When I gave him the point spreads from Eugene on the upcoming games, I tinkered with the lines. The Steelers, for instance, in their last game of the regular season, were giving twenty points to the Washington Redskins. Knowing Mr. Rosechild would bet the Steelers because he always did, just like everyone else, I inflated the line. I told Mr. Rosechild it was twenty-eight. Even if the Steelers actually beat the authentic line of twenty—the official book line filtered down to Eugene through Felix—but did not cover the fabricated twenty-eight, Mr. Rosechild would have to pay me. I did the same thing with a few other games—like the Pitt game. Rosechild refused to bet against Pitt, because he had gone to pharmacy school there.

Of course, he took the Steelers for $500 at twenty-eight—he was getting brave again—which meant they had to win by 29. To insure that I wouldn't get clipped, I covered myself by taking the Steelers at minus-twenty, the real line, for $500 with Eugene. If they won by twenty-one, but not by more than twenty-eight, I'd collect money from Eugene and Rosechild. The very worst I could do—say the Steelers lost outright or they won by twenty-nine—was break even. I'd have to pay Eugene, but Rosechild would have to pay me; or I'd have to pay Rosechild, but Eugene would have to pay me.

It was an ingenious plan, though I didn't feel good about doing it. Nevertheless, I consoled myself that it was business. I had no guarantee that Eugene wasn't doing the exact same thing to me: manipulating the lines he got from Felix. I had no choice but to try and bail out my family. Rosechild could have always gone the other way and bet against Pittsburgh. It was a free country. He could use his goddam head for once instead of his sentimentality. Furthermore, he could afford to lose, if that's what it came down to. He didn't have to suck salt pills, and sweat off ten pounds in an asbestos jumpsuit all day in front of a blast furnace like my father. If his Audi got totaled, the next day he'd be tooling around in a new one.

My parents were on the moon about the new car, and took every opportunity to announce that their son, Georgie, who was studying to be a lawyer, had bought it for them. My law board scores came back: 741, high enough to make me competitive anywhere.

Mr. Rosechild shook my hand and said "Mazel Tov" when I confided my scores. He insisted I borrow the pharmacy typewriter to type my applications.

"Sky's the limit, George. Sky's the limit. Think big." Then he winked. "JoAnn and I are having a little get-together on Sunday for the game with Washington. My daughter's coming in for the holidays. You two might enjoy talking. We'd love to see you."

I couldn't help thinking that all the hard work was starting to pay off. I enjoyed my life: school, studying, the pharmacy job; but, most of all, the little empire I had created around betting. Like Eugene, I had become a workhorse, a go-getter, a self-made man. Hadn't my dad always advised me to work for myself? There was an occasional pang over Mr. Rosechild, but Mr. Rosechild, I felt, had his own secrets concerning his business and his life. How a man made money was a private matter. I had mulled over it a thousand times: I had nothing to be ashamed of. On the days I lost, I stepped up and paid what I owed. In the next several weeks, I'd ship those applications off, graduate Summa Cum Laude in May, and by September be attending one of the most glamorous law schools in the world.

Reflecting on these things, as I drove through the beautiful mid-December city streets delivering prescriptions, sometimes I'd see Felix, jogging shirtless, even on the coldest days, around the reservoir, his compact upper body brown and tight with muscle, his gold neck chain catching the light, beating off his sweaty, hairy chest. Or playing tennis at the Stanton Avenue courts, charging the net, the yellow Celica parked at the curb, its sunroof open. I was nothing like Felix. Nothing like Eugene either, or my father, for that matter. I probably had more in common with Mr. Rosechild. Still, I always had the impulse to stop and talk to Felix on those days I spied him, ingratiate myself, see in his eyes an acknowledgment that I was a savvy guy who deserved his trust and admiration.

The day before the Steelers-Redskins game, my father came home, stood in the kitchen door, and announced that the mill had laid off two thousand men, and he was one of them. My mom, ankles round and blue as eggplants, sank heavily into a kitchen chair. The two of them stared at each other. My mom pulled Kleenex from the pocket of her housecoat and held it over her face.

"Sylvia, don't cry," my dad pleaded.

"What are we going to do? With Christmas two weeks away."

"In six weeks, I can start collecting unemployment."

"We could be dead in six weeks."

"I'll pick up something."

"I'll get a job."

"Jesus, Sylvia. You can't even walk."

"Is that my fault?"

My dad unpinned himself from the doorjamb and walked over to her. "We'll make out," he said, then crouched down in front of her and put his hand on her shoulder.

When I walked in from my last delivery, and found them like that, my mom began sobbing in earnest.

"I got laid off," said my father.

"Don't cry, Mom. We'll make out."

"That's what I told her. It's not like this hasn't happened before."

"I have money. I'll help out."

"It's your school money," choked my mom.

"Big deal. You two have always done everything for me."

"Your tuition's due at Duquesne next month," she said.

I knelt next to my father and took one of my mother's hands. "Mom, just until Dad goes back to work, I'll pay the tuition and help out around here a little bit."

"We still owe you for the car."

"You don't owe me anything."

"I'm not going to bleed my kid. I'll kill myself."

"Sylvia, calm down," whispered my dad.

"We need the help, Georgie," she managed, nearly unable to talk for her crying. "Honest to God. Or we'd never accept this from you."

"I know that."

"But it's just a loan," my dad insisted.

"So help me, God," echoed my mom.

"Of course. I understand. Just a loan."

I had a few thousand in the bank, maybe more, but how long would it last now that I was suddenly the breadwinner? This is doable, I assured myself as I dressed for the Rosechilds' party. My parents needed me and I wasn't about to let them down. Be smart. Be resolute. Be smooth. I'd work it out. I had my job at the pharmacy, and I could easily take in another three or four hundred a week—depending on how loose Rosechild got—by sliding those lines around on him, keeping his wagers, then covering myself by betting the legit line on the same team with Eugene. It was foolproof—a safe gamble. What regret I had entertained about feeding Rosechild manufactured lines was eased by my parents' situation. For them it was life and death. For Rosechild: a drop in the bucket.

Regarding myself in my bedroom mirror—navy blue blazer and ivory corduroy pants, blue Brooks Brothers shirt, red club tie, and gleaming oxblood penny loafers—I liked what I saw. When I walked down the stairs, my dad told me I looked sharp. My mom swooned: how handsome, like John Kennedy; someday, who knows, and why not, maybe I'd be a senator. I kissed both of them goodbye and took off in the enormous Chrysler.

The Rosechilds greeted me as if I was, indeed, a senator. Mr. Rosechild shook my hand warmly, and beamed.

"George, you look like a million bucks. What can I get you to drink?"

"Gin and tonic would be fine, Mr. Rosechild. Thanks."

"How long have we known each other? No more *Mister.* Call me Phil."

Mrs. Rosechild kissed me and said, "Very handsome, George."

"Thank you, Mrs. Rosechild."

"JoAnn."

She took my arm and led me through the house, introducing me to the guests, mostly married couples, roughly the ages of the Rosechilds. Holding tall silver drinks, breezy and confident, as if they'd just stepped off a yacht, they seemed genuinely glad to meet me. We've heard so many good things about you from Phil and JoAnn, they said. Phil tells me you're the next William Kunstler.

In the center of the dining room table plumed a voluptuous centerpiece: birds of paradise, iris, snapdragon, agapanthus, daisies, a score of furled crimson roses, and baby's breath. Orbiting it were pates and aspics, quiches, a monstrous compote of raw oysters, platters of chilled shrimp and cherrystone clams, fondues, a roasted turkey, baked Camembert, Gruyere, Mascarpone and fresh fruit. I shook hand after hand and confided how delighted I was to meet everybody. I smiled and thanked them for their warm words. I brimmed with a happiness I knew could never be duplicated in the realm of my own people. Light reflected off every surface of the Rosechild home. A fire twirled on the hearth.

Phil handed me a drink. JoAnn clutched my arm. A woman entered the room from the hall leading from the bedrooms. Black hair in a tight bun, black cocktail dress with a scooped neck. String of pearls and matching earrings. Young, maybe my age. Then it hit me: the Rosechilds' daughter. Small white teeth, black eyes, full black eyebrows, the most flawless skin I had ever seen. A vague fragrance, like rain or snow. The way the tendrils of her hair, pulled back from the severity of the bun, wisped up at the hairline, the deployment of the tiny pearls at the base of her neck, her bare unbraceleted forearms, the ringless fingers, how she lifted her chin and parted her teeth as she smiled, looked me square in the face and said, "Hi."

I had never been in love. I scolded myself that it was just her alarming beauty that distracted me from the football game. She was impossible not to gape at, impossible not to like. Her name was Sterling. A senior at Bryn Mawr, studying theatre. She already knew a bit about me: that I was a Political Science major with a Philosophy minor, at Duquesne, headed to some prestigious law school, that I had trumped the law board. Her parents thought the world of me. In fact, she told me almost immediately, as we strolled toward the food, that her father saw me as the son he had never had. Ridiculously flattered, I couldn't help imagining life as the Rosechilds' son-in-law: co-heir to a thriving business and what I was certain was a small fortune, country club memberships, dalliance with the city elite, vacations in Barbados, Paris, all over the world.

As we stood at the table, arranging food on cocktail plates—even though I was ravenous, I remained discreet—Sterling threaded her arm in mine, and I became a little lightheaded. She drank champagne and ate and laughed unabashedly. I drank more than usual, three or four tall glasses of Beefeater and tonic that Mr. Rosechild delivered to me the instant my glass went dry. I could have drained rivers of it and still been on my feet. Sterling's arm in mine was like a 220 line.

The Steelers jumped the Redskins for two quick touchdowns, but then Washington scratched its way back. I attempted not to stare at Sterling. She sat on the edge of one of the couches next to me with her chin on her fist, her elbow on her knee. She had kicked off her shoes and had one stockinged foot tucked under her. She said she liked football, and adored the Steelers. She sighed and laughed and threw up her arms in celebration, snapped her fingers in dejection. While these displays only endeared her even more to me, I was disappointed, even disgusted, when I witnessed them in the Rosechilds and their guests. They neither understood nor appreciated the intricacies of the game. The business of it. To them it was mere entertainment, an event around which they could throw a party. The Steelers had become chic. While I wasn't surprised at their behavior—I had witnessed it all along in Mr. Rosechild (or rather Phil) and his empty-headed wagering—their unschooled comments and silliness irritated me.

Nevertheless, as I sat there with the Rosechilds and their friends, becoming more bemused with every sip I took, and every glance I exchanged with Sterling, I abandoned a little more of myself to their world. I wouldn't have traded that afternoon for anything, and it looked like I would make a killing in the bargain. With a minute left, the Steelers, inside Washington's fifteen, were up 42–20. Most of the first team sat on the bench with their helmets off. Of course, they aimed to simply run out the clock.

Phil, on the other hand, figured they'd push to score again. He exhorted them to take it in for one last touchdown. I felt sorry for him, but a pinch of contempt too for his ignorance. When the Steelers ran a trap that went nowhere, the clock ticking—none of the players wearing black and gold in any hurry to get up from the turf and into the huddle—Phil shot me a doleful look.

"Why are they taking so long?" he blurted.

"Daddy," said Sterling innocently, "there's absolutely no chance of them losing."

The clock dragged down to its last clicks. Bradshaw strolled up to the line, put his hands under Mansfield, and waited there for nine seconds until the gun went off. Everyone in the Rosechilds' living room clapped and cheered and lifted glasses. I chanced a look at Phil. He was sunk into the loveseat next to JoAnn, his face an utter blank. Then he slapped his hands to his knees and jumped up.

"Let's have a drink," he crowed.

People assembled again around the food. I followed Sterling to the table. Admiring her as she snaked out an arm for a cracker, I felt badly. Had I given Phil the accurate line, he would have won his bet just as I had. I want to emphasize again that I liked Phil, and I liked JoAnn too. And now Sterling. Business, I reassured myself. You're just doing business. Supply and demand. Free enterprise.

Phil sidled over. "You bet Steelers?" he inquired under his breath.

"Yes." I was pleased to be telling the truth.

"Then I guess we both lose." Phil clapped me on the back and smiled. "C'est la vie."

In that instant, all of my regret vanished. I thought of my parents at home, dozing in front of *Sixty Minutes,* how "C'est la vie" for them meant worry and back-break and threadbare pockets. Not Rosechild's *What the hell, there's more where that came from.*

Sterling took my arm again. "Let's go out," she whispered . "Take a drive or something." Then, "George and I are going for a drive," she proclaimed.

The entire assemblage turned to us and conferred smiling benediction. Sterling kissed her mother and father and all the guests. I shook hands with the men; the women leaned in and kissed me. They wished me good luck. They looked forward to seeing me again.

"Have some fun," Phil told us, and handed Sterling a fifty and two twenties.

As I excused myself, so I could call my parents and let them know I'd be late, Phil turned to everyone: "That young man is one in a million. Some day he will make quite a mark in this world."

I stood at the passenger side of Sterling's brand new navy Mercedes convertible, a 1975 450-SL coupe, a twentieth birthday gift from her parents.

"Would you mind driving?" she asked, smiling.

I smiled back across the hood of the car. The way her collarbone stood out, the perfectly smooth expanse of flesh that filled in the large V her black dress made shoulder to shoulder, the tiny V where her small breasts joined and slid beneath the cloth. Her teeth as she smiled, the glint of the corner streetlight on them. She tossed me the keys and laughed: "You want to put the top down?"

We turned on the heat full blast and let the frigid air rush over us. I drove like a daredevil, but brilliantly, spurred by the elegant power of the Mercedes and the young woman beside me. Occasionally I stole glances at her, bundled on the white leather bucket seat in a long black coat, her face in profile as we sped past the nineteenth century stone mansions lining Fifth Avenue.

We ducked into the Gaslight Club in Shadyside. A black man named George Benson played the piano and there were guys playing sax, clarinet and drums, Harold Betters on trombone. I had never been in the Gaslight before. I didn't know a thing about jazz, wasn't sure I had ever even heard it until that night with Sterling. It seemed so right for the life I was about to enter: plaintive, mysterious, glittering. A bit like Sterling—sitting next to me in a curving, high, upholstered red leather booth with gold rivets shot into it. She drank Spanish coffee, steaming, laced with brandy, topped with whipped cream. After each sip, she dabbed with her tongue the whipped cream left on her lips.

Sterling confided that her father had a collection of jazz: Charlie Parker, Bix Beiderbecke, Stanley Turrentine. Her father had actually known Turrentine. I hadn't heard of them. Jazz was about improvisation, she said, not preoccupation—why she liked it.

I stared at myself in the bar mirror: eager, handsome, clutching my Beefeater and tonic, next to a stunning woman with her face turned to me, the chin and nose at forty-five degrees, the neck long and white between black hair and black dress, the garnet of fire from the cigarette lounging in her fingers, punctuating the invisible notes sawing through the smoke. Mad about Sterling, in love with our reflection in the mirror, I took her hand. I wanted to seal our bargain right then and there, make some protestation of love, some idiotic promise. She put her other hand on mine. We sat in silence, barely speaking.

On the way home, we kept our hands linked, even when I shifted gears. At the threshold of the Rosechilds' townhouse, I received from Sterling a kiss I'd taste the rest of my life. Then I climbed into the Newport, drove home, and immediately wrote a check for $1,200.00 to cover my last semester at Duquesne. This left me with only a couple of hundred dollars in savings. But

I had won several hundred that day and there were still another few weeks of pro football left, not to mention bowl games—and my job at the pharmacy.

I slid the check into an envelope, and trotted to the corner. Anticipating my parents' relief at being spared the heartache over tuition, I dropped it into the big blue mailbox. Standing in the spotlight of the streetlamp, the season's first snow floated over me. I touched the tip of my tongue to my lips and thought of Sterling. I had never been happier.

Chapter 5

My first five days in Queen, I slept on Crow's couch. Hiding out. Trying to keep at bay the magnitude of my suddenly shattered life, disguised in the tenebrous purple shroud of my heart. Crow took me in like she would an odd breed of dog, one she hadn't quite seen the like of before. She had a heart like that. Wide, capacious. For hard cases. But I wasn't a hard case. Not really. I just looked like one. More than anything, I had driven south in that stolen car in search of peace. But I wouldn't have known to call it that or what peace might have looked like if it had fallen across my path. Crow fancied herself another kind of dog, too, so she opened that heart and took me in. There wasn't another woman anywhere who would have done it.

I had been under the impression that in the South summer prevailed month in and out. But it was a cold January that year, bleak and often icy, nothing so soothing as snow, just dashed hopes for it. The world outside Crow's windows was a black slick of maudlin lights, dressed in vintage attire to the dire nines, a little tight and reckless: the city of Queen.

The apartment's sole source of heat was the dated gas range in the kitchen. Mornings Crow hiked the pilot of its four eyes and oven, the fumes instant and luxurious, then ignited it with a blue sulfur wood match. The flames *whooshed* up in lethal suspiration—you had to back off—and we left them in their burning blue dance, oven door wide open, until bedtime each night.

Crow and I ate restaurant food she fetched home: stolen, salvaged or discarded. Potato salad, cheese, bread, pies, beans, banana pudding. None of it mattered to me. Those first five days I mainly sat or laid on the couch in an amnesiac fog and gaped at the faded flaking wallpaper unscrolling from the high living room walls. Enormous blue hydrangeas blooming out of a yellowing white backdrop. Staring at the blue parchment flowers, I grew forgetful and, without realizing it, changed my last name, Dolce, to Roman, and my first name, George (actually *Giorgio* on my birth certificate) to Michael. Mike Roman: a durable investment in anonymity—though Crow took to calling me Romeo.

I left the couch only to wander in and out of the kitchen until the coffee Crow left in an old-fashioned percolator was gone. I ate raisins, canned fruit, and the biscuits she baked every morning. I drank water. I glimpsed myself, without recognition, in the bathroom mirror. Older, gaunt, apathetic. My hair seemed longer. A week or more of beard. My hand was a stiff raw clamp. An ugly machine. Like Dr. No's. I was empty. Disappeared. It wasn't me. I didn't care about anything.

I had washed up on the shoals and Crow plucked me up and cleaved me unto her like a foundling, and made up the couch like a bed every night for me. Clean sheets and a pillow with a fresh slip, a blanket and then the thickest, heaviest quilt I had ever seen. Made by Crow's grandmother. *Granny.* A field of green and upon it embroidered in rainbow thread wildflowers of every genus: goldenrod, thistle, violets, thrift, daisies, milkweed. Buried beneath that quilt those first nights, moonlight pooling in it, I envisioned lying in a glade, inseparable from it, and its considerable smothering weight, so very warm—the unholy cold beyond. Crow was gone by the time I got up each morning.

She owned a stereo console big as an altar. Blonde fake wood and plastic cane façade, great big speakers imbedded in it. Turntable, AM/FM and an eight-track tape player. It could belt it out. I played, over and over, a Janis Ian album of Crow's for the pleasure I took in her unremitting sadness. Something I could do to get the day started. Like Ian, I didn't want to "ride the milk train anymore." There was some Leon Russell and Dylan's *Blood on the Tracks,* but often they made it seem like there might be a life waiting out there for me, one I couldn't bear to think of. I wanted inside. I wanted interior. I wanted nothing.

On a windowsill in the living room, Crow had squeezed a stand of books between a pair of sinister porcelain rabbit bookends: *Contemporary American Poetry,* Jaspar Johns's crazy American flag—a 1954 encaustic, oil and collage on fabric, titled *Flag above White*—on its cover; Maurice Sendak's *Where the Wild Things Are; Alice's Adventures in Wonderland;* Flannery O'Connor's *The Complete Stories.* On the nightstand, next to her bed, presided a red leather-bound Bible her mother had given her when she was twelve years old, inscribed: "(December 24, 1967) John 14:14: *If ye shall ask anything in my name, I will do it.*" Secreted unceremoniously in the drawer, just beneath the red Bible, lurked Crow's slick black unlicensed .22 pistol.

I decided I'd read the Bible start to finish: from void and firmament through the redemption, and on to the final cautions of the Apocalypse—and all the turmoil in between. I made it through Genesis and Exodus, but stalled at the insane avalanche of *begats* and appellations in Numbers. So I skipped ahead to the gospels, which I had obviously misunderstood upon my first encounter with them.

In my home, we owned a Bible, a mammoth unliftable gilded tome that remained concealed, with the trove of other sacred untouchable family artifacts, in the cedar chest at the foot of my parents' marriage bed. The Bible had been a wedding present from Father Vecchio, the priest that had married them at Our Lady of the Help of Christians on Meadow Street on September 3, 1945. In my recollection, that Bible had never been touched. My parents seemed afraid of it. It was better left alone—the kind of book, if opened, that could unleash spells and machinations. Like Grazziella, the neighborhood *strega,* who had the power to curse you with the *malocchio,* the evil eye.

Yet my mother had somehow managed to clandestinely inscribe, in the appropriate brackets listed in the Bible's front matter, births and the dates of sacraments and marriages and above all deaths, longing on certain days that she could inscribe her own death-date. Our Bible's only practical use was as a press for flowers commemorating forgotten occasions. It was perhaps the most beautiful thing in our home. An expensive impractical bauble that, hocked, would bring more than a week of my dad's unemployment.

By the time Crow got home from waiting tables at The Tea Rose, her place, range and oven flames HIGH all day, was warm, sometimes fiery warm, in a heavenly way. You could smell the octane. I'd be on the couch, reading the Bible, the occasional poem from Crow's poetry book. I didn't know a thing about poetry beyond "Annabel Lee" and Kipling's "If," which a crazy professor of mine had us memorize in a freshman Political Science course. And a tiny bit of Frost: "The Road Not Taken" and "the woods are lovely, dark and deep." James Wright's poem, "Lying in a Hammock at William Duffy's Farm," seemed like my life: the promise and shimmer that precede that last withering line, "I have wasted my life." Pushing twenty-two, I was too young to have wasted my life. Maybe there was more ahead, but I felt wasted, discarded. In the space of twenty-four hours, fleeing Pittsburgh and landing inexplicably in Queen, North Carolina—500 lousy miles, the exact length, it seemed, of my destiny, my fate—I had wasted my life.

Crow witnessed an empty man when she breezed through the door. I had been reading the gospels and knew already how each ended. With sorrow mainly. And triumph. But a triumph inseparable from death. Jesus laying down His cryptic parabolic rap—in scarlet verses, multiple versions, different angles—of His unthinkable passion and execution. Hardship and confusion, and the Devil himself showing up every now and then. That's the life—some crazy kind of Biblical comeuppance—I had hurtled into. But I relished the miracles. Yes I did and, more than anything, I wanted Jesus to drop in on me.

And there was Sterling, beautiful, thoroughly exquisite Sterling, Phil Rosechild's daughter, my one true love, whom I had left behind in Pittsburgh—snuck out on, no explanation. Lying on the couch, Crow's red Bible winged across my chest as I closed my eyes, I smelled Sterling, heard her voice. I wanted to lay my cheek against her, whisper in her hair. Know that she was about to say something, then touch me, summon me back to the civilized world I had once inhabited, my certain future with her. I loved her inconsolably. Between us had floated a great pink cloud we would someday enter as man and wife.

Now I had no future, but I had Crow. No promises. Just the ephemeral blaze of now.

Often, I am moved to tell Crow I love her, because at given moments I do love her. But *love* her like I loved Sterling? Not out of obstinacy that I don't love Crow that way, but chemistry. Love is an addiction: pharmacopeia at its most profound. That's how I loved Sterling: a needle in my arm and a foot in Mount Carmel. Even now she fades like the geography I left in my wake, like the hand that once, at the end of my wrist, like a brother, kept me company. Not the capricious bastard it is now. Permanent clenched fist, grotesque manacle scrolling out of its sleeve.

Crow knew I had a big hole in me. Like she was the princess of empty. Its mediator. Through the door with a flourish, she threw her big red coat and hat off—an impish punk Myrna Loy—and sometimes she didn't stop until down to her white slip with its stanza of lace at the bodice, little pink sweetheart roses, and spriglets of incarnadine.

Like a little girl. All she needed was a pair of patent leather strap shoes and white anklets. A face that you might call cute, striking, dire, even adorable, but never pretty. Hair so irretrievably black, sliced to the bottom of her neck, razor-straight, lank, bangs curtaining her forehead to the eyebrows. Long, turned up nose. White perfect teeth, though big, that filled her wide mouth carnally when she smiled, and made me want to kiss her. Small intense striped golden eyes, beaded black at the pupil, a honey bee fizzing in each socket.

Atrociously thin, nearly transparent after a shower, the white complexion, the first time I saw her naked, startling, otherworldly white, her skin robing a visible emanating glow. Blindingly white against that chopped veil of jet hair and the prick of black beaming from her eyes—a disparity that stole my breath, the only other color the violet of her ample lips and aureoles of her chaste breasts. And absolutely hairless, except for her head and eyebrows, and not from shaving—as if she'd been scalded. An orchid, exotic, almost too much—in that way, Sterling's double—that frigid winter in Queen when the prismatic light that stole through the attic was smoky with frost, sword-length icicles knifing from the porous eaves into our bedroom. The winter I suffered from amnesia and couldn't remember if I had always known Crow.

Crow and I feed each other scraps of our stories, parsing out the chapters, even the sentences, often the syllables, like fixed rations the starving survive on until their lot improves or the rescuers kick down the door. In the purest sense, we reside in the moment. No past, no future, we are the quintessential minute by minute nowists. Between us exists an unspoken refusal to complicate matters with flashbacks and foreshadowing.

It's lovely: the existential not-giving-a shit about anything but the flat plane of her blinding breastbone, the long white downslope of her belly, then the harrowing plummet and ingress. Sometimes she sucks her thumb, just the tip of it, and turns her profile to the pillow like an exhausted child, black bangs adrift on the snowy pillowslip—she is meticulous about clean linen and knows how to keep a house (things my mother would admire in her)—and I read my future in the tea leaves scattered across her forehead.

I noticed the scars on her forehead the first time she came out of the shower, not naked then, not those first five days. Completely covered, wearing a thin red paisley robe. I sat at the kitchen table working a jigsaw puzzle. Monet's *Vétheuil in the Fog.* Sky and lake. Bluish green, the firmament sliding into the water, not a straight line in the painting, the shift in hue imperceptible, ultimately monochromatic as if, in searching for the interlocking puzzle fragments, I searched for cotton balls in a snowdrift.

Crow walked into the kitchen, running a comb through her wet hair, stuck to her head like penmanship. Combing it back off her forhead. The scars were smallish and seemingly uniform. Faded lavender bric-a-brac like Chinese characters. Angles. Petroglyphs. The divagations of a language I could not immediately decipher. I suppose I stared because she halted the comb in her hair, then simply sank into the chair opposite me across the table. Not looking at me, but out the window at the queue of long winter days while around her formed a brittle icy chrysalis.

She ceased to breathe or blink, her hand still holding the comb at her crown, a shock of black fezzed up in the tines. I neither stirred nor spoke. The slightest movement would have shattered her or, even worse, she'd disappear. And if that occurred, I would be alone—like my childhood nightmares of Limbo, neither on earth nor in Heaven, but marooned in the amnesiac ether of perished innocence—a mere half-saint whom no one would ever celebrate. So I stared at Crow—she had slipped off the earth—attempting by dint of my own desperation to reel her back into the kitchen as I read the story carved across her forehead.

Hardscrabble rural in Saint Joan's County, a forgotten backwater seventy miles or so east of Queen, Crow had come up headstrong, immersed in the writ covenant of Jesus Christ. In the red Bible she had given her daughter, Crow's mother had taken a blue pencil and underscored dozens of Jeremiads throughout its tissuey pages. In the margins, alongside the blue, Crow had written poems, typical perhaps for her age—twelve years—in which she lamented the cruelty of man to man and the absence of the Lamb's gentle light in the hearts of even the faithful.

Her father, a prison guard at the county road camp in the town of Coventry, worked the dead man's shift in single cell, 10 to 6, and fell into bed as his youngest daughter, the baby of the three—the eldest, the lone boy, Edney; then another girl, Charlene, prior to Ruby Lydia—hurried to catch the school bus. The Crow house allowed but one God, hoary, wrathful; one book, and its sacred offshoot tracts. They brooked not literature nor dancing nor music nor even the vestiges of secular pleasure. Sin was sin: tobacco and alcohol of any sort were anathema. The world was rife with meanness and above all the flesh was to be mortified.

Crow, as a girl, had often been described as *could be pretty.* Lank and frail, dressed plain and cheaply. Neither make-up nor scent, unable for years to even lay eyes upon her naked body in a mirror lest she sin. There is no way to know when a child might take up the righteous blowtorch of indignation. Crow's mama would blame it on all those libertine books urging folks to root deeper into the willing flesh; and that electric thrumming music that crept on its belly along the blacktop clean to Saint Joan's County out of Queen by way of Atlanta—those soul-riving chords that supplanted the Baptist Hymnal and lured from the bosom of the cropland, to Queen and worse, girls like Crow.

Crow, by the time I met her, laughed about it, after she had reconciled herself to her mama, Wanda, a woman I pictured stolid and sexless as a woodchuck; and after her father, Lon, had lapsed into a gelded senescence that left him occasionally mute and infantile, his sole activity circling the property cheerfully on a John Deere riding mower, its whipping rotors hacking the grass down to an inch of the millstone grit and gravel that coated the tallow of Saint Joan's County—indeed what it was famous for: a rare grade of rock.

Crow had one day come across in the corn crib loft—well before the stroke or conniption or whatever it was that tetched her daddy—his homemade robe in a rattan trunk. No more than shabby, stained, moth-egg-sequined, Halloween bed sheet, graffitied with his Klan rank and station, and the trinkets with which he dressed his hips as a chain gang dungeon boss: manacles, leg-irons, mace, the duct-taped blackjack—she remembered him buffing it each night, then beating it against his uniformed thigh, its supple dangle, before throwing it on the supper table, then seizing his chair at the table crest and returning thanks—even a ringlet of concertina.

Crow had known all along her Daddy's secrets. The club he belonged to that met under the guise of Kiwanis, in service to the halt and pitiful, that rallied every Wednesday after prayer meeting at Crumpler Baptist in the garret above Dossie's Schwinn Shop in downtown Dawson. The torches, the crosses, the hoods. Sodomy and Deuteronomy, moonshine and sweet tea. The marauders' ingenious bent of crossing sacred and secular. *I can do all things through Christ which strengtheneth me.* Braiding the writ into a lynch knot.

It could be argued that Crow had always heard whispers seducing her from outside the boundaries of Saint Joan's County where certain judgment lurked like disease. She wrote evenings by candlelight in the margins of that red Bible like she might a diary. She was twelve years old, staring into the blue-hooded writhing candle-flame, when the first voice whispered. She'd swear later that it had been Joan of Arc, the improbable patron of Saint Joan's county, and her testimony of 1429, commanding Crow to charge Sprague's Field that burning September in her big brother's black Belvedere. The mammoth cross flared regally into the night. Its acolytes, white-robed and peak-hooded in the black nave of the endless firmament, stood beneath it among the snowy swaddling left on swabs of harvested cotton.

She wheeled off the blacktop, through a ditch of brack and browning gentian, reared over a berm, and across the field corrugated in dazzling green furrows of winter wheat, a few hands high, the inquisitorial eyes of the Belvedere's headlamps blinding the robed men before they scattered, clutching their skirts above their hobnails. A few pulled guns, her father among them, but Crow never hesitated. She barreled into the fiery cross at sixty miles an hour, launching it in guttering fragments across the sky, meteoric embers hailing down on the fleeing shrouds, pocking them with brimstone.

Then *whomp,* the still intact transverse beam of the cross, roiling with fire, returned to earth—aslant the roof and hood of the car, shattering the windshield, spraying Crow with sparks. She shouldered open the door and crawled out, lay in the cool emerald wheat while the Belvedere sputtered, died, then took fire beside her.

They had all gone—except for her father who prayed above her a long moment, the hem of his robe knifing across the toes of his State-issue brogans, hood steepled on his head, its eye-ports smoking. Then he floated off across the field, like a revenant scarecrow in a dress unmoored from its haunted vigil on a post, dawn's ground-fog rising and with it the foraging ghosts of deer, votives of fire sputtering among the crop.

Crow lay in the wheat a few minutes more listening to Saint Joan whisper, or perhaps merely the whisper of the wheat, the Belvedere quietly expiring beneath its lavish flaming canopy. When she reached home, she went to work with an X-Acto knife on her forehead: barbs and crosses and runes, the ineffable embroidery not so much of despair, but declaration.

After her mother's hysteria, the insane invocations, the hospital and the stitches, she was arrested, given over to churchmen—the same men she had scattered that night in Sprague's Field—and tried for blasphemy as much as anything. There were the shrinks, adjudication, ongoing front page news in the *Saint Joan's Intelligencer* along with Crow's graduation portrait—a sweet, big-smiling girl, not big as a minute, dark bangs, tresses down to the black off-the-shoulder baccalaureate frock—side by side with the incinerated Belvedere.

Crow landed in a group home. Not long after, Lon had the spell that left him a quivering grinning buzzard. Photographs of her while detained at the Home highlight the bleached complexion, pellucid, as if her skin might drop like parchment, leaving but her skeleton crowned with its cropped black pillbox of hair and expressionless gaze. Often in the pictures—the photographer unknown, unaccounted for—she's half-clothed, a shoulder or thigh, neurasthenic breasts pouting out of her slashed blue shift stenciled with skeins of barbed wire abloom with black roses.

Across her sunken belly she had crudely tattooed with India ink, and a sharpened hawk's quill she'd found in the Home's high-fenced gravel quad, the word *time* in a palsied calligraphy. She attempted to starve herself, but the lack of food had no effect on her whatsoever, other than to steep her in the miasmic lucidity of the ascetic. Through all of it, she still believed in the body and blood of her savior. He was Che. He was Jesse James. That freak firestorm that would blow out of nowhere in the middle of the night.

With the other waif-girls, she smoked cigarettes and contraband weed, swilled smuggled beer. At lights out they tenderly entwined and kissed and held hands and sang love songs along with the turned-low radio, danced like prom dates, and sometimes fist-fought and self-mutilated. She caught the crabs, a colony of bugs scurrying along her pubis, then impetigo, called her house-parents *Mama* and *Papa,* told no one but God a thing about any of it.

Crow was canny enough to have invented the voices and visions, to feign lunacy, anything to escape her parents' house and Saint Joan's County—even if it meant a stretch in a kids' penitentiary. By the time I met her in Queen, that uncharacteristically frigid winter of 1975, she possessed for suffering the threshold of a martyr, and was similarly demented. Yet, in many ways, she is the most pliant, sweet-hearted—even innocent—woman I have ever known. But, by then, I myself had crossed over and, even Crow, in her most charitable moments, would have sworn I just wasn't right.

Chapter 6

After five days apprenticing in Crow's attic, she scored me a job at The Tea Rose washing dishes. The woman who owned the restaurant was Rosaria, a fierce, young blue-eyed black woman, nearly bare-breasted in a loose summer dress. A wedge of white hair plowed through the middle of her long bushy black afro, and across her face bloomed a blood-red Rorschach. She claimed to have been a witch in another life and burned at the stake. The blue eyes, the white hair, the scarlet birthmark: testimony to stages of fire she had endured in her past existence. She and Crow were friends, having in common a fascination with immolation. Often they crawled into the hotel ductwork and got stoned together.

Rosaria had taken one look at me, threw back her head and laughed long and richly. "I know you," she said, and wrapped her arms around me.

Rosaria knew everyone from her past lives. She confided that we had stood together at the foot of the cross the day Jesus was crucified. I tried to recall that moment, but it too had been pilfered, like so much, but I hoped, of all the memories that had seemingly vanished, that this one would surface with pristine clarity. For the moment, however, I couldn't be bothered with past lives.

A chain-smoking black ex-con named Too-Bad did the cooking along with Rosaria. Too-Bad instantly recognized in me, I imagine, the pedigree of trouble. In greeting, she raised the cleaver with which she was ravaging a bloody pork loin. "Got you a real man, Baby Crow," she said, then laughed along with Rosaria.

"Yeah, I reckon," Crow allowed, as she tied on her apron and threw one to me.

The busboy, Gabriel, a fat white man in his fifties, maybe older, wore a blue shirt laundered so many times it had a threadbare sheen, the sleeves rolled above his elbows. Thick hairy arms, but his hand mush when he stood with great difficulty, ash and crumbs tumbling off him, to shake mine. His large head was the smallest part of him: a barrel gut and knit pants with an adjustable beltless waistband that had curled over on itself, the shirttail swagging and his T-shirt visible where his buttons strained with each audible breath. He wore white socks, orthopedic shoes with Velcro straps.

He had the face of a palooka, gnarled and brownish, crooked, punched and pocked, but dear and splattered with melancholy. A face like a potato, poorly shaved, white stubble like frost clinging in rime at intervals and even the snow of shave cream just about his collar. White hair, and little to speak of at his crown, but the few dozen or so strands that remained were a foot long and electrified, so that about his countenance sprayed excelsior. He was a self-described poet; he'd read everything. He had the beautiful manners and accent of a true southern gentleman, suffering the twin curses of antebellum chivalry and Jim Crow guilt. He could be grossly effeminate when he drank badly, which he often did, sometimes ending the night weeping at our place. He adored Crow who was fiercely protective of him. He called me *compadre,* and rattled off lines of Cesare Pavese (*Someday, you think, your life will start all over . . .*) and Eugenio Montale (*The porcupine sips a quill of mercy.*) for my Mediterranean benefit, though I had never heard of them.

Hewitt, the Rose's manager, was a big man who showed every day in a tie, coat, and starched white shirt. Upon arrival, he removed the coat, placed it on a hanger in the walk-in, then prowled around all day in blazing shirtsleeves and loosened tie. "Good Morning, Rosaria," he greeted the boss every morning, then a spate of flirting, kissed her hand or even ran his fingers around her waist. She made no bones about wearing nothing under her flimsy dress. He meant nothing to Rosaria, but she required flattery, near adoration. Apparently Hewitt had never intruded upon her past lives.

"Good morning, Too-Bad."

Too-Bad bid Hewitt grudging good morning, though he knew not to push it too far with her. She wouldn't dirty her paring knife on him, but simply fell him with a sucker punch. She had done ten years in Women's Prison in Raleigh for killing her third husband. "I'd do it all over again," she liked to remind everyone.

"Good morning, Crow." He did his best to fondle her, even kiss her lips, run his hands across her flanks. I stayed detached. Detached was my assignation. Crow was more than capable of handling him. She was not my woman.

"Good morning, Gabriel." Then, over the course of the day, the vicious baiting, the jabs at Gabriel's homosexuality, at his slowness as the sorrow of his years weighed him down, that he needed to step it up, then *faggot* soto voce, then *faggot* out loud. Hewitt liked to make Gabriel cry. Gabriel was a disaster. He spent time in the walk-in freezer dabbing his eyes and nipping from the open mags of white wine.

Margaret, the other waitress, the woman Hewitt lived with, laughed her deep brogue at Hewitt's digs, though her voice was high-pitched and she was all hunky-dory. Every day was delightful; she was always just fine. Things were no problem. But she was treacherous, and treated restaurant work like it was theatre—with a grave operatic disposition. To my face, she was nice: but, in truth, a viper with pretensions to the throne. She and Crow hated each other. "Whore of Babylon," said Too-Bad of Margaret.

"Good Morning, Roman." He stared through me as if seeing my shambling heritage in steerage aboard the *Luisiana,* the seventh year of the 20th Century. In honor of my ancestry, my blood boiled: *dago, wop, guinea.* Because of him my father was out of work, my mother suffered arthritis, Alex jumped off the Meadow Street Bridge, and I lost Sterling.

My days at the Rose varied little, thank God. I carried cases of beer up from the cellar and put them in the cooler; cut meat and cheese on the lethal stainless steel slicer; buried my arms to the elbow in a vat of bloody ground beef and shaped dozens of hamburgers, stacking them between squares of wax paper four high on huge trays.

My final prep task was the whipped cream. Rosaria featured homemade strawberry shortcake; peanut butter pie; and a bourbon cake, each wedge of which purportedly contained a shot and a half of Rebel Yell. The desserts were served in a veil of whipped cream. Real whipped cream. So, every morning, as the breakfast crowd departed, I stood over a bowl and mixed with a giant whisk whipping cream and confectioner's sugar until it frothed up into a beautiful bride.

Crow, wearing a black beret, white shirt, black necktie, and gray and black striped shirt—like Margaret—sashayed by and dipped her finger into the whipped cream, licked off the tip, plopped the rest into my mouth, and that was it. The day had started in earnest. The cries of the flatware against cups and plates, the diners' congress with one another, Hewitt with theatrical airs marshaling the yapping staff, and then the dirty dishes bussed back to me in big black rubber tubs.

I found soothing the day's blessed rote: hosing out in the slop sink the clotted vessels before racking them; cups and glasses, upper tier; plates and saucers, lower; slipping the detergent puck into its niche and engaging the fuming industrial Hobart dishwasher until some minutes later it grinded to a foaming, watery halt and I released the hatch, a wall of steam engulfing me, the immaculate dishes smoking as I lifted them rack and all out of Hobart's maw and carried them to the prep stations. Then again and again as if running legs of a relay until Crow and I clocked out after lunch—often with a bag of scrounged food for our simple feast at Lark Terrace.

Once I started working, and we had a little more dough to burn, we headed after work for Ramon's, a garish alcove cafe we stumbled into one bitter cold night, not terribly long after I had landed in Queen. We had just seen at the Visulite the Ingmar Bergman film, *The Hour of the Wolf,* which haunted me from the first frame. Nothing could have prepared me for its bare cinematic nihilism: the stark marble of white, black fabric fastened over the orifice, the genitals like non sequiturs. I sat in a dim laboratory, not the movies, watching some vile experimental surveillance tapes. It made a kind of morbid sense, I suppose, that just before dawn most people die, that most people are born then as well. So that in the dingy passageway between life and death souls pass in the raw mist like refugees pressing toward and fleeing the invader at once, the retreating mute troops limping by the reinforcements on the road to cannibalism and necrophilia. I found myself despairingly influenced by something that completely befuddled me. Like a hallucinogen. That corpse on the slab. That morgue lab with its little gas jets and bottled specimens, formaldehyde, pickling sinks, petri dishes, Bunsen burners, cruets, beakers, test tubes. Jesus Christ. Where was He?

We staggered out of the theatre with the other shocked and bundled patrons into the anomalous Queen deep freeze. Ten degrees and a Norse gale keening. We all looked at one another, convinced for the moment that seeing that film had been a bad idea. It was two o'clock in the morning. Stars broke like china hurled against the frozen black firmament. An eerie light domed Queen. Like a portal had opened: filmic and artificial as outer space, but it was there and that was the freaker—like we had all been remanded to the black and white of Ingmar Bergman. No plot, no meaning. Maybe free will was just a line of nun bullshit to make kids feel bad every time they fucked up.

The small crowd hurried off. Crow so pale in the frigid night, so icily brittle that flashing car beams shone through her as she yawed apart. We held hands and trotted down Elizabeth Street. She wanted to smoke a joint, so we knifed in an alley behind a Wachovia branch, a spit away from where Elizabeth collided with Andromeda. She yanked out a little yellow Bic from her black-sequined antique pocketbook, then whipped out a number and torched it with Parisian flair even though she was scared to death by what we had just seen on the monstrous screen at the Visulite.

Crow possessed that panache—a couple of melodramatic drags seconds before the firing squad martyred her full of holes. Like she didn't give the least shit. Like she was from Little Italy, East Liberty, and not the intemperate backwater of Saint Joan's County. She'd exchanged the beret for a black stocking cap sheathed down over her eyes, those buzzing bees flickering off and on through the fabric, flaming hives abiding inside her cornea. She was a terrified waif, an alien genius. I stood there shivering with her. No hat. For gloves a pair of Crow's pink wool socks—like some kind of chooch. Like I didn't know better, my bum hand just giving it to me in the throbbing blue cold. Had my mother seen me, she would have perished on a dime. My father would merely shake his head. Both their hearts broken. What had happened to me?

Crow offered me the joint. As usual I waved it away. I didn't take dope. I'd witnessed it first hand whack out every third kid from my neighborhood. Kids way better than I. Mowed down like a tank had rolled over them. I wasn't going to do it. As if that moral high ground, or whatever it was, was the last tithe to my former life: some pretense of the clean-cut young man destined for Yale Law School and the string of guaranteed promises such a credential insured. We stood in front of the big drive-through teller's window, that silver-slotted futuristic circle they talk into when you're waiting in the car for your money to come sliding through to you in a two-way drawer.

Then I caught myself in the window. Crow there hunched up against me in black and white. I was all black and white too. My big head of black hair, with a few strands of silver, my big black beard, also a tad silvered, my oversized black Goodwill topcoat, my white face and black eyes. But what saved me were the pink socks on my hands. I laughed out loud. Crow looked worried—that I had cracked. She must have been expecting it. I saw in reflection the gloves, and Crow sidled against me like real love, as if we were some kind of remnant family, but a family nevertheless—all each other had. She told me right there she loved me. We were snared in a Bergman film, but it looked like I still had a shred of my sense of humor. I slipped off the sock on my left hand, took the joint from her and hit it.

I had never even smoked a cigarette before. This was the first smoke to infiltrate my lungs and, when I blew it out, it was inseparable from my frosted breath and the white billow of exhaust coming from the Dry Cleaner's steam vent next to the bank. Clouds and clouds of ether leaking out of everything, shrouding me, shrouding Crow, who looked pleased, but also astonished, and slightly worried, that every time she passed me the joint I took it, sucked smoke from it and huffed it out in growing baby-shaped clouds that hovered for a smiling instant and rushed off in rags on the fierce wind. It was a lovely moment—that seemed to please Crow. She burrowed deeper into my overcoat. The wind backed off and everything silenced. I put my arm around her and looked straight up above my head, deep into the cobalt. The stars had begun snowing on the planet. Big feathery twinkling flakes floated down onto my face, in my hair and beard. Faster and faster. Crow's black livery spotted white. The ground instantly covered. It never snowed in Queen.

Crow and I kissed, then arm in arm, matted with snow, resumed our walk. The minute we breached the turn at Andromeda, we heard the garish din from the Blue Shoe, a bar jackknifed between Plumley's, a pool joint, and Sky Pilot, a head shop. The wind had picked up again. Snow raced through the boulevard lights. Further off, the lights from Detox waxed and blurred—little pregnant girls from Gault hitting cigarettes—the snow so heavy our duplex, just a few blocks off, was invisible. To our left, the stadium gathered the snow in its great ellipsoid. Occasionally a car sloshed by.

The doors to the overflowing Blue Shoe were thrown wide. Smoke and steam and all manner of vapor flooded out into the night. They were in there screaming and dancing—a battalion of rowdy, stone-crazed pagans—to The Mother Night Band. Screeching electrons, the band's red fenders, the drummer's 50 caliber tantrum, toasting pitchers, busted glass, hooks of smoke in the footlights. Next to the Shoe, Sky Pilot's window twinkled with swirling blown glass bongs, pipes, and crystal Buddhas. Whiffs of jasmine incense. Scorched bowls of Marakesh. Chopped Harleys queued on the sidewalk outside the pool parlor, Hell's Angels snorting long bleached lines of coke and snow indistinguishable off black bike saddles.

Crow dug into her bosom and fingered from between her breasts a long pristine number, and singled out a biker, his crazy ancient battered head knotted in a blue paisley bandana, the rest of him grim black leather—like an amnesiac knight templar, keeper of the nocturne, who would die young in a swirl of sparks, red gravel blacktop and a band of angels.

Crow looked at him—he could have swallowed her whole—and asked, "Please, sir, may I trouble you for a light?" and held the joint to her generous mouth, the teeth, the red lipstick. She closed her eyes and waited until she felt the fire the biker held to her lips before inhaling. He stared at her, like maybe there was something about her request, the sheer apparition of Crow, that had undone him in a righteous way. Then he looked at me, like maybe he'd been out of line and given me cause to take offense.

He could have carried her off. Crow was the kind you'd see straddling a Harley, delicate white arms twined around an Angel. I wouldn't have stood in his way, but I had the mark of Cain and not even bikers wanted to trouble me. I was scared enough to kill someone if I had to.

We stood there, the three of us, not saying a word, and smoked the joint as the snow plummeted down. The guy offered us cocaine. Crow snuffed up a couple lines, but I refused. The Shoe was lifting up off its foundation. The band careened back on stage for its encore. The smell of beer and sweat wafted out into the night. Folks jammed together getting down, hands above their heads in praise, their shadows dancing on the wall beyond them, the rekindled voltage of Mother Night's guitars, the drummer hammering out of his skins hallelujahs.

Crow and I headed for Lark Terrace along the edge of the Little League outfield that backed Andromeda, a dark expanse of jagged winter weeds, absorbing the clout of snow. The Shoe revved, but then we made out other music: sitars and tambourines, vaguely, as if lilting down with the snow. Then we were upon a two-story old brick house just before the field. It had always been there, vacant—we had seen it before—but now it was lit up, and there was an electric blue neon scripted sign in English, along with Aramaic cuneiform: *Omar's*. Three stone stairs led to the front door. On either side of it crouched stone lions. Suddenly hungry, we looked at each other, smiled and kissed. We had forgotten Bergman. Just before I turned the doorknob, with my pink socked hand, and we stepped over the threshold, Crow slipped out a bottle of Visine and rinsed the smoke and blood out of her eyes. The bees were composed. They fluttered and hummed like Rimsky-Korsokov.

Omar stood just inside the door. A tuxedoed apparition spirited out of *Casablanca* or *Sirocco*. Spellbindingly handsome. Dark everything. Streaks of natural blue in his ungodly back hair, razored wavy. Dry and pressed and cool and dangerous as the sub-Sahara. His smile. His deep-browed anthracite eyes above the twin rows of blinding teeth. The sheer delight he blanketed us with the instant we walked in his front door. Quasars shooting off the blinding pleats of his foreboding starched white shirt, pearl studs, sapphire cuff links, satin cummerbund and lapels, a white rose boutonniere in the left. He was so beautiful Crow began to cry and I felt a shudder of sorrow and love.

Instantly his smile became a visage of great concern, even loving bemusement. He pulled out a chair from the closest table, and ushered Crow into it. The table was covered in blazing white linen. In its exact center: a silver and cranberry glass bud vase—a single opening red rose, sharp black leaves, curved thorns along the bright green stem.

"Please sit," he said softly—Omar always spoke softly—with a mysterious accent. He smiled again and walked quickly to the back of the restaurant, glided behind the bar and disappeared through a beaded curtain into the kitchen. The music came from speakers locked into the cornices of the back wall: a kind of somnolent screeking moan. Sexy. Subversive. Inevitable. Often excruciating—like a prelude to a door opening behind which the rest of one's life unravels.

On a platform to our right, a floor to ceiling mirror backing it, a tall, fleshy belly dancer, dark like Omar, undulated with the music. Her long black hair was banded across the forehead with a red and purple jeweled tiara. Over her large breasts cinched a purple sash trimmed in red sequins; then a long beaded ornate purple skirt, a jeweled, belled belt, red scarves tucked into the belt. On one hand a purple elbow-length glove, on the other a red one, both stitched with bells and bangles. Twirling colored footlights sprayed her as she shimmied, eyes closed, in a tinkling, glittering trance—as if she were completely alone.

Pinball machines clanged and knelled and occasional guttural exclamations and laughter issued from an alcove opposite the portal into which Ramon had disappeared. Two lambs tethered at its threshold.

In a moment Omar returned with a slender glass of water over ice and set it before Crow.

"I am so sorry," he said, again with the softness of someone practiced in the art of conciliation.

Crow smiled. The large luxurious smile, and swiped off her hat, her hair sparkling with electricity.

"You are better?" he asked.

"Yes, I'm fine."

"I am Omar. Welcome."

We introduced ourselves. I stood and smiled at Omar. He studied me with that same bemused appreciative affection, as if knowing and understanding perfectly my story—a story I could barely recollect. I knew patently nothing about him, but in his presence I felt a calm, oddly enough, like he was a man who would die to protect his friends.

We ordered Lebanese beer, Almaza, and when Omar delivered it in long conical pilsner glasses, he also brought Mezza: baba ghannouge, hommos, grape leaves, falafel, feta, and pink pickled turnips. It came on a pretty china platter with antique cracks spidering its dainty floral gold edges which Omar had decorated with crescents of carrot and cucumber, olives and peppers, triangles of thick pita. Exquisite pale green olive oil pooled in the platter's middle, then paprika over the oil.

"My compliments," he said and spun off again.

Crow and I stared at the food. It was beautiful; but, having never seen anything like it, we didn't know what to do with it. Suddenly very hungry, I picked up a piece of cheese, then an olive. Crow dabbed with the bread at the hommos and baba ghannouge.

Omar returned with menus, and smiled. "You like?"

"It's delicious," Crow said. "We've never had it before."

Omar named the foods, pointing to each, smiling, his teeth incandescent. He was an Egyptian. He and his wife owned the restaurant. We glimpsed her as she hurried from the kitchen to the bar. A black pensive woman with red hair and Asian features dressed in an ornate red brocade marbled gold caftan with a Nehru collar. She smiled with fortitude. Occasionally the pinball players slinked out of their alcove to the bar for drinks. Most were exchange students, glowering, agitated Middle-easterners, from Tyrone College in downtown Queen.

There was something about Omar. He reminded me of home: a certain comfort and familiarity, yet I wanted to assure myself without question that he was a good man just as I knew Felix was a bad man. There was no doubt, however, that Omar issued from that same brotherhood of danger as Felix, the one to which I now belonged; and for an instant I had the urge to drag Crow out of there and run. But Omar's mesmerizing smile, so unlike the murderous smile of Felix, held me there.

The restaurant was warm and smelled of cumin and coriander. The light was soft, perfect. Crow smiled and took into her voluptuous mouth with delicacy the food, her left hand resting on my thigh. Intermittently she removed it to place on my plate in precise designs portions of the mysterious, intoxicating food. We ordered more beer. I never wanted to leave that table, that room that held my life in what seemed like a shimmering glass crucible of perfection. I was suddenly out of my mind for Crow: electrified hair sticking in chopped black blades from her head, the ineffable Braille across her forehead, the mouth a declaration of gorgeous incendiary vulnerability. Bees spinning honey in her sockets.

It had kicked in the moment we crossed Omar's threshold—this reflex toward love. As if in sleepwalking through that bleak Bergman and out the door of the Visulite—the reefer, the sudden snow—then down Elizabeth and onto Andromeda in a blizzard until we crossed into this miraculous place, I had been restored, delivered. Both of us. We had come through something.

But, of course, that hadn't been the case at all. That interlude in Omar's: it was a mere moment of clarity or, more likely, fantasy. I didn't want to be in love with Crow. I didn't really want a future. I just wanted that night, that amnesty of Omar's, to never end. Crow was where I was—that in-between space, that interstice. She, too, loved me at that moment. She was happy. I lifted her hand and kissed it. She took my bad hand and laid it against her face, kissing it, tasting it, my tingling fingers flush against the desperation etched above her eyes, the vibration of the hive busy back there.

When we opened our eyes, Omar stood over us smiling in benediction—nothing at all like Felix, but rather our protector.

"You are in love?" he said, and we had no choice but to smile back and nod *yes,* not quite a lie, but certainly not the truth. Along with the beer, which he delivered on a tray, was a bottle of Mavrodaphne that Omar insisted, when we protested, was a gift. He set the wine on the table next to the red rose. "You are in love," he repeated, this time without the interrogative. By then it was as though the three of us had known one another always; such kinship forbade disappointing Omar. Crow and I turned to each other and smiled. Omar's wife melted through the beads and placed on the bar a cone of lit incense. A cleff of chartreuse smoke flitted up from it. The bottles along the bar shelves smirked. The belly dancer's arms were above her head, snaking along each other, the sound of tiny cymbals endlessly tumbling against each other melding with the clang and hazards of the pinball machines commandeered in the back room.

I ordered sheik-el-mashee. Crow ordered Middle-eastern Kefta—both upon the recommendation of Omar. Dishes we had never heard of, but that fact mattered little. We drank the Almaza, the Mavrodaphne, took in the last bits of the mezza—the food like a narcotic—and stared at the belly dancer, her eyes still closed, her hands now coursing over her round smooth belly, her breasts exposed except for the strip of purple cloth glittering red. Behind her, reflected in the mirror, the snow made every pretense of manna, edible, feathery, mounting into white fortresses of forgetfulness all over Queen.

Crow had my bad hand in both of hers, rubbing it gently between them. It was always cold and often numb. Blood, for some reason, couldn't get to it.

"Do you love me?" Crow asked. I didn't answer. "Here's what we're going to do. Just for tonight." My hand quickened between hers. "We are going to be a lovely couple."

"We're already a lovely couple."

"Well," said Crow, "we embody the essence of a lovely couple. But I'm sure that to other people we look like derelicts."

"Derelicts can make a lovely couple."

"I know this, Romeo. I do. But what I want, just for tonight, is to live entirely inside this illusion of having been rescued. Yanked out of the mist, just as I was vaporizing into it, because you know, we were trapped in that movie for a few frames. They sucked us in with their tractor beams. We were in bad trouble there for a while, but you pulled me out and we stumbled like wayfarers into this fairy tale. So I'm all aswoon over you, about as courtly as it's ever been for me. Right this minute, Romeo, I consider you not just my beau, but my betrothed, and you cannot refuse me—as I am a proper southern lady and you are, after all, an exotic Italian gentleman who knows how to treat such hothouse species. So we're in love and I'll entertain nothing less this evening because *though I bestow all my goods to feed the poor, and though I give my body to be burned, and have not charity, it profiteth me nothing.*"

"How, for the love of God, did you do that?"

"I can quote scripture on a dime. For the love of God. That was the King James. My favorite. The New Revised Standard is nice enough*: Love never ends. But as for prophecies, they will come to an end; as for tongues, they will cease; as for knowledge, it will come to an end.*"

Her eyes pollinated the three inches between our faces. *My beloved,* I wanted to say—because I felt it. I mustered my bad hand to squeeze the two of hers that cradled it, to make known to Crow that no matter what happened beyond the sacramental oddity of this night, that I did love her. I would always love her. But I said nothing. I didn't trust myself in the slightest. It was Sterling I loved. There could never be another like her.

"Then we're getting married?" Crow asked.

"Of course."

"When?"

"Tomorrow."

Had Crow been asked, she would have sworn she did not possess that thing, that aura, some very few women exude—that renders men nearly incoherent with pathological longing. Bad as being a drunkard or a dope fiend. Involuntary staggers, night sweats, obsessive dreams, juvenile insecurity, jackhammering heart.

Sterling had it. So powerfully it rolled off the air around her like compression waves of sound. The moment I laid eyes on her I was snared. Whatever she did. I adored every blessed thing about her. She was flawlessly beautiful. And kind. In a deluded pitiful way, I still expected to see her rising up into the clouds above me like an assumed saint. In my more lucid moments, I realized that she had never been real, but a mere figment—like my imagined former life. Those days in Queen, a quick glimpse at myself in a mirror assuaged the past. Gave it its due. I was somebody else now.

But I had a saint in Crow. She had that thing too—that Sterling had: that power, maybe more so—though, again, you'd hardly call her pretty—as her looks issued from a *gravitas,* a pessimism that lent her the mordant glory of a disgraced and fallen angel. Her brazen hairless nudity as she ambled forlorn through the flat, the tip of her thumb in her brilliant mouth intent on swallowing the beholder. Inky hair spilled across her white face, the drape parting intermittently to reveal the truth texted into her blue-scarred forehead. Eyes that stung once, then died; drowning kisses; nape of her naked bent neck. The skin, the blinding white complexion. Just the skin alone was enough. I stared and stared and never tired of staring. Even when she slept: a small child again, regressed, before whatever happened to make her sad and crazy had occurred—whatever happens to all of us—as she time-traveled in her twisted slumber, forgetting, I'm certain, who I, the man she lived with, was; or maybe it was all those others she had forgotten.

Suddenly I couldn't live without Crow. It was the marijuana, I told myself. Dope—the one thing I had stayed away from, the last cobblestone in the condemned high road I had stupidly clung to.

"Tell me you love me, Romeo."

"I love you."

"Thank you for saying that. I still possess a remnant of sweetness that thrills to those words."

It was ten minutes to 4 o'clock when we left Omar's. The instant we stepped onto the snow-covered sidewalk, the blue neon sign extinguished and the restaurant lights faded slowly until the building was invisible. It was still snowing. The city was silent. Everyone had gone away. We stood there peering through the gauze of snow at Memorial Stadium. Andromeda was an abandoned long white road to the sea.

We walked toward our flat, the snow over our shoe tops, in the cuffs of my tattered khakis. I led Crow across the baseball field out of deep left toward the alley beneath our window. We walked the foul line, though it was four inches under snow, toward the third base dugout, ducked inside and sat on the bench. Crow had left a lamp on beside our bed, the big square sash aglow with light. It looked a long way off. She fished a joint out of her purse and lit it. I stared at the field and blew frosted breath across the shrouded diamond.

A baseball field is the most beautiful, the most sublime, of all playing surfaces: the emerald grass, the blonde brushed burnished infield dirt, the livery, the sepulchral twilight. No other sport lends itself in quite the same way to daguerreotype, the elegiac collaboration between light and dark, day and night, the interplay of straight line and curve, aggregate and flora. No other sport has quite the relationship with the sky, with the past. Even blanketed, invisible, it was there.

"We're all alone in the world, Romeo. Just me and you tonight in this big powdery ball of beautiful believable lies and we're exonerated from the truth because we're in shock—not love. We're in shock with each other. You don't have to love me anymore. I'm releasing you from the love."

I leaned over and kissed her, took her hand, and led her into center field, imagining beneath us as I laid her down all that had been lost and forgotten on that very patch upon which she, white as the snow, disappeared beneath me.

It was the hour of the wolf. Souls rushed by one another in etherized anonymity, weighted with artefacts, catching the last trains into and out of their lives.

Chapter 7

Sunday. We catch a Greyhound out of Queen on our way to Saint Joan's County. Crow has decided I'm to meet her family. The bus is filled with earnest poor folk eating out of Tupperware. Their restive bored waif-like toddlers wander the aisle, weepy, besotted, staring at Crow and me.

The bus rumbles east over Andromeda until the crazy boulevard, once it leaves behind the precincts of Queen, becomes U.S. 74—the Andrew Jackson Highway. Civilization dwindles with each passing milepost until on either side of the sizzling road are but pasture and cropland, cows, horses, pillars of pines, orphaned houses, senescent farmsteads, a fish camp called the Fish Net, the County Line Tavern, and the endless emerald density of the Southland I have all along imagined. Dead possums and raccoons, even the occasional desiccated deer, lay at the shoulders, or gaping in dead bloody wonder on the blazing double yellow that splits the flat eternal road to the Atlantic.

At various mileposts, files of prison inmates clear right o'way with bush-axes and police the shoulders and medians of trash with long spiked sticks. A guard with a colossal shotgun walks alongside them. The prisoners wear brown drab fatigues, and keep their eyes on the earth until a car whizzes by. Then they lift their astonished faces, wave, and watch the car out of sight as if expecting it to halt and spirit them off.

Crow knows the names of the big eighteen wheelers and semis hauling timber and the famous native gravel west out of her homeland: Peterbilt, White, Freightliner, Mack. She recites the names of race car drivers: Richard Petty, Donny and Bobby Allison, Dale Earnhardt, Junior Johnson, Darryl

Waltrip, Bill Elliot, the counties they were born in and the names of their wives. We buzz through a tiny town with one grand dilapidated white-columned plantation house with a café called the Klondike across the road from it, and she whispers that it's the town where that son-of-a-bitch, Jesse Helms, a man I've never heard of, was born.

The voice in which Crow narrates takes on more and more of a southern inflection the further we get from Queen. She calls me her Yankee boy, holds my bad hand, which she is partial to, and lays her head on my shoulder. We pass Cuddy and Holly Farms chicken plants where convicts on work release pull craw with their bare hands. Everybody's doing time.

"Uh-huh," whispers Crow. I'm her baby, she tells me. By the time we rumble into Saint Joan's County, her voice has slowed an octave and the softened protracted vowels fall slowly out of her mouth. Gs disappear entirely from her suffixes. She says *caint* for can't and *own* for on, nuances that must have been there all along, but swallowed by the thrum of Queen.

Again and again, as we pass a crop or a yellow hulking farm contraption, she asks, "I bet you don't know what that is?" I don't know what anything is: the winter wheat, the gleaner and combine. Even the churches, little clapboard shanties with petroglyphic crosses and graveyards off their doorsteps, stymie me. I don't know what so much uncolonized land could mean—the sheer expanse. Enough room to hoard secrets, to remain hidden in, to remain unheard, and ultimately forgotten.

A starveling passionate girl in black, a haiku of woe marching along her brow, has her head on my shoulder, recounting in a voice cured in smoke and jasmine how she hopes her mama has fried corn and okra, cracklin' bread, leather britches, how delicious cornbread crumbled in milk is. More than anything, I don't know who or what I am. Since fleeing Pittsburgh, I've neither shaved nor trimmed my hair. I look out from a revenant's cowl. The green wheat dances.

"It's alright, baby," Crow shushes. "You don't have to know anything. You know me." I wonder what it means to be Crow's baby.

I haven't talked to or seen my mother now in months. My disappearance has aged her, accelerated her determined journey toward the dirt of Mount Carmel. One afternoon, not long after holing up in Queen, I walked into a phone booth in a chewed-out airport neighborhood off Wilkinson Boulevard with the intention of ringing her up. She'd be in front of the television watching the noon news. Ironically a tiny steel mill called Little Pittsburgh leered from the other side of Wilkinson, a dirty road of adult shops and wet T-shirt contests in cowboy bars, and derelict stores where pissed-off black guys lingered in the smog with the gas pumps. Cigarettes, nasty wine, prostitutes, malt liquor and broken bottles.

I had chosen the phone booth for its promise of anonymity. A filthy glass square in a seething vector of concrete that shimmied and melted each time a plane took off or landed deafeningly at nearby Queen International, a gray plume of spent jet fuel spooled across the sky, blurring everything. I never felt more like a criminal, gazing out over the corrugated sky of Queen, scouring earth and sky for Felix.

Part of me, my irises especially, toils round the clock, on panic alert for Felix. In the lore, of what has been written and foretold, he will find me. I see him everywhere—just as I saw him that day I stood in the Queen phone booth, the receiver in my hand, the index finger of my good hand jabbed in the first digit of my parents' phone number.

As I dialed, he very deliberately crossed Wilkinson. Dressed immaculately: in a navy blue suit, white shirt and red tie. His alabaster teeth and black shoes sparkled. His hair gleamed. His mustache was enormous. That pimpy bop to his walk—I'd recognize it anywhere—all muscle, cock strong, and coiled. Picking up velocity, the vents of his suit coat flapping, the red tie lolling like a tongue, he trotted straight toward me with every intention of crashing through the glass and seizing me by the throat. It's a set-up—a stock scene for a gangster hit, reprisal written all over it. Cliché-death. *Morto* nevertheless. Of course, it wasn't Felix, but a businessman desiring only to use the phone. I staggered out of the phone booth, and ran all the way back to Lark Terrace.

From then on, I have conversations with my mother in my head. I call sporadically, always on Sundays, my way of keeping holy the Sabbath. Initially she is overjoyed. Her voice lovely, youthful, when she first hears mine. Her accent on *hell* in *hello* has not changed in the nearly twenty-two years I've known her. It still delights me, in that first instant, when the world still holds promise. Often enough, the news is bad.

"Hi Honey," she sings, then calls to my dad: "George. It's Georgie." In a few seconds, my dad picks up the upstairs extension, sparing my mother the climb, her arthritis now unbearable, and snaps, like a football coach gearing up his team, "Whattayasay, Son?"

We have nothing really to talk about, but the exchange of our voices is enough. Apart from assuring her I'm alright—which is the only information safe to volunteer—I say little. She talks about the weather: bitter cold, hot as hell. Never fails to mention the first robins in the yard when finally spring arrives. But, in the main, she prattles about stories on television or in the newspaper. Cops getting shot, drive-bys, gangs, black and white. Inexplicable explosions. Life-flight. The burn unit. Even a monkey that escaped from the zoo and lived down the Hollow for a while and ended up drowning in Highland Park Pond.

My dad sporadically chimes in with news of the Steelers and the Pirates. Usually, however, he remains silent. Even though my mother's stories are grim, it cheers me in an odd way to hear her tell them—the impassioned way she internalizes the various *infamia,* as if they are personal affronts. *Those son-of-a-bitches.* I can't help but laugh.

The pedestrian facts of what little we have in common keep us going like a sputtering engine guzzling its last trickle of fuel until finally she asks, suddenly hysterical, *Where are you? Why did you leave? When are you coming home? What have you got yourself mixed up in?* My father trying to soothe her: *Sylvia, calm down. You'll make yourself sick.* She tells him that what makes her sick is his constant fussing at her. He's the one that makes her sick. Then she is shouting at him through the phone, my mother at the kitchen table, my father on the extension upstairs, seated on his side of their marriage bed—that he made up earlier, after she finally woke and struggled out of it, along with the rest of his daily housework, now that my mother can no longer stand for more than ten minutes at a time on her swollen legs, jointless, lumpy and blue, that look like they've been stuffed with marbles. Legs that no longer can support her corpulent trunk, her fearful depressed heart, the doleful music ransacking her brain. That keep her even from Mass on Sundays. In grottoes all over the house lurk rosaries, prayer books and statues, with which she superstitiously barters.

These days my father wanders his home with a char-rag instead of a pipe wrench in his pocket. He knows he'll never be summoned back to the mill, that this last layoff is his final severance from the world of steel. Nevertheless, to stop hoping in the hopeless is not in him. He'll make my mother a cup of tea. He'll get her calmed down, put her to bed, and start the sauce, fry the eggplant. My father likes to say that if he doesn't eat pasta on Sunday, then he'll be confused all week as to what day it is. Maybe he'll roast a chicken. Make a big dinner. My mother will feel better after she lies down. They'll eat early, then maybe sit on the porch for a while or watch television: *Ed Sullivan* and *Bonanza.* A little ice cream and coffee.

More than anything, he is resolved to not yell through the phone at his wife, so like a child now, yelling at him. His voice is permanently keyed to the octave to soothe restive babies. He can take it; let her dish it out. But *Sweet Jesus, how did it all come to this? Whatever in the world happened to his boy, Georgie, his beautiful son?*

Up in the bedroom, he is but a few feet above my mother's gray head a floor below where she sits stooped and weepy at the small wooden table, its sharp edges filed, then sanded smooth by him, so she does not scrape herself when she totters into it passing through the kitchen; and if the floor gave way beneath him, he would drop into the cold sunless kitchen and be face to face with her—the living oracle of his destiny.

I have taken the phone from my ear. I look at it, this deranged odd-shaped black vessel inside which my bickering parents are immured for all time. But I can still hear them. My mother keens. She pleads with me to tell her where I am, to come home, that I'm killing her. Then she blames it all on Sterling, that rich little Jew streetwalker, and her showoff family with all their airs, who buried her hooks in me, till I turned against my own family. Suddenly I was too good for them—with all my education and big plans.

Standing there, in my glass confessional, in Queen's outlying industrial sump, my mother's plaintive broken voice chastising me as if she were standing next to me, I do understand: people sometimes walk away and are never heard from again.

By the time I hang up, an eye out for Felix—the call could be traced, he has spies everywhere—she is apologizing: *I didn't mean it, Georgie. Please come home. Come home and sit down and have a dish of macaroni like a normal human being. Then we'll all feel better. I don't even know what I'm saying.* And my dad: *She's just upset, Son. You have to understand. Sylvia, honey, calm down. You're gonna make yourself sick.*

I should weep, and I try to, with all my heart, but I can't. I can remember, *O my God, I am heartily sorry* from The Act of Contrition, but I can't bridge past *sorry.* I simply stare at the planes, artificial, toy-like props in an old movie; the drunks in midafternoon, sidling out of the strip clubs and porno shops. I think of destination, but not the future. I don't want a future, and the past is fluid as an acid flashback. The present and Crow in Queen: this is life now, something I have no vocabulary to explain—not even to God, who still exists, but remains indifferent.

The Greyhound drops us in Dawson, the county seat. The moment we're off the bus, I'm robed in heat. Heat like another language, one I can't understand. Crow understands it. Its catatonic stillness. Its murmuring. Like a forgetful, forgotten old woman alone at the oven talking quietly to herself. Saint Joan herself, perhaps, yet smoldering in the molten corridors between worlds.

I have never seen Crow sweat. Rather her albumen skin when heated takes on a silvery translucent sheen. As though gauging my true mettle, she watches carefully as my foot for the first time touches Saint Joan's County.

The temperature is not merely a fact of geography, proximity to the equator, that I have crossed on the map the imaginary seam, Mason-Dixon, segregating North from South. The heat that drops its ponderous damp garment over me hordes the history and lore, the scholarship, the witness and testimony, the theology of heat: the myth and memory of heat, and of all who have passed this way.

This heat is the South, what I sought when I fled Pittsburgh. Endless. Disincarnate Purgatorial heat. Ancient and glorious and filled with rectitude. That old woman at the stove, her bony parched fingers reaching through me: Negroid, shrunken, Saint Joan blackened by the stake. Her skin bears the snaky bituminous gleam of ancient cloth about to disintegrate. Yet her touch is cool. Everyone and everything forgotten. Even the trees have lost their memories. That heat, when I put my foot on it, separates me from my breath and, for a moment, lifts me off the ground. And the smell: dust after too little rainfall, the violent fecundity of swamp. With my foot on that boiling blacktop, I feel a calling. Like a priest. Like I mainlined the evangelical secret unction of Jesus God; and perhaps I smile, or what passes for one under the heavy beard, because Crow kisses me for a long time, then leads me by the hand across the highway.

We stand in the parking lot of the Tastee Freeze, eating ice cream, waiting for Crow's sister, Charlene, to pick us up. White ice cream rolls down our arms. Crow licks her arm, then mine. Five hundred miles away, my mother watches the noon news. There she will find any number of tangible catastrophes to focus on and store until the next time we talk.

"When I was growing up," Crow reflects, "this was the heart of social action in Saint Joan's County."

"I see."

"This is where we used to hang out."

"Doing what?"

"Nothing much. Pack of kids in cars, driving in circles in this very parking lot all night. Hanging out the window, yelling *hey* to your friends. Sweet tea and slushies, foot longs, banana splits. Making romance through eye contact. That sort of thing."

"Sounds innocent enough."

"I reckon. You know, my mama is going to interrogate you."

"About what?"

Well, you can sure expect some inquiries into your personal relationship with the Lord. She's especially inquisitive about things that aren't any of her business, especially folks' religious practices. And I don't know what else."

"That's fine. I got one just like her back where I come from."

An exaggeratedly long bright mustard yellow Cadillac Coupe de Ville convertible, top down, streams through the lot and halts with a predatory quiver in front of Crow and me. At the wheel is Crow's older sister, Charlene, a cigarette in her mouth. Sunglasses, her hair the color of the Caddy. Short shorts, a halter, a dozen turquoise bracelets and a big turquoise cross around her neck. Early May, but she is already sun-browned. She whistles out a plume of smoke, drops her shades to the tip of her nose—her blue eyes garish with turquoise eye shadow—then stares over them at us, back and forth between me and Crow, for a long moment, before opening her red-lipsticked mouth in a toothy neon smile, the same outrageous set of teeth as Crow's. Charlie Daniels's music blazes from the speakers.

"Get your asses in this vehicle," she says in a voice like a National guitar, takes a gorgeous drag, then flicks the cigarette onto the asphalt.

Crow throws herself in the front seat against Charlene and the two of them hold on to each other for a half-minute. I stand there gaping, then slip in next to Crow and stick out my good hand toward Charlene. She ignores it, grabs me by the shirtfront, hauls me across Crow, and kisses me hard on the mouth.

"Tastes like trouble, Baby Sister," she says.

"Takes one to know one," Crow answers. "Romeo, this is my big sister, Charlene."

"We've met," I say.

"I like him already, Liddie. Even if he is a Yankee. Sense of humor's hard to come by in men."

Charlene floors it, cuts across four lanes of Jackson Highway, and spins us south down Highway 109. In the backseat sits a cooler of beer, between Charlene's legs a pint of George Dickel. "Reach inside that glove box, boy, and see what you find," she orders.

We are already well into the outbrake of Saint Joan's, its shroud of forgetfulness canopying the brilliant Sabbath, balling 90 over narrow blacktop, knifing through a breach of shimmering holographic green that breaks my heart with promise. I am fearful of lifting my sunglasses. It is the blinding light itself, the exultation of the ordinary, the inclusion of our lives in an instant of light and elevation whiter than angels. We pass the Dickel and chase it with cold cans of Schaeffer. Without a time machine, Felix will never find me out here.

I pull three fat joints, fastened with pink ribbon, out of the glove box.

"Light one of those sons o'bitches," orders Charlene, punching in the Caddy's lighter. "Hell, light all three." She turns to me: "Hope you don't mind me cussing."

"Not at all."

"Real Yankee manners, Baby Sister."

I hand the joints to Crow.

"You gonna partake?" she asks me.

I just shake my head.

"Romeo doesn't take drugs," volunteers Crow as she yanks out the dash lighter and puts its coiling orange fire to the number.

"Clean liver too. Goddam, what a find. I might have to steal him."

"He's all yours," Crow answers, hitting the joint and passing it to Charlene.

Nothing at all out here, dense swarming green, the early crop of corn, luscious emerald, but already fighting for its life. What is now already dry will be brittle in July. Come August, the plowsoles will shrivel and crack. The corn will faint, lie there expiring in its flaming shucks and tassels. Half of it won't make it into the grain siloes. But today, it encamps with blinding fortitude along 109. And the mighty prehistoric kudzu, swallowing the few shacks sinking off the road, mainly abandoned, but a few with black folks on the porches who wave as we jet by.

Something launches out of a tree along the brake, slices into the windshield, as though it aims to decapitate Charlene, and caroms off. We all duck. Charlene runs the car off the flint shoulder, mowing down a skirmish of corn stalks.

"Good God Almighty," yelps Crow. "What was that?"

Charlene whips the car into a U-turn, slaps over another dozen plants, and heads back. There in the road twitches a juvenile owl, one wing flapping and the other dangling in a regal black and tawny fan across the faded white middle line. He twists his head toward us. 180 degrees. Must be his heart ticking so loudly. Like a bellows, it puffs in, then out, one wing twitching uselessly, the other already quite dead. Dignified, imperious, like a little gangster, he takes us in in turn as though marking us. He won't forget. A mere child, he understands the way things are. He dares us to kill him, looks at us not so much imploring for mercy, or even understanding, but dispatch.

"Shit," Charlene hisses. Then she aims and slowly rolls over the owl. Its death spreads through the chassis for one long instant. Charlene engineers another U-turn, assassinating more of the corn, and we sail breakneck again north on 109.

"Jesus, Charlene!" Crow exclaims.

"I couldn't just let him suffer."

"An owl is a bad omen."

"Only if you're Mama. And not a word of this to her. She'll have us tying knots in the bed sheets and Lord only knows what else."

"Owls are powerful medicine, Charlene. Emissaries of wisdom. Take heed."

"If that windshield hadn't been between us, that emissary of wisdom'd be sticking out of my forehead like a tomahawk."

Crow turns to me: "Charlene kills things like that all the time."

"I don't kill them. I have encounters."

"In one of her encounters, she was driving well above the speed limit along this very road and sliced a blue jay in half with her aerial."

"I felt bad about that one."

The sisters laugh a little nervously, as if leading up to weeping, then break down laughing madly. Charlene guns it up to 95, and passes the Dickel. "Goddam, it's hot," she says. "Fire up another number."

I take a swig of the whiskey, drink some beer. It's okay, I tell myself, the vision of that baby owl, like a dead hat those burning miles behind us, imprinted in both frames of my eyes. The girls laugh. They whoop. On the windshield, at the point of impact, a foot from Charlene's face, is a smeared halo.

"He always this quiet?" Charlene asks. When Crow, patiently holding in a hit, doesn't answer, she says, "He's kinda dark. You sure he's not Negro or Mexican?"

Crow sings out in a cloud of smoke, "He's Italian."

"Out here Italian's close to black."

"Charlene, you're scaring my beau. I wish you'd hush."

The roads we zoom over have no names, but rather mere numbers, faded to Sanskrit, imprinted on stakes in the gravel roadbed. Murdered stop signs, punctured by jagged bullet holes, root where one road veers into another. We lurch into a fen, the ordained rot of the season as it creeps toward the solstice. Banners of mist rise from brackish water.

"Alligators in there," Charlene says.

It doesn't matter to me. I'm further from home than I've ever been. Bugs tick off the windshield like buckshot. In the dust the Caddy's wheels churn up, the heat and rot smell like semen. Burning sweat runnels beneath my beard.

On either side of the road, peach orchards appear, acres and acres of twisted little trees with bandaged trunks, furzy balls of fruit, the ground confettied with shed blossoms, catching in the brilliant fallen light like pink cellophane. The sun is a furious yellow peach buzz-sawing as it drops through the crop and rolls into the road.

Charlene never brakes. She drives right through the mammoth yellow ball in the interminably long yellow Cadillac as it liquefies around us and we find ourselves parked on the other side of it at the edge of a rock escarpment. Beneath us, stretching for miles, is a lake, walls of sheer rock containing its jade-green water. A quarry, called the Ballast Pits by the indigenous, the aftermath of excavation. Saint Joan's County is renowned for its gravel, a rare grade of granite and quartzite, a vein of prehistoric rock, found nowhere else in the world.

Charlene explains all this as she and Crow strip off every shred of their clothing and stand poised at the jagged brink. The Ballast Pits reach all the way to the prison in Coventry where their daddy made his living for thirty years. Convicts once mined the rock, and many of them, drowned while dredging, or shot out of caprice by guards, are still preserved in freezing astral pockets on the fathomless pit floors, monstrous gilled felons that prey on the young lovers who queue in cars along the quarry to spoon. The prison graveyard is up on a bluff and, on a clear day, you can see the spraddled crosses listing across the horizon.

"Don't listen to a word she says, Baby," Crow says.

"Gospel truth," avers Charlene. She is darker by half than Crow, yet still fair. They favor each other only in the mouth, the generous wet lips, their tongues that poise on the tips of their glistening large teeth. They stand there stitchless, and powdery, silhouetted inches from the falloff like sister virgins about to appease a volcano. Not an ounce of shame to them, Charlene endowed where Crow isn't, Crow hairless where Charlene isn't. A big cobalt cloud and chuffing wind sit dormant, miles off, atop the corrugated bluff on the other side of the water.

I take off my shirt and stare at them staring at me, then everything else until I'm unclothed as the rock I tiptoe over. Crow takes my bad hand, and leads me to Charlene, now looking out over the vast green water. With each cloud shift in the oncoming darkness, a shadow plummets into it and light ripples well beneath the surface. My instinct is to pull back—I don't know how to swim—but it's too late. Charlene takes my other hand and we stand there at the end of everything looking thirty, maybe forty, feet down into the rock water.

Dead sedans nose out of the water's edge and, on a gouged ledge, two bleached elephant skeletons stave out of the shallows like a pair of ruined temples, the tusks brandished against the sky. Relics of the mythic 1952 cyclone that heaved up Saint Joan's County and shook it till everything fell out of it. Even elephants—visiting with a traveling circus in Dawson. Panicked by the twister, they ripped out of their cages, through town buildings and citizens, along the Andrew Jackson highway, then rampaged through the woods like bulldozers until finally stampeding over the edge of the ballast pits where they drowned, and eventually beached to rot once the water abated. Crow hadn't been born yet, but she knew all about it.

"I know," Crow is saying to me. "It's alright. We're gonna count to three."

There's no counting at all. The sisters leap off the escarpment holding me in their soft hands. The plunge is long enough for me to wonder if my life is at an end, but I don't have my usual dread at the prospect of submersion. I say the Hail Mary and stare at the hyperventilating clouds on the far cliff of the ballast pits.

The water is blessedly warm. We sink through marbled rills of white and green. When I open my eyes, Crow and Charlene, whiter, even more unclothed, exaggerations of nudity, in the phosphorescent water, stare at me, smiling, from a distance. Then they laugh, and I hear the laughter in the bubbles that squeal out of their mouths and envelope me. Torpedo-sized golden koi swim among us. On the quarry floor shimmers the congress of all that has been lost or mislaid in this gouge: Saint Joan's Lover's Lane where the county progeny first endure love and often die for it. Their souls—with the buttons, coins and jewelry, trousseaux and dowries, automobiles and bones, the crowning syllables of their last day here—drift with the ballast at the bottom to which I slowly sink until I am walking among the forgotten still trysting in their gravel beds. The smoky coils of their limbs, the utter hush of spirit coitus. Crow and Charlene have disappeared.

Something gathers above. Darkness, yes, but some ponderous weight the sky bears. It is in this rocky water, too, filled with dark sky. Drowned lovers beckon as if I am one of them. Dark robes of murk churn toward me. Long bone-white arms encircle me and I am buoyed up, away from the perpetual light, toward the ever-growing darkness until suddenly I break the surface, shrieking for oxygen, hooded by the brutal sky. Then Crow, who has delivered me, shrieks as well; and, with her help, I make it to the bank where we keel panting in a mound of mica and cordite.

We don't bother to dress. Just scrape with our clothes toward Charlene's Caddy. Quartzite and feldspar stud my hair and beard, the hair that has somehow sprouted on my chest and stomach, even curling across my shoulders and back, since arriving south, the pelt between my legs; so that when the first fender of lightning scissors down from the black canopy enveloping the ballast pits, Crow and I light up like x-rays.

The trees shimmy. They know what's about to go down.

Charlene's at the wheel with a lit cigarette, her bare dripping torso around the massive steering wheel, kicking it into *Drive* before we can even reach her. Crow leaps in first, catches my good hand, and I run along the car until I can vault in between them.

It won't rain. Not just yet. The sky gargles and rolls back on itself in wave after wave of ever-blacker, until it's a skillet of bubbling black glass crackling with capillaries of light, big as arsoned houses. At each ignition, flashes of the past play as if the dead have been herded back to earth, along with apparitions of the living, and even the premonitory shades of the yet-to-be. We speed along the curves, out of the Ballast Pits, rusted lorries and dump trucks and cast off tools littering the scarred road.

A little boy in the window of his block shed house pushes against the pane. The bones in his little hands flash when the lightning spears the tin roof. Clothes drying in a burdock tree blow off and disintegrate. A hawk knifes down and snares up a rabbit from the road, but cannot summon the lift. The rabbit, a curio of a rabbit, so perfect, the ears at attention—it might already be dead—hooked in its talons. The hawk, beating its massive wings, still reluctant to give up its prey, but stopped in the gale, time stilled. A cross wind skives the tin roof off the boy's home. The roof, divested, rendered anomalous, stuck too in that cross wind. The hawk with the rabbit in its talons, and the rusted patch of tin, side by side in midair, the house like an open shoe box, the little boy gone.

Charlene: a cigarette smoldering in her mouth, a beer between her naked legs, flooring it, fiddling with the radio, but all that coughs out is static. As we race along the crude red road, grouted in gravel, we pass under the roof and the hawk. Hovering just above us. A Saint Joan's County icon. The wind keening like the Point South and Comfort spearing out of Coventry along the Pistol River with a hundred pearly tons of gravel.

Charlene swerves into a ditch, where snakes and vermin congregate to wait out the storm, then crashes through a moldering cedar and brittle barbed wire fence a man three hundred years gone had built. A man I see through God's stereopticon in a burlap jerkin, pelt hat, spade and mallet.

I see my mother and father. At Saint Joseph's altar at Saints Peter and Paul Church in East Liberty. My mother in a wheelchair. My father with a cane. He tucks a dollar in the alms-box. My mother leans over and lights a candle among the bank of red-glassed votives. It flares up and I smell frankincense. Magazines of lightning spray the Caddy. My mother begins to cry. My father places his hand on her arm. My grandfathers roll bocce balls across the shaggy electrocuted face of the swales. The Italian dead of Mount Carmel lurch through the toppling woods. The stone carver, fitting bit to the ledger stone, taps out ponderous epitaphs.

Then Felix, dressed like the undertaker, a pink Forget-Me-Not in his double-breasted black suit. He moves easily among the living and the dead, at will jimmying open their worlds, smiling, greeting each in turn, asking if they've seen me: George Dolce, a good friend of his, from the old neighborhood, East Liberty, his boy, really, a good looking kid, on his way to some big shot law school, twenty-one, twenty-two, with a busted-up right hand. He and George go way back. Felix is looking right at me. I shield my face. Things hurl at us. But I am no longer George Dolce. I no longer wear his countenance. Still Felix knows it's me. He raises his hand, the blazing white cuff of his shirt sliding out from his black coat sleeve, the hairy wrist strapped in a gold Rolex, wedding band and star sapphire on his last two fingers. He smiles like the day I first met him and he pretended he was joking when he warned, "You don't want to fuck with me."

I say nothing of these apparitions to Charlene and Crow—like two of the Furies, deranged and iconic, after a run-in with the Gods. They glance back and forth at each other, across me, grim, but self-collected, as if there is little for whatever we're driving into or away from, but to accept it. Like we have tripped into prophecy, and there is no way to wheedle out of it. Porcelain bookends on either side of me, their breasts dignified, strange, and I hoary with rock, intent on the spirits toiling in each seam of lightning.

The bright yellow Caddy with its black-walls and chrome is flying. Like a mammoth goldfinch. The land bosky, the black-green sky, silvered on the half-minute with slabs of lightning. The heat veering out of the swamp is tropical. Deer huddle on the sandy spits where tulip poplars sway. Snakes twine the upper limbs of the voluptuous sycamores lording over the banks. Rabbits everywhere, and starlings settling, then going up again, like blankets shaken out and redraped, then grackles, and two bald eagles. A bobcat. The soil smokes. The underhouses have caught fire.

Then hail, like baseballs, bombs us, hammering the car, leaving declivities in the hood, landing in the back seat, in the few inches between the three of us in the front seat, accumulating freak snow on the black top. I take one in my shoulder, off my knee. Crow soughs quietly as one slams into her thigh. Two break across Charlene's hands on the steering wheel. She cries out and for an instant lets go of the wheel. Trees drop their leaves like October and swoon along the iced road bed.

We skid off the road, through the mucky brake and into a clearing where deer have gathered in congress—thirty, forty, all bucks with great swirling racks webbed with ice. As though marble, they simply stare as Charlene rights the Caddy, then swipes it in a careening U-turn back toward the road. It's airborne when we hear the whistle of that twister train ripping through its appointed railhead—no brakeman nor stoker, no conductor. Just the unholy caprice of that one mutant cloud, like placenta, its umbilici drooling down, vacuuming up the earth.

Saint Joan's Chapel stands sanctuary at the apex of a curving green rise vaulting out of the swamp, another road with its forgotten black numbers on a white stick nailed to a cedar post.

Above its red double doors, recessed in the grottoed eave, lords a statue of Joan, but a girl, in full armor, black hair chopped to her nape, eyes heavenward in delusionary transports—a 15th century likeness of Crow. Fixed above the statue is a neon cross that sprays inextinguishable light across the ancient churchyard.

Charlene slams on the brakes and cuts it hard into a raw gravel lot between the church and a small graveyard held in a black wrought iron fence. The name *Gaddy* furls across the front gate, its brass ball handle turned green, then beneath the ledger the vendor's imprint: *Stewart Iron Works, 3rd and Culverts Streets, Cincinnati, Ohio.*

We jump out of the car and sprint in the crossfire of hail for the church. My hand curls around the black porcelain doorknob. Miraculously, one of those nearly two hundred year old red doors is open. Once inside, we bar the doors with the pike that fits across the iron slats bolted to them.

In the minute narthex is a greening bronze plaque. Saint Joan's was built in 1783, the earliest place of worship for Methodists in the county. It was served by a circuit minister, Jonathan Jackson, purportedly kin to Andrew Jackson who obtained his law degree in Saint Joan's County. Ladybugs coat the walls. Ornate cobwebs, littered with fly and gnat carcasses, spill from the cornices. Goldfinches and indigo buntings flit about the three storey beadboard ceiling, at intervals roosting, on the cane ceiling fan paddles.

It's just before dark. But time is divested of itself, neither day nor night. Green Old Testament light slants prophetically in from windows that span near to the ceiling, and line the two side walls of the nave. Panes big as writ pages, crinkled with age, sills but two feet from the wide cracked pine slab floor, and sponged on the outside with honeycombs.

A regiment of crude benches on either side of the center aisle, Cokesbury Worship Hymnals at intervals along their seats. Toward the chancel, through refracted ramparts of limelight, we walk in the footprints of the departed, the scuff and brush of shoe and frock.

Flanked by primitive oak deacon chairs, the altar is a misshapen slab of granite. On its shoulder, resting on a moth-eaten purple velvet antimacassar is a twenty-pound King James Bible, printed in Philadelphia by A. J. Holman Company, signed in memorable penmanship in the frontispiece by each member of the congregation, Sunday, August 25, 1783. It is thrown open to Acts, Chapter 2, Peter's address at Pentecost, Verses 20, all caps: THE SUN SHALL BE TURNED INTO DARKNESS, AND THE MOON INTO BLOOD, BEFORE THAT GREAT AND NOTABLE DAY OF THE LORD COME. On either side of the Bible are tall golden candelabra, long yellow tapers inexplicably lit. Forty-two cents loll in a brass collection plate.

A Denon black pump organ sits off to the side with two rows of benches for the choir, *Denon* in gilt Gothic glyphs ablaze across its face above the keys. At each octave of wind the chapel quakes, the candle flames rear, and there comes the steady toll of the church bell strafed with hail.

To cover their naked bodies, Crow and Charlene don sky blue, fluted, silky choir robes, and throw a third to me. Crow sits at the organ. She works her feet against the brass pedals and fingers the keys. A pneumatic keen that mixes eerily with the howl beyond the chapel and the contrapuntal gong of the church bell. She plays "There Is a Fountain Filled with Blood." She and Charlene sing like doomed angels. The massive windows, spackled with birds, foliage, dragonflies and lost garments, wheeze in and out. *There is a fountain filled with blood drawn from Immanuel's veins; And sinners, plunged beneath that flood, lose all their guilty stains. The dying thief rejoiced to see that fountain in his day; And there may I, though vile as he, wash all my sins away.*

I mumble a song to keep up with Crow and Charlene, who seem to know we're going to die. But all the sounds have become one insatiable deafening entreaty, the wind begging God to let it rest. Detonation upon detonation: the end of the world. *Per Omnia Saecula Saculorum.*

The smell—what already I know for the smell of the South: a hush to that smell, a sacred hush, the word made flesh, the land itself and all its props having absorbed its own mythography. The old country church you might have occasion to seek sanctuary in: still furnished, the haunted furniture shrouded in bedsheets, whole wars fought to keep the dowry extant. Something fecund, forbidden, on the evening air.

A parcel of late sun suddenly prisms the dripping windows. It's how I know I'm alive. That smell. The incense of must and old. Pentecostal pigheadedness. In Saint Joan's Chapel, after the storm, Crow and Charlene on either side of me, those candles atop the altar burning.

When I throw open both big red doors—studded with jackdaws, some spiked to them beak-first, their glistering eyes onyx periods—white light streams the narthex and trickles through the nave. Trees sprawl along the ditch banks. Contorted limbs bric-a-brac the road. Runoff floods the churchyard. In the far woods beyond deer gallop the swales. Flocks of birds sing above them. The warm hush: and out of it the crickets and cicadas and even the whippoorwill, insisting beyond count, that he is the whippoorwill, have resumed their tally of time. And further, beyond the fen and Ballast Pits, and the swollen Pistol, vaults a rainbow, its raiment—scarlet, orange, maize, green, blue, indigo, violet—stacked in a parabola of concentric bands. Saint Joan and her inextinguishable cross shine above us. Behind her rests the plump red evening sun. Crow takes my arm. She and Charlene stare at the rainbow.

"Lord God," whispers Charlene.

The Caddillac is swamped. Waterlogged and littered with leaves and twigs. Sparrows and voles drowned in pools on the floorboard. Charlene picks our sodden clothes out of the back seat and begins wringing them out. A black snake slides out of them and slithers into the graveyard.

"I don't believe we can show up at Mama and Daddy's in choir robes," she says, laying the wrung clothes across the Caddy's hood."

I follow the girls toward the graveyard where the snake has curled on a gravehead yet in the full sun. It's a small cemetery, and we move about it without speaking, hefting the limbs off the stones and setting aright the markers that have fallen, brushing away the detritus from the epitaphs: *Beautiful, lovely, queenly she was. Faithful to her trust even unto death.*

A passel of *Gaddys,* then *Sheppard, Capel, Liles, Maness, Poplin, Webb, Usrey, Icemorelee.* Cracked. Pocked with stonewort. Effaced by years and weather. 1600s and back. Evermore. Brushing with our hands the angel stones and soul effigies, little tablets no bigger than picture books, bleached and calcified. The keen work of the stone carver: the endless story of love's pittance flaked in Gothic script with chisel and mallet. Some have names. Some just *Baby.*

The sun speads across the horizon. Berobed, we sit in puddled seats and hold our clothes in the wake to dry. There is Schaeffer and Dickel, Johnny Cash on the radio, the last weed number blessedly dry when Crow whips it out of the glove compartment.

Charlene wheels into a clearing where stand four giant blighted dead cottonwoods. *The Sisters,* Crow and Charlene call them. Haunted trees, where escaped slaves were lynched and left hanging, naked as we are once we strip off the robes before wiggling into our still-wet clothes.

Crow and Charlene recount how as teenagers they got dolled up—perfume, make-up, jewelry—and came here to *The Sisters* at dusk, smoked a joint and waited for aliens to abduct them. They'd read up on it: how blinding hovercraft would drift over its prey, young women desirous of escape, and assume them into its belly in a magnetic shaft of light. Aliens, Charlene and Crow say, have long favored Saint Joan's County.

We drape our glory robes in the lower arms of the Sisters and speed through the peach orchards, dazed and swooning from the blow, at the feet of the wispy trees piles of plucked infant peaches.

The swamp has overflowed its rim. It laps the road. The ditches gorge with brown water. Downed power lines fizz in the trees. The blacktop scrawls with drowned snakes and birds, frogs and terrapins, rabbits, possums, crows and skunks. Charlene never slows, but steers around them. We pass the bottle. Charlene and Crow smoke cigarettes.

Charlene makes a right on Prison Camp Road, a slight incline. In the distance, in the laser sunlight, hover coils of silvery clouds trussed in razors. It's phenomenally beautiful, mesmerizing—like the rainbow, some wonder smelted out by meteorological violence. Up over the rise, as things level out, a compound, like a concentration camp, with little shacks on stilts—guard towers—at its four corners, surrounded by tall chain link fence, barbed wire. Along its spine, swirling, overflowing, gleams concertina: razor wire—named for the Italian squeezebox, like the one my grandfather played as he sang Napolitano folks songs to the children on holidays—patented as a medium for laceration in 1844 by Sir Charles Wheatstone.

Along the fence, men, dressed identically in green fatigues, stand in a quagmire facing the highway. Uniformed men with shotguns pace behind them. Fallen power lines writhe across a concrete basketball court with. One of the goals is down. A tree leans against the fence.

"That's Daddy's prison," Crow prompts.

The prison is built against the quarry, at the northern reaches of the Ballast Pit. Prisoners smashed, then drayed, those rocks out of the cavity and built their own jailhouse with them. Mist wafts up from the fathomless vast green water behind the line of stone buildings at the back of the compound.

"Our daddy lost his mind behind that fence, on that yard right yonder," Charlene declares.

Charlene honks the horn as we fly by. The men raise their hands, and the girls throw big exaggerated waves.

"Mama won't say it," confides Crow, "but we got a brother doing time back there."

Chapter 8

Holiday season was frantic at the pharmacy. With things so stretched at home, the extra hours on the clock there were especially important. But I was torn by my desire to see Sterling who did not have to return to Bryn Mawr until after the Super Bowl. Phil raised my wages again, and encouraged me to cut back on my hours.

"Why are you pushing like this?" he asked. "Enjoy yourself while you can. Next year you'll be in New Haven or Boston, Washington, wherever you want to be, with all the responsibility. This year, relax."

"But you need me here, Phil. We're swamped."

"We'll manage, George. JoAnn is in here every afternoon. Why don't you work till twelve or one and then have lunch with Sterling? Enjoy each other's company. Have fun. Two weeks and she's back at school. Don't be silly. Life is short."

But I needed those hours delivering pills, and every dollar they put in my pocket—in my family's pocket. How often had I heard my father say, "Make hay while the sun shines." Meaning: Never take a break and *never* depend on tomorrow because you might be in a wheelchair. This ethic superseded everything. Superseded God, though I would never confide this to my mother. But my father understood it perfectly. It was in his gait and in his eyes when he was out of work. A beaten-downness and impotence as he needlessly whitewashed the immaculate cellar and painted the garbage drums just to keep busy. So he could feel like he wasn't completely worthless.

Phil Rosechild didn't understand this. He had money. An unlimited supply, it seemed. When he used the word, *manage,* he meant having enough money to piss away. When my parents used it, they meant cutting to the bone, staying a half-crippled step ahead of the poor house. So I worked every hour I could despite the protest of Phil and even JoAnn when she rolled in at two o'clock every day to work the register.

There was one adage, however, that the Rosechilds and my parents invoked alike: *Life is short.* Pushing twenty-two, I already knew this. Sterling would head back to Bryn Mawr on January 13. And then what would happen? I knew I shouldn't even think of this. It softened my resolve. But I couldn't help it. She and I spent nearly every evening together. I drove the Newport to the Rosechilds, had a drink with Phil and JoAnn while I waited for Sterling, then we took off with me behind the wheel of her Mercedes.

Sterling had a curiosity about my life that made me uncomfortable. She didn't want to talk about what I studied at Duquesne, or my career plans—the easy things we chatted about the afternoon we met at the Rosechilds'. She wanted to talk about the part of me I hardly ever considered: the part of me rooted exactly where I stood in time; and she wanted to hear about my past.

I didn't share that same curiosity about her. I loved being with her, looking at her, her touch, her scent, everything about her. But I wasn't intent on what she was thinking. And I wasn't necessarily interested in her past. At the Rosechilds', I had seen her high school and coming-out portraits. As an only child, like me, her photographs, from the time she was an infant, were displayed everywhere. But they were mere images, outside of me and anything I could ever know.

What thrilled me most about Sterling, however, was contemplating a future with her. An impressionistic vision, a cross between Madison Avenue and Tahiti. There were three piece suits; airplanes; tan skin; the smell of Ban de Soleil; fragrant children in sailor blouses; automobiles like the ones I parked at parties in Squirrel Hill; an enormous, white house arbored in Sycamores, a fire in the hearth, a laid sparkling table and, hovering in every perfect room, black-haired Sterling, in a white linen dress flowing about her like wings, so unspeakably beautiful that when she walked the wind whipped up outside and the first leaves of the Sycamores fell to the sod lawn.

It was a borrowed vision—though I didn't realize this at the time—extrapolated from a subscription to *Esquire* I had taken on a whim the year before. The magazine bored me; I never read it. But I pored over the photographs of the better life with real longing, and the certainty that one day it would all be mine. There simply existed no alternative, and I never imagined that Sterling, or anybody, really, would want something different. I didn't consider the fact that after graduation from Brynn Mawr her plan was to go to New York and chase down her dream of acting, whatever that took. New York was a routine commute to New Haven—Yale was at the top of my list—and we'd see each other regularly, perhaps even live together, though I was determined not to marry until I'd completed law school and passed the Bar. She'd have the theatre, I'd be wrought up with my studies, and in three years we'd start our lives together in earnest.

That I had led a life so far of any interest had never occurred to me, and why anyone, especially someone like Sterling, would want to know about it stymied me. I fancied myself a guy on his way somewhere, not someone stalled in the here and now—or, worse, in the past—like those laid-off has-beens who sat all day in Caprino's nursing shots and beers, worrying about when their unemployment would run out.

What could I tell her? That my dad was a laid-off steelworker? That my mother had had four back operations and was crimped over with arthritis so badly she could barely walk? That the two of them sat together at night, with the television on or listening to Mario Lanza records, and made gaudy Christmas ornaments out of costume jewelry for the Catholic War Veterans to distribute to the poor kids in the projects even though my parents had bitterly fought the construction of the projects, didn't like black people at all, but had a soft spot for the children?

That was the house I had grown up in: pasta on Thursday and Sunday, fish on Friday, soup on Monday. Mass and the sacraments until I graduated high school and started college, then my parents didn't bother me about my immortal soul anymore. They didn't bother me about anything. They had complete faith in my vision of the future and subscribed to it themselves.

I paused a moment, surprised at what had come out of my mouth about my parents. Sterling and I had been in the shallow end of the swimming pool at the University Club, where the Rosechilds had a membership. Her legs were wrapped around my waist, her arms around my neck. She wore a black tank suit, and pink ear plugs. Her plastered hair dripped in my face.

"I want to meet them," Sterling said.

"My parents?"

"Uh huh."

"Why?"

"Because I know they're nice people and I want to meet them."

"I don't know."

"You're ashamed of me."

"That's it."

"When can I meet them?"

"I don't know."

She fell back into the water and backstroked to the other end of the pool, then back and forth, free style. I could not swim. I stood there in the shallows and watched her cut effortlessly through the water, flip-turning at the walls.

I envisioned my mom and dad, Sterling and I in our living room. The television was on: *Lawrence Welk.* My mother, in her housecoat, sitting on the heating pad, had her feet propped on the hassock, stockings rolled down to her ankles, lap filled with thread and little red and green beads while Sterling went on about how she loved the ornaments my mom was making, how beautiful the Christmas tree was.

"This is the last year we're putting one up," my mother declared.

"You say that every year, Mom," I responded.

"We're getting too old for all this. Your father can't handle it."

"Who can't?" growled my dad.

"You," shot back my mom.

"Oh, I'll bet you'd miss it," said Sterling.

"Your people don't put up a tree, do they?" asked my mom.

I knew this was coming. *Your people.* My mother's way of saying, *You're a Jew.*

"Oh, we always have a tree."

"But you don't celebrate Christmas."

"Mother," I interrupted.

"What did I say?"

"It's fine," Sterling said, smiling. "Jews, as a rule, don't celebrate Christmas, but our family always has."

"What about your own religion?" my mom inquired.

"I wasn't raised to believe in a particular religion."

My mother looked at me, like *How about this*? Then said, "Hmmm," smiled at Sterling and turned to Lawrence Welk, surrounded by champagne bubbles, his wand poised in midair.

My dad was trying to keep awake. Looking to change the subject, I tried talking to him about the Steelers' chances against Buffalo. But the instant I turned away to acknowledge something Sterling had said, he dropped off and started snoring.

"George, my God, you'll wake the dead," my mother snapped.

My dad came out of it like a man doused with ice water.

"Wake up, sleeping Jesus," my mom said. Then to Sterling: "He's exhausted. He painted the whole cellar today. He still thinks he's twenty years old. When he's laid-off, he doesn't know what to do with himself. Do you, George?"

"What?" said my dad, still not completely awake.

"What," mocked my mom. "You're snoring in front of Georgie's company."

"I'm sorry, honey," said my dad to Sterling.

"Oh, that's alright. I hadn't noticed."

"How could you not notice?"

I wanted to strangle my mother. What an idiot I had been to let Sterling talk me into this. My darling Sterling, sitting there next to me on the couch with her hands folded in the lap of her jeans, hair in a loose pony tail. She just smiled.

My mother, with great sighs, removed one leg, then another from the hassock, then gripped the chair arms and hoisted herself from it with a moan.

"*Jesu Christe,*" she said.

Sterling shot to her feet. "Let me help you, Mrs. Dolce."

"I can manage." She grabbed her cane. "I hate this son-of-a-bitching thing." Then she tottered side to side out of the room.

Her profanity infuriated and embarrassed me. I wanted to say something, but I knew that in the mood she was in—it was obvious to my dad and me that she didn't feel good—the least thing could set her off.

"Where you going, Sylvia?" asked my dad.

"I'm going to put something out. These kids need to eat."

"Please don't go to any trouble, Mrs. Dolce," Sterling said.

"It's no trouble."

"Mom, we're fine," I said. "Sit down."

"You sit down," she snapped without turning.

My dad looked at me like: *Save your breath. You know she's going to do what she wants.*

"I'll give you a hand, Mrs. Dolce," offered Sterling.

"No, thank you. I'll do it myself."

Sterling caught up to my mom, twice her width, and patted her back. "I really have to insist," she said, smiling.

My mother shrugged and they disappeared into the kitchen together.

I sat at the table with my dad and watched the women bring out the food. Things I really loved, but which seemed to me, that night, coarse, common: eggplant and salami and capacola, hot green peppers, Sicilian olives, aged provolone, big haunches of Italian bread. Food that could take the skin off the roof of your mouth.

Sterling had some of everything, even the peppers—my dad's favorites—that I couldn't eat because they went down like boiling oil and doubled me up with cramps. My dad eyed her approvingly.

"Don't let her eat those," my mom warned me. "They'll make her sick."

"They're delicious," Sterling said.

"God bless her," said my dad.

"How can you eat them?" asked my mom.

"I love hot things."

"Not me. My God, they turn my intestines to mush. I can't digest them."

"You like hot sausage?" my dad asked Sterling.

"She wouldn't eat that," said my mom.

"No. I love it."

"Next time I make it, you come over."

"I'd love to."

My parents were impressed by Sterling's mettle at the table. If she had turned up her nose at any of it, that would have been the end. But she dug in with respect and appreciation, and chipped in in the kitchen with my mom. The two of them were back in there, chatting and laughing as they made coffee and loaded a platter with sweets. My dad had gone back into the living room to watch the rest of Lawrence Welk, and was snoring away in his chair.

Sitting alone at the table, I glanced around the room, at the side by side oval portraits of Jesus and Mary that my parents had received as wedding presents, their hearts lolling on their robes like pomegranates stitched with thorns. On the big, white stereo sat my graduation picture and two orange glass bowls with a huge orange vase between them. The carpet was burnt orange. In the china cabinet was displayed the set of fancy dishes that my father and I had bought for my mother one Christmas several years ago. We had put them on layaway at J.M. Roberts and Son, Jewelers, at East Hills Shopping Center; then, every Friday evening, we traveled clear out there and put five dollars toward the bill. They were still beautiful: blue flowers in the middle of a white plate, goblets with a silver glaze about the rims. Those dishes had never been used. Instead we dined on grape-green plastic dishes my mom had collected, piece by piece, with coupons from the milkman.

I love my parents. I refuse to be ashamed of them or the world they inhabit. It is not, however, my world. I fully acknowledge I'm of it, though my complete exodus from it—Sterling by then fixed in my mind as its most obvious symbol—was, at that time, a matter of mere months. Even so, I worried that Sterling would see them as freaks. Her world was sculpted out of Waterford crystal, cushioned by Persian carpets. Surely she had never broken bread in such a home before; there would be the temptation for anyone not raised in that world to see it as garish and small. She didn't know a damn thing about a day's work, what a cake of soap looks like after you wash your greasy hands with it, what hands look like after thirty years of shoveling slag out of a blast furnace, how a man and his wife shrivel after only a few days, let alone, weeks, or God forbid months, out of work. I bristled at the thought that, to Sterling, the evening in my home might be no more than a social experiment, that what I had opened for her was not a family album, but an ethnography. I chided myself all over again for giving in to her requests to visit my home.

But the instant she reappeared from the kitchen with my mother, and sat back down beside me, I forgot all this. The flames of her world encircled me like a halo. I loved her like you might love the sun were it possible to stand on.

My mother yelled at my father, still snoring: "My God, George, do you think this girl wants to hear you grunting like a pig in there?"

He opened his eyes and gaped at my mom in astonishment, then smeared back his disheveled hair. "I'm sorry."

I shot a murderous look at my mother, and started to say something. I would have if Sterling hadn't been there. I couldn't wait to get out of that house. Out of that town. Far away.

"We're waiting for you to have coffee. Turn off the TV."

My dad obediently stumbled to the TV, then into the dining room.

"One of these days," he said, smiling, and wagged his fist at my mother. "I'm going to give you a free trip to the moon."

"Yeah, any old day," she countered. "You'll be pushing up daisies."

Sterling laughed. She seemed genuinely charmed.

"Your little girlfriend here says I should take yoga to help my arthritis," said my mom, then laughed and laughed.

My mother hardly ever laughed. And referring to Sterling as my *little girlfriend.*

"What's yoga?" my dad asked.

"A kind of exercise," answered my mom.

"They offer classes at the Irene Kaufmann Center," Sterling said.

"I'm not Jewish," said my mom.

"You don't have to be Jewish," my dad assured her.

"What do you know about it?" my mom turned on him. "That whole neighborhood is overrun with blacks anyway."

We had cake and coffee and hard chocolate cookies my mother called *niggertoes.* I winced each time she said it, but Sterling didn't seem to notice.

As we were leaving, my mom presented Sterling with a mound of the cookies wrapped in aluminum foil. She thanked my parents for their hospitality, then hugged them, and promised to visit again if they would have her.

"Don't be silly," said my mom.

"You're welcome any time, honey," chimed in my dad.

For the rest of the night, Sterling raved about how much she had loved the visit, how sweet my parents were. When could she visit again? I was merely pleased that she hadn't been horrified.

When I returned home from the Rosechilds', my parents were in front of Johnny Carson. My mother woke with a start and put her hand over her heart.

"My God, you scared me. George, wake up," she pealed. Then, about Johnny Carson: "I hate him. He's so in love with himself."

Anxious to get upstairs and study, I kissed my parents goodnight, and started up the stairs.

"I liked your little girlfriend," said my mother. A comment I knew was merely a prelude to the postmortem. I knew, as well, to excuse myself on that high note, but I paused for a moment. In spite of everything, I wanted so much for them to approve of Sterling.

"I told your father. She has respect. Doesn't she, George?"

"Yes, she does."

"And she knew her way around the kitchen. I bet she didn't learn that from her mother."

Here it comes, I figured. One of my mother's ingenious diatribes. Compliments laced with invective. I sat down. Might as well get it over with. My dad had gone back to sleep.

"She could use a little meat on her bones. I don't know how she stays so skinny if she always eats that much. You can tell she doesn't get that kind of food at home."

"She was just being polite, Mother."

"If she's so rich, why wasn't she dressed better?"

"Who says she's rich?"

"Please. Her father's a millionaire twice over. She didn't look any snazzier than any of the other girls I see."

"How snazzy do you have to look to eat a salami sandwich?"

"What? Salami's not good enough for her?"

"What's going on here, Mom? I thought you said you liked her."

"I do like her. She has beautiful skin. What worries me is she has no religion."

"What are you talking about? And what does that have to do with anything anyhow?"

"I just know that a lot of heartache goes along with mixed marriages."

"I just met her. Nobody's getting married. And what do you mean by mixed marriages? You talk about her like she's black or something."

"Hey! I don't like that kind of kidding. Nobody said a word about being black. I think she's darling. But Jews and Catholics, Jews and Italians. Like oil and water. Just promise me you'll raise the kids Catholic."

At that point, I clicked off the switch in my head and laid the vision to rest. Taking Sterling by to visit my parents would be too delicate an operation. My mother was too unpredictable, too explosive. She'd be sure to say the wrong thing.

I watched Sterling emerge at the other end of the pool, climb the ladder to the high dive, and wave to me. She was just beautiful. Every inch. I waved back. Then she flung herself into the air, and hovered there for instant, her arms like pinions, before bringing them together in a steeple and falling head-first into the blue water.

At lunch upstairs in the club dining room, Sterling asked me if I knew anyone in the Mafia. The waiters wore maroon waistcoats, black bowties and white gloves. They poured coffee out of lidded silver pots.

"Are you serious?"

"Not entirely, but not not entirely. Do you?"

Those guys in carnal, point-blank suits and big snap-brims who stood outside Genevieve's on Larimer Avenue, guys my dad would say, "Whatta ya say?" to when we walked down to Labriola's for lunch meat and cheese. *Racketeers,* my mother called them, half of them politicians. She used the two terms interchangeably: *rackateers* and *politicians.* Those guys never worked—not like my dad—a real job. That was for sure. About themselves they had cultivated the illusion of ennobled privilege simply because they weren't like the other dumb stiffs who toiled for a living. If you were tight with them, you felt like a million bucks. That's how my dad felt. He prided himself on knowing them. He had grown up with them. He had become one of the dumb stiffs. And where had it gotten him? he'd ask. Laid-off. Back in the bread line. On his ass all day doing crossword puzzles without a pot to piss in. And those guys—who hadn't once broken a sweat in all the years he'd known them—they drove new Lincolns and Cadillacs, vacationed two weeks every summer at Wildwood, then Las Vegas over the holidays.

They had it all figured out. They sold smokes out of their trunks. Nylons, tennis rackets, cameras, wristwatches. You name it. They always had an angle. Plenty of them made book. Like Eugene. But Eugene was different, my mom was quick to point out. He was a working man. An electrician earning a good living for his family. Not a showoff. Not a slicker. Not a man who stays up all night and sleeps all day. Not a *gavone.* She almost spit when she said it.

Those guys down on the Avenue weren't criminal, just shady. Not a bonafide gangster among them. No guns. No blood. They all had wives and kids and were members of the Holy Name Society. In their ways, lovable. But they too were something I wanted to leave behind. Those petty wise guys. Nevertheless, I was intrigued by them. Life is short. Why be someone else's stooge?

I attempted to explain all of this to Sterling, but what I said fell flat, monochromatic. She wanted to understand. She even smiled and reached across the table for my hand, as if to make easier the disclosures she seemed certain I'd confide.

"So you don't know anyone like in *The Godfather*?"

"No, I really don't. Why are you so interested in all this?"

"I just am. It's unusual."

"I guess."

I pulled out my wallet to pay for lunch, but Sterling signed for it. One of the waiters handed her a pen and a piece of paper and she merely scrawled her name.

Holding hands, we walked to the Carnegie Museum to look at paintings. Sterling wore a red beret and bright red lipstick, tiny red Christmas bulb earrings. Her cheeks were red. Every few minutes, she squeezed my hand. She told me I was sweet to indulge her this way. She knew I didn't want to go to the museum, but she loved being seen with me. She was going to drag me to all of her favorite boring things all over the city for the duration of the holidays and I'd just have to put up with it.

It was viciously cold and windy. The sky hoarded snow. I brushed the blowing hair away from her mouth, took her face in my hands and kissed her for a long time. I told myself that this was happiness. Love. Sterling peered at me so tenderly when we came apart from the kiss, I worried I might begin to cry.

"What?" she asked.

This was the juncture in a relationship where you told the other person you loved her. I stalled a moment, weighing what such an admission would cost me. "Nothing," I muttered.

During my childhood, I had been to the museum dozens of times with my dad: dinosaurs, mummies, suits of armor, the impenetrable hush of the marble, like a gigantic tabernacle, magnifying every breath. But I had never once visited the wing in which the paintings hung.

Sterling paced among them, warily, nearly trembling, as she studied them. For something I didn't even know to look for. I tiptoed into another room and was instantly mesmerized by an oil that lit the chamber with buzzsaws of light and color. It vibrated in its frame, threatening—so brilliant, so dire—to spring off the wall. Slowly, I walked toward it. *Wheat Field with Crows.* Van Gogh. A Dutch painter who sliced off part of his ear with a razor and presented it to a woman he'd been jilted by. When he was 37, he shot himself in the chest while at work on this very painting, and a few days later died of the wound. I had seen his work reproduced in books, but the anxiety, the turbulence, the loneliness of the actual canvas was like a drug: the crows, just black-V-slashes like child-drawn birds, moiling out of a cobalt-indigo sky crushing the sun-colored wheat blowing in a thousand directions at once, an indeterminate path swirling through it, Vincent's impastoed paint rising out of the field in three dimensions, all of it promising to detonate at any moment. I touched my right index finger to a crow, nimbused in a bruised round of faint-blue cloud, an upraised nub of stony eighty-five year old paint.

Two arms encircled me, then I smelled Sterling. She squeezed herself against me, and I gripped her hands linked at my sternum.

"Hey, I'm going to take you for a ride," I said.

"Now you're starting to sound like a gangster."

"Let's go, Baby."

Chapter 9

What the hell, I thought, as I drove Sterling's Mercedes through the old neighborhood. This would be better than taking her to visit my parents. My memory was imbedded in those streets, but that didn't make anything true. I'd let the omniscient landscape do the telling.

My mother would have pronounced that, for all my education, I sure didn't have much common sense. I was crazy to take a girl down there, especially in that flashy car. It was bad. Nothing but black gangs. Drive-bys. And those *gavone* racketeers who never grew up. All the decent people had left.

My dad still bought Italian bread at Rimini's, sausage and cheese and olives at Labriola's and Pompa's. "It's getting bad down there," he liked to say.

I fixed a wary eye on the black kids walking across Meadow Street Bridge. Young men, really, but it was difficult to tell since they were bundled against the cold in long overcoats and ski caps. They held cigarettes in gloves with the fingers snipped off them. Smoke from the cigarettes and the sixteen degree temperature launched out of their mouths as their heads swiveled to check out the conspicuous blue automobile.

Sterling was so innocent; she didn't even know how to be scared. We caught the light at the corner of Larimer and Meadow. An enclave of weathered-looking hatless white guys in leather jackets with the collars turned up, smoking, and blowing into their fists, stood outside the falling-down corner store that used to be Johnny and Carlo's Dairy. In 1968, during the riots, a fifty caliber machine gun had been mounted on its roof.

"Is that true?" Sterling asked.

"Yeah." But I didn't know if it was true.

Only a handful of stooped, grim old women dressed in black trudged up and down the street, stopping to browse the storefronts. Bins of produce and fish sat on the sidewalks. The stores had metal jail bars over their windows.

"Who are those women, George?"

"Those are Italian widows. Once their husbands die, they wear black for the rest of their lives, down to their underwear. Even if they're only nineteen when it happens. Deadlier than the black widow."

"They seem so unhappy."

"That's their job. To haunt the living with their unhappiness. They're walking unhappiness generators."

"Why are you so cynical about them? Don't you think it's sad?"

"I do think it's sad. When I was a kid I was afraid of them. We ran like hell when we saw them. We thought they were witches, and could cast spells just by looking at us. The *malocchio.* The evil eye. You've seen those gold horns guys where around their necks with their holy medals? That's to ward off the *malocchio.* Very important piece of equipment in these parts."

I pointed out three men in suits across the street in front of The Meadow Grill. "There's the Mafia."

"Really?"

I laughed. "Naw. They're just guys who like to dress up like gangsters. It's part of the mystique of the neighborhood. What's left of it. My mother calls them racketeers. But that's because they're not brick layers or tailors."

"They look quite authentic."

"Actually, I do have a gangster story for you." I made the left at Larimer and slowly wheeled up the avenue. "You see right there." I pointed to a spot in front of Labriola's Grocery. "A local politician named Alfred DiStefano was shot to pieces right on that sidewalk about five, six years ago. My parents were in the store buying salami. Classic gangland hit. Big black Caddy cruised by. Burst of machine gun fire. No one was ever charged."

"Oh, my God."

"Yes, indeed."

"You're giving me the business."

"Documented fact. You can look it up."

"That's terrible."

"You want to hear something else terrible?"

"Yes."

"See those long black things sticking out of those bushel-baskets in front of that grocery store?"

"Uh-huh. What are they?"

"Codfish. Frozen solid. The Italian word for it is *baccala.* Eaten especially during Christmas. Christmas eve. When I was little, my mother and father, would say, just kidding, that they were going to give me a *baccala.* Like a spanking."

"Why did they call it that?"

"Because some of the old Italian people used to beat their kids with the frozen *baccala.* Use it for a paddle. True story. *Unusual.* Your word."

"I *guess.* Your word."

Driving along Larimer was like reading in a child's hand the first chapters of my autobiography and, as it spilled from my mouth to Sterling, I was touched by it. Its power, how it all came back so vividly, how successfully I had cut myself off from it.

Larimer Field: a weedy lot of broken glass and crack fugitives, where I had played Little League. Across the avenue from the field bulged Larimer School, boarded and sprayed with graffiti, one of its front columns gone. Past Joseph Street where Isaac Bond had lived. My dad and Isaac had been friends, millwrights together on the open hearth at Edgar Thomson. Isaac hadn't owned a car, so my dad gave him a lift whenever they shared turns. Light-skinned, bald, with a fringe of sandpapery white hair above his ears and a white nub mustache thumb-tacked to his lip, Isaac had a voice like God the Father and was a consummate, joyless gentleman.

Isaac's son, Kevin, black as a Steelers helmet, had been a schoolmate of mine. Kevin was nothing like his father. A gangly, flighty, effeminate, smart, very African-looking boy whom everyone picked on, including me. The very first day of first grade at Saints Peter and Paul, in 1959, Kevin wet his pants. Sister Sarah escorted him to the cloakroom. When he emerged, he was wearing a dress and blubbering, tears dripping off his face to the desktop. From that day forward, Kevin became the whipping boy. He failed two grades, entered the Bishop's Latin School with the intentions of becoming a priest, recanted his vocation, became openly homosexual, then a junky, and was shot squabbling over dope in a bar on Frankstown Avenue. Paralyzed for life, he spent his days scooting along the avenue, trying to cop, in a wheelchair.

At dawn, buying bread at Rimini's, my father sometimes came upon Kevin, hunched, nodding, in that chair, and Kevin never recognized him. He'd mumble thanks for the couple bucks my dad habitually laid on him. "You're a fool," my mom admonished him for giving Kevin money.

"What the hell," he replied. My little *compadre,* my dad referred to Kevin. He had been Kevin's Confirmation sponsor. Isaac had claimed he didn't know any decent colored Catholic men, so he approached my dad. On the appointed Saturday in May, with the gift wristwatch wrapped in his pocket, my father swung by Joseph Street and drove Kevin to church, as was the custom; then stood with him at the altar rail, and took an oath as his new Godfather, in the sacred rite, to exemplify and uphold Kevin's apostolic life. After the ceremony, my dad had driven back to Joseph Street for Kevin's party. In secret, the lone white, he had sat at the Bond family supper table, broken bread with them, and had his picture taken with Kevin as he presented him with the watch. I have never seen the picture, but I remember the ribbing my father had to put up with from my aunts and uncles—and especially from my mother—for standing up for that little *melanzano.*

When I think of Kevin—the morning he reappeared from the cloakroom in that calico dress, that poor little mortified boy, his life at that moment transmogrified for all time—I feel murderous all over again. Not merely because of what Sister Sarah had done to Kevin, but my own realization, as a six year old, like an injection of ice water, that the world was cruel beyond words, that if you expected kindness from it, it would rut you into whoring for life. I vowed that day, back in first grade, 1959, that they would never put a dress on me, that rather than submit to such humiliation, I would hurl myself through one of the huge windows that ringed the classroom, bleeding to death from the lacerations as I fell three stories to the concrete schoolyard below.

Sterling and I drove across Larimer Bridge over which Sidney Jackson had jumped—five, six, seven stories, maybe more—and only broke his leg. Sidney had robbed Murabito's, a gas station there at the edge of the bridge guarded by two ferocious German Shepherds. Sidney took off with the dough across the bridge and, rather than be eaten by the chasing dogs, he leapt over the rail right in the middle of it. Landed on the roof of a red Studebaker footling along the slow lane of Washington Boulevard, then bounced off it like a rubber ball and came down on the pavement. That's when he broke his leg. Hitting the car hadn't harmed him at all. They loaded the old lady who had been driving the car in the ambulance along with Sidney, as the shock of a large black boy falling from the sky on to her automobile had caused her to hyperventilate. Murabito declared anybody crazy enough to jump off a bridge, and lucky enough to only break a leg, is entitled to something. He let Sidney keep the money.

Up Lincoln Avenue, past Corpus Christi Church, where I made a furtive Sign of the Cross, until it dead-ended at the streetcar barn. Two more turns through potholed war-zone streets and we were at Mount Carmel Cemetery.

I hadn't been there since the day my grandmother had been buried, fourteen years earlier, when I was seven. We parked where I remembered the stone to be, but I couldn't find it. It was late afternoon. What had been a bright day had turned somber, the sky one huge dirty chrome snow cloud spilling gray light on acre upon acre of Italian dead. The fantastic Mediterranean names trembled across the tombs like declarations of amnesia, the cemetery all but deserted. Just the grave-scrubbers and rosary-sayers. The demented survivors. We searched until there was too little light to see, then gave up and got back in the car.

My grandmother, Giovanna, my mother's mother, the only grandparent I had known, the daughter of a Roman architect who was a confidant of Pope Saint Pius X, educated in Florentine convents, fluent in six languages and world-traveled, came to the United States with her mother after her father drowned in the Adriatic. Early photographs verify her loveliness and grace. Apparently the family was quite wealthy, but whatever had happened to the fortune remained, like their reasons for leaving Italy, a mystery.

Giovanna married a marble mason immigrant from Umbria, my mother's father, who spent his meager paycheck being a "bigshot, a playboy, the son-of-a-bitch," as my mother recounted it. He was a bad drinker, violent whenever he had too much, and frequently beat his nine children, though never laid a finger on his wife who helped make ends meet by giving spinet lessons until her husband chopped up the spinet for stove-wood during the Depression. My mother and her brothers and sisters hated their father and rejoiced when he died of pneumonia the day before Pearl Harbor. He left no insurance money, no legacy. Penniless. But, as my mother pointed out, he left them alone, and that was a blessing.

Giovanna lived the next twenty-seven years of her life a widow who refused black, but wore instead quiet blue and pink and yellow dresses. My mother spoke of her mother elegiacally, as she might of the Blessed Virgin Mary, and could not get through the first sentence without breaking down. I've adopted as a fixed portrait of my grandmother my mother's version of Giovanna, though her account is so laced with sentimentality, and seasoned with venom for her father, that it can't be trusted. The truth, suspect as it must always remain, is that I had never really known my grandmother, and have only the vaguest memory of her, though my mother has always insisted that above all the other grandchildren she adored me.

What sustains Giovanna in my psyche, however, is not her purported love for me, though I find it attractive and believable, but the notion of her lofty bearing and noble blood—the ancestor from whom I had hatched: brilliantly educated, erudite, charming. My mother possesses none of her mother's gentility. My other grandparents, all Italian immigrants, as well, were of humble origin. Simple laborers and tradesmen.

The one true memory I have concerning Giovanna is the day she suddenly took ill and died. The call had come and my parents rushed off, leaving me in the house with Judy Marmo, the seventeen year old daughter of our next-door neighbor. After supper I went into the refrigerator and pulled out what was left of the chocolate pie my grandmother had baked and sent over just the day before. It was a rich, dense dessert I loved like no other, and when it was in the house I could not rest for thinking of it.

I had been sitting in front of television, gouging at the pie, still in its pan, when my parents came in from the hospital with news of my grandmother's death. My mother, held up by my father, wept uncontrollably. When she saw me and the pie, she lunged at me, grabbed the pie and threw it across the room. She stood over me with her fists balled until my father led her upstairs to bed where she cried all night and into the next morning. The last thing I remember of the night is my father, standing on a chair, sponging chocolate pie off the ceiling. The real truth: I don't remember my grandmother at all; I remember a pie.

The neighborhood looked less dingy, less abandoned, as the darkness furled over it. A few of the houses and stores had Christmas lights strung along their gutters. Driving back over the Meadow Street Bridge, I remembered the pellet gun and Dave Mazzotti. A crew of us—Dave, Alex Caprio, and I—decided we needed a pellet rifle. To shoot birds. Shoot whatever. Targets. Streetlights. We had been about thirteen, fourteen. Alex was a good artist and could draw anything. He sold inspection stickers he copied by hand to people whose cars couldn't pass inspection. You couldn't tell the difference. They looked like they had just come in the mail from Harrisburg.

To raise the bread for the gun, Alex had drawn three pictures of a cute little pitiful boy on crutches, holding in his hand like a Valentine a big red heart with *Please Give* printed across it, and *Children's Hospital* with the hospital logo at the very top. Perfect in every detail. Sherlock Holmes couldn't tell the difference. The pictures were glued around three empty Ajax cans and we collected door to door in the neighborhood until we had enough money.

One afternoon, Alex and I had been shooting at sparrows in an alley behind some abandoned houses on Collins Avenue. Dave walked into the mouth of the alley, a good way off. Alex said he didn't think he could hit Dave. He shot four times. When Dave reached us, he was holding his stomach. Two pellets had struck him. Blood rolled over his fingers and dripped onto the alley floor. He started to cry and sunk to a sitting position. Dave sat in the gravel looking helplessly up at us, his tears falling with the blood, drop by drop.

We stashed the gun under the rotting floorboards of one of the houses, got Dave to his feet and half-walked, half-carried him to my house. My mother couldn't drive, so she called an ambulance, crying the whole time, punctuated by a litany of "Oh, my God." Then she called Mrs. Mazzotti who ran all the way to the house in her slip and hair curlers and became hysterical when she saw Dave.

We blamed it on the blacks. We had been walking along Sheridan Avenue when an ice-blue Buick LeSabre stopped and a tall guy with an afro and a red sweater jumped out and started shooting. We were pretty sure the other guys in the LeSabre had shot at us too. There were three of them in all, but we only got a decent look at the guy with the gun. We were scared witless and had, of course, started running. No, we did not get the license plate number.

The two white detectives had taken this all down on their pads and told us and our parents, all gathered in the Mazzottis' living room, how lucky we had been. All nodded their heads in assent. The parents said things like, "Thank God," and "Animals." We remained silent and sobered. Dave sat there in his bathrobe and bedroom slippers. He betrayed nothing. His guardian angel had been working overtime, one of the cops said before they left. "Amen," Mrs. Mazzotti intoned, and began to weep. "Goddam niggers," said her husband.

It had been on TV and in the newspapers: *East Liberty Youth Shot Twice by Unidentified Assailant* and *Shooting Fuels Racial Tension.* Our fabrication about the black men nearly resurrected the race wars of the late sixties. For the next two weeks, the neighborhoods stayed on red alert. Every black was eyed with well more in the way of the usual suspicion, and there were a number of fights. But no more incidents, and things eventually settled into the old predictable antipathy between the races.

As I listened to myself relate these stories to Sterling, I couldn't quite believe them myself, though they had been there all along, residing in the attic of my brain with the rest of the discarded and forgotten memorabilia. Things I thought I'd methodically eradicated from my memory over the years tumbled out of me in words. Sterling, tears in her eyes, placed her hand upon my thigh. Why in the world had I told her all this? What would she think of me now? More than anything, my own sentiment shocked me. I had never supposed nostalgia played any part in my life. It was like recovering from amnesia.

At the end of the bridge, I made a hard left at Saint Marie Street, not far from my home, and cruised slowly until I hit the stop sign at Sheridan across from Chookie's store. Standing in front of the store in a huddle were a half dozen stooped men dressed in overcoats, smoking cigarettes, passing a paper bag around.

"I know all those guys. I grew up with them. Three of them are in my Little League team picture on the wall above my bed."

"Why are they standing out there in the cold?"

"That's what they do. Day in and day out. They stand there. Cold, warm, rain. It's in the script."

Sterling looked at me.

"They're hoods, bums, junkies, drunks, the neighborhood discards. They're who I'd be."

"I don't understand."

"In this neighborhood, there have to be the sufferers. Like a quota, a barter the founders of East Liberty made to appease God. You know, like throwing a virgin into the volcano. Then the rest of us are safe. Every generation has its sacrificial lambs, and those guys are my generation's. They stand there jonesing in the freezing cold so I and my rosy future can sit in this very expensive warm car with a beautiful woman and plot my way out of here."

"You're talking metaphysics, George. Do you feel guilty because you're not a drug addict?"

"I don't know."

The guys on the corner stared at the Mercedes, lingering so long at the stop sign. Two of them dropped off the curb and started across the street. I pressed a button and my window disappeared into the door.

"What's up, Dave?" I called.

"Who is that?" hollered one of them.

"It's George. Dolce."

"Hey, Georgie-boy," said Dave, carrying the paper bag and walking unsteadily toward the car. The other guy turned back and sat down on the curb.

Dave stuck his head in the car window. He smelled like an old guy. Piss, sweat, smoke, booze, confusion. His beard was long and his hair teased out under a wool cap snugged down to his eyebrows. Beneath his eyes rutted deep dirty creases. His teeth were rotten, but he smiled broadly. He thrust his hand at me.

I took it and smiled. "How you doing, Dave?"

"Not as good as you, boy. Where the hell'd you come by this car? Where the hell'd you come by this girl?"

"I'm just the driver. Sterling Rosechild, this is my old friend, David Mazzotti."

Dave slapped the hat from his head and held it over his heart. "It is a pleasure to meet you, Madam," he said. "Can I offer you a drink?" He held up the paper bag.

"No, thank you, Dave. It's nice to meet you too."

"Yeah, well," Dave muttered, staggering a little, nodding. "We're just holding down the fort here."

"I thought I'd say hello, Dave," I said, putting the car in gear.

"Well, Merry Christmas, George. Come back when you can stay longer. And bring your little girl here with you." Dave smiled and looked past George at Sterling. "You know, Miss, Georgie always did have a horseshoe up his ass. He has a secret life buried in him that passed the rest of us by. He's going to make something of himself some day. We're proud of him. We really are, George." Dave clapped me on the shoulder.

I handed him a rolled-up twenty dollar bill.

"Thanks, man," he said.

"I'll see you later, Dave."

"He didn't seem so bad," Sterling said as we drove off.

"He isn't so bad. He's just not human any more. None of them are. If we walked away from this car for five minutes—even though I've known those guys since we were babies—when we came back it would be sitting on blocks, nothing but the chassis left, everything gone for dope. If you were down here by yourself in it, and they didn't know you, they'd do worse. Believe me. Once they start riding that horse, they'll sell their mother's wooden leg for a fix. They'll sell their mothers."

"Why did you give him money, then, if he'll just buy more dope?"

"Guilt. More than anything it's a bribe, a payoff. I pay him to be the junky on the corner instead of me. If that makes any sense. He's doing my time for me in Purgatory."

"Do you really think of it that way?"

"I don't know. It's why I want to get the hell out of here."

"Isn't Dave the guy Alex shot?"

"Yeah."

"What happened to Alex?"

"One night he got out of bed in his pajamas—I don't know, four years ago, right after high school—and threw himself over the bridge you and I just drove across."

"Oh, George. My God. Why?"

"Nobody knows. Like the Trinity. It's a mystery."

"But you said he was such a good artist."

"He was. Won every scholastic art award in the city. A genius. He had a full scholarship to Carnegie-Mellon. Everyone of those specimens down on that corner are smart as hell. Talented."

"I don't understand."

"Nobody does. It's like when they get to the point where things are really starting to work out for them, that it looks like all the promises are going to be kept, that they're going to actually be happy, they panic. The day before graduation they drop out of school, or tell off the boss, or break up with their saintly girlfriend. Whatever. Mainline smack. Jump off a bridge. I don't know. They want to succeed, but they want to fail more. And fail with great passion, I might add. My mother and father, people like that, they see these guys as scum-of-the-earth, but it's way more complicated."

"Is that why you've worked out this little schema about quotas to explain why you are you and they're who they are?"

"Maybe so. I just can't accept it's merely random."

I wasn't sure whether I was trying to endear myself to Sterling or drive her away. Holding my hand, she gazed at me with absolution in her eyes. The more horrible things I told her, the better she seemed to like me. She couldn't have been that good. No one could be. She probably simply found it fascinating. Like anthropology. Maybe she just felt sorry for me.

"Now that I've trotted out my sordid past, and spent the day traumatizing you, what do you think of me?"

"I love you, George."

That word had not been used before between us. The very sound of it withered me. I absolutely loved Sterling. No doubt in my mind. But the actual word loose and sizzling through the car was like having that syringe jammed into my forearm. Too sweet to be true, an illusion in all likelihood. Like heroin. Like I might lapse out of consciousness. But instead I uttered the pure truth: "I love you too." Then we kissed. There at the corner of Highland and Saint Marie, the Seminary clock tolling the hour as if something had been decided, just a block west of my past from which I had long ago so thoroughly distanced myself.

We drove around the city, holding hands, kissing at lights and stop signs. I had to bring myself back to earth. I hadn't talked to Eugene in three days, had even missed payday, and the weekend was nearly upon me: first round of playoffs, including the Steelers-Bills game. I was the breadwinner. My parents were depending on me, though they had no idea that most of my money came from gambling.

Christmas was seven days away. But it was hard to shift my thoughts from Sterling. I couldn't help but envision myself in a yarmulke, stepping under the hoopah, the glass breaking; the new territory, starting with the European honeymoon, I'd blaze with her far far from East Liberty. But all these things, despite the love beating in me like the speeding car I manned, sported pendulous price tags. Sterling, herself, for that matter. As sweet and unpretentious as she was. No sense kidding myself. I had been to her home. I knew her parents. Money was a must. For my own integrity, if nothing else. Otherwise you spend your life kissing asses. I valued humility in others, but I did not wish to be humble. Not the way my parents were.

We weren't far from Eugene's house. It was Wednesday, the early lines available.

"I'm going to take you to see some old friends of the family. Five minutes. Just to say hello and Merry Christmas."

"I'd love to meet them."

"They'll be a letdown after Dave."

The Pappas' house was outlined in thousands of colored lights: windows, stairs, porch railings, doorjamb, roof and chimney. It resembled from a distance a child's colorful, geometric sketch of a house.

The front door opened directly into the Pappas' living room, lit to match the outside. Every line, every angle, was strung with lights. An episode of *One Day at a Time* blared from the TV. Wrapped gifts bunched under the Christmas tree. Eugene Junior and Michelle sat playing on the floor in a pile of baby dolls. Connie hugged and kissed me, then did the same with Sterling after I introduced her. Eugene kissed her too and wished her Merry Christmas.

"You any relation to the pharmacist?" he asked.

"He's my father."

"Good guy. He's always gone the extra mile with my mother whenever she has questions about her medicine. She's old. Has to take a lot of pills. Very patient. I appreciate it. George always has nothing but praise for him."

"That's very nice of you to say," said Sterling. "I love all your lights."

"Can you tell Eugene's an electrician?" quipped Connie. "Our house is like a celebrity in this neighborhood. Here. You two sit down. Have something to eat. It's junk, but what are you going to do? It's the holidays."

On the coffee table were bowls of potato chips and chex party mix and little chocolate balls wrapped in red and green foil.

Sterling sat on the couch next to Connie and took a handful of the chex mix. "I love chex mix. My mother always makes it at Christmas."

"It's not the holidays without it," said Connie.

Michelle, dangling a doll by an arm, stared from the other side of the coffee table at Sterling.

"C'mere, honey," Sterling coaxed, and held out her hands.

Michelle very deliberately toddled around the coffee table and walked into Sterling's arms. Sterling hugged and kissed her, then boosted her onto her lap where Michelle, still clutching the baby doll, continued to stare at her impassively.

"Well, aren't you just the sweetest thing? What's your baby's name?"

"Man," I said, "I've known Michelle all her life and she's never done that with me. You have the touch."

"Well, she's a little prettier than you," cracked Eugene.

"No, no. You do have the touch," said Connie. "She doesn't go to just anyone. That's remarkable."

"Well, I'm flattered," said Sterling, looking into Michelle's eyes, then dipping in to rub noses with her.

Lovely. The lights, the tree, the kids. Eugene had a nice family. This wouldn't be so bad. And Sterling: she had the touch. But something was missing. I was tempted to say it was Sterling, except she was sitting right there in front of me. My life. It was too ever-present. The hereness. The nowness. Its proximity: East Liberty, Pittsburgh, the twenty-one-plus years snagged in a geography I could not rise above without leaving. Go some place where I had no history, no ancestry. That long ride I had taken with Sterling had hammered this home. Ghosts crawled out of every sidewalk crack. If I didn't get out soon, I'd turn into one of them.

Those streets were waiting to claim me. Like Dave. And Alex. Poor, angelic Alex. Gone. Deader than hell. No note, no clue, no nothing. Just gone. And the pity was that people, myself included, I foremost, had blanked him out as if he'd never existed. As if thinking too hard on it would send me over the bridge too. Get me hooked on Horse. Anything to not think about how grotesque everything was. I was leaving—hell yes—and I wouldn't come back until I could buy and sell the lot of them. Next year, this time, I'd have half a year in at Yale, Georgetown. Somewhere. The Pappas living room would be a plane ride away.

On the floor, Eugene Junior repeatedly slammed two dolls into each other.

"He's getting ready for the Steelers game," Eugene laughed.

"Be nice, EJ," cautioned Connie. "Santa's watching you."

"Hey, George. Walk downstairs with me. I want to show you something," Eugene said.

"I'll just be a second," I said to Sterling.

"I won't let anything happen to her, Georgie," Connie said.

The cellar was small and tidy. A washing machine and dryer, a couple of washtubs, clothesline with clean white diapers and bibs clothes-pinned to it. A sink and a toilet. A work table, above which tools hung on hooks, and under which were two huge tool chests and Eugene's electrician's equipment.

In one corner was a tiny room Eugene opened with a key. I had never seen it. A desk, with a telephone, adding machine, pads of paper with numbers and notes scribbled on them, and a picture of Connie and the kids. Three tubes of parallel fluorescent lights ran across the ceiling. On the bare concrete floor was a dorm refrigerator. Eugene opened it, took out two pony bottles of Miller High Life, twisted off the caps, and handed one to me. He sat in his desk chair and motioned me to sit in a chair jammed between the wall and desk.

"*Saluto,*" Eugene said, and took a long swig.

"*Saluto.*" I held the beer in my mouth for a few seconds before swallowing.

"Let me give you your sheet." Eugene handed me a page from one of the desk stacks. "It's got the latest lines. As of this minute. And here's your loot."

"Thanks very much."

"You're doing good."

"Yeah, it's been working out well." I folded the envelope in half and slid it in my pocket.

"You not going to count it? You should always count it."

I smiled. "This is nice," I said, looking around the office.

"It gets the job done. The kids don't know a thing about what I do down here."

"Right."

"Where were you yesterday?"

"I got hung up."

"Not like you, Cuz."

"If I had owed, I would've been here."

"I know that. That's not what I'm saying. It's just not like you to not show up on a Tuesday. What I'm saying is I missed you. That's all. How's your mum and dad?"

"They're okay. You know. My dad's getting stir crazy. My mother's driving him nuts. They go to the grocery store about twelve times a day."

"Those son-of-a-bitches. All those years, and then they lay him off at Christmas."

"It'll work out. It always does."

"What do they think of your girlfriend?"

My reflex was to tell Eugene to mind his damn business. "They haven't met her."

"She's nice."

"Thanks. I think so too."

"You're really stepping out on this one, Cuz. She's a little outside your element."

"How so?"

"She's a Jew broad, isn't she?"

"She's not a fucking Martian, Eugene."

"Look. I don't mean any offense. But I think you're taking a chance bringing this girl over here."

I started to speak, but Eugene cut me off. "I know, I know. You just stopped in to say hello, share a little Christmas cheer. And here I am jumping you. I understand. And I also understand that I'm pissing you off. But you can't mix business with pleasure. Don't let the little head tell the big head what to do. *Capisco*?"

That Eugene would take it upon himself to dole out counsel about how I should conduct my love life—as if he could ever appreciate a woman like Sterling, much less comprehend my relationship with her. I knew better than to say a word.

"Let me tell you something. And I'm telling you this because you're like family. I've known you since you were born. Your mum and dad are like second parents to me. If you want to get in on this, this business, make a little book yourself, the time is right. I got more than I can handle, and Connie stays too tied up with the kids to help out steady with it. If you're interested."

"I'm not set up for anything like that."

"You can come over here on game days. That's when it gets really crazy. We'll put in another phone. You'd be working for me. I don't mean being somebody's jerk. Something a little further along. Taking your own action, for instance. Felix thinks a lot of you."

"He doesn't even know me."

"Believe me, Cuz. He knows you, and my say-so is everything in this matter. What do you say?"

The proposition appealed to me. Very much. I could deliver for Mr. Rosechild, keep up my own betting, and work a little for Eugene. Maybe, eventually, I'd install a phone in my bedroom at home and study when it wasn't ringing. I needed the bread. At least until my parents got on their feet. Another seven-eight months. Then I'd be out of Pittsburgh, this phase of my life, except for Sterling, wiped clean.

"You'd get a percentage of every piece of action that comes through you. I get a bigger chunk and Felix gets the jackpot. But you have to understand; he's the bank. It's his money we're playing with. Think about it. Easy, clean work. Very simple. The fridge is full of these little Millers."

"I'll do it, but I want to wait until after football season. I'm pretty busy right now."

"Now, during playoffs, is when we do the most volume. People bet like lunatics on these games. The cabbage rolls in. But you do whatever you want. No pressure. After football, we got basketball, then baseball. Whatever you want to do."

It was Sterling and nothing else keeping me from this extra money my family was desperate for, and so crucial to my future. Soon she'd head back to school, and I wanted to be with her every moment I could spare. Still, it made me queasy that my own sentiment, a softness I had always prided myself on not being swayed by, would divert me. I wondered if Sterling would do the same for me. But she didn't have my worries. Her education was paid for, and the car and the clothes, and everything else. The pressing issues in her daily existence were what time to wake up, whether to go out for lunch or not, where to spend her glittering evenings. Like all the rich girls, she undoubtedly had a trust fund that would provide for her the rest of her life. She had the world by the ass. And why not? Isn't that what I wanted?

"Well, like I said, just think about it."

"I will. Thanks, Eugene. Thanks a lot for thinking about me."

"Don't mention it. And no offense."

"No. No offense."

We got up from our chairs and shook hands.

Upstairs, Sterling had both children on her lap, and was reading to them.

"This one's a natural, Georgie," said Connie. "You better hang on to her."

Chapter 10

I don't know what you'd call the Crow house—in terms of architecture. Fronting an interminable field of corn, it's off a gravel road, mitered into the woods, and of the same hues: brown, then green, then sun-shot dappled and churchy. Homemade. Like they had built a room, then another and another like connecting children's building blocks from different sets. Nothing matches. One storey of incongruity: dips and disparate angles and varying heights. All painted a dismal beige with white trim and a crude plank porch propped on four by fours and roofed with sheets of rusted corrugated tin like the rest of the house. There's a smokehouse and a backhouse, a corncrib spread out behind it, then the dark forest stretching to eternity.

It could only be Mr. Crow, the sad old chain gang man, who putts along on a beat green John Deere riding mower. He is shirtless, his torso scarred and emaciated. On his head, a John Deere baseball cap, the same faded green as the little tractor, with a stitched deer in mid-leap above the bill. His blank face brightens when Charlene's Caddy zooms by him and parks in the yard.

He switches off the deafening engine and slouches to the car. He wears high-lace steel-toed clodhoppers. His pants are so short, you can see where his shoelaces knot up on his ankles. He removes his hat and hugs his daughters in turn. They embrace him the way one might a beloved dead thorn bush, gingerly and with great care to neither be punctured nor crack it. His hair is silvery-white and yellow. Like an egg, the yolk sundered, cracked on his skull. His otherwise unremarkable face is a writ of blame, oddly childlike; its wonderment is informed by enormity, the thing that has left him speechless.

"Daddy, this is Michael Roman," Crow says.

"How do you do, Mr. Crow," I say. He holds out his right hand and I take it with my left, my good hand. I realize this is the first time I've had occasion to shake hands since I got hurt. His grip is powerful.

"I know you," he says, raking me with his innocent watery eyes.

"That's the first he's spoke in ten days, I'd say."

I turn to the house. There on the porch stands Wanda Crow. Charlene and Crow rush to her and throw themselves on her. She kisses each on the mouth, holds them for a moment in each arm, seems to lift them, then place them back on the porch where they stand on either side of her like handmaids. Mrs. Crow is fantastically beautiful. I had expected a pinched ascetic, like the cronish habited nuns I'd been taught by in grade school, sexless and formless, a sharpened pointer in her hand or a pitch-pipe to cue our praise.

In Wanda's big hands, however, is a rolling pin powdered with flour. She is voluptuous, tall and powerful, smooth thick arms in a sleeveless summery dress that scoops over her big breasts—a scar necklace left by the thyroid surgeon—six inches of cleavage swooning into the flowered pink fabric. Her hair is long blonde and wavy. She has the eyes of her daughter, Ruby Lydia, huge black and gold queen bees hovering abuzz in each of them. Not a speck of make-up. Roseate skin like a fair white peach. And Crow's teeth—with an overbite. Yet she and Crow don't favor each other in the least. Maybe it's Charlene she favors. She looks like she could birth Crow and Charlene in their current incarnation and swallow her husband while at it.

"You must have the power of God in you," she follows, "to get Mr. Crow to speak. It's a miracle every time a words drops out of his mouth."

"He does have the touch, Mama," Crow says, coming down from the porch and taking my arm.

"That's what I been hearing," Wanda allows.

"I can vouch for that, Mama," Charlene says.

"I expected y'all much earlier," Wanda charges, hands now on her hips. Ample. High. Surprisingly small in the waist given her size.

"We got caught in a tornado, Mama," Charlene volunteers.

"Is that right?

"Yes, ma'am, that's so," Crow seconds.

"Y'all look pretty rough," Wanda says. "Like you might've been in a tornado. We didn't have any weather here. A little wind, maybe. Got dark for a spell."

"Well, we pretty near got blown off the planet, Mama," Charlene says. "Mama is scared breathless by tornados."

"Thunderstorms too," adds Wanda.

"It was like the Apocalypse, Mama," vows Crow.

"Don't tempt fate, Girl." Then to me, the least bit of a smile on her lips: "You should shut your mouth, and put your eyes back in your head, Son, lest a fly light in it."

I've been staring at Wanda like a fool. Mr. Crow stands next to me. He is a tall man who has wizened into the posture of an old Italian man who has stood too long over vendetta, and forgotten his grudge. He sneaks a look at his wife, then lowers his eyes to study the patchy, scrub grass we stand on under the shade of a Gum tree. It's May 6, I think, and the temperature is 104. An aggregate of talc and flour twinkles atop the patina of sweat glistening on Wanda's breasts.

"Mama, this is Michael Roman," Crow says.

I approach the porch, hold out my left hand. "It's a pleasure to meet you, Mrs. Crow."

She drops the rolling pin into a rocker. "Nice to meet you," she says, taking my hand in her floury soft fingers. "What's the matter with your other hand?"

My bad hand has gone to sleep. Distracted. Senile. It has aged into my father's hand, brown and seamed, oversized and knuckly, grouted with labor, though I have never done a day of real man's work with it. Often I can't lift it. Can't control it, as if it has a mind of its own. A hand out of Greek myth. For my sins, cursed.

"Romeo was in a terrible fight defending my honor, Mama."

"Is that so, Mr. Roman?" Wanda asks.

She looks at me, and I lower my eyes to the parched soil, the green stubble that passes for grass, the spiked gum buds that have tallied over the years around the old tree's pocked trunk. And Quartzite. And every grade of igneous. The earth here shovels it up. Stokers in the underhouses feeding the engines, driving the planet recklessly into the indifferent galaxy. It's so motherless hot because we're standing on the roof of Purgatory.

I am mesmerized by what can only be a snake, inching along the scrabble, nearly imperceptible, a long soft cylinder of blown brown and yellow glass just out of the glassblower's pipe, still molten, lethal.

My eyes still on the earth, like a guilty catechist, I'm wondering how to answer Wanda. I feel her eyes on me and the snake at once. This could be a gambit: everyone sees the snake—how could they not? It is writing a long sentence on the ground that says: *The wages of sin is death* . . . But we are not permitted to speak of it. When I look up, the queen bees in Wanda's eyes hover, brandishing their stings. I have to shade my eyes, though the sun sits atop the corn.

"That's not quite the truth, Mrs. Crow," I say.

"What is the truth, Mr. Roman?"

The snake has chosen me. It lifts its head. Its tongue switchblades, in and out, a tiny black trident. In and out. Forked. Revolting. Obscene. It's an emissary sent by Felix to assassinate me. I contemplate the truth, the true story, I'll relate to Wanda. Every bit of it, start to finish: my narcissism and greed, my callow ambition, my pitiful beloved parents, Sterling (already a cameo of something cherished gone), the gambling and Sterling's father, my duplicity and flight, and Felix. Felix's snake at my shoe. That demon one inch from the sole of my tattered second-hand shoes. The levitating triangular head, the pit between eye and nostril. The tongue. I have been seeing this snake all my life since Genesis. That *gavone* operator serpent who seduced Eve right there on Eden's mossy floor, and all the iconography that followed.

Dogs have yowled ever since we skidded up in Charlene's Caddy; and, suddenly, they flare through and over and under a barbed wire fence that skeins off the Crow property from a field of tobacco, and one cow with its washtub of dirty water. They aren't sure whether to love up on Crow and Charlene, who coo and chortle at them, go at me or the viper—that finally strikes. Not at me, thank God. But at the lead dog, a big collie named Robert who ricochets back at the injection and wheedles off under a cedar along the fence and never ceases his hoarse bark.

Two other dogs: one named Mutt, a feisty calico mess, probably the smartest of the lot, dibs in and out at the snake like some apprentice hood from Larimer Avenue with a Mafia death wish. Trailing is Annie, old and pissy, her white fur gone yellow, like an old woman's mane turning. A beauty in her day, still trying to maintain that carriage, but her legs have shortened and her belly isn't six inches off the earth. Sour and complaining, wolf-face, her brushy white tail threaded with briar, beholden to only one mistress—Wanda, of course—no loyalty to the others, and impatient with children.

Annie broaches the snake with protocol and pride; you can tell right off she's Wanda's dog. Wanda who doesn't say a thing, who has a smile on her face that is nothing about pleasure. Wanda who reaches out and pulls me by my nasty sodden shirt to her, clear of the snake. Charlene and Crow screaming for Annie to get away from the copperhead. They whisper *copperhead* again and again like it's a secret. *Copperhead. Sweet Jesus.*

I've seen maybe two snakes all my life—garter snakes, at that—and, without thinking much about it, I'm scared of them. I've been seeing snakes, however, since I was able to walk into the zoo holding my father's hand, and climb the three stairs that little ones ascended to peep in the window behind which the captive vipers lolled. Their faces: that exquisite regretless detachment. The eyes: inked opalescent periods. But also in the face: hard sinister mouths of assassins, hitmen, hideous carnal amusement smeared across them.

My mother talked about them sometimes, those professional hitters, and it was always the mouth, *that ugly mouth,* not the eyes, that terrified her. Like they wouldn't just shoot her or chop her up, but shove a six foot poison needle in her, and they'd bite her, until she'd been eaten, swallowed.

A pit viper is like the worst kind of cockstrong hood—a fighter, possessed of an apocalyptic temper. Down on Chookie's corner, just debuting with junk—used to be a nice kid, now wearing an oily black leather jacket, drinking sweet pink rotgut wine. Mogen-David. Manischewitz.

But this snake. He's still not beaten down enough yet by junk, into the slump and nod, that narcotized immobilization. No. This guy's still driving a car, has change in his pockets for gas and cigarettes, a girlfriend. Can still throw a baseball. He's given up the church, but that's not unusual. Growing a trifling mustache. Taken to wearing a little Frank Sinatra fedora, brim curled up in the front. Looks more like a greenhorn huckster than a desperado. Swears by his mother and father.

That'll change. In half a year he'll loot their house. He'll stand by while his wasted associates jump his dad for junk money. He'll sidle up to old women and sucker punch them. When they fall to the sidewalk, he'll kick their teeth out. For pennies. Destroy cars with tire irons. Carry a switchblade until he fences that too. His mother will pray that his death comes soon and mercifully, that he'll be remanded to Purgatory rather than Hell.

Right now, however, this minute—under the gum tree in Saint Joan's County, or down in front of Chookie's on the corner of Sheridan and Saint Marie in East Liberty—he's a junky at his peak, at the top of his game. But—and he doesn't know this, he can't—it's just before his long long interminable never-ending plummet. My father, a steelworker, who climbed cranes on the open hearth at the Edgar Thomson Works in Braddock, the first of Andrew Carnegie's mills in America, has a favorite saying: "It's not the fall, Son, but the sudden stop."

A venomous snake, like a hood, is not all one thing. Sometimes lewd, sometimes charming. Lucifer was the most beautiful angel.

Annie minces. Lurches. In and out. The snake's head levitates. Strikes. Misses. The old dog staggering like a punchy fighter playing possum, then knifes in and clamps in her mouth the copperhead at its middle and rears up, two-legged, like a horse. The snake loops back, striking, coiling over Annie's back and then falls from her mouth in a heap. Cinches up again from the earth, the tongue stabbing in and out, eyes like caviar. Annie whimpers. Can't tell if she's hit. Charlene and Crow call her back. Mutt sits on his haunches watching. Robert groans that same bark. Mr. Crow runs into the house.

"Please don't get the gun, Daddy," Crow yells.

Annie and the snake rip into one another again.

Wanda. Silent. Still clutching my shirt. Mr. Crow hurries out with the gun, a twelve-gauge with its long black twin barrels. He hefts it level and hands it to his wife. The girls are screeching. Annie wobbles. The snake preens, flattens out, wiggles and flattens, then glides at Annie. Wanda steps barefoot into the snake's path, drops the gun barrels, bore down, on its triangular head, the stock pointing at the serene indigo sky, and presses with both hands, pinning the snake to the earth. It lashes back and forth, curls back over on itself, flops grossly, lasciviously, the sandix patches and amber hourglasses swirling fitfully. The girls have Annie—panting raw cotton.

Mama, they are saying, as Wanda lifts one of her bare feet and steps with it upon the middle of the snake's writhing belly. One hand still pressing with the shotgun the snake's head into the gravel tallow, with the other she whips from her dress pocket a filet knife. Pauses voluptuously like the Virgin for one avenging moment over the serpent. Then in a deft plie severs the grinning head from the body.

A gasp goes up from us all, even Mutt and Annie, and a thin whistling hiss from the snake. Now two snakes. The long-end hysterical, shimmying itself into a coiled pile of offal. The face-end ever-leering, fangs translucent, deadly. The stench of the vent fluids as it fixes its final stare on me, though we all stare at Wanda until Mr. Crow reaches down, picks up the head and lopes around the side of the house. Annie walks to the still-fidgeting body, grips it—lapping down from her grizzled mouth—and trots after him, Mutt following, then Robert who has finally hushed and seems not punctured at all.

Wanda finally looks at us, the slippery dripping knife in her hand.

"Lord God, Mama," says Charlene.

"Amen and amen," Wanda responds. To me: "We live in a topography of snakes, Mr Roman. Mischief of the revolting sort is abroad. It is not an accident that the Lord allows the snake to prosper. A reminder to remain vigilant."

"Yes, ma'am," I say, having learned *ma'am* from Crow, suddenly at my side, her arm twined through mine. "We're all crazy here," she whispers.

"Ya'll been drinking," Wanda declares. "I smell it. You believe in drink, Mr. Roman?"

I simply gape at her. The sun is disappearing down behind her dress, her hair afire.

"He doesn't believe in anything, Mama," Crow interrupts. "He's a Catholic."

"And a Yankee on top of it," adds Charlene.

"Lord have mercy," sighs Wanda. "Y'all come on in the house and change those damp clothes."

The inside of the house is dark, filled with heavy brooding heirloom furniture. Tiger oak chifferobes and sideboards, carven slope-back brocade davenports.

Streaked unsilvering ornate mirrors. Flowery wallpaper ruffling off the walls. Antimaccassars on every surface. And dust and cobwebs and the same timeless hush and smell as the church. Forboding antiquity. Yet, as I make my way through the dining room, which adjoins the kitchen, I smell food, and the light is better, though the sudden black night pours through the screen door and bugs flick at it unceasingly.

Crow hands me a pair of green work pants with matching shirt, leads me down a hall, pushes me into the bathroom, then steps in and closes the door. She kisses me long and hard, then, "I told you they were crazy."

"They're fine. It doesn't matter."

"My mother catches me in here with you, it's not certain who she'd kill first." She kisses me again, and flies out the door.

I so rarely look in mirrors these days that my reflection startles me: the morass of hair, graying more daily; the big beard, shot gray, too, that reaches nearly the wells of my eye sockets. And the eyes themselves. Clearly the eyes of a stranger. Michael Roman's eyes. Snake-black opaque. Astonished.

I strip, and stand for a moment gazing at my naked reflection, the glittering silt and gravel still studded into my chest and stomach hair, through the mats of my crotch and thighs. I've gained weight. Felix will never know me.

The bathroom is determinedly pink. Toilet seat cover, mat and throw rug. Pink toilet and toilet paper. Pink lampshades. The tile. The bathtub and towels. Pink. Like the Dolce bathroom on Saint Marie Street.

The long vanity into which the pink sink is embedded is stacked with pamphlets and tracts: *The Last Call, Revival or Martyrdom, False Comfort for Sinners, Guideposts.* On the mirror is a placard with instructions of what to do if you start choking, another with the number for Poison Control, then hand-written on a scrap of paper emergency numbers for every conceivable catastrophe. An unlidded shoe box of eight tracks: George Beverly Shea, Andre Crouch and the Disciples, a series of lectures by Charles Stanley.

Then Pond's, nail polish remover, aspirin, paregoric, witch hazel, a curling iron, and sitting on their chargers a compliment of electric hair rollers clotted with blond hair. A folded white brassiere.

Wearing Mr. Crow's green work fatigues, walking the hall back to the dining room, I glance in an adjacent room where a lamp glows—Mr. and Mrs. Crow's bedroom—and there I see my mother sitting on the side of the bed in her housecoat, her feet inside heelless turquoise terry cloth slippers. Stranded there, in between things, before a bath or after, the moment before undressing for bed or donning clothes for her long day of ennui, she struggles not to cry, but her tired brown eyes float in pools of water, magnified by heavy bifocals, and her lips move. Imperceptibly. Her hands, in her lap, fret something. She is saying the rosary. She asks the Blessed Mother to bring her son, George, back home. He is lost.

I walk to my mother, but she is not there. But her bed is there in Wanda's room. My parents' bed—four-poster cherry, with the inlaid scrolled and notched massive headboard, the bed in which I was conceived—is unmistakably here. As is their entire bedroom suite—along with the bed, the dressers, nightstand and vanity with its cushioned seat—that they bought at May Stern those first months of matrimony with saved steel money. The oval ornate brass fixtures. Identical. I have never seen anywhere another suite like this. Now here, over five hundred miles away, in Saint Joan's County.

On one wall, a picture of Jesus at Gethsemane. Distraught, He kneels, His hands folded upon a boulder, a shaft of light from on high bathing them. On the opposite wall a water color of the Jesus-stripped cross, the bloody spikes gleaming in their triangulated equation, a purple shroud draped along the transverse beam. *INRI* where the savior's head had lolled. That same shaft of numinous light. Bibles on the dresser and vanity.

The bed is covered in a wreath-ribbon quilt. Foxed in one corner of the vanity mirror is a Polaroid of a man in a coffin. Dusty shears blow in and out of the opened windows: the music of the deep country.

Mr. Crow is already at the big table, at its head, a crumbling stone fireplace raised up behind him, a saber and a musket crossed over the mantle. He now wears a shirt; we're dressed identically. He glances up at me and smiles.

Wanda and her daughters carry platters to the table, then finally sit. Charlene and Crow have changed clothes, both in loose summer dresses. We link hands for the blessing. Crow's chopped hair is swept back off her forehead with barrettes. The blue Braille scars comfort me. Seated next to me, she squeezes my good hand at intervals as her mother, flanking me on the other side, prays over us and the food, a longish anthem to "Our Kind Father."

The Crows close their eyes and bow their heads. Wanda goes on about the prevalence of meanness and iniquity. She entreats the Lord to place his healing touch upon us all, asks Him to move in me, in particular, to ease the weight I so visibly carry, to bloom in my heart like a thorny weed. Crow squeezes my hand ferociously. Her mother's voice breaks. Wanda too squeezes my hand, the bad hand, and in it I feel as she squeezes harder and harder a prickly current crackling through it. Wanda finally ends with "in Jesus's name we pray." There comes a whispered sigh of "Amen," then the Crows raise their heads and look at Wanda's gorgeous tears.

"God is good," she says, dabs at her eyes with a napkin. "Y'all help yourselves."

The table is laden with fried chicken, country ham, hoe cakes, crab apple jelly, black-eyed peas, boiled as well as fried okra, turnips, pickled peaches, collard greens, hominy, red-eye gravy, and a pitcher of sweet sweet iced tea. All in beautiful crockery and china, cloth napkins and a brocade lime table cloth—every bit of it dignified and elegantly worn, chipped, and threadbare. Like one of the numbered final tableaux of lost Saint Joan's County grandeur.

Other than the ham and chicken, everything is foreign to me, yet when the platters arrive in front of me, I help myself. Next to me, Crow coaches me through things: what to do with the red-eye gravy, made with coffee she tells me, how I should avoid the boiled okra and eat the fried, how grits and hominy are related. To sprinkle raw onion on my black-eyed peas, then dowse them and my collards with chow-chow and hot pepper vinegar.

"Where are your people from, Mr. Roman?" Wanda asks.

I'm not sure what to say. Wanda has pulled her hair back in a clip, and put on lipstick. She dabs at her forehead and stunning neck with a flowery handkerchief.

"Romeo's from Pennsylvania," Crow prompts.

"Is that right?" says Wanda.

"Yes, ma'am. All of my grandparents are from Italy."

Wanda looks at me inquisitorially, suspiciously, then says, "Mr. Crow was in Italy during the war."

"Anzio," gasps Mr. Crow without looking up from his plate.

"Daddy's right talkative today," Charlene offers.

"It's Mr. Roman. He has the touch, I believe. And you say you're a Catholic?"

"I was raised Catholic and educated in Catholic schools."

"And where would you go this instant were you to drop dead?"

"Mama," chides Crow.

"It's alright," I say. But it's not alright at all. The world slips out from under me for a moment. I forget where I am, who I am, and stare at the hives revving in Wanda's eyes, golden bands across the queen's black body. *Where would I go?* I finally answer: "Purgatory."

"We don't believe in Purgatory," counters Wanda. "There's heaven and there's hell. No in between."

"Purgatory's like junior hell, Mama," volunteers Crow. "You're sent there for a while to get your sins cooked out of you. Then you get to go to heaven."

"Then you haven't been saved?" Wanda asks.

I'm looking at her, that delicate phosphorescent scar where her throat was cut that scoops across her snowy bosom. "I don't know."

"As Southern Baptists we believe that once you're saved, then it's a done deal," says Charlene. "No matter what you do after that, that seal of approval cannot be revoked. Lifetime membership in the Saved Club. You can murder, pillage, and fornicate to your heart's desire without consequence."

Wanda lowers the hand clutching the handkerchief, makes a fist of it, and strikes the table. Not hard. Not at all. But the flatware quakes and the dogs huddled on the porch yammer. "My daughters like to show out in front of company, Mr. Roman. They actually know better."

The girls' heads are down. Mr. Crow eats without surcease, yet steals a moment to look at me and wink. I realize with shame that I too have not stopped eating. Like a man rescued. With my mouth open, as if without breeding, as if to deny my own kith. Like an *animale.* A peasant. *Gavone.*

"And you pray to the Pope?"

"Mama," interjects Crow.

"It's an innocent question, Liddy," Wanda answers.

"No, ma'am," I say. "I do not pray to the Pope."

"Well, that's a relief. It's getting late, I reckon. Would anyone care for some cobbler?"

After I bathe, Crow beds me down in sheets of linen on an old brass fainting couch tucked under an open window in the living room. She undresses, switches off the lamp, and slips in, twining around me so we fit snugly on the narrow couch. She is smooth and pale as paper. The moon, white-washing her in the suddenly dark room, sets up in her eyes.

Crow kisses me. "I hope that wasn't too unbearable."

"It was nothing."

"Mama can be obnoxious about all that."

"I didn't mind."

"Well, you handled it better than I would've. She likes you. Daddy too. But she can have a spell any time, and get ugly. It pays to be afraid of her."

The house is quiet, except for the clumsy shadows of ghosts, and despite the mad keen and propagation of insects across the cropland, the occasional long and sorrowful moan of a cow, a catbird impersonating a cat, bullfrogs groaning, whining coyotes slinking under the bright stars and cresting moon.

A grandfather clock tocks, minute taps of time against the surging night. The quiet of old and forgetful. The house. The land. Putting me to sleep, Crow reaching for me, pulling me over on top of her, and I must tell myself I am here, I am a man, this is my life. Yet I have no ballast, no whenness, no nowness to keep me moored to this moment. Crow beneath me. So lovely. Tenderly guiding me through what must be love, saying my name over and over, not my name at all. This is love, I tell myself. *This. This This. You have landed in this place.*

Yet I am floating off, astrally projected above the fainting couch where Crow and I, Crow and I, Crow and I. Crow growing smaller and smaller, translucent, her skin paling into the sheets so that I can no longer see her and I merely mate with an apparition, the hacked message of love and desperation transposed from her forehead to her now-vacated pillow upon which my head summons sleep, the fireflies so plentiful, so brilliant, they infiltrate the stars; and, even after I convulse into dream, they fire beyond the drawn curtains of my eyelids.

Thunder. Rolling mythic claps bulling in over the meadows and orchards and slaglands, shrouding the penitents at Coventry Prison, across the Confederate War Dead in Bethlehem Cemetery, as far north in the county as the little town of Saint Joan's itself where Wanda was born and she and Lon married, and all the Crow children baptized in the chapel of All Souls.

Out of the thunder comes a voice, not Jehovah's, but from one of his living angels, Wanda Crow, whispering, though she is already feeling for me along the edge of the day bed: *Mr. Roman, might I climb in here with you? I'm deathly afraid of the thunder. Simply paralyzed.* Then she is next to me. Twice my age and then some, my mother's age. The utter softness in that narrow bed where she curls as had her daughter Ruby Lydia mere moments, it seemed, before. Up against me, Wanda, her powdered bodice, the heft of her, the heaving of the oncoming rain and even the thunder that paralyzes her. Lightning lights the room. She wears a lacy long white gown. Her hair streaks with sparks, currents running from the roots to the ash tips. Her lips are red and the bucked teeth luminous. Her eyes buzz and gleam.

Put your arms around me, Mr. Roman.

I wrap my arms around her and gather her to me. Thunder and lightning fire at the same instant. The house shudders. The room ignites with white light. The gown slips from her shoulders. The storm subsumes the house, rocks it, boom and torrent, hail gattling the tin roof and cedar-shake walls. Rain washing over us through the opened window. Wanda whimpers against me. I lock her against me, my eyes in the crook of her neck, my cheek against her breast. It's me. Crying. All along. She holding me. All along it's she holding me, cooing, whispering in my ear as she pets me: *It's alright, Giorgio, sweet boy, my lamb, my sinner.*

And then: as the storm subsides. The flimsy curtains: in and out. In and out. The storm: thrusts off into the forest, then slinks into the outer of supernal, the cane and brake of Saint Joan's, where deer dream of suicide and copperheads mate with King snakes, then trundles up the Pistol River in disguise. In and out. In and out. We lay there and watch the storm pass, its last paroxysm quaking the house a final definitive time. Fog sucked into space with the fleeing inhalation, and the fireflies again, infesting the drenched land. Off and on. Like fairies. The moon drops back to its orbit as Wanda rises, like my guardian angel with her robe dangerously off her shoulders, arranges her gown and hair, takes my hand.

When we step onto the porch, the dogs slink out from under the house. Annie follows. Wanda raises a hand to the others and they halt, sit and whine. We walk through the meadow. Fireflies congregate on each rain-bent stalk, firing contrapuntally, lighting all over us. In Wanda's hair and flickering on her gown, and beneath it against her skin, beneath even her skin in beaded strands of electricity. Throughout Annie's matted fur.

Then between two tobacco siloes, the sweet deep rust aroma of curing tobacco, down a grown-over logging road, fireflies spread over the impenetrable gorse, every now and then a clearing where massive piles of felled pine trunks smolder, the smoky fecund stench of pitch and brack. Turpentine. The stars now gathering around the unleavened moon. Until we break through to the Pistol, a bank of clay, marble smooth, lined with colossal sycamores, their white exposed roots runging down to the water's face upon which the stars float south into the Atlantic.

We sit on the bank and look across the river at an open fallow field. Annie stays off in the shadows of the trees. My hand is still in Wanda's. I'm afraid to look at her. The fireflies in the field mate. They drape in rosaries over the wildflowers. Each time they fire the green earth flashes. From a bank of thunderheads, further off, heat lightening gasps and crackles. The same quadrant of sky flashes pink. Among the fireflies spark blue flashes—the blue hood of flame that crowns a candle flame. Blue and bright yellow fireflies all through the vast field as the river, brown with the white stars on its back, glides by.

On the banks of the Pistol, across from where we sit, Theodosia Burr, Aaron Burr's alluring daughter, was last seen. In the early winter of 1812, she and her husband had stopped for the night at the Knox Inn at Sneedsborough, at one time the new world's largest inland port. The next day they boarded The *Prince Frederick* bound for Georgetown, South Carolina. The ship and all aboard were never heard from again. Shipwreck? Marauders? Captured by the

Pee Dee Indians? Theories abound; the mystery remains. There is the legend in Saint Joan's County that if you keep vigil at this spot on the Pistol, during a storm, you will see the body of Theodosia, in layers of silken white livery, tossing in the swells, still chained by her ankle to the bulkhead of the *Prince Frederick.*

"I see her, Mr. Roman. Do you?" Wanda is on her feet. "Sometimes she wears nothing at all."

I gaze out across the river at the foaming water: roiling white fabric, swirling tresses.

When I turn to Wanda, she is naked, her white body, now the gypsum white of Ruby Lydia, punctuated with fireflies. Her hair, long, white like the unfurled mane of an old beautiful queen's, cloistered too long, is shot with them too, even the blue ones. I realize I'm still crying.

"Yes," she says. "I've come to baptize you."

She helps me out of my clothes and, with my bad hand in hers, I follow her down the root ladder into the river. The water is warm, convincing. We stand to our waists and look across the wide river where ground fog shreds out of trees and envelops the field. Instantly the fireflies disappear. Distant claps of thunder echo off the rippling river. Small explosions that light up Wanda and mirror her statuesque torso among the stars on the river spine. Her body so much like a gorgeous saint's. Saint Bridgette or even Saint Joan. Or Diana, her unclothed body so taboo, the Gods cursed Actaeon to be ravaged by his own dogs just for having glimpsed her. To look at Wanda seems sinful, but she wants me to look—as it is on the water, as it is in the flesh—and I cannot look away. Her ploy all along has been to get me to look—as if she is not merely a saint or an angel or goddess, but the Blessed Mother herself and that somehow I will be evangelized at the forbidden sight of her.

She rocks me back. The warm welcoming water pulls me down. Cottonmouths bind my wrists and ankles. As I am lured under, I gaze through the fathom hooding me at the stars on the river's ceiling, those stars the diadem in the hair of Wanda, the necklaces and brooches upon her breasts. The voices of the souls that have preceded me on the ancient Pistol, once the most powerful river in colonial America, chant *Jubilate Deo. Requiescat in Pace.*

Then I panic because my eyes are open and there appear in my baptism the drowned in their timeless tumescent reveries, floating in amnions of amnesia and regret: the missed appointment, the unfathered children, the foreshortened dreams and aspirations, the eternity of time wasted. In frock coats and tri-cornered hats, Pee Dee and Creek Indians in tanned leggings, Confederate dead in grandiose regalia, manacled escapees from Coventry Prison, artifacts from a gone world: spinning wheels and cotton gins, pie safes, butter churns, parasols, petticoats, martingales, ploughshares.

Then the *memento mori* of my ancestry. Aunts, uncles, cousins, beloved *paesani;* my grandmothers in black, grandfathers with flint mustaches, colicky *bambini* in steerage. All the way across the Atlantic from Formicola, Naples, Manfredonia in Foggia, querulous and dark, seduced by America, but always water, this water, that led them here. Even those I never knew who wear as well my jutting black brow and aquiline nose. My blood. Then Alex, sleepy, befuddled, fearful—blonde and ringleted as a girl—looking to cop in the watery underworld, still half-asleep in the red flannel pajamas he wore the night he woke and leapt off the Meadow Street Bridge.

Nor do they quicken, these water-bound apparitions, only nod piteously like mourners at grave-time as, if all along, they've been waiting for me just to say goodbye.

Wanda lifts my head from the water: "Michael Roman, ' . . . if thou shalt confess with thy mouth the Lord Jesus, and shalt believe in thine heart that God hath raised him from the dead, thou shalt be saved.'" Her voice echoes over the water and across the cropland. I had once believed all of that, and now I do not disbelieve it. I simply believe in nothing.

"Say it," Wanda commands. "Say it. You must say it."

"I believe it," I whisper. "I confess it."

She grips my right hand, my bad hand, between the two of hers, kisses each finger, the palm, its knuckled back, holds it against her breasts, palm down, whispers, "Amen."

The river tides over us in waves of hallucination until, curled around each other, we sound, in the shallows, kissing—or maybe she is simply lending me breath. I run my tongue along her teeth. I open my eyes. She looks deeply into them, the queens' stingers preening lewdly; and, before they can strike and blind me, she steps away and simply stands there, the water lapping against the confluence of her hips and thighs slightly parted.

"Now you're saved," she says. "Nothing can ever touch you." She kisses me deeply. Whispers in my ear, her teeth against it: "Like a thief in the night." Then takes my face and brings it between her breasts. Rocks me there in the suddenly rushing river. I fall to my knees, wrap my arms tightly about Wanda, let my head slide to her soft belly and weep. Up to my neck in the Pistol, I kneel in the river mud. The wind whips up; the river whirlpools. Theodosia Burr rushes by in a current of taffeta. The ground fog disperses. Suddenly the fireflies, blue and yellow, quadrupled, larger, reappear in the field. That once-distant heat storm hovers above. Thunder. Lightning. The wind rushes out of the land across the river, gathers in its fists the field of fireflies and blows them in a wall, a million whits of flame, instant aurora, strafing us, then into the river, where they extinguish in cleffs of hissing smoke.

Saved.

A siren. Ugly. Blaring. Coming from somewhere inside the Crow house. A cycle of two seconds deafening, a second of silence, climbing a decibel at each interval; and for a moment it is 1962 and I am back in Sister Cabrini's class at Saints Peter and Paul's, the Air Raid siren shrieking as we rise by rote from our cast iron desks and find our "Purgatory Partners." Mine is Dave Mazzotti, brilliant, handsome, athletic, still a decade away from his tryst with Heroin. We link hands and fall in the column of twos and, at the snap of Sister's fingers, trot behind her out the room.

The other seven rooms of the haunted schoolhouse empty silently behind us, save for the tread of our identical oxfords on the polished naked floors. The nuns prepare to perish in the odor of sanctity, have no expression. Behind their wire spectacles and promontories of towering wimples, their chalky pocked faces are expressionless. Our jobs are to die with them. Purgatory promises cleansing flame for each of us no matter how good we might think we've been—a pittance for some, relentless unbearable plenty for others. Index fingers to their lips, adjuring us to silence, regardless of the pain and terror of the atomic bombs Khrushchev and his Communist minions are about to rain on us, they betray not the slightest trepidation. Beneath their floor-length ebon robes, their feet are invisible. They glide as if assayed by wheels and armatures. Jesus on his cross dangles at the center of the blazing white bibs scooped over their breasts. Rosaries—beads radiated to the size of thumbs, crucifixes big as daggers—girdle their hips.

Down the marble staircase, past the milk machine and the janitor's snow shovel, mop and slop bucket, to the fusty basement where we crouch beneath the long lunch tables as we've been drilled, reciting in the tiny bomb shelters we've made of our consciences failed Acts of Contrition. The Air Raid siren bellows. Stray dogs just beyond the melting windows cut their throats.

This is the dream out of which I surface and find myself naked and sweating where Crow left me hours ago on the fainting couch in the parlor of the Crow house, Saint Joan's County, North Carolina—not the dream of Wanda and the river, if it was indeed a dream—but the interminable honk of that alarm that issues from somewhere within its walls.

I sit up. Outside a dreary light bonnets the house. The dogs pull at a shank of rubbery deer gristle shaped like a boomerang, nip at each other, as they squabble. Maybe I hear thunder punctuating the siren—from the kitchen, it seems—exploding each second of this new day. The contiguous lament of the poor souls in Purgatory denied the Godhead—as foretold by Sister Cabrini.

I scuffle into my green fatigues and rise, stumble toward the kitchen, a kettle keening, the radio rattling off its morning news. Dirty gray light shimmies along the fluorescent ceiling tubes, presses its face to the café-curtained kitchen window. Another day of no sun. Dark clouds spill into the yard.

A terrible storm. That's what the woman sitting there at the table would prognosticate. My mother. She pulls tightly about her the pilled gray velour robe over her nightgown. Her hair is pinned up, and gathered in a gauzy rag. She drops her glasses to the tip of her nose, looks over them, parsing out her medicine, tablets from one bottle, then another, counting, her lips soundlessly tallying, gathering them to her with a hand that is still white and soft, the gold band tithing her to my father.

Crouched across from her at the table, the pain sips tea. It is a little girl. My mother snubs it, pretends it's not there. Like a twin she despises, a self she must deny. But her crippled back speaks: "You bastard." To a little girl. "You bastard." My mother turns her face away from the pain, cinches its pretty pink neck with a noose of silence, and drops the pills, one by one into her mouth, swallowing each in tandem with palsied sips of tea.

There. Almost instantaneous. Like she's a junkhead and her fix has just kicked in. A softening in her bearing as if the pain is disappearing, taking its last pulls of oxygen as it asphyxiates. Then. She hikes the volume on the radio when the announcer breaks in with a news bulletin. Northwest of Pittsburgh, near Neville Island, miles down the Monongahela where steel is starting to play out, some of the mills and foundries still running, all night, but with spectres alone.

A P&LE brakeman, on a twenty storey trestle spanning the Mon, has somehow caught his leg in the coupling gears of two coal cars. They've stopped the train, but he's up there bleeding to death. They can't get to him. Too high. No catwalk. And this terrible storm sweeping in. Tornado force winds. You can hear him screaming above the wind, the announcer says. They lower through one of the threatening black clouds a surgeon from a helicopter. There's nothing he can do, but amputate the leg. No proper anaesthesia. He saws the leg off right there in the howling wind and the first wave of rain. Then, through spools of lightening, they reel in the physician and the brakeman, blown sideways in the gale, and rush him to Montefiore Hospital.

My mother sits there listening, sipping her tea, shaking her head, and cries. Against the kitchen window, hail peens. She covers her face with Kleenex from the pocket of her robe and sobs. This is life, she thinks. A man leaves for work one morning and look what happens. How unprotected we are: as if this—a leg chopped off—is what has happened to her. She dresses her pain in bad news. She coats it with thunder. The lightning is a dagger she stabs herself with. She has not seen her son in six months. "Oh, my God," she says aloud, lowers her head to folded arms and heaves against the table top for a long moment, as the storm snatches the house in its teeth.

I place my hand on her shoulder. "Mother?"

She lifts her head. Wanda. In her robe and nightgown, hair hemmed into a frayed scarf. Clutching her Bible. An exact replica of the one that sits on our bedside table at Lark Terrace. Looks up at me as if we've never met. Then stares at the big black weather alert radio, out of which the siren, that has never let up, blares louder and louder. The dogs howl.

Crow barges into the room—I'm finally awake—reaches over and switches off the radio, then to the stove to remove the shrieking kettle. A bar of lightning lights up the room, and Wanda cries out softly, brings her hands to her mouth, runs them through her hair, and whimpers.

Charlene runs in, says, "Lord God, Mama. You got to get a grip."

"It's that crazy radio," Crow says to no one.

The girls encircle their mother, get her hands away from her head, hold them between their own, pat them. Mr. Crow enters the room.

"Sit with me a moment, Lon," says Wanda. She has aged twenty years since my dream. Crow flashes me a coded look.

Mr. Crow sits next to his wife, swipes off his hat and takes her hand, like a baby might his mama's. Does not say a word. Does not look at me as I walk through the house and out to the front porch. Nor does Wanda.

A witching light envelopes the Crow house and far off beyond the swales floats the storm, black, swirling, a constellation of foreboding. Veins of lightening crack through it. The dogs, huddled under the gum tree, stand when I step off the porch and follow me around the side of the house. Behind the smokehouse is a garden: staked tomato plants, yellow squash writhing in long vines, pitty-pat and butternut squash, cucumbers, half runners starting to climb. Flowers crawl out of rusted tins and basins, junked boots, and lard buckets: morning glory, azuratum, Sweet William, daisies, purple iris, gypsophila. A wicker jug spouts ivy on a warped treadle-driven Singer. Troughs of jonquils line the barbed wire fencing the pasture, entangled with gnarled yellow tea rose with two inch thorns. Nailed to the smoke house wall a skirmish of snake heads leer: triangular, ossified, the fangs arrested in an iconic cameo of assassination. Thunder sounds. But it's distant and, when I turn, the incendiary sky across the swales has fragmented into a thousand black rags the sun burns into the original blue of the firmament. Beneath the mounted snake heads sleep the dogs at my feet. I remind myself that I am saved. Like a day lily on its lone day of bloom, my bad hand unfurls.

Chapter 11

Gabriel toddles in an hour late, not even into his hangover yet, but bottomed on his drunk, maudlin in an inconsolable way. Aged a year overnight, having wept out the last minutes of it mere hours before in Old Settlers Cemetery behind First Presbyterian on Church Street, among Queen's sacred dead and Trial Street's ferocious hookers. What he does there with other men, those fallen angels, the red lording light of the church's stained glass: St. George, horseback, spearing a simpering dragon.

He stinks of timeless regret, unrequited love. His dirty white shirt flaps about his thighs, a plaid necktie drooping from the loose flyaway collar. Beige Velcro tennis shoes. When he slumps into the kitchen, Rosaria greets him with a glance at her watch, the other hand on her jutting hip, her hair standing in two wire pyramids on either side of her head, the streaks parting them like jagged lines of cocaine. One of her dress straps is off her shoulder, half her breast exposed. She doesn't shave her legs or under her arms.

The Allman Brothers rip through the kitchen speakers, making the already fiery kitchen torrid, filling it with trouble and Gabriel's pitiful longing. Electric guitars wired to detonators. Each lick screeches like brakes locking. Gracious plenty trouble up ahead, bad trouble, and it's not but May.

"I'm so sorry," Gabriel says, reaching for his apron docked on a nail next to the walk-in.

"Goddam," Rosaria says. Turns and walks out to the bar where Crow cuts lemons and limes.

Too-Bad, sautéing mushrooms in clarified butter, never turns from the burner. She likes Gabriel well enough, but he's sloppy and weak, and falters on the job. I stand in front of Hobart with a scalded rack of wine glasses just out of the machine. Steam rises behind me. My T-shirt is soaked.

"What's up, Gabriel?" I say.

He looks over at me and says, "I'm sorry, Mike. I'm a fucking mess today."

"You don't have to apologize to me."

Too-Bad is about to turn and spit, "You're a fucking mess every day," and she'd be right, but instead she asks him if he's had anything to eat, and hands him a plate with two hard-boiled eggs and the heel of a baguette. “Get you some coffee and pull yourself together, man,” she says.” A bib of sweat scoops across her shirt front. Beads of it stand out on her brown face.

Gabriel takes the plate. “I know. I know. I’m sorry.” He sits on a stool at the big stainless steel prep table in the middle of the kitchen.

“Just get your damn self together,” Too-Bad snaps.

Crow saunters into the kitchen and, when Gabriel sees her, he starts to cry, his hairy lips corrugating around the mash of egg in his mouth. Crow walks to where he sits and takes his big head in her arms and pulls it against her chest. Gabriel’s another breed of dog Crow just can’t help befriending.

Too long a sacrifice can make a stone of the heart, Gabriel blubbers.

I lug the glasses out to the bar where Rosaria sits with a pencil behind her ear, and another in her hand, checking off the produce shipment IPA just dropped off. She drinks white wine and doesn’t look at me, reaches across the bar and cuts the music in the middle of “Melissa,” a song she hates: *Or will you hide the dead man’s ghost?* Her heart: she says it’s broken. She hates men. In past lives they scourged her. Her lit cigarette smolders in a crystal ashtray.

I dry each glass with a towel and slot them upside-down in the overhead wooden rack above the long polished bar. I have to reach across Rosaria, but she never looks up. Behind her, in a booth, sit Hewitt and Margaret. They drink coffee and smoke cigarettes. He’s writing down the lunch specials on a square of paper. Margaret stares toward Rosaria and me, abstractedly dragging on the cigarette, but we don’t register. She is all alone; this is the finest moment of her day. Above her and Hewitt, recessed into the stucco wall, is a single pane window. Light ranges over them and, for an instant, they are two of Hopper’s strange stalled figures, something unpredictable and inevitable about them. As if doomed. Hewitt hunches exaggeratedly close to his work, his hand crawling slowly over the table. His earring ignites. Light skates up and down Margaret’s long long blonde hair, and she is wholly transformed, beautifully tragic in the brilliant sudden silence, and the mysterious cigarette smoke that wends through feinting sunlight across the empty restaurant. Then I hear Hobart grunting with the last load of glasses I shoved in, and the vague warbling of Gabriel as he pours it all out to Crow.

Hewitt hands Margaret the paper. She gets up, and steps out of the light, back into her life. She swings her arms as she walks, the hair under a beret like Crow’s—the same outfit as Crow—no longer golden, but very long, and spread across her wide back down to her broad hips. There comes the sound of the chalk on the easeled blackboard just inside the locked door as she scrawls the specials. It’s two minutes after eleven. We open the doors at 11:30 sharp. Usually there’s a line.

Back in the kitchen, Too-Bad and Crow stand next to Gabriel, still on the stool. He's calmed down and the three of them smoke cigarettes—which isn't supposed to happen in the kitchen, but everyone does it, including Rosaria.

Crow and Too-Bad get Gabriel to his feet. Too-Bad heads back to the burners and grills, the two big pots of soup, the Shrimp Creole, today's entrée special. Crow leads Gabriel into the big walk-in cooler and the Sauterne that he'll hit to get his ballast back. If he wasn't so fat, she'd squeeze him into the ductwork and share a number with him.

Hobart idles out of its last rinse cycle and halts. I crank it open, dig into the steaming cave and hoist out another heavy tray of glasses. As I walk into the bar, Hewitt strides into the kitchen, and we pass in the narrow doorway. I have the load, but nevertheless juke to the side to let him pass. He stops there and looks at me. He doesn't smile. His mouth is small and pursed beneath his tiny hooked nose. He brushes, deliberately, it seems, against the heavy tray of hot dripping glasses and it digs into my stomach. I barely hang onto it. My bad hand. He nods, almost a smile, as if we both clearly understand the dynamic between us.

He steps into the kitchen. "Smells like a fucking chicken house in here."

At the bar, putting up the glasses, I hear him: "Only one person smells like that. The elegant marriage of shit and rotgut."

Rosaria looks up. At me. I imagine my expression, over the course of time, never changes: locked on the same speed of impassive. My face is gone. What's left is a mask. I live inside myself. Rosaria, with her gift, knows this, and she knows that something is about to happen. It's 11:18. But she doesn't care. That's it. She doesn't care and I see it in the white streaks and the birthmark. The iceberg blue eyes out of which her cigarette smoke seems to emanate.

"Where's the lardass?" Hewitt continues. "Late again, and the usual crocodile tears."

The door to the walk-in opens. Rosaria's eyes are back on her list. She takes a sip of wine. Hits the cigarette.

"The tears of a clown. A big faggot clown."

I set the nearly emptied tray on the bar, wipe my hands on my towel and stuff it in my back pocket. Walk back into the kitchen. Too-Bad's back is to the stove. All the burners roar, yet there is nothing on them. In her hand is the serrated bread knife she uses to slice bagels. She is staring into the walk-in.

Gabriel sits on the cooler's slick plank floor. Hewitt stands above him, yanking him by his necktie and pouring over his head a mag of Sauterne. Gabriel's massive head lolls shoulder to shoulder. He sputters, unable to catch his breath, drowning in the wine, his hair and beard limp and dripping, his legs splayed out. One of the crummy Velcro shoes has come off. On the shelves around him are massive wheels of cheese, bins of produce, cases of beer and white wine. Flour and rice and potatoes. Hanging tuns of swaying meat dangle from ceiling hooks. A 60 watt bulb above the door is the only light. *Where's Crow?* Then I see her scrambling out of a corner, chaste, furious, on her hands and knees. Scared too, but ready. Her striped skirt's soaked.

Hewitt's back is to me. He's dumped flour on Gabriel. It sets up in curds all through his hair and beard. Coats him white as he sits there, a bulbous pantomime, worrying his caked white lips.

Crow sees me. Stays poised like a wildcat, one front paw off the ground. Her black and gold eyes: yellow jackets. Blazing red lipstick. Cocks her head. Her beret, like a black halo, caps her short black hair. Face white as whipping cream. Opens her mouth. Her teeth flash.

Hewitt believes that he'll just stroll out of the walk-in. After he's abused and humiliated Gabriel. After whatever he might have done to Crow to put her on the floor. As if he is immune to consequences. Walk through me as if I'm mist, kiss his buxom Margaret, unlock the doors to the restaurant, smile and begin handing the patrons menus. He has faultily reasoned that brains and bearing and position are protection against will and savagery—an illusion people that grew up in my neighborhood, East Liberty, reject. It is exactly such vanity, and hubris, that made a fugitive of me.

I stand in the doorway of a restaurant walk-in cooler in Queen, North Carolina, precisely because of payback. This instant is a point on the parabola my life has charted since I stiffed a Pittsburgh bookie named Felix Costa for $11,000 and had to flee the city. A calculated play that went haywire.

I abide in the purifying aesthetic of reprisal, so that when Hewitt pivots and sees me, I have already thrown my fist at his smiling face, a face so smug and lordly that he does not see the fist hurtling toward him. He sees only Crow's scudzy boyfriend, Mike, the tattered loser dishwasher who wouldn't say shit if he had a mouthful.

My right hand has a mind of its own. Some days it minds me; some it doesn't. It is hurt and broken and, in truth, a symbol of my heart, roughly the same size, scarred and riven, a remnant of my former charmed life, ruined in a fight over a girl—though I am not a fighter. Far from it. My right hand, like me, is a fugitive; therefore I throw at Hewitt my left, my other hand. The hand that inhabits my new unprotected life. The hand that remains to fight for Crow.

Hewitt feels protected, like I used to feel. I want to see that expression of superiority change when he realizes he is now unprotected. And it does—when he steps into that punch and recoils: a subtle pirouette, a quarter turn, and slight buckling of his knees, the creases of each bent pant leg still parallel in that pirouette, his hair and necktie whipping out with centrifugal force. Eyes rubbed clean of anything he recognizes. Then slowly reassembles himself, twists back to an erect position like a film in reverse. There in his refocused eyes I see myself reflected: the crazy beard and hair, the stinking soiled T-shirt; evangelized, no longer deluded that my life is charmed or the universe gives the first damn about me. My desolation and triumph, my moment of grace.

Then, before he can say a thing, because that's what's about to happen, because I know him like the back of my bad hand—an apology, some wheedling excuse, tears, even begging, though his contrition, however abject, would be false, and he'd return another time to assassinate me and Crow and Gabriel—I pop him again. Open-handed. Then two more quick ones. The way the nuns slapped hell out of you if you cut your eyes at them the wrong way. His mouth is bloody. His hands are in front of his face.

Crow has crawled across the floor to Gabriel and is wiping the flour out of his eyes with the hem of her skirt. He tries to get to his feet, but they go out from under him each time he attempts to rise.

"Put your hands down," I command Hewitt.

He's making little noises. His sports jacket dangles from the ceiling on its hanger.

With my bad hand, I pick up an ice pick from a shelf. "Put your hands down or I'll stick this in your eye."

Crow says, "Romeo," but I'm not sure if she's asking me to give it up or drive a hole in Hewitt.

"Mike," I hear from behind and I know it's Too-Bad with her knife. Then Margaret screeching.

"Hands down," I say evenly, brandishing the ice pick.

He drops his hands, whimpering.

"You lift your hands and I'll skewer your eyeball like a cocktail olive. You understand?"

He nods.

"Okay. Now you may go, but first you have to thank Gabriel for affording you this lesson."

Suddenly an old man, older than Gabriel, Hewitt turns and says, "Thank you, Gabriel."

"Very good. Now tell Crow how terribly sorry you are."

"I'm terribly sorry, Crow."

"Yes, you are," answers Crow.

"Nicely done," I say, rip his coat from the hanger and pin it to the wall with the ice pick. "Now go in peace and sin no more."

Hewitt staggers by me out into the kitchen. I help Crow get Gabriel to his feet. Hewitt sits on a stool where Margaret, now sobbing, engulfs him. "You're a monster," she says to me.

Still clutching the knife, Too-Bad smiles. But Rosaria, who stands in the center of the room with her hands on her hips, does not. "You're fired," she pronounces.

Crow unties her apron, and lifts it over her head.

"Not you, Crow," says Rosaria.

"I quit," Crow replies and drops the apron.

She takes my arm and we walk out of the restaurant, out of The Tea Rose, out of the Pfeiffer, into the late spring streets of Queen.

Holding hands, we walk in silence down 7th Street. When it hits Andromeda, at our place, instead of going in, we stroll up the boulevard and duck into Omar's where Middle-eastern students from the college huddle religiously over rice and lamb. The music loud: sitars, tambourines.

Instantly, Omar stands over our table, dressed in white shirt and white pants, white bucks on his feet, twinkling eyes, the dazzling smile.

"Mr. Roman. Miss Crow," he says, bowing slightly. "What a pleasure to see you."

I stand and hold out my left hand to shake his right. "Omar, my good friend," I say. Crow smiles up at him. He places his palms together in the attitude of prayer and bows to her. The restaurant is sultry. The ceiling fan above us stirs the tassels hanging from our tablecloth. We order Almazas and stare out the huge window at the students dodging traffic as they cross the boulevard. A cadre of jet-black-haired dark-faced young students enter Omar's and take tables for lunch. Others disappear behind the alcove where the sound of the pinball machines and exclamations filters into the dining room along with the vague scent of hashish.

Omar's wife hurries from the kitchen to wait on the students. She smiles meekly at Crow and me. She rarely speaks. Crow and I have not said a word to each other since the scene at The Tea Rose. Crow lights a cigarette. We finish the beer. I motion to Omar, standing behind the bar—three lambs, small and grayish, peek for a moment around the side of it—and when he brings us two more Almazas we order mezza and the special: a chicken stew with stuffed vegetables.

When I rise to use the lavatory, I kiss Crow. The restaurant is suddenly crowded. We are the only Americans. I have to pass the alcove with the pinball machines commandeered by wild-eyed cursing students. The hash is strong. And cigarette smoke. They don't look up, but notice me. There is about them an eternal vigilance. Not unlike my own aesthetic since fleeing Pittsburgh.

I open the door to the tiny lavatory. A toilet with a mirror above it, sink and blow dryer on the wall. Stinking of reefer. It's occupied—by a Vietnamese man—so I immediately begin to close the door. This man, however, beckons me to enter. I go in, not wanting to at all, but for some reason feeling too awkward to refuse. He's finished, so I step to the toilet, nodding to him as he passes on his way out. There's urine, a good-sized marijuana roach and a cigarette butt in the bowl. I lift my foot and press the flush-handle.

But he doesn't leave. He stands directly behind me—I watch him in the mirror—combing his long black greasy hair with a huge pink comb. He's short, slight, clothed entirely in denim. His face is pocked with blemishes and, down each cheek, dives a deep rut. When I catch his eye in the mirror, he stares directly at me and protractedly combs his hair until I drop my eyes. I stand there like an idiot with my zipper down trying to piss, but too agitated to make it happen. I'm figuring this man has no intention of leaving, that he's trouble, that he has something very specific in mind for me. An emissary: Felix's boy.

I outweigh him by seventy-five pounds. I'm a foot taller than him. But it doesn't matter. Against him I'll be powerless. I drop my eyes and concentrate on my task, praying he's not packing a gun or a knife—though I've heard stories about the gruesome work a comb can do. The fact that he's Vietnamese completely terrifies me. Through the flimsy sheetrock that walls the lavatory, the crazy pinballs chime, the canned carnival voices that play out of the machines, the maniacal jockeying of the students. Suddenly the man turns and leaves. I bolt the door with trembling hands and finally complete my business.

On the way back to the table, I quickly scan the restaurant for the Vietnamese. Nowhere to be seen. The mezza sits in the middle of the table. Crow, still in her beret and necktie, smokes and looks out the window, sips the beer directly from the bottle. The restaurant is filled, the music louder, the students' conversation animated, loud as well. I eat an olive and finish my beer. Look back out the window at the flag blowing over Memorial Stadium, its green grass, water shooting in perpendicular arcs from huge sprinklers.

The restaurant is unbearably loud. The students habitually argue. They jeer and knock on the tables, tap their forks against their saucers. They choreograph everything they say with their hands. I never know what they are saying, but the overall context is passion. Like the Italians I grew up with, my family. A kind of familiar grandiosity: *emozione.* I have learned to ignore what does not concern me; and, like Crow, I'm preoccupied. We no longer have jobs.

From the din emerges the hiss and snarl of ferocious anger, distinguishable in any tongue. I turn. Omar stands behind the bar, gesticulating wildly at the man I had seen in the lavatory. Spitting words at an incredible rate, they argue in what I assume is Vietnamese.

It is soon obvious to everyone that theirs is not another heated debate. Eyes slowly lift to study the combatants. Conversation ceases. There is a Middle-eastern fellow, Khalil, who always sits at the same table closest to Omar near the bar. Early forties, wild head of black hair, thick horned rim glasses, ears jutting from his head at right angles. With him is a very young strikingly handsome man with one arm, dressed in camouflage fatigues.

When Omar suddenly charges around the bar to get at the Vietnamese, Khalil jumps to his feet, but does not move. Omar, still gesturing maniacally, towers over the Vietnamese, who gives no ground. They waltz to the middle of the room, jostling, shouting. Omar's wife darts out of the kitchen, throws herself on Omar and shrieks in English, "This is a business. This is a business."

Omar pushes her away and says, "Shut up."

She flings herself upon him again and, this time, he slaps her across the face. Hand to her cheek, she staggers along the floor, then collapses, weeping, in a chair at Khalil's table. Taking advantage of the diversion, the Vietnamese goes for a chair and is lifting it as I, instinctively, though regrettably, shout, "Omar." But Khalil springs from where he's been rooted and manages to wrestle the chair from the Vietnamese who then flees through the kitchen and, presumably, through the rear entrance to the alley as we hear the heavy thud of the door.

"Call the police," Omar says to no one.

"No police, Omar. Please," sobs his wife.

Omar walks toward the kitchen. His wife, still weeping, rises and follows. Khalil says something to Omar as he passes, then takes his seat again. The students return sullenly to their lunches.

"Jesus Christ," says Crow. "What was that all about?"

"I don't know. That Vietnamese guy was in the bathroom when I went in. I was trying to take a piss and he wouldn't leave. He just stood behind me combing his hair. Like he had it in for me."

"What do you mean?"

"Like he was going to kill me."

"Why would you think that?"

"You know why. I'm ready to get the hell out of here. Just lam it out of this town."

There is a sudden wailing from the back of the restaurant. Khalil has already disappeared through the beaded portal into the kitchen, along with the one-armed guy whose lone hand disappears into the blouse of his fatigues.

I jump to my feet.

Crow puts her hand on my arm. "What the hell are you doing, Romeo?"

I take off for the kitchen, towing Crow by the hand.

There is blood all over the floor. Jets of it streak the walls. Omar is on his knees, in the blood, keening back and forth. He makes a humming noise through his hands with which he's covered his face. His wife, draped across his back, chokes out an in comprehensible high-pitched lament. Khalil hovers over them. The young one-armed man dashes out the rear door.

The lambs are dead: their throats cut and they've been mutilated. Sacrificed, in their bright red wool, they stare into each other's astonished gray eyes. Students gather in the doorway. Khalil sets about herding them back to their tables.

Crow and I are left alone with Omar and his wife. He looks deadly.

I must return to Cairo," he says, rising and sitting heavily in a chair as if contemplating his own execution. The knees of his pant legs are drenched in blood. His wife, still weeping, crumbles at his feet. He runs a hand across her hair, looks up, smiles: "There can be no more Omar's."

I stare at the massacred lambs, the bloody kitchen. Crow holds onto me, trembling, urging me out of the building with the electric thrum of her pulse. Not just danger, but a kind of evil—as if someone is slipping over my head a black hood, and all I can think of is Felix, that whatever has happened here has been meant for me. Even the police sirens, not unusual in this neighborhood, as they grow louder and closer.

"My friend," says Omar. He turns slightly and lifts his hand—an old and weary gesture filled with futility and benediction—and pulls from somewhere behind him a bottle of Mavrodaphne. "The things we must do," he says sadly. Then he sighs, breaks the bottle neck against the wall, drinks deeply from the jagged mouth and offers it to me.

I take the bottle. Omar's lips bleed. His wife is prostrate in the blood, her hands around his ankles. I lift the bottle. Omar's blood poises on the jagged crown of glass I'm about to drink from—for what reason I'm unsure—when Crow commands, "Don't."

Then in slow motion, in a precise replica of a classic stage faint, she twirls toward the bloody floor, her eyes lolling in her still open sockets, her white throat exposed, bangs parting to reveal in the blue characters on her forehead the future.

The cop sirens cease.

I drop the bottle—it shatters on the tile—slide over and catch Crow before she hits the floor. At that moment, bedlam erupts in the dining room:

shouting, broken glass, crashing furniture, cops from Andromeda on the bullhorn, and the insane recital of bodies breaking against one another.

Omar stares at his wife and pets her head. Drops of blood fall from his mouth into her red hair. A handful of students, handkerchiefs over their mouths, blow by us and streak out the back door, still thrown wide from the Vietnamese. The air is suddenly peppery, unbreathable. More sirens. Omar coughs in steady iambic beats.

I hold my breath, throw Crow over my shoulder and follow bloody footprints out the door into the alley. Police cruisers race down Andromeda, blue lights wiggling in the afternoon sun. I cut left, take another alley, lined with the white millhouses we see from the bedroom window of our attic apartment, just on the other side of the little league field, and slide down the grassy embankment into foul territory along the left field line. Cops everywhere. I don't want to risk crossing the outfield, waist-high in bunch grass and blackberry, old soldiers lurking at the roots, to Lark Terrace, especially with an unconscious woman crimped over my shoulder. I slip into the stone dugout between the plate and third base, and prop Crow in a corner on the bench.

She comes around instantly, that same incredulous look upon her face. "I fainted, didn't I?"

"Yep."

"Jesus Christ. What do you think was going on back there?"

"I don't know. Omar is obviously into something."

"Those dear little lambs. My God. That's the most horrible thing I've ever seen. And what'll happen to Omar?"

Crow buries her face in her hands and cries, long and beautifully, without quarter or regret, every inch of her quaking as I hold her and say, at decent intervals, "Don't cry," though it makes perfect sense to weep.

I lean in to kiss her. She smiles. Tears pour out of her eyes and rush down her cheeks. "Rough day, huh?" she says. "Let's go to the movies."

"Okay, and then let's get out of town for a while."

Chapter 12

The second I reported for work the next morning, Phil buttonholed me about the Buffalo game. What was the early line? Did I think it would move? What about the other games? The actual line that Eugene had given me was Steelers by 10—a load of points to be fronting a team tough as Buffalo, especially during the playoffs. Even so, people would bet hometown without even thinking. Knowing that line would inevitably creep up as game time neared, I decided to try and middle Phil again. I told him the Steelers were favored by 17.

"What are you going to do?" he asked.

"I don't know. Probably bet Steelers. But we need to grab this early spread. Come Sunday, who knows what it'll be."

"Okay. I want the Steelers for a thousand dollars."

"A thousand dollars?"

"Is that too much? Tell me if it is. I don't want to queer things between you and your connection."

"No, it's fine. No problem. A thousand on the Steelers giving 17."

"Correct."

"Okay. What else?"

"Just Steelers this week. And, George, I hope you'll be our guest for the game again this Sunday. Same crowd."

"Sure," I answered without even thinking.

Later that afternoon, I called Eugene and took the Steelers for myself at 10 for a thousand dollars. I had never before bet more than five hundred. Just saying *a thousand* made me nervous, even though I was holding on to Phil's bet, at 17. Same deal as the Washington game: the worst I could do was break even.

Eugene whistled. "You sure, my man?"

"Yep."

"Then you got it."

I bet the other playoff games too, modestly, except for the Oakland-Miami game. On a hunch I plunked down $400 on the Dolphins, a three point underdog.

"Here." Phil handed me an envelope. "Tickets to *The Nutcracker.* It's Sterling's favorite. I take her every year."

"I can't accept these, Phil. You go with Sterling."

"Believe me, my boy. She'd rather go with you. Besides I plan to work late this evening and catch up filling some of those prescriptions for tomorrow."

"Thanks, Phil. Thanks very much."

Phil's habitual kindness flooded me with guilt as I walked home with the ballet tickets in my pocket. It had begun snowing an hour before, and was still wafting down steadily, big feathery flakes in the full dark—beautiful up high against the sky in the orbs of light the streetlamps shed. At least two inches on the ground. I scooped a handful off a parked car and packed it into a baseball-sized snowball.

A city bus, the 73 Highland, rumbled slowly along, throwing up a wave of sooty slush, then stopped, its air brakes suspiring, to drop off a few riders. The inside of the bus was lit. Row on row of grim, bundled strangers skidding home from making a living. A stooped-over old lady, a shopping bag in each hand, stumped down the bus steps. She peered suspiciously out of a royal blue coat, frayed at her shoe tops, and a clear plastic rain-bonnet. She teetered side to side as she walked, using the shopping bags for ballast. When she and I passed each other, she gave me the eye, like those demented Italian widows down on Larimer Avenue, and mumbled something.

Holding in my hand that plump, perfect snowball, I was tempted to whip it at her, watch the white circle flair on her blue coat, run off as her invective chased me down the street. As a kid, my friends and I pelted buses with snowballs, jumped out in ambush, then ran like hell. After school, one afternoon, Alex and I bolted into the middle of Highland Avenue and blasted the windshield of a city bus depositing its passengers in front of Sears. The driver jumped off the bus and chased us. We cut into Sears—the furious driver chasing, screaming for us to stop—and dodged through the racks, knocking things over, banging into customers. We exited the store through Will Call into the icy back parking lot and kept running. The driver finally gave up and returned to his bus and the long line of horn-blaring barricaded traffic it had created.

Poor Alex. He had apparently lived for a while after he had crashed into the boulevard. Jesus Christ. How could they have known that? I hadn't thought about it in a long long time. Alex and I were no longer tight when he jumped. I'd see him on the corner sometimes. We'd wave. I'd spot him a fin. He was a junky by then. To get high, he would have yanked my teeth with ice tongs. Even wasted, however, he could still draw anything—whatever that was worth.

I fired the snowball at a stop sign, hit it dead center, and kept walking.

And Phil. He was free to bet any way he wanted. He could have taken the points. Anybody who knew anything about football would have taken Buffalo with 17. Still: I liked Phil very much.

When I got home, before going in, I shoveled and salted the walk. In my head, I heard my mother lament: *That's just what I need. To fall on the ice and break a hip.*

Inside, my parents were both asleep in front of the six o'clock news. The only light was from the tiny Christmas tree in the corner of the room. In my mother's lap lay the ornaments she had been working on. My father, in a beat-up gray cardigan, snored in the chair across from her. They looked old. I tiptoed up the stairs to get ready for the ballet.

When I came back down, wearing a suit and a white shirt and tie, they were wide awake, and I smelled food from the kitchen.

"What are you all dolled up for? I didn't even hear you come in," my mother said. "Where are you going? You're not going to sit down and eat with us?"

"To see *The Nutcracker* with Sterling. The ballet."

"I know what it is. What do you know about ballet?"

"Nothing. But I'm going to learn all I can tonight."

"When did you buy the tickets? Why don't you mention things any more? Everything's such a big secret."

"No big secret, Mom. Mr. Rosechild just gave them to me today."

"What's he giving you these tickets for? They're not free."

"He couldn't go himself, so he gave them to me."

"Why doesn't the mother go with her daughter?"

"I don't know, Mom."

"Sylvia," said my dad. "Leave him alone."

"I just want to know what the big attraction is with this girl?"

"I like her."

"He likes her. I think she's chasing you," countered my mother.

"You don't even know her."

"Which is my point. When do we get the privilege?"

"Don't start, Mom."

"Sylvia," interjected my dad.

"Don't Sylvia me. I would at least like to lay eyes on this mystery girl. If that's not too much to ask?"

"I'll arrange something. I got to go." I kissed my parents, and started out the door.

"Let me look at you, Georgie," said my mother.

I turned.

"You look very handsome," she squeaked, then started to cry.

Jesus Christ. I joined my father who had bounded toward her the second her voice cracked.

"What's the matter, Mom?" I held one of her hands.

"I don't want to lose you."

"You're not going to lose me."

"She's just tired," said my dad.

"I'm tired of you telling me I'm tired. Just be home at a decent hour and watch yourself in this weather."

We had first row Grand Tier seats. A spectacular view of the gilt, ornate vaulted architecture of Heinz Hall. Towering columns. Massive dripping chandeliers. Sterling in profile against the faint blue light, escaped wisps of hair from her French twist like smoke, a just-off-the shoulders golden dress, the sparkle of her necklace and earrings. The rise and fall of the dreamy music, the barely audible tap of the ballerinas' slippers.

But I was preoccupied by what had become my precarious relationship with Sterling's father. Could I trust Phil to not blurt out that I had turned him on to a little harmless gambling? How would I rationalize that to JoAnn and Sterling? That betting a few bucks on sports with a bookie, as long as you knew the bookie, was innocent as Bingo. That I, George Dolce, was engineering the entire operation and their husband and father was under my protection. Completely safe. In fact, Sterling had met the bookie, his sweet little wife and family, just a couple of days before, and had pronounced him a nice man.

The ballerinas whirled across the stage. At all costs, I had to keep Sterling out of it until I shook Phil. Sitting there in my plush red seat, holding her hand, I tried to sort out my dilemma. I could feed Phil a story: that my bookie had been busted or had moved away, shut down—anything. There was no reason for Phil not to believe me. That would be the most expedient end to it all. I could continue my own betting through Eugene.

But, if I cut Phil loose, I could no longer manipulate the lines and keep Phil's bets, depriving myself of the extra income I desperately needed. My parents were depending on me until they could get back on their feet. It might be another six months until my dad was called back to the mill. Maybe more. Maybe never. God forbid. He was sixty-four. With her arthritis, my mother, in a few years, could be in a wheelchair. And I absolutely had to have that money for law school. What if I did get into Yale? Every school I had applied to cost a fortune. I could take loans, but I didn't want to be in hock the rest of my life. Law school was my ticket out of town and, then, once an attorney—in three years—I'd take care of my parents in style. The first thing would be to send them on a trip to Italy—something they had yearned for all their lives. See the old country once before they died. I wasn't about to forget about them—my blood. The hell with Phil. Was he going to take care of Big George and Sylvia Dolce?

The complicating factor, of course, was Sterling. How could I have dreamed I'd fall wildly in love with Phil's daughter when I entered into this arrangement with him? I took a long look at her. She was too lovely, so innocent, her dark eyes impetuous, brooding as she studied the ballet, as if she might laugh or cry or both. I had never known a girl like her.

No, there could be no leveling with her about what was going on between me and her father. She wouldn't understand. She had no conception of money. All her life, it had poured out of faucets and tumbled from closets. When she looked up into the sky, it rained down upon her. I couldn't risk losing her. No one ever told the real truth anyhow. I was convinced of this. Just versions of the truth. And my version was above reproach.

After football season, I'd break it off with Phil. Besides, Phil wasn't betting enormous amounts. Certainly not more than he could cover. He was rolling in it. Early on, Phil had requested I keep our gambling relationship in confidence. There was no reason to believe he would ever betray me to Sterling. Or to JoAnn. Especially after our betting relationship had halted. By that time, Sterling would be back at Brynn Mawr. Maybe I'd quit the pharmacy. If I could earn enough money making a little book, throw in as an apprentice with Eugene and Felix. Put some distance between me and Phil. I decided at that instant I'd accept Eugene's offer—once Sterling returned to school. I thought of his comment about straying outside my *element*. But, for now, there was no turning back. Guilt was for chumps. All I had to do was keep my head, be a man. Things would blow over.

The audience was applauding. Clara's dream had ended. Curled up on the sofa, the nutcracker returned to its original inanimate state, she clutched it to her and slept until the curtain collapsed over the set. The applause heightened through the curtain calls, wave after wave, as the audience stood and bravoed, and finally died out as the lights dimmed on and there came the collective noise of people rustling from their seats and into the night.

I didn't want to leave—as if my own dream had slammed shut. I didn't want to walk outside into the gleaming winter streets, and throttle a cold automobile to life.

Someone tapped me on the shoulder. When I turned, I recognized the man. But the context was skewed and it took me a few seconds to identify him, dressed in a blue three piece suit, a camel topcoat and white silk scarf.

"You don't remember me?" queried the man.

He was with a woman with a prominent nose. A mouth that spread across her face as she smiled. Blondish, streaky brown hair parted in the middle that swooped around her face, and nearly touched at her chin. Under a white fur coat, she wore a very short silver-sequined dress.

"Felix. Of course I remember you. I just . . ."

"What? You didn't expect to see me here. Right?" Felix smiled, but he made my skin crawl.

"That isn't what I was going to say."

"It's okay. But you might be surprised that I know quite a bit about ballet. And opera too. You think you have the market cornered when it comes to culture, college boy?"

"Believe me, I don't know a thing about it."

"He's just pulling your leg, honey," said the woman. "I'm Marie Costa, Felix's wife."

She held out her hand to me and then to Sterling, who had taken my arm the moment Felix started talking

"I'm Sterling Rosechild."

"You related to the pharmacist?" Felix asked.

"My father."

Felix darted in and kissed Sterling on the cheek. The mustache bristled against her cheek, his razor-cut blue-black hair at the collar of his white shirt. "Merry Christmas, Beautiful," he said.

"Merry Christmas," answered Sterling.

"George is going to be a lawyer some day," Felix said to Marie.

"Good for you, honey."

I smelled Felix's cologne on Sterling. She held me tighter and smiled.

"We're going up the street for a drink. Why don't you two join us?" Felix offered.

I stood there, fumbling for an excuse.

"I think these two lovebirds want to be alone. Not with a couple of old married people like us," said Marie, smiling warmly.

The theatre had almost cleared out. The women walked ahead and chatted. Felix and I lagged a few yards behind. He put his arm around me.

"You giving me the ass on having a drink?"

"No, Felix. We can have a drink."

Felix smiled. His icy teeth, shellacked with spittle as he talked, flashed in the now-raised house lights. "Look, Georgie. I'm just jagging you. What are you so tender about? You okay?"

"Yeah, I'm just fine."

"How about mum and dad?"

"They're good. Thank you."

"Eugene talk to you about that thing?"

"He did."

"Well?"

"That you very much. I'm considering it."

"Well, I want you to know that I like you, and I like the work you been doing for us. But don't keep us dangling." He squeezed the back of my neck. "That's a pretty little piece you got."

I needed to say something—to show I was flattered. Respect. But I despised Felix for bringing up Sterling like this—*a pretty little piece*—for kissing her—he had done it just to needle me, because he knew he could, son of a bitch—for assuming that everything that everyone else had really belonged to him, and was merely out on loan. Petty, pretend-gangster with more balls than brains. Crude, ignorant. A real *gavone.* The silence resounded between us for another minute until we hit the freezing sidewalk on Sixth Street. Felix clamped my neck again, hard, and then removed his arm. There was a round of farewells. The women hugged.

Marie said, "God bless you both."

Felix, no longer smiling, winked. At me. He raised his hand and said, "Ciao."

The Costas clipped one way up Sixth. Sterling and I, holding hands, strolled the other toward the parking garage.

It had stopped snowing, but there was a fresh coat on the sidewalk and street. I wrapped my arm around Sterling's waist to steady her. The shoes she wore were no more than slippers. She kissed my cheek. I smelled Felix again.

"How do you know them?" she asked.

"I know Felix from the neighborhood. We bump into each other up the park sometimes. He's a running fanatic. I had never met his wife."

"She was nice."

"Yeah, I liked her."

"Didn't you think she looked like Barbra Streisand?"

What I had been thinking, even though I really had liked Marie, was that she was trampy-looking. But just to get back at Felix. I pictured myself confronting him, ripping that big cashmere topcoat off, shredding his expensive suit, tearing the white shirt to rags, strangling him by his gold chains, divesting him of all his gangster pretensions and just kicking the living shit out of him in front of his wife who, after it was all over, would thank me for finally putting him in his place.

But I could never take Felix. That packed, ruthless, cockstrong body. An assassin's temper. He'd never stop until he killed you or you killed him. Felix and Eugene had grown up together on the Avenue. Eugene had related a couple of tales. About Felix massacring people in fights. Going on and on way after they were down and beaten on the alley floor. Blood and teeth. Felix was bad news. The kind it was best to just steer clear of. I was no fighter anyway. And there I was on the verge of entering into business with Felix. Eugene was like family, but this guy . . . I realized again how passionately I wanted to leave Pittsburgh, how badly I needed money. I reminded myself again that I had to keep my head, bide my time. Then I wondered if Felix carried a gun.

"Yeah, I guess she did look like Barbra Streisand, now that you mention it."

"What's the matter, George?"

"Nothing."

"You seem pretty preoccupied. You have that pensive troubled look. Your future counsel-for-the-defense look."

"I don't even know how a guy like Felix gets a wife." I wanted to spill the whole thing to Sterling, everything, start to finish, have her grant absolution right there on the dark, snowy cement, then fuel up the little Mercedes and drive to California together. There was no one on the streets. The frozen sky wore black. Salt trucks rumbled across the bridges from the Northside.

"He seemed nice enough," she said.

"It's nothing. He's just a little too slick. He gives me the creeps. I was going to say 'What the heck's he doing at the ballet?' but then I guess he could be wondering the same thing about me."

"You're a funny boy." She kissed my cheek again.

Chapter 13

The parking garage was deserted except for the woman in the ticket booth reading a paperback. Sterling and I took the nasty, graffiti-fouled elevator up to the fourth floor, our steps echoing as we walked toward the car, parked at the river side of the far end of the deck. The Allegheny lay beneath us, black pewter in the city lights, its grim, holographic face pocked with crisscrossing boiling wakes that shoveled up the light falling from the skyscrapers fronting it. The wind ripped at twenty-five knots. Half a mile downstream, where the river plowed into the Monongahela to forge the Ohio, Three Rivers Stadium hulked silently in the darkness.

As a high school football player at Saint Sebastian's, an all boys preparatory school—referred to by my mother as "a private school for Catholic hoodlums"—I had been on the first secondary school team to ever play in Three Rivers. When the stadium was brand new, before the Steelers had risen from the sump of the NFL. Bradshaw's rookie year. Saint Sebastian's had met there a much vaunted, nationally-ranked Saint Isaac Jogues High School for the Pittsburgh City Diocesan Championship.

Coach Noonan had given each player two sleeping tablets to take the night before the game, but I had not closed my eyes. We received a police escort to the stadium and were quartered in the Steelers' luxurious locker room. I dressed in Bradshaw's cubicle, the Louisiana quarterback's practice jerseys inscribed with number *12* hanging from hooks, a dozen pair of spikes littering its carpeted floor.

The night had been frigid. The coaches spread dollops of analgesic at the bases of our spines, taped our ankles one last time. Then in a massive huddle we prayed to Our Lady of Victory, each of us straining to touch Noonan, a red-headed, Jameson's-drinking, ex-pug with a mangled face who had played two seasons pro with the Rams after his boxing career tanked. Above us, in the stadium, reverberating with 15,000 spectators pummeling steel, Saint Sebastian's band played the fight song over and over.

We took a quick lead. Lenny DePaolo snatched a fumble and raced ninety-six yards before anyone knew what had happened. The gargantuan lights burned in assent. Blue and gold banners waved. The crowd sung, *Nah, nah, nah, nah. Nah, nah, nah, nah. Hey, hey, hey, we're number one.* I had had the impression that if I kept my eyes closed long enough, I would doze off and come to an hour later with the game ball in my hand, flashbulbs exploding, all the promises kept.

But I rarely played. I ran scout team in practice, fodder for the first string, one of the sacrificial lambs during scrimmages and tackling drills.

Lenny's score was followed by drought. Jogues horded the ball, methodically grinding up and down the field. Sebastian's defense back-pedaled all night, yard marker to yard marker, hash mark to hash mark. One collision after another, Three Rivers' Tartan turf skiving them like oranges. Noonan put me and the rest of the scrubs in the game only when it was obvious it was out of reach. The final was 33–6. But after it was all over, after I had peeled myself off the artificial grass and watched the last integer on the game clock round into a zero to match the other two, then wept in the Steelers' clubhouse with my teammates, I never wanted to see any of them again.

I endured the ovation we received from parents and girlfriends—I had no sweetheart, my mother had cried—when we emerged from the locker room, showered, in neckties and blue blazers, and boarded the bus to chug sorrowfully back to the school and what was to have been the victory dance in the gym. I was ashamed of losing, ashamed of crying. More than anything, I was ashamed to have not been out there on the field the entire time taking a beating with the others. What I wanted most was to be far away from all of it, all of them, the topography, the rivers and bridges and tunnels.

When we got back to Saint Sebastian's, music spilled into the parking lot. With a few of my teammates—guys who were starters—I walked down to the State Store on Craig Street, and paid a drunk five bucks to stumble inside and buy us a half-gallon of cheap vodka to mix with orange juice. We drank it in the black piss-smelling stone train tunnel behind Sebastian's gym. The matches we lit cigarettes with bathed our faces like icons. As if it was our last night on earth. We would die young, we pledged. At the least we'd never part. We cried a little more, and laughed and passed the vodka. I had felt wonderfully tragic. And smart. Like I had seen something for the first time in that inky narrow tunnel. A way through all the bullshit.

As we stood on the rails, there came a noise: remote, like a quill scratched across parchment. At first I thought my brain was grinding out a story or my teeth chattering. The tunnel walls were sheathed in ice.

Then the rails began to jitter and hum; the crossties checked. The train was coming. We felt it far off—the tunnel sizzled—driving toward us in our catacomb, getting bigger and bigger. Bats unroosted from the ceiling and drilled out of the tunnel. It was time to run, yet nobody moved. The whistle howled as the train crossed the Oakland trestle. The walls vibrated. The gravel in the rail-bed jumped. I opened my mouth to say it was time to get the hell out, but still the others drank. Then I knew they weren't fleeing, that this was just an extension of the game, a way of salvaging something.

I had had enough vodka to fancy such stupidity romantic, but mainly I was terrified, yet even more terrified to show it. I thought of my parents, their monumental grief at the death of their only child. My mother and father, in the living room, the TV rattling, trapped with each other for the rest of their lives, rehearsing what had never happened. The reams of black fabric they'd shroud their lives in.

"Here we go," one of guys said.

Up the track appeared a pinprick of light growing larger and larger, drawing a bead on us. The thrumming tunnel closed in. Pages of ice clawed off its walls. Gunk rained from the ceiling, then the thunder from the approaching train took over, the locomotive beam, searing, blinding, like the moon, bowled down the tracks. The last thing I saw before subsumed in the Pentecostal light were my friends plastered against the train walls. Then everything went black, blacker than before.

If I had so much as stuck my tongue out, I could have licked the highballing freighter. Spiriting down Two Mile Run to the Hazlewood mill where the deadman's shift cranked out steel by light of acetylene, it toted car after open car of coal. Grit bathed us. Black unbreathable oxygen rushed by in the wake of each car. My back wettened from the sweating wall that seemed about to break apart. Car after interminable car. A din that threatened to split us open. Just another kind of ovation, the tide of night sweeping me away.

When it was over, as the train disappeared, and a brakeman lounging on the steps of the caboose waved, as if he had known all along we had been there, I laughed with the others, brushed myself off and took another pull of vodka.

We barged into the dance, wet and filthy. The gym was crowded, hot and dark, the shiny floor, along which the young dancers shuddered, slippery with sawdust. For a while I simply stood in the crush. Like the loners, looking but not looking, wandering through the packed gym. The ones who are never asked, and never ask, the never-named Saturday night faces, amnesiac photos in the school yearbook. There is a song for them, but it's never played—so they never dance. I was not one of the team stars, merely a number on the program. Forgettable. Forgotten. I watched those around me fall in love, and make out on the top row of bleachers. The sad plush music: *High on a Hill* and *Harlem Nocturne.* It was either break down and cry bluesily on the gym floor or cling slow-dragging to any girl who would raise her face to mine until the needle lifted from the turntable.

There were girls who had their own reasons for not dancing. In small enclaves, their dropped hands cupped like flowers in front of them, as if to ward off loneliness, they sung silently along with music. Sometimes they even danced together. I made my way to one of those girls: in a plaid skirt and dark sweater, out of which a white rounded blouse collar peeked, a gold cross pinned to her throat. We danced for the rest of the evening. She was shy and I was nobody. It was late and dark. She laid her head against my neck. I smelled her hair, felt her thin fingers firm across my shoulders. Her name was Regina. In my mind, as I held her, I imagined I was telling her my troubles. I felt in the music her understanding: first the game, nailed to the bench; how I had almost died in the train tunnel; how it didn't matter, how nothing mattered; lost, lost, lost. The music testified, throwing its longing like a net over the two of us, her heart pounding against mine, sweat streaming beneath my blazer.

The DJ laid Marvin Gaye's *Forever* on the turntable; and I did what no boy in my state should have done: I sang softly in her ear. Whispered, really.

Forever had no weight for me. But the sheer ache of the song. Marvin Gaye crooning like he had lost the big game and nearly been run down by a train, and now all that remained was to, by God, secure in a girl a shot glass of comfort. I had never kissed a girl before. Hadn't known what a mouth might feel like on mine. The way she raised her eyes to me. How could I not press her against me and kiss and kiss and kiss her, swept away, so happy in my ignorance there in the dark gym, while the others too clung to each other like sleepwalkers under the crepe and bunting streaming from one hoop to the other? I opened an eye to catch the time on the clock above Coach Noonan's office, but it was too dark to see. There was nothing but now.

Then a stabbing in my shoulder, an insistent, painful jab. Brother Gregorian, my English teacher, one of the chaperones, loomed above me like Ichabod Crane in the floor-length ebony vestments of St. John de LaSalle, his giant hands separating Regina and me, shaking his pruned head in condemnation. Then the lights burst on and Regina and I looked into each other's embarrassed faces.

She was tiny with a spray of black down on her upper lip. Her hair was wiry. In her ears were the gold studs favored by the little crinkly-haired Italian immigrant girls who spoke broken English back in grade school. Her brows were dark, nearly knitted. Too dark. Too conspiratorial. There would be secrets. There would be silence. I didn't want an Italian, but a Nordic woman, fair and temperate, not some mercurial Mediterranean like my mother. It wouldn't be fair to say Regina wasn't pretty. But she was too eager, the way she clung to my hand with both of hers, and sidled against me like the song. *Forever.*

She would be an angel of a wife, bear me a dozen babies, have my dinner ready the moment I crossed the threshold. My word would be law. I would never have to change a diaper or make a bed. On Sundays I would wake to the aroma of tomato sauce and we would all go to Mass. She would know how it was with children. She would never raise her voice. Little by little, our relationship would take on a Victorian formality. Old age would push her further and further toward the church. Dutiful she would always remain, but *love* a word mired in duty and hierarchy. If I went before her, she would wear black down to her skin until the day she joined me at Mount Carmel, and in the meantime anoint my grave at the Proper of the Seasons and say rosaries daily for the repose of my soul.

Brother Gregorian unchained the double doors leading to the parking lot, and the gym emptied. Holding Regina's hand, I fought through the crowd, and led her onto the practice field. The ancient, wooden goalposts at either end trembled in the breeze. We walked to the far end zone and sat at the base of the Monster, a sixty degree clay hill Noonan ran us up and down every day after practice.

I kissed her: her hair, her eyes. I held her hands to my face and kissed the open palms. I told her I loved her, and she was silent. Even when I slipped my hand under her sweater, she made not a sound—though inside her were noises—as though it were her lot to suffer me this way—drunken, overtaken by sentiment, pushing her against the clammy slick hill hulking above us. She closed her eyes. She held on to me. Headlights from the departing cars swept the grassless field. Tires whispered on the black asphalt. Regina fell back crushed in the dust under me. She did not tell me she loved me, nor did she utter one word to absolve me. I simply could not go on seducing her—precisely because she was prepared to endure whatever I desired.

I jumped up from her and raced to the blocking sled, banging each pad with a shoulder and spinning to the next, banging and spinning, to the next and banging, spinning to the next bang, and spin. The screak of the metal as the sled recoiled at each hit echoed across the field. It had begun to drizzle. Regina was on her feet, smoothing her skirt, looking up into the sky. I dropped to my knees and vomited. She got down next to me and stayed with me in the rain, until with her help I clambered to my feet. She raked the hair out of my eyes, cleansed my face with her handkerchief.

Arm in arm, we walked to Cathedral Pharmacy where her girlfriends waited. She wrote her phone number in red lipstick on my gold necktie, kissed me goodbye, and helped me onto the bus home. In its empty unearthly glare, I cried quietly in the last seat. Then the driver was shaking me, telling me to wake up, last stop. Outside it was black and raining. I ripped off my tie and threw it into the street.

Maybe, I could have played college ball at a small school. I toyed with going out at Duquesne, but didn't have the heart for it. No allure for me, either, in the dope that my boyhood friends were pumping in their arms. Even marijuana I refused to try. I needed new dreams. It was time to grow up, start being a man. I would make myself smart, and then I would make money.

Lenny DePaolo drove a bread truck for Stagno's. He was twice his playing size, as if he had swallowed himself, and already had two kids. I'd run into him occasionally, but I didn't speak, and Lenny didn't seem to recognize me. Mr. Noonan, of all people—I had loved Mr. Noonan—became a muttering, panhandling, homeless drunk pushing a shopping cart around downtown, so fat it took him all day to cover a city block.

The world that night, under the gargantuan lights of Three Rivers, had been large; then it got suddenly smaller. Like looking at things from inside a train tunnel with a freighter barreling at you.

Lounging on the ledge of the garage wall the Mercedes was parked against were three black guys with big afros, smoking cigarettes and drinking Iron City quarts out of paper bags. One of them wore a Pirates baseball cap. Another had a pick sliced into his hair. Young, sixteen or seventeen, they stared at Sterling and me as we approached the car. Even seated, they were long and lank with an air at once of apathy and militancy.

I eyed them once, warily, then looked away—as I had been coached all my life. To look away. Nevertheless, with one eye, I held onto them. With the other, I looked inside myself; and spied fear, even hate, though I held no special animosity for their race. I had grown up with blacks, though back then the most inoffensive, even respectful, reference to them was *colored.* East Liberty had always been integrated. Not by design, but happenstance and poverty—the strangle-hold the rent-man had on the working man. Blacks and Italians hammering their own brains out against the walls of ignorance they lived behind.

I had always gotten along with blacks. Of the fourteen boys posed in my Little League photograph, still hanging in my bedroom—Coach Big George, far right, second row—five were black. Sidney Jackson, embarrassed, smiling and demure, right next to Big George, not a clue in his broad, open, little boy's face that hidden within his heart was larceny. And Kevin Bond, crouched in the front row with the taller boys: querulous, sprawling, wearing spectacles and wristwatch, hard black street shoes instead of sneakers like the rest of the team. My dad had chosen Kevin in tryouts as a favor to Isaac. Kevin was a disaster, and had become a scapegoat all over again. His capering and giggling, his terrible, clumsy play. Everyone laughed at him. *Sissy.* My dad just shook his head and remained patient, Isaac looking away with fury and shame each time Kevin flailed like a woodchopper aimlessly at a pitch, then dragged his bat back to the bench after he struck out.

I can name every one of those boys, but they all disappeared and, as I got older, I found myself without black friends, no occasion to even speak to black people. Like all the rest of the white people in East Liberty, I sidestepped them. I lived through 1968, the riots and curfews, the borrowed pistol I had found among my father's tools in the cellar, the smell of incineration clear from the Hill District. The day after King's assassination, I had written a required class theme on what I had called *the tragedy of a great man passing.* When I brought it home with the A+ circled at the top, my mother had cracked, "What are you writing about him for?"

Holding tightly to Sterling's arm, I guided her around the car to the passenger side. Not ten feet from where the black guys sat, now talking in hushed mumbles, smoke twirling out of their mouths as they laughed—probably about Sterling. I thought of that gun lying under the wire cutters in my father's toolbox, how the day I found it I had wanted to pluck it out and feel it in my hand. I had never seen a real gun other than in a policeman's holster. But I had just stared at it, sure that if I touched it, it would kill me. Or my mother and father. Sizing up the three blacks kids, I wished I was caressing a gun. Then, when they came towards me, when they reached for Sterling. If I could just get her into the car.

"Get in," I said, nudging her a touch.

Taking her time, she looked at me and smiled. So naive. Rich girl. Always prepared to think the best of everyone.

"Hey, man, what's happenin'?" the one with the pick said out of the side of his mouth. On the back of the hand he smoked with was sloppily hacked a braided, upraised scar forming a horshoe-like omega, the last letter of the Greek alphabet.

"How you doing?" I answered. "Get in the car," I whispered to Sterling.

She paused and looked at me, then at the black guys, and smiled. The wrong thing to do. I could have taken one of them. I could have done okay for a little while with two if I had to. But three . . . I looked for something lying around. A bottle, a brick. Felix probably carried a gun; he would have pulled it out right there and settled things. My father kept a blackjack under the driver's seat of the Newport. Maybe I could rush them, plunge them along with myself over the deck wall and into the icy gunmetal river. Then I would swim away, but I couldn't swim. I'd die then, but I wasn't going to allow them to hurt Sterling. If she had just gotten in the goddam car.

The three of them got to their feet. One of them flicked his cigarette over the wall into the night. I imagined hearing it fizz as it hit the water, joining the mutant carp and drowned lovers wintering there.

The black guys nodded and walked off, their steps echoing off the concrete ramp corkscrewing down to the street. Left behind on the ledge sat their bottles, sheathed to the necks in brown paper.

The decorated downtown streets had been deserted, except for people huddled at bus stops, and the deranged vagrant angels doomed to haunt every city despite the hour or weather. The U.S. Steel Building, eighty stories of stacked rust, the tallest building between New York and Chicago, swayed imperceptibly in the wind. Beneath it stood a life-sized creche. Jesus, Mary, the mangered baby, the entire cast of characters, including the cattle, in a slab-wood shack, roofed with straw, a big lit star clamped to its peak. A couple of bums, swaddled in the bulldog edition of *The Pittsburgh Press,* curled at the feet of the wise men.

On Liberty Avenue, the silhouetted insides of porn shops glowed behind filmed, barred windows. Sterling and I drove in silence, lavish yule lights italicizing the sky, stars dying every millisecond, the colossal Christmas tree, stories and stories high, lording in the Golden Triangle. The high-storied lights of the Hilton and William Penn hotels where lodgers, at least for the night, lived dream lives.

I envisioned Sterling and I walking into one of those hotel suites—I had never spent the night in a hotel, not even a motor court—its perfect, burnished surfaces, the softness of the carpet, the opulent bed, the white, gleaming tile bathroom, brass, crystal, chandeliers, candelabra, a wall of windows framing the sheer immensity of the twinkling, holographic city. In a long embrace, I would kiss Sterling and take her coat from her. Hang it in the closet alongside my own. She would disappear into one of the other rooms. From behind the door, I'd catch the occasional rustle of her linen. Peering down on my city, the congress of the three mighty rivers, I would wait, drinking champagne in shirt-sleeves, the room dimmed with candles until she reappeared in a white peignoir, and turned down the bedclothes. White silk sheets. Like Ecclesiastes. The drapes left open. Across the river, Saint Mary's of the Mount perched on a cliff like a toy church under the Christmas tree.

Or Sterling and I escaping: West. Or even south. South where it's always warm and poinsettias grow wild. Take the first bridge over the Monongahela and accelerate until the weather turned pink and we could turn the car heater off, peel off wool for cotton, sink in just our skins into warm water and sand.

Once over the bridge, however, we did not head south, but turned right on the McCardle Roadway and scaled its narrow back to the peak of Mount Washington. The wind was outrageous. Thick storm clouds lumbered east along the moiling Ohio, shrouding the parapet upon which we stood clinging to each other. Spread for miles beneath us, the city resided in ruin and glory, the rivers patched with ice, black tugs pushing black barges of snow-decked coal. Christmas lights from the skyscrapers reflected in the current, along with the sputtering stack-fire of what was left of the mills, ladling out the very last of its white melts of steel, spraying sparks like shrapnel along the wharf walls where it was so bitter the lapping water froze on contact. As if Christmas had already departed. Or Jesus had elected this year not to be born.

We kissed up there on Mount Washington, like sad lovers, tenderly, decidedly, as the city winced at our feet. We had planned to eat somewhere, but neither of us had an appetite.

"Let's just go home," Sterling said.

She held on to me tightly, desperately, it seemed. Against the gale, entwined, we struggled back to the car. *Home,* she had said. As if there were a home somewhere we shared. Our home. Such promise in her voice. Ever so carefully, I drove, contemplating our lives together: our bedroom; our children; her jewelry on the night-stand; the scent of her livery; the sound of water running behind the closed door, candlelight visible beneath it, and knowing she was bathing, the water against her. What she'd wear to bed. She, pregnant, turning toward me in her sleep.

Back at the Rosechilds, Phil and JoAnn, surrounded by their glittering townhouse, were glad to see us. A spectacular noble fir, decorated with bubbling lights and antique Christmas ornaments preened in a corner. At its tip an androgynous china angel decked in frothy silk scraped the ceiling. Opera sailed out of the big stereo. They asked about the ballet, and the weather. More snow was expected, Phil said. By kickoff Sunday, it would be merely in the teens, and with the wind-chill, no telling. I still planned to watch the game with them? How about a drink?

Sterling, seated close to me on the couch, squeezed my arm. I assured them, of course I'd be there, a drink would be fine. Phil padded over to the bar. On one end of it rested a large aquarium streaming with goldfish. Bubbles from the filter played through the water. A little treasure chest opened and closed. A deep-sea diver raised and lowered a hand.

"I'll bring something in to snack on," JoAnn said, and left for the kitchen.

Sterling kissed me on the cheek. Ira, the fat blond tabby, jumped up on the couch. Sterling took him in her lap and stroked him. I reached over and scratched him behind the ears. This time, Sterling kissed my mouth.

Phil's back was to us as he fixed the drinks. Glass and ice clinking, the metallic rush of the vodka, then tonic flooding the glass, ice cracking, the smell of sliced lime. A small circle of hairless flesh sat like a yarmulke at the back of Phil's head, his brown hair graying, his neck above the collar crisscrossed with sun wrinkles. Patch-madras pants, white polo shirt and bedroom slippers, his glasses dangling from his neck. He inclined his head one way and then another as he hummed along with the music.

JoAnn breezed in with a tray of roast beef sandwiches. On white sliced Town Talk bread, the crusts trimmed off. Pickle spears. Paper plates and plastic cutlery. Jars of mayonnaise and Grey Poupon. My mother would have made fun of this food. Called the Rosechilds *Americanos,* her catch-all indictment for non-Italians. Because of their chic home, their clothes and music, she would have accused them of making the *emozione,* putting on airs, even though their high class furniture was lousy with cat hair, and for supper they ate sandwiches in the living room on paper plates. With all their money. Piss on them. She'd pronounce them booze hounds for drinking gin and vodka. Shot-glasses of cheap Canadian blends, Iron City beer, and pitchers of home-made red wine were the only alcohol allowed in her house; and, make no mistake, as someone who would not so much as allow a drop to pass her lips, she merely tolerated it.

While we ate, the Rosechilds' phone rang. Mrs. Kannakas. An old pushy Greek woman to whom I regularly delivered. She had run out of blood pressure pills. She had to have them. Right away. Or she'd miss her evening dose. Six days from Christmas. Looking at me, his wife and daughter, seated side by side on the coach, *La Boheme* still belting out of the speakers, Phil smiled and raised his eyebrows. He told Mrs. Kannakas not to cry, that he'd deliver the pills to her immediately. He just had to put on his coat and run down to the pharmacy.

Chapter 14

My mother laid it on so heavy that come Sunday I decided to stay home to watch the first half of the game with my father. Having never had a serious girlfriend before Sterling—no one I had really cared about—I had never witnessed this side of her. Why was I spending so much time with Sterling? Why did I prefer the company of the Rosechilds to my own family? When was I going to introduce this girl to my mother and father? What was the mystery? Was she too grand for the Dolces? I spent every extra minute with her and her family. Was I ashamed of my own family?

My first impulse was to retaliate, but there was no way to win an argument with my mother. She lived to be right. I didn't want to give her the least cause to have it in for Sterling. If she set against someone, she would never relent. Never. Not even death. Grudges, to her, were sacraments.

In truth I had been feeling a little guilty about not watching the game with my dad, especially now that he was home on Sundays. He seemed a little low. He had whitewashed the basement; sanded, primed and repainted all of the wrought iron on the front porch; shampooed the carpets; repaired every little thing my mother scrounged up for him. By then, he had little to do. It was tough being out of work in the winter when it's too miserable to do much outside. He had that caged, doleful look. My mother had begun to harp at him about sleeping too much in the day. Having him underfoot all the time was getting on her nerves.

I was horrified to hear myself promise to escort Sterling to the family Christmas Eve celebration at Aunt Lucia's. It would be unbearable, but Sterling would love it, and it would hopefully placate my mother.

"They don't have Christmas," she stated.

Here we go, I thought. "Who doesn't have Christmas, Mother?"

"Jews. They killed Christ."

"Can I bring her anyhow? The Christ killer."

"Don't talk about her like that. Of course you can bring her. She's perfectly welcome."

"Good."

"George," my mom said to my dad. "Georgie's bringing his little girlfriend to Lucia's on Christmas Eve."

"That's very nice."

"Very nice," Mrs. Dolce repeated, but it sounded like she was mimicking him.

The first quarter ended with the Bills ahead 7–3. It looked like it was going to be a very close game. I couldn't get out of my head the thousand bucks Phil had riding on the game, not to mention my own grand. God! What was I doing? So tangled up in it. If Sterling ever got wise. Studying my father, however, slumped in his easy chair, I remained convinced I had opted for the right course. The family had to have the money. What the hell was I going to do? Let my parents go on welfare? I'd be leaving Pittsburgh soon enough, and the arrangement with Phil would simply evaporate. There was no reason why Sterling would ever have to find out. Unless Phil told her. But why would he do that? Perhaps at some point I'd make a clean breast of it myself to Sterling.

More than anything, I needed to middle this game and pull down that two grand. But the Steelers were sluggish. There seemed no way they'd be able to beat the spot. It didn't even look like they'd win the game.

My mother, baking Christmas cookies, limped in and out of the living room long enough to make cutting remarks about the black players, or swat at my dad with a tea-towel and order him to look alive and sit up in his chair.

She brought in a tray of cookies warm from the oven and set them on an end-table, handed me and my father napkins and placemats to set in our laps and threatened, "If you drop one crumb, you'll be sorry." My dad exchanged a glance with me, sighed and picked up a cookie.

In the second quarter, the Steelers began dismantling the Bills. Bradshaw threw four touchdowns. Buffalo's virtuoso halfback, O.J. Simpson, couldn't do a thing. He juked and scuffled parallel to the line of scrimmage until a gang of black jerseys smothered him. Suddenly the Steelers looked invincible again. Now the problem was reversed. If the Steelers crushed Buffalo, then I would only break even. It was 29–7 at the half.

I ran upstairs, washed my face, brushed my teeth, and put on a coat and tie. When I came back down, my parents were dozing. My mother's swollen, rubbery legs were gray and blue like Gorgonzola. Her beige-tinted hair was curled tight to her skull, the tea-towel thrown over her shoulder. My dad's hair was the color of freshly mixed mortar. He was starting to lose a little of it at the crown. He idled evenly, like a well-tuned car in neutral, his mouth wide open.

I shook my mother gently. She woke with a start, raked my face as if unsure who I was, then croaked breathlessly, "What's the matter?"

"Nothing, Mom. I'm getting ready to leave."

"My God. You scared me."

"I'm sorry. I just wanted to say goodbye."

"George," she barked at my dad.

He came out of his stupor like a slapstick comedian being revived after a safe had fallen on him. "Wha-What? What?" he mumbled, darting his eyes off the walls and faces until they focused on my mom and he realized he was awake.

"Georgie is leaving," she said.

"What?"

"God, George, I'm getting you a Belltone for Christmas."

"Well, I'd better get going," I said. "The second half's getting ready to start."

The halftime show was concluding: a feature on Franco Harris and his Italian Army. Franco, a black man, had an Italian mother. So a contingent of Pittsburgh Italians, led by Tony Stagno of Stagno's Bakery, rallied behind him and formed the Army. They showed up at games waving Italian flags and loaves of Sicilian bread. They had even enlisted Frank Sinatra in the Army, who purportedly sent telegrams before each game urging them to victory, and signed them *Colonel Francis Sinatra.*

"Oh, please," my mother said. "They're taking this all too far. This Franco thing. He's not even Italian."

"What do you mean, Mom? All you have to do is look at him."

"Maybe he's mixed, which is a disgrace, but he's not Italian."

"Don't you want to join Franco's army, Sylvia?" my dad asked.

"Very funny. I wouldn't have anything to do with anything Frank Sinatra's involved in. He's nothing but a racketeer."

"Well, I gotta go," I repeated.

"Just a minute," said my mom.

With great effort, she rose from her chair, and wobbled into the kitchen. She returned carrying a mounded heavy cardboard Santa plate of cookies covered in ice-blue Saran wrap. *Cavalluccis.* An Italian spice cookie she made only at Christmas. Hard as stone, of the same size, with a thumb print in their middles. The best way to eat them was to soak them in coffee or milk. My dad liked to soften them in red wine.

"Here. For your girlfriend and her family."

"Thanks, Mom. That's really nice." I put an arm around her waist, then suddenly dipped down with the other arm toward her legs as if I were going to scoop her up like a child.

"Don't you dare," she said. "You'll put me in the hospital."

"I don't think I could get all that freight off the ground anyhow," I replied, smiling.

My dad laughed, and I laughed too.

"Go ahead and laugh. I know I'm getting fat."

"Aw, Mom. You still have the figure of a school girl."

"Yeah, go on. We'll see what you look like when you're sixty-four."

"And you," she said to my dad who was still chuckling. "Sitting around doing nothing all day. Look at the gut on you. Like you're about to deliver."

"I'd like to stay for this discussion, but I'm already late." I grabbed the *cavalluccis*, kissed my parents and ran out the door.

The Rosechilds' driveway and the curb in front of their house were crowded with sleek foreign automobiles. I left the Newport across the street, several houses down, and lifted my mother's cookies out of the back seat. I took two steps toward the Rosechilds, then turned around and put the cookies back in the car.

Sterling met me at the door.

"I want you to go to a big family get-together with me on Christmas Eve," I blurted. "It could be excruciating, but I promised my parents that I'd invite you."

"Well, of course. I'd be honored. You know I've been dying to meet your family."

She kissed me openly and led me into the living room. Many of the same people I remembered from the Washington game were there. They wanted to know how I'd been. They told me how well I looked, what an adorable couple Sterling and I made. Had I decided where I'd be going to law school? The women kissed my cheek and sidled so close I smelled what they'd been drinking. Their husbands beamed, squeezed my hand and nodded like they were all in collusion over my certain star-studded future.

The Steelers, in the second half, could do no wrong, and Buffalo was terrible. The people at the Rosechilds went crazy every time the Steelers ran a play. Drinking my customary Beefeater and tonic, I sat with Sterling on a red and white striped loveseat and watched them shriek and clap. They didn't even know what was going on. Occasionally Phil would look at me and smile a thousand-dollar smile that said, *Things are going very well.*

I politely returned the smiles, then glanced at Sterling to see if she noticed these exchanges, but she seemed oblivious. So did JoAnn. It was more gambling than I was interested in. I had to lose Phil—but not right away. I drank gin and sat there, Sterling warm against me.

Finally Buffalo scored another touchdown and conversion. Good for me, bad for Phil.

Phil jumped up and said loudly, "Jesus Christ." It was the first time I had ever heard him raise his voice, or use anything other than the gentlest diction. "Dammit," he said as he walked over to the bar and fixed another drink.

"Phil, what are you worried about? They're winning by fifteen," JoAnn said. "Buffalo'll never catch them."

"Oh, I know," Phil responded. "I just want them to win."

I kept my eyes on the TV screen as the Steelers lined up to kick off. I wished I had stayed home.

The game went into the fourth quarter with the Steelers ahead 29–14. Two grand in my pocket if it just stayed that way. And there was no reason why it wouldn't. Buffalo was sputtering, and the Steelers would elect to simply chew up the clock on the ground with Franco and Rocky. I felt bad about Phil losing a thousand. He wasn't flashing those smiles toward me any longer, but hunkered down in the sofa, his eyes glued to the TV. What the money would mean to me and my parents, however, anesthetized me more than all the gin I'd been drinking.

But Buffalo was too hapless. Unbelievably so. The Steelers churned away, sweeping and trapping, the clock ticking, but not fast enough. As they bulled into Buffalo territory, the crowd in the Rosechilds' townhouse cheered them on like an audience of high-schoolers. Sterling dug her hand into my thigh as if there were something at stake. Phil leaned forward, his hands steepled together at his chin.

Then the Steelers did the unthinkable. Instead of just going for it on fourth down, to keep the clock running, or even punting because the game was in the bag, they lined up for a field goal. Their place-kicker, Roy Gerela, puttered shyly on to the field, his bemused, koala-like face beaming out above his single bar. The camera cut to the end zone where his admirers, Gerela's Gorillas, jumped up and down in gorilla costumes.

The kick was perfect. The stadium and the Rosechild living room went wild. Phil jumped up and threw a fist in the air, then turned to me and pumped it up toward the ceiling again. Sterling threw herself into my arms. I remembered Phil muttering *C'est la vie* after dropping that five hundred on the Redskins game. It was only then that I realized how desperately I had wanted that two thousand dollars. After nearly forty years at the mill, my father didn't make that much in a month, even with overtime and working weekends. Eugene would have to pay me a thousand, since the Steelers covered the legitimate line of 10. But, because they'd also covered, by one measly point, the phony line of 17, I would have to turn around and fork over to Phil a thousand he didn't even need. A wash.

A sudden revulsion for all of it seized me: the betting, the anxiety over money, this pampered, childish, overdressed assembly now moving toward the bar and the food as the game clock wound down and the Bills blooped one hopeless pass after another into the snowstorm. Above all, the duplicity.

Phil, absolutely beaming, walked over and shook hands with me.

"Let me buy you a drink," he chirped, pulling me up from my seat toward the bar. "Well, we did it, my boy," he half-whispered. "I guess you raked in a little too."

"Yeah. I did."

To stop my lie from choking me, I took a long swallow of the Beefeater and tonic Phil placed in my hand. That stupid Beefeater in his ludicrous tights and pleated, puffy collar. Phil wore a pair of red corduroy pants sprinkled with tiny crossed tennis rackets. The collar of his polo shirt was open, revealing the top of his white lumpy chest, a few strands of gray hair smudged over the navy fabric.

I had grown up alongside kids who would have punched Phil, turned over a table and toppled the china cabinet, broken every goddam piece of glass in the house just to see the Rosechilds and all their perfect friends grovel.

Now, those hoods would oath, as if they had turned a page in the book, and the undeniable story of what was really what had finally revealed itself. For half a second, I fancied myself such a person. But then the cameo, upon which in my mind's eye I habitually saw my handsome face in relief, seduced me. I took a breath. *C'est la vie.* What the hell. I had taken a calculated risk and lost. Broken even actually. No harm done. I took another sip of gin. And smiled.

Phil had his arm around me. "You know," he confided, "Sterling really likes you. We've never seen her so happy. She had been in this relationship—a very serious relationship—with this boy from Haverford. A real shmuck. The manners of a caveman. Not a speck of your brains and industry. He treated her like you would your yard shoes. I don't know what all went on, but when it finally ended, thank God, at our urging, I don't mind telling you—she's still our little girl, you have to understand, our only child—Sterling thought her life was over. Really down in the dumps. We had to bring her home for a semester. Crying. Didn't want to eat or get dressed. Then, little by little, she finally pulled herself together. We knew she would. She's a very strong person. But naturally, you understand, we were worried. Maybe I'm talking out of school here. Listen to me. Why am I apologizing? You're like family. I just want you to know that having you around has meant a lot to us. We owe you a debt of gratitude."

"You don't owe me a thing, Mr. Rosechild."

Phil wagged a finger. "Phil. Remember. Call me Phil."

"Phil."

"You and I, George, we discuss money a lot. All this wagering and winning and losing and up and down, but we're talking about ball games and lousy pieces of paper. Replaceable. Ephemeral. Money is not everything. Love is. *Love.*"

Phil turned toward Sterling and gestured. Still seated across the room in the loveseat, she watched her father and me with a bemused look. I turned toward her as well. She smiled and waved. I didn't know what to make of Phil's epistle. Why had he told me all that? And the old love versus money equation? Had it been a parable, coded and layered with what Phil really wanted me to know? Yet I could have sworn that Phil had been entirely sincere. Hearing all that about Sterling and the Haverford guy, however, introduced a Sterling I had never contemplated: involved *very seriously* with someone else, depressed, unstable.

"Love," Phil said, turning back to me. "That's why I'm telling you all this. JoAnn and I love you. Like a son. You've been very loyal to this family, to the business, and I wish you the greatest happiness. And I don't want you to get the impression that this is just the gin talking."

Then Phil hugged me, held me until I had no choice but to put my arms around him in embrace.

"What was that all about?" Sterling asked a minute later. "I didn't want to interrupt."

"Just your dad. He's a good guy."

"So are you."

"I'm glad you think so."

"You're pretty sober. Aren't you thrilled that the Steelers won?"

"Yeah, of course."

I wandered back to the television where a jubilant, but humble, Terry Bradshaw was being interviewed. The reporter recapped Bradshaw's up and down, frequently turbulent, career with the Steelers, how he had been dubbed a loser, a bonehead, and now here he was a hero, just one game away from the American Football Conference title. Bradshaw just hung his head and smiled like a country boy. He gave all the credit to his teammates, to Chuck Noll for having the confidence to stick with him. Sure there had been tough times, but he had endured, and the real credit went to the Lord.

I recalled the Cincinnati game, Bradshaw being led off the field with a dislocated shoulder, the number 12 on his throwing sleeve hanging near his hip. That's how badly the bone had been ripped from the socket. The fans had cheered, happy that Bradshaw had been injured. They poured beer over his head as he left the field for the clubhouse. Kids, outside the Thrill Rivers, gave him the finger as he lay in the back of the racing ambulance. The papers reported that Bradshaw had wept. Now here he was: their golden boy.

Across the bottom of the screen, the network flashed the Miami-Oakland score. The Raiders had beaten the spot. I was out another $400, $440 all told with the juice. Pittsburgh would face Oakland for the AFC Championship in one week. The crowd at the Rosechilds cheered and toasted. Out of sheer enervation, I sunk into one of the loveseats and sighed. I suddenly felt the gin.

Sterling plopped down beside me with a plate of food. Four crackers smeared with caviar, and two strawberries. She lifted one of the crackers to my mouth. I looked down on it. People watched us, smiling. The caviar, black as grease, hung off the cracker. I couldn't stomach it. I wanted to knock Sterling's hand away and run out of the Rosechilds. But she was so delighted, so lovely, feeding me in front of these people. I opened my mouth, then choked it down with a long pull of gin.

Chapter 15

I had had too much to drink. I knew it the moment I hit the street, and didn't see the Newport. Then I remembered I had parked it in the next block. Even before starting the car, I plucked my mother's cookies from the backseat and threw them down the sewer. To clear my head, I drove home with the windows down.

My parents, as usual, were asleep in front of the television. They woke when I opened the door.

"How'd they like the cookies?" was the first thing out of my mother's mouth.

"Good. They liked them a lot."

"What did they say?"

"Just that they were good. They liked them."

"You didn't give them to them."

"What do mean I didn't give them to them?"

"Because I know you didn't. You're lying. I can see it in your face."

"I am not lying. I gave them the cookies, Mother."

"Swear. Swear you gave them to them."

"I don't have to swear on anything. I gave them the cookies."

"Sylvia," my dad stepped in. "Let up. He says he gave them the cookies."

"Swear on your Grandmother Giovanna. Swear on her eyes."

"I'm not going to swear on anyone's eyes, for Christ's sake. I gave them the goddam cookies."

"Don't you dare disgrace your grandmother with that filthy mouth."

My father shot to his feet. "You watch how you talk to your mother, buddy."

"I'm sorry, Mom."

I approached her to put my arms around her. She launched out a hand to halt me.

"You've had too much to drink," she said. "I smelled it when you came in. What's the matter? Those cookies weren't good enough for your high class friends? Are you ashamed? I dragged my crippled body in that kitchen and baked so you'd have a little offering when you walked in. To make you look good. To show respect. My flour. My sugar. With your father out of work. Are you so ashamed of your own family?"

"Mom, I'm not ashamed of anyone. I'm really sorry about what I said."

I attempted to embrace her again, but again the hand came up.

"Sorry about what? That we're not some bigshot Jews putting on all the *emozione*?"

"Sylvia, let it go now. He said he's sorry."

My mother looked at her husband, then me, her son. "You can both go to hell." She grabbed her cane, and mounted the stairs for bed, at each step wincing, then groaning heavily at the top.

"What was that all about?" I asked once she had disappeared.

"Ah, she's pretty worked up. I found out today that my unemployment won't start now for another six weeks. I been standing in line down there like a stooge for two hours, twice a week, just to hear that. Then the dryer went out. I been putzing around with it, but I can't get it to work. It's shot. We bought it used ten years ago. So your mother, you know, she takes these things pretty hard. I'm going upstairs now, see if I can't get her settled." Then: "George, did you give those people your mother's cookies?"

"Yeah, Dad. I did."

"Good. I knew you did."

First thing Monday morning, I went to the bank and made a withdrawal from what was left of my savings account. I set aside $440 dollars to pay off Eugene. Then I went to Sears and bought my parents a new dryer—to be delivered. Then I drove downtown to Tiffany's and bought a white gold heart locket and chain for Sterling that I got on sale for just under a thousand dollars.

I just had to hold out a little longer. Until the holidays and football season were over and I would be quits with Phil and start making book for Eugene and Felix. Once my dad's unemployment kicked in, things would look up, and I had decided that no matter what I'd keep my job at the pharmacy. Six months, eight months, tops, I'd be out of Pittsburgh. By then my dad would be back at the mill. My future with Sterling, certainly—that was number one. But keeping in mind that nothing, like in betting, was a certainty. For now, above all, I had to handle Phil, my future father-in-law, perhaps, with real delicacy, and not let go of another nickel myself.

When I got home the Sears truck was just pulling away from the house. My parents met me at the door, my mother crying.

"God bless you, Georgie," she said, kissing me. "You're so good to us."

"Remember, Son, just a loan. As soon as we get on our feet," my dad threw in.

"My God, yes. Enough's enough," agreed my mom.

"It's just an early Christmas present," I said, smiling, pleased that the dryer had made the peace between me and my mother.

"So they liked the cookies?" she asked, smiling.

"Absolutely. Very much."

"They sound like nice people."

"Very nice."

"And you're bringing your little girlfriend over to Lucia's for Christmas Eve?"

"Yep. It's all set."

By 4:30 on Christmas Eve, the CLOSED sign hung in the window of Rosechild Pharmacy. In the back room, among the legions of medicines and painkillers shelved to the roof, Phil Rosechild and I sat at a little table drinking gin on the rocks. No tonic. No lime.

I handed Phil the envelope Eugene had only minutes before slipped me, lined with ten brand new, never-folded, slippery hundred dollar bills. The line on the Pittsburgh-Oakland game was 12. Pittsburgh by 12. A sucker line. Way, way too many points to give Oakland, a team just as nasty as the Steelers, especially at home, during playoffs. The smart move was to take the points and bet Oakland. But the bookies knew their sentimental clientele would back the Steelers no matter what, and they aimed to stick them for their loyalty.

I planned to middle things again on the thousand dollars I figured Phil would want to put up. Move the line five-six points. Not get too cute. Break even, or make a couple grand. Same arrangement as the Buffalo game. However, before I could even throw out my manufactured line, Phil blurted that he was plunking down ten grand on the Steelers.

"I haven't even told you the line, Phil."

"I don't care. I feel confident. Ten thousand dollars."

As my mind raced over the arithmetic, the implications, the complications, I stared at Phil: his pink hand curled around the gin glass, the pink face and oily mottled forehead shimmering under the fluorescent light, little glasses at the very tip of his nose, striped shirt, knit tie, unbuttoned sweater vest, bottom lip suctioned up under his yellowed front teeth.

A shroud of greed outlined Phil like a nimbus. His small watery blue eyes looked directly through me at another place on the other side of money, a mythic shore he would never reach before drowning. The notion that Phil might be unhappy—he had everything—had never occurred to me before that moment. I felt deeply sorry for him. He was a very good man, but a sucker. A sucker who could afford to be a sucker. Something I could not afford to be. In that instant, I decided that after this I'd never take another bet from Phil. He had become a liability. This part of our life together was soon to be over.

"That's a lot of money. Why so much?" I asked.

"Why not, my boy? The iron is hot and, more to the point, the Steelers are on fire."

Phil smiled his lovable smile, twirled up out of his seat, and gestured grandly about his kingdom of pills. "I really have nothing to lose."

I smiled back.

"You're worried about the amount, aren't you?" Phil asked.

"Well, yes. It's a load of money. Ten thousand, plus the additional thousand in juice if you lose. Eleven thousand bucks. It's unreal. Don't you even want to hear the line?"

"What is it?"

"Eighteen," I said without hesitating, knowing at the sound of my voice I had been in all along. Keep Phil's bet with the bogus line, and bet the true line myself with Eugene. It was I, not Phil, who had nothing to lose. Break even or middle the lines and take home a jackpot of twenty-one grand, all my prayers answered. One more job. Then jilt Phil, come hell or high water.

"Fine," said Phil. "Would you mind calling your man right now and secure that line? I'll step out of the room."

"Steelers?"

"Who else?

Phil was nuts. A fool. Giving the Raiders eighteen points. He'd take the Steelers against an atom bomb.

"I'll be glad to lay it in your palm, right now. Cash. If that'll make you feel better," Phil said.

"It's not a problem. I know you're good for it."

"Geez, Cuz. That's a lotta green," Eugene said when I announced my bet. "You sure about this?"

"If you need the money up front, I understand. I can run it by this evening."

"Not necessary, Brother. Your word is gospel. I know you're good for it. Steelers giving twelve for ten big ones."

"Thanks, Eug."

"Forget about it. Merry Christmas."

I dropped off my parents at Aunt Lucia's before picking up Sterling for the first time in the Newport. She, along with her parents, met me at the door, then led me into the living room, presided over by the magnificent Christmas tree and banked with white poinsettias. JoAnn handed me a drink in a Santa glass. Sterling kissed me on the cheek. Her black hair was down on her shoulders, and swept back on one side with a rhinestone barrette. She wore a bright red corduroy dress. When I was situated on the couch, Phil handed me an envelope. They all took seats around me. I gazed at their familiar, strange faces.

"Please open it," Phil said.

I ripped open the envelope. Inside was a round-trip plane ticket to New Orleans, and a ticket to the Super Bowl, January 12, in Tulane Stadium.

"Merry Christmas, George," Phil said.

"This is for me?" I managed.

"Yes, indeed," Phil assured me.

"The four of us are going to the Super Bowl," JoAnn said.

"You're kidding? I can't accept this."

Sterling had tears in her eyes. She and JoAnn held hands.

"You most certainly can," said Phil.

"It's too much. I don't even have anything for you."

"You have enlarged our lives, George," Phil intoned. "You're family."

I lowered my head. I wanted to throw myself into Phil's arms.

Things were already at full tilt when Sterling and I walked into Aunt Lucia's enormous old house up on Lemington Avenue. The smell of food, loud talk, laughter, a pack of little children running through the house, up and down the stairs, banging on the piano, Dean Martin on the stereo singing Christmas songs in Italian. Face after face came at us, kissing, hugging, making over Sterling. Then Aunt Lucia led us through the house, introducing Sterling as *Georgie's little girlfriend, the pharmacist's daughter.* She took us into the kitchen, reeking of fish, where the women cooked and the men played poker, drank and ate smelts at the kitchen table.

My father got up and shyly, ceremoniously, kissed Sterling. My mom was at the stove tending all four burners. Three pots of different sauces and, in the fourth, whiptailing in boiling water, hypodermic needles to inject my grandfather with his asthma medicine.

"I am so glad to finally get to meet you. I've been begging this one forever to bring you over to the house." She raised her wooden spoon at me, then stepped up to Sterling and gave her a hug and kiss.

"I've been begging him too," Sterling said. "But he just won't listen to me."

"You're not telling me anything. He's got a head like rock. Just like his father. What a beautiful dress."

"Thank you, Mrs. Dolce. What can I do to help?"

"Not a thing. You just make yourself at home. We're getting ready to sit down and eat."

The meal started with the Sign of the Cross, and Grace. Then my ninety-five year old grandfather creaked up from his chair at the head of the table. He wore a smoky blue suit with a vest and watch chain. His face was the color of potash, his ears enormous, his eyes so thickly cataracted they were like mirrors. On top of his head sprung a thick crop of uncombed ivory hair that swayed as he levered up the wine in his hand and invoked in a cracked Foggia dialect the absent beloved. But the names were unmistakable, and at each came a tiny murmur of assent as if the dead had just stepped hungrily into the house with the new fallen snow on their shoulders. Then all drank in unison. "*Saluto, Buono Natale.*"

Sterling wanted to know why we ate fish on Christmas Eve. *Tradition,* someone said. *It's a Fast Day decreed by the church. But the church says nothing about it. You always have seven kinds of fish. Seven because of the seven sacraments. No that's not why. Then why?*

"Papa," someone asked my grandfather, "why are there seven kinds of fish on Christmas Eve?"

But he did not understand. So he was asked in Italian. But no one was skilled enough in the dialect. He waved them away and told them to use their mouths for eating. Old Aunt Concetta, my grandfather's sister, who could get around only with a walker, but still brought every year mushroom caps stuffed with crab, said she didn't know. Then one of the little ones said there were ten types of fish on the table, not seven, so they all counted them, singing out the names: *calamari, octopus, smelts, shrimp, scungilli, baccala, eel, scrod, crab, clams.* Ten. The children were right. We drank to the children. No one knew, then, why there were so many kinds of fish.

Sterling ate everything, even the unspeakable baby octopi floating in the fish sauce along with the balloon-like calamari. The men watched in admiration. My grandfather passed her each dish, made sure her wine glass stayed full. "*Mangiare,*" he'd say, and Sterling would comply.

"Honey, you don't have to eat that," my mother told her.

The old man was delighted. He laughed a bray-laugh like the donkey that the little ones liked to imitate. "*Italiano*?" he asked.

"No, Papa. She's Jewish," I replied.

"Oh, oh," my mother said.

"Did he ask if I'm Italian?" asked Sterling.

"Yes. Your appetite has him convinced," I answered.

"*Che cosaè, Giorgio*?"

"Jewish, Papa. She's Jewish."

The children brayed like their great-grandfather. Their mothers slapped the table and looked at them, lifted fingers, until they hushed.

"*Ebraica,*" Aunt Concetta translated for her younger brother. Jewish.

"*Ebraica,*" he repeated gravely, pretending he was displeased, and shook his flinty head. Then he laughed his bray, and the children picked it up again until the mothers told them they would get the *baccala.*

Sterling said that she knew what that meant, that I had taken her down Larimer Avenue.

"You with all your brains. Look where you take her," my mother snapped. "Your putting this girl's life in danger taking her down there. I'd kill you if she was my daughter."

"Mother, please."

"Don't *mother please* me. Honey, don't ever let him take you down there again."

Then it started. The blacks this, the blacks that. How the neighborhood was going to hell. They were animals. Like apes. Drive-bys. Crips. Bloods. A litany of all the things they had stolen over the years: two years in a row Georgie's football and helmet he got for Christmas, Big George's car from right in front of the house. They found it stripped up in the Hill District. And the three break-ins at Bella's apartment before she was even married a year. Aunt Nellie had had her purse snatched by one right under Kaufmann's clock downtown. In broad daylight. Who was the one always horning in downtown with the mayor? H. Rap Brown. Nothing but an agitator. Black power, my ass. There were some nice ones, though. Refined. They weren't all bad. My mother declared she liked the ones who acted like white people.

Sterling simply smiled and nodded. I kept my mouth shut, knowing if I disputed anything my mother said she'd double her attack. The best thing was to ignore her.

Papa abruptly stood, clamped the table edge with his claw-hands, stuck out his bottom teeth and raked the table with his fierce chrome eyes. Some pronouncement was imminent. He was fond of toasts and curses. But then the eyes rolled back and fired like dying stars. He lifted the table half an inch—the silver pealed, two glasses went over—before reaching for his throat, and speaking in a voice of smoke. Not words, but what's left of words when trapped between two languages.

"It's his asthma," my mom exclaimed, everyone on their feet at once and moving toward the old man who staggered away from his overturned chair and collapsed.

"Oh, my God," Aunt Lucia wailed.

My dad had bolted for the kitchen and returned running with the syringe. I loosened Papa's necktie and ripped open his collar, fleeced off his suit coat and rolled up a white cuff. Lucia had his head in her lap, his hair a tuft of snow against her green dress. His breaths were gravelly. The children cried. Sterling and my mom held hands. Once the needle slid in, he relaxed and began moaning like a hired mourner. My father and I helped him to his feet and got him settled in his chair. He smiled and took a long swallow of wine.

"My God, Papa, right away with the wine. You just nearly died," chided Aunt Lucia.

"Honest to God," said my mother.

"*Mi sento meglio,*" said the old man after he had drunk. Better. Then he smiled, and began the donkey laugh. The children joined in, and he motioned them to him. He uprooted himself from his chair and sang in his concrete voice: *"O Bambino, Mio Divino, Io Ti vedo, qui a tremare."*

He bade the little ones join him. He sang again, and waved his hands. His fingers were like parsnips. The children spouted nonsense syllables trying to follow him, but sang loudly with the rest of the family when they came to *O Bambino.* My grandfather went on alone for several verses, then Aunt Concetta accompanied him.

Sterling sang with the rest. "What does that mean?" she asked George, when the clapping began at the song's conclusion.

"I don't know. *The Baby.* I know that much. Aunt Concetta," I called out. "What does the song mean?"

"It's about the baby," she said in broken English. "*Jesu.*" She crossed herself. "Born *una grotta.*"

"I don't understand," Sterling said.

"A cave," Mrs. Dolce said. "The baby was born in a cave. I bet you don't know that story."

"Mother," I said.

"What? Why would she know the story? Am I offending you, honey?" she asked Sterling.

"No, of course not. But I do know the story of Jesus's birth."

"Then I give you a lot of credit. This one," she gestured at me, then began whispering, "he's just like his father's family. Dramatic. The singing. The crying. One performance after another. See what I mean?" She pointed to the head of the table where my grandfather, now quiet, but smiling, had just lit a short, tar-colored cigar. He yanked a pen knife out of his vest pocket and cut up pears and apples to soak in his wine glass and give to the children.

"Two minutes after he's on the floor asphyxiating, he's putting that garbage in his lungs. So he can do it again. Give everybody another heart attack. I think he does it on purpose. Ninety-five and he can't grow up."

"What's she saying?" I asked Sterling.

"You. Mind your own business. We have things to talk about," snapped my mother.

I was happy. Chalk it up to the season, but so what? I had impressed my family, picked a good girl, durable, affable, someone with backbone, who didn't shy away from Italian sentiment and ten kinds of fish. Sterling provided me with status, an importance, I had never felt before among my family. That a woman like her would fall for me seemed another validation of my promise, of the fact that among them all I was the one. This is happiness, I told myself. I sat back and drank with the men and watched Sterling do the Twist with the children. She let them wear her shoes, her barrettes, play with her hair. She could have been an Italian woman standing ringed with dark-eyed, dark-haired children as Uncle Marty closed in on them all with his movie camera, the bar of blinding, blazing mammoth bulbs, stealing the moment in a bank of obliterating light.

"Was that enough opera for you?" I asked Sterling on the way to the Rosechilds after dropping off my parents in a snow storm.

"I loved every minute of it."

"You were a big hit."

"They're such warm, generous people."

"Yes, they are. Southern Italians. Thankful for everything they have, and willing to share it. Good old-fashioned peasant ethos."

"You sound a little condescending."

"I don't mean to be. Sometimes I get tired of all the humility."

"It's a wonderful virtue, Giorgio."

"Don't start that."

"Is that a nickname?"

"It's actually my given name. It's on my birth certificate. My father's too. And Papa's, my grandfather."

I pulled into the Rosechilds' driveway and killed the engine. The houselights were on. The vague echo of music leaked into the Newport.

"Why did you change it, Giorgio?"

"We didn't change it. We just don't go by it."

"I think you should. It's rather grand."

"And Dolce means sweet."

"I know that, sweet Giorgio. And I've thought about it many times."
"How did you know that?"
"*La Dolce Vita.*"
"What's that?"
"The movie. *The Sweet Life.* Fellini."
"I don't like movies with subtitles."
"I think it's the most beautiful depiction of love ever filmed."
"Then I want to see it. With you."
"You've obviously already seen it, Giorgio. My sweet Giorgio."
"I don't want you to call me that."
"Oh, let me. A little humility, please?"
"I'd rather you didn't."
"Giorgio, Giorgio, sweet Giorgio."
I laughed, then lightly kissed her.
"I like this big car." She moved over against me, took my arm and put it around her. "I can sit right next to you and you can put your arm around me. We can pretend we're in high school and make out."
She slid over onto my lap and kissed me fiercely. The hard cold window against my cheek. I opened my eyes. The windshield was glazed with snow. The Rosechilds' lights twinkled through it. When she came away, we stared at each other.
"We're in love. Aren't we?"
"I think we must be," I said. "Look what I have." I switched on the interior light, reached across her and pulled a small wrapped box from the glove compartment. "Merry Christmas."
Sterling cried when she saw the locket. Cried as if her heart had broken. With her face in her hands. Fastening it around her neck, sweeping aside her black hair, kissing the little twirl of black baby hair riding up her nape, I felt a touch of heartbreak myself. The tenderness. The vulnerability. The big car in the soft snow, Sterling turning to me with the new heart on the bib of her red dress. Switching the car light off.

Chapter 16

Awakened by the song of dead millwrights on the wings of darkness along the Ohio, through Aliquippa and Neville Island—the ghostly husk of Hussey Copper—bridges stringing the black river like phosphorescent necklaces, sooty zodiac constellated in a rendition of past and future at once, we rumble in a predawn Sunday mizzle into the Pennsylvania Station on Liberty Avenue in downtown Pittsburgh.

In the station, I barely recognize Dave Mazzotti. He wears his sobriety like a seared still-smoldering robe of glory. Hair short. Clean-shaven. The face a diary of scars and divots: each drink, toke, pill, each punch and puncture, blade, bludgeon, insult. Each scorching fix he drove into his veins. The shearing aged him, shrunk him, as if all those years under the long hair and beard and scurvy clothes a wise older man had been hiding. His once black hair is lighter, not quite grey, thinner, thread-like, colorless. But his brown eyes are clear. They have stared into the blinding light long enough to have assumed it—the shocked witness the lightning-struck carry with them into eternity—as if sin had been pried out of him with a crowbar. Shriven, he is now a living martyr: plaid shirt, khakis, tennis shoes and a cigarette clamped in his broken yellow teeth.

Before leaving Queen, to sneak into Pittsburgh and see my parents, I decided I had to talk to Dave, my communion partner. I guess I needed someone from my past, someone who had known me all my life, and grew up like I had in East Liberty. I called his parents' house—the number long ago locked into memory—fully prepared to hang up when Mr. or Mrs. Mazzotti answered. No telling what might have become of Dave in the months I'd been gone. Smart money had him dead. I don't know what I expected, but Dave answered the phone, like a professional angel, and I laid out the entire story of my new life south as a lammist and asked him to meet me and Crow at the train station.

It takes him a while too before he realizes it's me. The hair he discarded hoods and masks me, and I am aged as well, having studied now for too long that same blinding light.

"Georgie," he cries, races to me, pulls me to him in a fatherly embrace.

"Dave," I say. "Dave. Dave." There, in the anonymous train station, that looks like a bomb shelter, travelers laden with baggage, slumped in the plastic chairs, waiting for their connections, the TV babbling on—a room full of homeless strangers with nothing but the illusion of destination to keep them going—I weep in Dave's arms. As if delivered, but that is not so. I'm simply back home where all the trouble started and I realize—as much as anything by looking at this shape-shifted Dave Mazzotti—the irrevocable metamorphosis I've endured.

"Hey, man, it's alright. I know all about it. We'll go get some coffee. It's okay." He pats my back. Crow has her arm around my waist. "How you doing?" he says to Crow. "I'm Georgie's friend, Dave."

"I'm Crow."

Dave lets go of me and hugs Crow, grabs the mangled valise we have between us and says, "Let's get out of here."

We end up at Finnegan's, an all-night diner on Baum Boulevard.

"I don't know about this," I say to Dave. "Felix could walk in here any minute."

"Naw. He's graduated to swankier dives, I assure you. And he wouldn't know you anyhow. You look like Robinson fucking Crusoe."

"He'd know me."

"Eat something, man. You'll feel better. Both of you."

Dave drinks a hundred cups of coffee and never stops smoking. Pack of Kools on the table that he and Crow dip into. Wreaths of smoke above us joining the storm of smoke that wraps the rafters and fluorescent lights caked in cobweb.

He relates his conversion story. Saint Patrick's Day, a couple months after I split, he was staggering up Highland Avenue, one, two in the morning, cranked on Horse and spodi-odi, scaggy reefer, a couple of Quaaludes, didn't remember where he had been. Maybe Kelly's down on Center Avenue. Big drinking bash and guys starting to get pissy. Wanted to kill someone. So he booked.

Bitter cold night, snowing like a bitch, four days from spring time and it's a blizzard, his nasty overcoat matted with ice and cooties, like Aqualung—not a friend in the world, except for his associates down on Chookie's corner. Cars plowing by, throwing shit in the street. Gunshots. A couple drive-bys a day in East Liberty at the time. Back to the old days of blacks and whites dying to kill each other. Same old shit. Dave's mom shaking in her boots each time a brother walks by the Mazzotti stoop, bad news from the TV and radio like a needle in her arm.

So here comes Dave, kind of daring someone to fuck with him, but nobody wants to because he's so dangerously tetched—it's in those junk-filled sockets, teased into the long ratty beard and hair capped with a Steelers stocking hat—up Highland right through the gut of it: Fashion Hosiery, Myers Sporting Goods, Italian Pastry Shop, Cowboy DeLuca's, Gammon's, Alex Reich. All gone or boarded up. The only thing open is the William Penn Pipe Shop, but you can't go in. Jail bars over bullet-proof glass. The guy does business with you through a drawer. Cruising cop cars paying no attention, and you can't really blame them.

Dave passes the fire-bombed church across from Sears, up another couple of storefronts, where he ducks into Vento's Pizza for a couple of cuts. Filled with wasted black dudes. Stands there at the counter bullshitting with Carmen. The blazing heat of the ovens every time Carmen lifts a pie out on the long wooden split. Then he's back out on Highland. Lurches into Fox's for a quart of malt liquor. Same old derelicts: yellow, skeletal, who've been boozing there for forty years, waiting for the wrecking ball. Then he's on the street again sipping from the quart, the snow wrapping all of East Liberty in a blessed mantle of forgetfulness.

And that's the last image he has of his old self—a filthy junky trudging shakily up Highland in a white maelstrom sucking a quart of Mustang—before a ring of black dudes with baseball bats close in on him. They pound him with the bats, just tee off on him, but they can't score a head shot. Takes most of it in the shield he makes of his arms and the big overcoat absorbs a lot of the damage, but by this time both arms are busted and three ribs. Somehow he manages to wrest a bat away from one of them, then beats them off—roaring out there in the blizzard, finally driven insane, flailing with his broken bones long after they've run off.

He scrapes the few blocks home, lets himself in, writes the note with his bloody hand dangling from his busted arm, leaves it on the kitchen table, saying who he wants to get what—not much anyhow, he's sold everything for his habit—absolves his parents, each labored letter limned in contrition. He wants them to know how sorry he is. Then back out the door—there's half a foot out there by now—and down Saint Marie, just two lousy blocks, to the Meadow Street Bridge that Alex launched himself from. He's going to go on and catch up with Alex.

But his body's shot. Fractured arms and ribs. Still high as ten men. Barely able to stumble off his mom and dad's stoop. No juice left, but still he has his hard head. Then he sits down on the sidewalk and lets the snow shroud him like a statue forgotten under a sheet and, when he is utterly exhausted by the pain, he topples over, his cheek resting in the snow, his new aim to die right there on the sidewalk in front of his house.

He tells me and Crow that all he thought about was Alex. What he wants to say is that Alex visited him, and by that sheer presence, that apparition, dissuaded him from dying. That's what I see too. Alex bathed in the blinding light. Of course it was Alex who stepped in. It happens all the time. Everyone in East Liberty believes in spirits: *spiritus mundi*. The Sacrifice of the Mass is a grave consort of spirits. But, again, it's Dave's burning humility that will not allow him to say all that has happened, all that he sees. He's been cast into the miraculous. A sudden Jesuit, the circuit preacher at Saint Joan's Chapel. All he says, though, is he thought about Alex, and then his new soul exploded in him and he began to scream for his mother and father. He gave it all up right there with his face in the snow on the sidewalk he'd taken his first steps on—no more dope, no more drinking—before his parents made it to him and called the ambulance.

"I was in the hospital like two days. I'm glad I didn't jump off the bridge. It's a cliché around here. Sheer plagiarism. The East Liberty story. Told too often by too many. But each time with a little twist. So I'm still living at home, painting houses with my old man. Like your dad, he never got called back to the mill. You know, all those years of hell I put them through, they never threw me out, never even threatened with it. My mother's novenas finally kicked in."

"Jesus Christ," I finally say.

Crow, in a crummy infamous diner in Pittsburgh listening to Dave Mazzotti testify like a Pentecostal, has melted against me, stunned, nearly vanished except for her silent breath.

One of the Greek owners marches over with our food, lays the platters in front of us. Drops the kits of silverware in the middle and turns away from us. Dave: two plain cake doughnuts. Crow: fish sticks and French fries. Fried egg sandwich and home fries for me.

"*Mangiare,*" says Dave

"Means *eat* in Italian," I explain to Crow. She still hasn't said a word, sits there staring at Dave as he dunks one of the doughnuts in his coffee.

"So that's my drunkalogue. Almost. I have something for you."

He dips into the breast pocket on his shirt, pulls out a tiny black velvet pouch and hands it to me. Inside the pouch is a black rosary, gold links and gold crucifix. The nexus is a relief of Jesus elevating above a chalice the consecrated host. Engraved on the opposite side: *Remembrance: First Holy Communion.* The day of our First Communion, May 14, 1962, each boy was given a rosary exactly like this. The girls too, though theirs were white. I have no idea where mine is. Probably in the cedar chest at the foot of my parents' bed.

"You know what that is?" Dave asks.

"Yeah, I know what it is. But why are you giving it to me?"

"Because that's what I left you when I decided to do myself in that night. I had it in the note that I wanted you to have this rosary. Because we were communion partners. So now I'm giving it to you because I've given away all the stuff I said I was going to give away. Even though I'm still here."

"Geez, Dave. It doesn't seem right for me to take this."

"Look, man, that's the bargain I made. With myself. With God. It's the pact. It's no longer mine. You gotta take it."

"Okay, man. I'm honored. Really."

"And Georgie?"

"Yeah?"

"You should say that rosary every now and then. Pray without ceasing, my man. No shit."

Crow takes the rosary from my palm and studies it. She runs a finger over the glittering spread-eagled savior, fingers the beads, places it against her cheek.

"Do you pray?" she asks Dave.

"I pray all the time," Dave says. "I think I always have. You know I was this close to dying. My mom and dad, the old people in the neighborhood, they went on forever like crazy people about those black guys who busted me up on St. Patty's. Niggers. *Tizzones. Melanzanos.* How East Liberty went to hell because of them. *Animales.* The whole manifesto. But those black guys were emissaries, angels dispatched to give me the ass-whipping I needed. They saved my life."

"I want to say the rosary," Crow says.

"Georgie'll teach you. You still remember, don't you, buddy?"

Crow places the rosary around her neck like a necklace, then drops the crucifix inside her blouse.

"Yeah, I remember. Listen, Dave, you can't call me Georgie or George or Dolce or any of that any more. I have a new name: Michael Roman."

"Alright. Michael Roman. Pleased to meet you. David Mazzotti." He reaches his hand across the table to shake mine. I clasp it with my left hand. My right hand, filled with shame, sits on the table. I thought I was too good for the people in my life, too good for East Liberty, too good to pray, too good for God. What a fool to think that intellect can protect you from anything.

"What's wrong with your other hand, *Michele*?

"It's a little embarrassing, but I ruined it in a fight."

"You a fighter now, too?" Then to Crow: "You better eat your food, Miss. You got a long day of Pittsburgh ahead of you."

Dave drops us off on Penn Avenue in Garfield in front of Saint Francis Hospital. I get out and walk over to his window. Crow hugs him and slips out. "I enjoyed meeting you," she says. "Come see us."

"I just might do that. Take care of yourself, and my communion partner here."

"I'll be right there," I say to her. She whips out a cigarette, waves to Dave with a teary smile and walks toward the hospital entrance.

Dave climbs out of the car and lights a cigarette. "I always said you had a horseshoe up your ass, Georgie. I mean Michael. Even an ugly you can still snag the good women. Whatever happened to that Rosechild girl?"

"Shit, Dave. I blew that to pieces."

"What the fuck happened to you, Michael Roman? You were the neighborhood messiah, the sure bet, the blue-plate, good-looking, genius prince with the first class ticket out of here."

"That's what happened to me."

"I don't follow."

"Doesn't matter."

"Listen, you tell your mom and dad I send my love, and tell them too that I'm praying for them. You know, no one'll ever love us like our mothers and fathers. Crazy Italians from East Liberty."

"I know that. I really do."

"And take care of that nice girl too. You got my number. Call me if you need me. I mean it. I'll take you on as a project. Hey, you wanna see something?" Dave pulls out his wallet. "Look what I keep in my wallet. You don't even know what it is."

"What is it?"

"It's the ticket to the Super Bowl you gave me the night you split." He hands me the ticket. "You remember?"

The black and gold ticket has printed at one end: *January 12, 1975, New Orleans, LA.* At the other end: *$200.* There's a photograph in its middle of the Super Dome with the figure of Terry Bradshaw firing a pass superimposed over it.

"Yeah. Yeah. I remember. Guess you didn't make it."

"Naw. Didn't make it. But I'll bet it'll be worth something someday. I'd wait around and run you back to the station later, but I gotta get to work."

"No, man. I understand. You've done so much already." I hand him the ticket.

"I got one more thing to show you." As he tucks the ticket back into his wallet, he yanks out five hundred dollar bills and holds them toward me.

"What's this? I can't take it."

"It's yours."

"Dave, I appreciate it so much, but I can't take it."

"You won it. The number hit. I played Alex's birthday. Straight up for $1000. Both of us. $500 to the good."

"You're serious?"

"On my mom and dad. It's yours. Take it."

I grab the bills, fold them, button them up in my shirt pocket. "Thanks, Dave. Thanks for everything."

Dave takes me into his arms again. "I love you, Georgie Boy."

"I love you too. I just don't know how it is we came to love each other."

"Back in '62 up on the altar when we knelt side by side and Father Guissina laid the host on our tongues for the first time and said *Corpus Christi.*"

Holy Communion. The very thing that I was sure would deliver me, that I had invested with the tangible miraculous: the presence of Jesus, flaming inside my soul like the burning bush. No metaphors. No mysteries. Rather: the corporeal presence, the word made flesh. *Corpus Christi.* Saved once and for all. Like Crow's people. Saved. Romans 10:9.

But the host made me sick. The unleavened arid pasty wafer gagged me with nausea. My great fear was that I would vomit it in some gothic Pre-Raphaelite scene on my way back down the center aisle to my pew at High Mass. While the congregation belted out "Holy God," I'd commit sacrilege—so loathsome that Jesus, who turned my stomach, refused my roof. The nuns had instructed that should we ever throw up after Communion, canon law instructed we retrieve the *vomitus,* as they called it, in a clean handkerchief, and bury it. Otherwise, a mortal sin had been committed and, should we be run down by an automobile crossing Larimer Avenue on our way home from school, we would go straight to hell and abide there in unrelieved agony for all of eternity. The only way to exempt yourself with any surety from that fate was to receive, every day, the sacrament of Holy Eucharist and remain in the state of sanctifying grace. My unworthiness—that I could not stomach, literally, my Savior's promise of everlasting life—was a parable of irony. The cruelest, most insupportable thing that has ever happened to me. Now, I'm an outlaw.

"Instant karma," says Dave and smiles, fires up another smoke.

"Maybe it doesn't take right away with everyone."

"Patience, my man. That's what sobriety teaches. Listen, keep your eyes peeled for angels—blacks ones, with Louisville Sluggers. That mangled hand might be a gift, not a curse. Good shit is often disguised."

"I'll keep all that in mind, Brother. I'm glad you've turned it around."

"Work in progress, buddy. We all are."

He jumps in the car, sticks his hand out the window. I take it with my left and squeeze. Pops it in gear and drifts off. Says: "Yo, Mike Roman. You are still better than everybody else." Then down Penn Avenue back to East Liberty to paint houses with his dad.

I catch up to Crow in the hospital lobby. Seated on a bench, sober and fidgety, her eyes rim with tears. Pitifully thin, so young. So far from home. I lay my hand on her head, then along her cheek. I don't even know who she is or why we're together, but she's all that's keeping me from being sucked through the glass cupola ceiling into the troposphere. We smile at each other and walk hand in hand to the elevator.

I punch 8: the psychiatric wing. Another of my mother's self-fulfilling prophesies. How often have I heard her say she would end up at Mayview or Woodville or Saint Francis. My father and I were driving her to such places. And, now, here she is. The crazy house. She finally made it, the place she had warned she was headed, apart from Mount Carmel, all her life.

The elevator opens on an information desk at which sits a nurse in an old fashioned white uniform and shoes, the soft white cap. Rather beautiful–like an advertisement for a nurse. And a security guard: a badge and gun and cop hat, a patch on his gray starched sleeve that says *Wackenhut.*

On either side of the desk are huge double doors with signs: *No Admittance. Authorized Personnel Only.* Nothing else. Just the sterile hum of the fluorescent lights on the polished tile. I tell them we're here to see Sylvia Dolce. We have to show ID. Crow is nervous, trembling slightly as she hands her driver's license to the guard.

He stares at her a moment, and finally says, "North Carolina."

"Yes, Sir," she answers.

I still have my Pennsylvania license: George Dolce, a twenty year old clean cut, clear-eyed young man smiling confidently. The guard looks at the license, then at me, back and forth, trying to make the connection.

"It was taken a while ago," I say.

He says, "I guess."

"I'm here to see my mother."

"She's in 819," says the nurse. "Go through those doors"—she points to the left—"and make a right at the first hall. It'll be the first room on your right."

She pushes a button and the big doors swing inward. I take Crow's hand. Once we pass through, they swing shut behind us. The corridor is empty. The doors to all the rooms are closed. Not a sound. The lights are so exaggeratedly bright—like the laboratory lights in *The Hour of the Wolf.* As if my mother has the entire wing to herself—as she would prefer it.

It has been over a year, maybe fourteen months, since I've seen my mother. I have missed my father deeply, and he has suffered in my absence. But he can weather if he has to and, even if his heart has broken, he will not burden others with his sorrow. He still knows how to throw up a hand and say, "No use kicking."

But my mother: fourteen months, maybe more. A criminally long time for anyone in the Dolce family to go without seeing his mother. My aunts and uncles and cousins—they understand why I had to leave the city and they'll stand by me no matter what—no matter what—but nevertheless they feel betrayed. They had expected more. I, above all, had expected more. *Disgrazia.* I am a disgrace. There is no dispute about this. They can stand my disgrace if they have to. Because they love me, and are loyal to my mother and father. But all this time—over a year. Maybe I've had no control over such a lapse. Circumstances. Fate. Say what you will. But fourteen months is a tragedy. *Infamia.*

In my position, to apologize for anything, at this point, seems merely another version of disrespect, a coward's pact with an oblivious God. No one cares what I've buried in my heart. My mother has been impossible, and crazy, but I love her. Because she is my mother, and that's that. Something between us that I can't possibly understand.

It is my father's voice that bids us enter when I knock upon 819—Crow and I walk into the room—and I remind myself to play that number.

My mother is somehow perfected, tucked in billows of her vanished pain, the wholly white light of peace streaming from her eyes. Her gown is spring-grass green, her hair silvery and soft against the starched pillow. She glows. As if the pilot has been stoked from within by some long-hidden spirit, disguised these many years by care and bitterness. She smiles. To ease the fractured hip, every four hours the steady narrative of Morphine is injected into the gossamer I-V line braceleting her wrist. In the vernacular, my mother, a lifelong teetotaler, is flying. A rosary and a devotional booklet to the Blessed Mother rest on the bedside table.

My father, archetypal, papal, sits chiseled in the bedside recliner, his eyes darting from my mother to me and Crow. He wears a tie and sports jacket. He holds his hat in his lap. Behind him, the window gives way to the sky draping Garfield, eight stories below, a neighborhood of narrow streets and narrow houses piled on top of one another.

As though expecting me to walk out of the clouds into her room at that instant, my mother sits up in bed and sighs, "My little boy." Then she smiles and claps her hands. "Georgie. My God, George"—to my dad—"it's Georgie." And she begins to cry. Not piteously, nor even sorrowfully, but a deep soulful sanctified cry, a sound I've never heard spring from her, as if within her the ineffable rapture of the Holy Spirit has just sprouted wings. A cry that casts over Crow its evangelical glory, so that she bursts into tears and it is she, not I, who reaches my mother first and they entwine as if having known each other a long time.

My father intercepts me on my way to my mother, his bones quaking as he kisses me, then holds me and says, "Son" and I whisper, "Dad." Then I am with him at my mother's bedside, and she is holding me, telling me she loves me as I stroke her hair and kiss each of her hands in turn—as if the holy has ignited in me as well. She has been praying for me all along: lighting candles, making novenas on her swollen legs, saying rosaries. And here I am.

"Who's your little friend, Georgie?"

Crow sits right there in the bed with her. They are holding hands.

"This is Lydia."

"Ah, that's a nice name? Is she the little Jewish girl? The pharmacist's daughter? Lydia's a Jewish name, isn't it?"

"Sylvia, this is someone else," explains my dad. He looks over at me. Like *I hope you understand.*

"Ah, someone else. Very good. You can see she had a home life, that she was raised right. Very down to earth. How long can you kids stay?"

"We can only stay a little while."

"How nice. Isn't that nice, George? The kids can stay a little while."

"That's beautiful, Sylvia. What a surprise."

"Are you kids hungry?"

"We're fine, Mom."

"George, fix these kids something."

"We're really fine, Mrs. Dolce. But you're sweet to offer."

"This one"—she gestures to Crow—"skin and bones. How do you stay so thin, Honey? God bless you."

"George, put some food on the table. The kids are hungry."

"We're not at home, Sylvia. We're at the hospital."

"Oh my God, yes. I keep forgetting. They have me *stonare* with all this medicine." And then she laughs—I can't remember the last time she laughed—and closes her eyes, dozes for a few seconds, the lovely smile still breaking across her lips. She looks ten years younger. But not my father. The days I've been gone have settled over him like ore dust. He's thinner, stooped. He glances at me again, purses his lips, shakes his head and walks to the window.

"I broke my hip, Georgie," says my mother. Then to Crow: "Don't ever get old, Honey." She laughs. Looks at me. "You," she says, smiling and wagging a finger, "need a haircut—and a shave." Her eyes flutter and, that quickly, she's asleep.

I'll wager my sober mother would never leave her bed, would accept this calamity as God's fixed judgment. She's been threatening to die for as long as I've known her. But this Mother Morphine, this wasted angel, like someone on leave from the underworld, thankful for this new crack at life, suddenly claims half-dozing, "But I still got a little fight left in me. Me and your father. Don't we, George?"

My dad, holding his bewildered hat, turns from the window. "You better believe it."

The doctors expect it will take her at least two months before she's able to get around, a minimum of two to three weeks before she can even put her right foot on the floor. Of course we don't discuss her breakdown.

"We still want to take a trip to Italy. Don't we, George?"

This time, my father, his back now to the window, doesn't answer. Behind him, across the horizon, rage the stack fires of the Jones and Laughlin plant along the Monongahela; then, across the river on the Southside, a string of failing mills, in the dwindling light of steel in Pittsburgh. The Duquesne Incline, no longer packed with immigrant open-hearthers descending the cables to feed blast furnaces coke all night and day, scales tourists to Mount Washington. My father will never return to the mill and he knows it. He blames himself for all this: me, my mother.

"I'm crazy, Georgie," says my mother, suddenly awake again.

"No, you're not, Mrs. Dolce. You're just resting," Crow assures her.

"She just played out. That's all," says my dad.

"*Christina a puzza,*" chirps my mother, then giggles.

My dad shakes his head and turns back to the window.

"We need to be going, Mom," I say.

"When does your law school start, Georgie?"

"Pretty soon."

"You better visit the barber shop first, or they won't let you in." She laughs and I smile, then turn my eyes to my father's back as he gazes out into the streaked sky, the sun almost level with the window.

"Crazy," she mumbles.

"We have to go."

My father turns. "Sylvia, I'm going to walk out with Georgie. I'll be right back. You gonna be okay?"

"Where am I going? Take your time."

My father bends to my mother, kisses each of her cheeks, then her lips, and she raises her arms and wraps them around his neck. He kisses her mouth again and smiles. "I love you very much, Honey."

"I love you, too, George."

I've never seen them kiss on the lips before or confess their love for each other.

Crow slides out of the bed, then leans in, brushes my mother's pretty white hair from her forehead and strokes it for a moment, then bends and kisses her brow, then her cheek and whispers, "I love you."

"What's written on your forehead?" my mother asks.

"I love you," says Crow.

"Is that what it says?" my mother asks.

Crow kisses her again and pivots out of the room, trying not to cry. My father pats my mother's hand and follows Crow into the hall.

"I gotta get going, Mom."

"Of course. You kids have things to do. Enjoy yourself. Whatta you want to spend all your time with a couple of old fogeys? Before you know it . . . "

I take my mother in my arms. I don't know when or if ever I'll see her again. She's so beautiful. How did I mistake her for someone else all those years? How did I mistake myself for someone else all those years?

"I love you so much," she says, looking into my eyes, as her eyes close and flutter, and, though she seems now thoroughly asleep, she continues to murmur.

"I love you too, Mom." But she doesn't hear me. She is listening to her friend, Morphine. It has slowed the future to a watery trickle. The present is no more than the portal to the past. She mumbles and hesitates, smiles at her inability to land a single sentence, then nods off in earnest like a junky before she can finish. I like her this way, the least bit dotty. Endearing, like Aunt Clara, from *Bewitched,* or the tattered elegance of Auntie Mame.

I kiss her forehead, each cheek. I take her hand in mine, and stare for a moment into her face. My mother. Without thinking, I make the Sign of the Cross. "I'm sorry," I say and walk out of the room.

The hall is now filled with people. Old snowy people in patterned hospital gowns tied off at the neck and wide open in back. Some amble solo. Others tethered to I-V trees, others led by attendants. Ancient people lost. That is clear. Some so far out in the mist they are mere shapes, peering out from their skulls as though from the rail of a vast ship disappearing further into the murk. They mumble and drool, titter and mewl, clump over the gleaming corridor like zombies. They stare at us with no comprehension. At the end of the long hall, a crane-like apparatus lowers in a sling onto a port-o-potty a spindly naked old man in a Pirates cap. In a small alcove rests a battered desk with writing paper, pencils, and a black telephone.

I trot down the hall, past an empty waiting room, a television clacking a morning talk show from its bracket in a corner of the ceiling. I catch up to Crow and my father talking at the elevator. She has her hand on his upper arm. His hands clasp in front of him, the hat dangling from them. His eyes are on the floor; he's shaking his head.

"Your father was telling me that your mother won't go home when she's released," Crow says when she sees me.

"They're going to send her to some kind of place for rehab. She doesn't need to go somewhere. I can take her home and take care of her myself."

"I was telling him that she'll get better care wherever they send her. Professional care. She'll get better faster."

"That's right, Dad."

He looks up. He hasn't shaved in two days. His hair is white and wild. I swear I smell whiskey on his breath. "You," he says and points a wrathful finger at me. "You. Don't act like you know. Like you have any say in this, goddam it."

Crow says tenderly, "Mr. Dolce," steps up to him in embrace. But he bars her with his hand.

"No, no. None of this with me now. I don't even know this girl. The both of you. Not now—with your mother in there like that. Like them." He motions to the flimsy levitating bodies in the hall about us.

"Dad."

"Uh-uh, Georgie. You did this to us. Your mother was a nervous wreck to begin with. Then I get laid off, and you get yourself in this terrible trouble. You know what that did to her? This thing with you. She never stopped carrying on. How we just lost our kid. We don't even know where he is. If you're laying in a ditch somewhere bleeding to death. The whole family took it bad. Not even a phone call. Your mother worshipped the ground you walked on. Both of us. You were our whole lives. Then she falls and breaks a hip and, bing, she finally cracks up. So how is she supposed to bounce back? You hear her in there? A mental case. I brush things off all the time, like I'm some kind of chooch with no feelings. But how am I supposed to get over all this? And on top of it, the hospital bills—even with the insurance—will send us to the poor house. All the tough is gone, Georgie. I've aged twenty years in the year you been gone. Jesus Christ. I'm not far from the bridge myself."

The bridge. Like a giant magnet hung over the hollow abyss. The candlelit procession, cardinals and monsignors leading the suicidal mothers and fathers of East Liberty to the wrought iron bridge deck rails where they queue like communicants awaiting Extreme Unction. Then their sacramental leaps into rectitude, the boulevard littered with the sacrificial first generation *Americanos,* driven into the concrete by their insatiable children.

"You did this to us, Georgie. My father would have disowned me."

"Mr. Dolce," Crow says, tears in her eyes.

He looks at Crow, and for a moment softens. "You'll have to excuse me, Honey, but I don't know you or where you're from or who your people are. The two of you look like gypsies. Worse. I'm sorry, but this is what comes from waiting sixty-five years to speak my mind."

The hall swarms with the crazy doddering pilgrims. They are close enough to touch. They hum and mumble. Their scalps are pink. They peer at us and listen. An old woman wiggles out of her shift and stands before us naked, a twisted column of smoke, androgynous, transparent. Looking through her, I watch Crow begin one of her balletic twirling faints, but I can't get to her before she lands softly like a floating scarf on the floor. Then it's a sudden melee. A nurse rushing to Crow, an attendant trying to get the old woman covered—her eyes chocked wide, her toothless mouth open in a death mask of silence. Herding the rest of them, cooing and warbling, back toward their rooms.

The nurse props Crow against the wall just beneath a red fire extinguisher in a glass cabinet. She crouches to her with a cup of water. Crow is conscious, crying like a little girl, wearing a short orange dress from the Magic Attic, in Queen, with rhinestones embroidered on the bodice and the hem, her long fingers slanted across her face.

"Thank you. She's just upset," I say to the nurse. I'm bent over Crow, the back of my hand on one cheek, the other stroking her hair.

I have never known my father to not have a handkerchief. He pulls it out of his pocket—white, immaculate, ironed in a crisp square by my mother. With some difficulty he gets down on his knees and holds the handkerchief toward Crow. "Honey, I'm sorry."

Crow removes her hands from her face. Her black and gold eyes are circled red. It's time to go. She takes the hanky and my dad begins to cry, tries to get to his feet, but can't. Crow throws her arms around him. I motion to the nurse that it's okay, and she walks off, trailing the old ones jabbering ahead of her, that old man in the sling now suspended up in the air fast asleep.

My father composes himself hurriedly, laboriously clambers to his feet, and jams the hat on his head as if he's going somewhere. He holds out his hand to Crow. She gets up and stands close to him. They look like a pair of scared immigrants just off the boat.

"I gotta get back to your mother."

"I know, Dad."

"And it's no good—you hanging around here too long." He pulls out his wallet. "You know, I talked to Eugene. He feels real bad about all this."

"It's not his fault."

"I only have a couple of dollars to give you."

"Dad, I'm not going to take your money. I got some money for you." I pull the folded hundreds out of my shirt pocket.

"Where the hell did you get that?"

"Never mind."

"Whatta you mean never mind? I am an honest man, godammit."

"I didn't steal it, Dad. What do think I am?"

"I don't know what you are. I don't know what anything is."

"Look, I played a number. It hit, and I want to give you and mom a few dollars."

"I'm not going to take the money. Gambling's how this whole mess got started."

"I was just trying to help."

"Did you do all those things? Rob the pharmacy? Steal the car? The drugs? Jesus Christ, boy."

My father's clothes are too big for him. His mouth hangs open. His eyes rip into me through the whorl of tears in each of them.

"Don't tell me. I don't want to know. That goddam scum on the corner. They finally got to you."

"Dad, it didn't have anything to do with them. Or you and mom. Now take this money."

"I don't want the money."

"What are you doing for money, Dad?"

"I still have a few more weeks unemployment. Sam said I can pick up a couple days short order and washing dishes at the Kennilworth. We'll make out."

"Dad, take the money."

He shouts, "*Basta* with the money."

The people in the hall start at the sound of his voice. One old woman shrinks against the wall and snickers. Others smile, or fret their hands. The attendants look up, concerned. My father holds out his hands, as if to show they are empty. He smiles. "It's okay," he says to them. Then to us: "You kids get on the road and get the hell out of here. You watch yourself, Georgie. That Felix Costa's a bad seed, an *animale.*" He turns to Crow. "Honey, I'm sorry. It's not a good time for me. I have all these bad feelings."

The black telephone at the end of the hall rings.

"You have nothing to be sorry for," says Crow. She links her arm through his.

"Well," he says and shrugs, tries to smile. "You two better get going. And I better get back to my wife. I don't like to leave her for long."

The intercom barks a *Code Yellow* over and over. *Code Yellow.* The amblers put their hands over their ears. One old woman screams. Takes a breath. Screams. Just keeps screaming. A couple of nurses sprint down the hall. Past my mother's room. The phone ringing and ringing.

"I should get back down there, kids," says my dad apologetically. Crow hugs him, but he no longer notices her.

"Dad, I just got caught in a jackpot. I was up to my ears before I knew what was going on."

"Holy God, Son. You broke our hearts. You should have known better. I love you very much, but I have all this hate in me. I gotta go to your mother, and you sure as hell better get out of town."

He takes me into his arms and shudders for ten long seconds, lets me go, wipes his eyes with those mangled millwright's hands and turns, walks past the screaming woman, the rest of them with their hands over their ears, though the intercom has gone dead.

"Dad," I call, but he can't hear me. I watch him, swallowed inside his immense coat, until he turns into my mother's room.

Chapter 17

Two days after Christmas, Sterling and I went to a party thrown by Jamie Ledge, one of Sterling's high school friends, at her parents' lodge in Hidden Valley, a ski resort ninety minutes out of the city. I hadn't wanted to go. I had never skied, and I wasn't in the mood for a crowd, especially people I didn't know. People from money—like Sterling. My first instinct was to beg off, but Sterling was excited about skiing and seeing her old friends.

In that day's mail, I had received my first law school acceptance—from Georgetown. I was elated, but, instead of comforting me, it made me feel petulant, edgy. I worried I wouldn't get into Yale and Columbia. I was nervous about the Pittsburgh-Oakland game. Not just the ton of money riding on it, but my future and my parents' future. How would I ever pay for Georgetown? Or any of those schools? How could I afford Sterling in my future—which, by that time, I couldn't envision without her.

My mother cried when I told her and my father about the Georgetown acceptance. She lamented I'd be moving away, and joining a better class of people, that I'd forget about them. What would they do without me? But she didn't blame me. Go, she told me. I was smart to better myself. She and my dad were over the hill. But, she said, and she held up a finger as if to imprint this moment in the cosmos once and for all, she remembered changing my nasty diapers, she remembered every meal she stood on her crippled legs to prepare for me. Every load of wash. Did I not always have the best clothes? Some things you forget, she said. She was perfectly willing to admit that she was not as young as she once was. Who is? But other things you don't forget.

"Am I right, George?" she asked my dad.

"Sylvia, you've always been a devoted mother."

"You always side with your son, don't you?"

"Sylvia, please."

"Mom, there's no side one way or another. I thought you'd be happy I got in."

"She is happy," my dad said.

"You, I can tell him myself. I'm happy. I'm very happy. My God, we're so proud." She broke into a fresh round of sobbing. "But what good am I to you? Neither of us. Not two nickels to rub together. In another month we'll be on welfare. Go ahead and go to your party. Get your new life started tonight. You and your rich Jewish girlfriend. I won't live to see my grandchildren. God bless you. I'm on my way out."

I stood it as long as I could, then kissed my parents goodnight and walked out into the snow.

I told the Rosechilds about Georgetown the minute I walked into the house to pick up Sterling. They were jubilant. Hugs and kisses. Phil poured drinks. The four of us, as if already tithed to one another, crowded together on the couch. Phil and JoAnn plotted my future. I wanted to ask Sterling to marry me right then and there before it all evaporated.

It snowed the entire way to Hidden Valley. Sterling held my free hand and insisted that Washington was an easy jaunt from New York, and I'd probably get into Yale and Columbia too. Besides, her plans were still up in the air. She was waiting to hear from NYU and the New School. Everything would work out. She called me her sweet Giorgio.

From a distance, the lighted slopes of Hidden Valley looked like heaven in a blizzard, chairlifts floating the tiny people up the mountain, snow castling down, skiers shooting like quasars out of the lit night.

The houses in the village, referred to as cottages, were enormous stone mansions. They were decorated exclusively with white lights. It was an ordinance, Sterling informed me. No colored lights.

We parked the Mercedes in the Ledges' circular drive, and walked through four inches of fresh snow to a door of varnished, slabbed oak belted in cast iron, a small window of Tiffany glass at face level and a holly wreath swagged in red and white satin ribbon.

Sterling clunked the door knocker three times, and we stepped in. A leaping blaze in a fireplace immense enough to house a Volkswagen, a fantastic Christmas tree, around and beneath which, instead of gifts, lounged a dozen people my age who wore their perfection like models, as if there had never existed an alternative to beauty. I felt like a threadbare immigrant pressed by a hundred years of scrutiny, as though I were there to answer for my people.

The girls told me they had heard about me from Sterling. The boys shook my hand firmly, looked me dead in the eye. Guys who'd gone to Kiski Prep and Shadyside Academy, girls from Winchester Thurston and the Ellis School where Sterling had gone. Not Saint Sebastian kids from East Liberty whose parish had had to subsidize their tuition because their parents couldn't afford it. Sterling's crowd was from Churchhill and Fox Chapel, Sewickley and Ben Avon Heights, places I had entered only as Mr. Rosechild's delivery boy. They belonged to country clubs, had grown up spending summers at tennis and golf camps. My tongue failed. I smiled like some greenhorn monkey, sizing them up the way any *dago* hood from East Liberty might. Maybe I'd bring Dave and all those scurvy junk-bags from the corner out there and kick their pampered asses. Or just appall them to death.

We drank shots of Jose Cuervo and chased them with Heineken. Sterling stayed close to me and held my hand. At intervals, she kissed my cheek, my mouth. It made me uncomfortable. She told her friends that I, Giorgio—having had three shots, she laughed as she said my name—had just gotten into law school at Georgetown. I was brilliant. Her family adored me.

"*Giorgio,*" one of the guys said, smiling. "Is that your real name?"

"Well, it's what I call him," Sterling said. "My sweet Giorgio."

I knew to be pleased. Sterling was going out of her way to let her friends know I was not just another fellow escorting her to a party.

"Actually, it is my name," I said. "But I go by George."

"*Parla Italiano*?" asked one of the girls.

"No, I don't speak."

"You're kidding? It's such a beautiful language. Have you been to Italy?"

"No, I haven't."

"You have to go. There's nothing like it."

They were all handsome and smart. I was handsome and smart too. But many of them, as we talked, had been to Italy—and across Europe—and it was as if they knew something about me that I didn't know myself. These *Americanos* even owned the old country. It was silly, really, my blaming them for having all the things I wanted. Their blue blood and blond hair, their trips to Italy, the way they could stand back from things, from people, especially, and possess them.

Sterling's friends called me Giorgio, and I was fine with it. I smiled and remained silent. I drank when they drank, and when they all stepped outside to ski down the long, long hill of the Ledges' front lawn, I followed. About three hundred yards. It even had its own rope tow to get back up to the top.

I had never been on skis before. Sterling taught me to snowplow, how to shift my weight from ski to ski to change direction, and use the poles for balance. Nothing to it, I told myself, as I took my first run, the white floor of the earth rushing by me with a hiss, the fiery cold fogging my eyes with tears. I was good; they'd all see it, standing below waiting for me. At the bottom, the hill stopped abruptly; then, after a short expanse, the road. Had it rolled out a bit, I would have snowplowed to a gradual halt. However, going too fast to make my legs mind enough to snowplow, I had no choice but to voluntarily go over in a great sliding whirl-about that left me clotted with snow and upside down in a snow bank, one ski flapping from my ankle, my poles buried.

It was a good thing that Sterling, after assuring herself that I was alright, had laughed too, harder than the others, that she didn't seem embarrassed. She congratulated me on my spectacular fall, retrieved my poles, brushed the net of snow from my face and hair, licked my eyelashes. I smelled her sweet boozy breath. We kissed. I wasn't going to let myself get pissed off at these people laughing at me. I would have laughed too. But then I couldn't make my skis cooperate as I clung to the rope-tow back up the slope. They kept getting tangled. I slipped again and again, and was half-dragged to the top.

They laughed again, but this time not Sterling. I wouldn't have minded Dave Mazzotti and those guys laughing, but not these people. *Okay,* I told myself, *okay,* and took another run down the hill. I was as good as any of them going down, but I couldn't get the hang of braking without a protracted slapstick fall. Wet and frozen, I continued to charge up out of the snow and wrestle that tow to the peak of the Ledges' lawn until finally the rest of them had had enough and went inside to drink some more.

I was drinking too much, but didn't know how else to compensate for the drubbing I'd taken on my skis. I wanted these people, the males especially, to know I was a man. A man of taste and discretion and destiny. I sat in front of the fire with Sterling at my feet. Lights off, candles lit. Stevie Wonder on the stereo. A few of them danced.

Jamie's boyfriend, Bill, threw a bag of dope on the coffee table and began rolling a joint. I didn't like Bill, the way he rubbed against Sterling when we'd first arrived at the Ledges', how he had kissed her mouth, the way he looked at me, like he wanted to wink, as if he knew something deep about me and Sterling. As if he had been down that road and back before, way before. I had watched Bill drink too much all night. His square jaw, blue eyes and naturally bleached wavy hair that he never worried about combing. His beauty. He was utterly beautiful—in that unearned patrician manner. Tall and muscular, Bill played rugby at Bucknell.

Yet Bill had been perfectly decent all night with me, congratulated me on my acceptance to Georgetown—he'd be attending law school at Duke in the fall—served me beer and inquired repeatedly if I was comfortable. But he had prattled on all night about how Terry Bradshaw was a lunk-head who would ultimately fold because of his intellectual inferiority, and how his counterpart, Ken Stabler of Oakland, was an aesthete, a kind of Sweet Jesus-Buddha combined who would lay waste to the Steelers in righteous fashion. Bill had been born in California. He had learned to surf before he walked. He was full of poetry and shit. Maybe he was kidding, just fooling around. It was Christmas, old friends getting together. But Bill, an expert skier, had laughed the hardest at my falls. Now here he was with the dope, and asking Sterling to dance.

I thought of Felix, of all people, that son of a bitch, that *gavone.* What he might do in this situation. How he might feel. It was not a matter of action, really, but rather of comportment. A wise man, a man who ultimately knew how to get his way by gauging people, by manipulating them because of his superior take on the human psyche, knew the difference between the two. Some things you have to forget about, let go.

Nothing to it, I told myself, passed on the joint as it made its way to me. I laid back and drank beer, watched the swirling dancers, tried to keep my eyes off Sterling as she danced with Bill. Joints floated around the room. A fifth of Bellows bourbon, rotgut cheap and campy, along with somebody's daddy's Courvoisier, bumped hand to hand to mouth, chased by beer, wrapped in reefer smoke.

Little Stevie was clearly Little Stevie no more. He no longer wore *high-topped shoes and shirttails;* and Susie, the old *childhood sweetheart,* was damn sure no longer wearing *pigtails.* His ass had been scratched clean to *Hard Times, Mississippi.* He lived *in a house the size of a matchbox.* A house infested with cockroaches.

Roaches. My mother talked about them all the time. She was obsessed by them, ancient unkillable avatars of poverty and filth. *You're going to bring home roaches,* she'd harp at my dad about the mill, and to me about the fields and gyms where I had played ball in high school, about the locker rooms where I'd changed clothes. *Roaches.* They had followed certain people from Italy. The dark gypsy ones. The Calabrians. The *pigshit* Irish too. The blacks in the projects cultivated them. When they opened their cabinets, they spilled out like buttons. They mated in sewers and garbage; they wormed out of drains and toilets the moment the lights were snuffed.

Only the most repressive Calvinist zeal could keep them at bay. My mother's life was a war against uncleanliness. The ditch separating refinement and squalor overflowed with roaches. She had always admonished me never to put my mouth directly to the spigot for water. She knew somebody who had had a roach dash right into his mouth like that, then down his throat into his stomach where it hatched babies like a battalion of mortal sins. She had a story for everything: the kid whose hand had turned to stone and stuck up out of the grave after he died because he had dared strike his mother.

Getting back. Somebody, something, would always be there to get back at you. So you better be clean, cleaner than the next person. Immaculate. Because you couldn't be sure of love or money, but you could be clean. That didn't take a fortune or a college education or even somebody telling you they loved you. If you were clean, God would smile on you.

When I was little, she'd ask me sometimes if I could imagine roaches in heaven. I'd admit that I couldn't. I didn't even know what a roach was. "There," she'd say. "You see? The bigshots are no better than we are. God doesn't give a damn about money. But He cares about who's clean and who's not. It's cleanliness that's next to Godliness. Not money. Not a big car or big house. Not good looks."

The well-off didn't have to clean their own houses. They had daygirls and yard men. Left to their own devices, they were nothing but hogs. Sure they had money, but they drank too much and had to take pills to go to sleep. Every stitch of money they had acquired came from wiping their feet on the poor. Not a one of those glamor girls knew how to cook or iron a shirt. Even my mother's doctor's white shirt—and he lived in a hundred thousand dollar home out in Fox Chapel—was tattletale gray.

What good was money if you didn't even know how to boil water or get down on your hands and knees and scrub the kitchen floor? If you sent your family out of the house each day looking like *straccioni*? Ragamuffins. Nobody's children. It was a disgrace. *Consunto*—my mother's ultimate indictment. Threadbare, wasted, worn-out. And even more: a kind of piteous, moral and spiritual decrepitude that she had also assigned to those who were *consunto*—that kept her and hers always at least one rung above them in God's eyes.

My mother lumped the Rosechilds in with the rest of them. They were Jews and she had never liked Jews. Christ killers. She changed the noun *Jew* to a verb. *To jew. Old Man Rosehild, Old Lady Rosechild,* as she referred to Sterling's parents. Where did their money come from? Did they have to beat their heads bloody against a wall for every nickel? No. Someone had left it to them. Like all of them got their money. And before that, they stole it from someone. Please. She was tired of their bellyaching over the war. Everyone had suffered. You want to hear about suffering? Macaroni, if you were lucky, every day during the Depression. Breakfast, lunch and supper. What about the Italian people? What they went through with Mussolini? She could tell them about hard times. *Couldn't we, George*? she'd bark at my dad, who would open his eyes long enough to say, *Yes, Sylvia,* then fall back to sleep.

Look at her carrying on with this other kid, my mother would have said about Bill and Sterling, banging like everyone else through the room. *Fluffing you off for that showoff playboy. Right in front of everybody. I wouldn't let her make a fool of me. They're all laughing at you.* And there I was among them, convinced, despite my uncompromising drive to have all they had, that I cared for them no more, less even, than my mother.

I couldn't take my eyes from Sterling, wiggling in her black cashmere sweater, black silky hair slashing the tiny space between her and Bill. Bill with a look on his face like he owned her. Owned me. Owned everything. *Let it go,* I told myself, but when Sterling shot-gunned Bill, took the lit end of a joint into her mouth and exhaled a torrent of smoke into his waiting mouth, like they were kissing, passing fire back and forth, teeth to teeth, I jumped to my feet, my rage great enough to turn that grand house over, to at least stop Bill's black heart.

Sterling saw me stand. My eyes blew two holes into her. Bill studied me too as I strode over to them. *Doo-doo-doo-doo-doo-doot* piped the brass from Stevie's backup. This was where in the song, and on the streets of East Liberty, the offended party threw down on the pretender. What Felix would do. Look at Sterling, then look away, a little eye-fake and jab-step, like a tailback running a counter, then *Boom.* Drop Bill like a piker, and spit on him: *Now, pretty boy?*

I forced myself to smile. A trace of Sterling's lipstick gleamed like a target on Bill's mouth. I swooped in and kissed Sterling on the cheek. Her face was bright with candlelight, a tiny rime of sweat on her upper lip. She smiled back, the crimson of her lipstick exaggerating the moment. Like a detonator. It was more romance than I could stand. My legs clabbered: arrhythmia and vertigo. The lethal jackhammering of my heart. *Doo-doo-doo-doo-doo-doot.* As my hand galvanized into a fist, rising up like a wrecking ball to demolish Bill like a condemned tenement, Jamie hooked my arm and asked me to dance.

Eugene had told me the story of how Felix had once sucker-punched a guy who had cut him off on The Boulevard of the Allies. Felix jumped out at the next light, but the guy quickly zipped his Mercedes window up airtight and locked the car. One button. Then this automatic genius smirked at Felix. The light was turning. Up by the big Isaly's across from McGee Hospital where all the rich women have their kids. Felix popped him through the glass, suckered him right through the window. A quarter inch of glass. Knocked the guy out. Then took a tire iron and beat the shit out of the Mercedes. People in the Isaly's looking out from their booths against the giant windows, eating skyscraper cones like it was television. They all but applauded. Felix busted his hand all to hell, but he didn't care. He parked his car, walked over to the emergency room at McGee, came back to Isaly's two hours later with stitches and a cast, and took home a half gallon of rainbow to Marie.

"He claims he's the only man ever treated at McGee," Eugene had said. "Honest to God, Georgie. He's not the bird to fuck with. I'll tell you what, though. He likes you."

"I never believed that story," Connie had asserted. "Anything that comes out of Felix's mouth is ninety percent exaggeration. Especially if he's talking about himself."

"True story, Babe," Eugene testified.

"Frankly, I think Marie is embarrassed by him."

"What are you talking about? When it comes to street-fighting, Marie makes Felix look like Shirley Temple. She's the homicidal one."

"I just want to say to you, George, that Felix is no example. I love him like a brother, and I'd pull out my eyes for Marie—they're wonderful people, Godparents to the children—but few women would put up with a man like Felix Costa. I certainly wouldn't."

"You put up with me," said Eugene, sliding over on the couch to Connie, and putting his arm around her.

"You're a gentle man who knows how to do a day's work. Felix has never worked a day in his life. And he can be mean. Very mean. I've seen it. Am I right, Eugene?"

"Honey, you're always right."

"Maybe he won't say it," Connie said, gesturing toward her husband. "But I will."

"Georgie knows what the score is, Con."

I only vaguely knew what the score was. I was exhausted from playing away, playing catch-up, and my patience, as well as the clock, was running out. With a sick feeling, I realized I'd been foolish to come to the party. My youth, good looks, intelligence, Brooks Brothers livery and burnished future that charmed the Rosechilds' friends, were nullified at this gathering. This was just another version of *Lord of the Flies.* There was no gentlemanly way to go about things. No codes that adults at the Rosechilds' parties had adopted to get along. Just loud music, booze, reefer, libidos, a bunch of rich friends—all still kids—and me. At least with Dave Mazzotti and the rest of Chookie's thugs I had history. A face and a name. Ancestry. Some gut recognition of blood. They'd walk away from this charade or bust it all to pieces. Or sell it for Heroin.

I danced with Jamie for a while, snapping my fingers, throwing my arms, clapping my hands, caught in the crossfire of brass and bass. I didn't know what I was doing. I felt like a fool, though minded less and less. Then a slow song struck: Stevie's *My Cherie Amore.* I pulled Jamie in to me and, for a few moments, we reeled around the room until colliding with Bill and Sterling. My eyes involuntarily stabbed Bill. Without a word, I let go of Jamie, grabbed Sterling's hand out of Bill's and spun her to me.

She curled a hand around the back of my neck and played with my hair; pressed the other, tucked in mine, against her breast. The music was heady. I was a tad drunk. My face in Sterling's hair, her scent, her fingers gripping my nape, the cashmere give of her breasts against our clenched hands. I closed my eyes and sang to her, like I had sung to Regina, that little working class Italian girl, at the Saint Sebastian's dance, I had deleted from my memory. With Sterling, I didn't care that I was a romantic fool. Perhaps I sang a little too loud, but Sterling seemed to like it. She dropped her cheek to my shoulder and sang with me.

Someone passed a spit-dampened joint to her. She took a hit and offered it to me as we danced.

"No thanks."

"Giorgio?"

"No thanks."

"Take one hit."

"Why?"

"For me."

"I don't believe in it, Sterling. You saw Dave and those guys."

"You think one toke's going to turn you into a junky?"

"I don't know what one toke would do to me."

"Maybe it'll loosen you up." She took another hit and blew it in my face. "C'mon, Giorgio."

"You want me to loosen up?"

"Yeah, I do. Kiss me."

"Right here?"

"Yeah. Right here."

I leaned down and brushed her lips lightly, but she drew me to her, dug her nails into my neck, my hand deeper into her sweater, and kissed me, sucking the life out of me.

Chapter 18

When we leave the hospital, we don't say a word. Crow and I. Scared—surely in shock from Saint Francis's, the scenes with my parents, what the uncontrollable future will bring, the granite weight of sorrow—we're fine with what we aren't talking about. Sunday. Everything still. Mass bells chime across the city. I have five hundred bucks in my pocket, so we grab a cab all the way down Penn Avenue, back to the station to catch the train back to Queen that won't leave for hours. We must traverse five hundred miles, and I have a dollar for each of them. Through the dismal haunted mountains of West Virginia—and its skirmishes of Coffindaffer crosses, trinities of rectitude; and carcasses of deer littering the shoulders—to my hideout in North Carolina.

We wander about, stalling into the Strip District where guys on the docks unload produce from boxcars, and the smell of fried fish and salami is overpowering. The front doors to the taverns hang open. Millwrights, dressed in asbestos, just punched out of the deadman's turn, their day just beginning, sit at the bars nursing boilermakers. The glow of the open hearth still envelopes them, glints off the shot glasses they lift to their lips.

Crow shivers. I put my arm around her. I can't remember when we've eaten last. Then we see Primanti's. A place my dad used to take me, not a joint my mother would venture into. Founded in 1934 to accommodate the shift-work of steelworkers, teamsters and the dockworkers, the restaurant stays open all night. It serves a monstrous legendary sandwich that Joe Primanti invented during the Depression—all the sides, including French fries, between the bread with the meat and cheese.

We walk in and take stools at the long wooden counter beneath a high ceiling from which lit globes dangle from long black chains. Handful of booths. A floor of scuffed discolored tile. The grill, with the menu in plastic letters above it. Coca-Cola sign. Pirates and Steelers memorabilia. A juke box. That's about it. Not another soul in the place—except for a guy at the grill with his back to us. He knows we're here, but he takes a minute before strolling over to us.

He's not much older than me, but ancient, timeless, so Italian he's Estruscan, as if chiseled out of marble, and I want to break into the language I've left so far behind. Endearingly handsome—a movie star—but shadily so like a gangster archangel undercover; and it's apparent, the way it is in some, that he'll keep his mysterious dark good looks all through his long robust life. A gold crucifix around his neck, and the horn to stave off the *malocchio.* Bound to be from lower Oakland—which pegs him for an athlete. Combed back coal black hair, heavy brow and black eyes. Aloof. Perfect teeth and, though he shaved mere hours ago, a blue sheen, like a mirror, sparks off every little bit off his perfectly smooth face. Muscular white gleaming T-shirt, *Steelers,* in black, stamped on it. Like those really are the Steelers on his chest.

He wipes down the counter in front of us and asks "What'll it be?"

Crow starts to cry, then I tear up and put my arm around her as she swivels, back and forth, in a little semi-circle on the stool.

This guy stands there—silent, attentive, unfazed—with a miniature golf pencil poised above a pad as if we are merely indecisive, or even a couple of quirks who just fell apart while trying to figure out what kind of sandwich to order. As if he is there solely for us.

Crow's looking over his head at the menu, tears washing down her cheeks, dropping to the counter. She tries to speak, to order. He nods a few times, but never smiles. Looks at me like he has all the time in the world, then suddenly, without a word, whips up two Iron City beers from behind the counter, twists off the caps and eases them down before us.

We look up at him, and he just nods.

Crow and I grab the Irons and take long swigs.

"You know what you want?"

We look at him, look at the menu and shake our heads—like we'll never know what we want.

"Leave it to me." He turns to the grill.

Crow and I sip the beer. In a few minutes, he deposits in front of us on squares of wax paper giant sandwiches, cut in half. Capicola and provolone, vinegar cole slaw, tomatoes and French fries—all of it between two thick slabs of Italian bread. Plops down two more beers.

Crow laughs. "What is this?" she asks me. She can barely get her hand around the sandwich; it's so thick. French fries spill onto the counter.

We eat the food and drink the beer. The sandwiches are phenomenal, almost as if they're not meant to be eaten. You can't control them. They fall apart, and we rebuild them. We laugh and drink a third beer, slop up the counter as we eat—mopping up every bit of it with our fingers—then sit there and watch what passes for sunlight spread through the big front windows across the counter.

The guy swipes up the soggy wax paper, our empties. He drags his rag across the counter. I pull out the creased bills.

"It's Sunday," he says.

"I know, but what's that mean?" I answer.

"It means I'm not taking any money from you."

Crow, tears again in her eyes, leans across the counter and kisses his cheek.

"God Bless you," he says, holding his hands in front of him. Like the priest proffering his hands to the congregation during Offertory after the Lavabo and saying *Orate Fratres.* Pray, Brethren. Then he smiles wryly and turns back to the grill.

It's late morning, but still a few hours before the train leaves. We walk up toward the Civic Arena and the Church of Saint Benedict the Moor. Its bells toll. People pour into its massive red front doors. Organ music swells over its threshold. A shriveled black guy in a motorized wheelchair buzzes by us. Vagrants slump in doorjambs on the sidewalk. Ambulances screech and hurtle toward Mercy Hospital.

We drift back toward the train station, then keep walking, drop a couple bucks into each panhandler's jar, past the all-night porno shops and massage parlors on Liberty Avenue where call-girls spike by in tiny skirts and garish furs.

Downtown is all but abandoned, smoky with morning, gauzy newspapers blowing like ground fog delicately along the sidewalks, into the street as if someone had stopped reading in the middle of a sentence. Dropped the story right there, then disappeared on a ray into the firmament.

Pittsburgh is self-consciously mythic, over-determined in its symbolism: all these bridges and tunnels, the sage and capricious divagations of the Monongahela and Allegheny spawning against banks of steel the juggernaut Ohio. You don't think about these things if you're born here and you sure as hell don't use language like this. Words are risky, another way to get your ass kicked; though, in East Liberty, where I grew up, on Saint Marie Street, it was custom, a sanctified rite, for people to disparage one another. The parable of the boy whose face froze with his cruel impersonation of the octoroon with Bell's Palsy, or the paralytic who sat gargoyle-like on his porch in a wheelchair because he had dived into the forbidden river and broken his back in the shallows, the half-dozen wanderers with plates in their heads. But there's food on your table, and your kids are healthy. You get down on your knees and thank God.

You never stop talking, as if to stop is giving in to the silence that will eventually outlast you. So you talk. About the way it used to be, the way it's not any more, how you die a little bit every time the price of sugar and coffee go up, how people are standing in line to buy gasoline. You talk about the time Nixon came in to give a speech at the Hilton and they had to bring him in through an underground entrance because the hotel, the entire Golden Triangle, was mobbed with pissed-off steelworkers about to lose everything when the mills shut down. You talk about the Steelers. John Baker's hit on Y.A. Tittle, Maz's 1960 homer, the death of Clemente. You talk about the kid who took the bridge. Before the neighborhood went to hell. You don't know if you'll ever see your mom and dad again and there's a madman with a vendetta against you. People understand what you're trying to say. *Shot and a beer for my friend here.* You just keep talking because mouth and swagger are all you possess to prove you know how to suffer. It's more than pigheadedness; it's pig iron. Immigrant blood.

I hear those voices as if caught in webs across the skyline. Crow smokes cigarettes and gazes up at the sky, the interminable rise of the buildings hemming the streets into grids. Iridescent pigeons scutter at her feet. Big square buses huff over cold cobbled streets, dispensing loners bundled in weathered black and gold Steelers regalia and toting shopping bags. The same old guys with their unlit soggy stogies: Steelers parka, Pirates cap. The insane and homeless, the amputees and Jesus freaks in cruddy cast-off colors: black and gold, the default raiment of The City of Champions. Like apocalyptic troubadours, the only ones left. Steelers banners from the Super Bowl still hang everywhere. Grates in the sidewalk chuff out the steaming breath from whatever beast has been immured forever in the city's underworld.

Crow is the rarest thing on the streets today: a waif in an orange dress and crown of raven hair, toting an antique carpet valise, her skin so frantically pale, her black eyes leaking golden light onto the sidewalk as her head finally drops and she sags against me. Everything about her exaggerated, pixilated, electrified as if she just spilled out of stained-glass.

We stumble into Market Square. Inexplicably the sun shines on it, a beam dead out of God's flashlight, though it is one of those implacable steely grey bitter Pittsburgh Sundays, the holidays and football season over. The winter of hearts. The town I was born and raised in, and love so devotedly like a deranged favorite grandfather from Foggia: the contradictions, the glorious bitter mystery, silence, vendetta, all the tender ablutions, the caprice of love. It doesn't feel like home at all. In hiding, stripped of my name in the city of my birth, I am more than anything lost here too.

A man in buckle-Arctics and a gold Steelers watch cap hoses down the sidewalk in front of Walt Harper's Attic, a jazz joint, then sprinkles it with rock salt. In the air sill hang the last smoky licks of trombone and trumpet, snares still whispering that the vanished night, gone but a few hours, is still young.

First hours of late winter Sabbath. At this moment, spring has agreed to nothing. Ghosts, dropping bits of bread to the pigeons, sit on benches lining the Square. One of them glances up and catches my eye. He wears a hat, but I recognize the mustache, the furious teeth, the blade-glint in his eye that matches the gold chain around his neck, the hairy hand that disappears inside his overcoat as he stands, though he's no longer looking at me.

"Let's go," I say to Crow. "I gotta get out of here." I grab her arm and break into a trot. By chance, I glance at the implacable sky. Far off, on Mount Washington, across the river, Saint Mary's nestles into the cliff face, a place I might find answers to a few things. But I wouldn't be welcome in that house.

By the time we hit Liberty Avenue, it's begun to flurry: a hurried parsimonious snow, frigid, grudging. It will not lay, however, though it is cold enough. Just this much, not nearly enough, but more than you can stand. Winter has the stamina, the color, of steel. The light fades; it was never really here.

Chapter 19

I anchored myself at the three foot end of the Ledges' pool and drank beer. Snow fell out of the frigid sky. Every so often I submerged to my head in the heated water to warm myself. *Go ahead and catch pneumonia,* my mother would chide. *You and your bigshot friends.*

Half-asleep, I watched the others, passing bottles and joints, through the scrim of snow. In a poolside bath house, a mirror scrawled with cocaine sat on a table. They all took their turns, except me. Sterling too. She wore a black bikini, while I flopped around inside a pair of Phil Rosechild's flowery trunks that Sterling had packed for me. Just in case, she had said. She hadn't really thought we'd swim. I pondered that: whether or not she had deliberately not told me because I don't know how to swim and might have balked at the party.

It didn't matter. I was content to simply wait it out. Sterling stayed close to me. We kissed. She called me *angel.* But she grew increasingly sloppy. She was merely having a good time with her friends. Why should I care?

The others called me *Giorgio,* even Bill, who had kidded me about Phil's trunks. *Paisano,* Bill called me. "*Como esta, Paesano?*" Bill asked every so often after butterflying the length of the pool, throwing a geyser all over me and Sterling when he surfaced. I merely smiled. The soothing tepid water, the beer, the snow heaping out of the cold black night, Sterling wrapped wetly around me. Refusing to be perturbed, I made the face of contentment, even when she left the water to hit the bathhouse for another jolt.

A naked girl stood poised, statuesque, on the diving board, the snow driving down behind her in the spotlights. She hoisted her arms above her head and held them there, palms together, then plunged headfirst into the water. Sterling traipsed out of the bathhouse. Snow glanced off her as she walked barefoot through the tiny drifts building around the pool. Steam roiled along the surface. She jumped in and kissed me. Several of the others had shed their bathing suits. Some danced. I could barely make out the faces.

Dave, Alex and I used to ride our bikes along Allegheny River Boulevard where a concrete slab from an old barge lock shelved over the water. We'd strip on the bank, climb the wall and jump off it naked, except for shoes, into the mint green brackish water, one-eyed carp big as footballs muscling by us as we sluiced into the sludge bottom. I feared treading on the face of a drowned millwright who would quicken and pull me under. Dave, Alex and I—none of us could swim. The warm water reeked of sulphur. Slag piles loomed on the banks. Rust. Sewage.

Yet across the river preened marinas strung with pleasure boats. Occasionally, the Gateway Clipper, painted red, white and blue, like a Dixie showboat, paddled by, its giant waterwheel throwing up goblets of water into the sun, the entire river held in its silver wake. The glorious passengers dining on deck never noticed us, but once a trio of girls gazing out over the rail spotted us, and lifted their middle fingers. Beautiful girls with long blond hair out on the river.

One day we spied on a man and woman trussed together in the backseat of a canary-yellow Galaxy junked into the riverbank. The front end was buried in muck, scurvy water eddying at the windshield. The guy was wedged on top of the woman, flailing away, yanking her bra off. She had bright yellow hair and black horned-rimmed glasses she kept adjusting on her brow every time the guy rammed her, the car shimmying and squishing in and out of the sump. We chunked rocks at the Galaxy, and the man tottered out—his trousers ballooned around his knees—and chased us. The woman swung her legs, like two lumpy columns of buttermilk, out of the car, and crossed her arms over her stupendous breasts. Clutching our clothes, we pedaled nude for a mile down the boulevard before realizing the man had given up.

That was the last thing I really remember doing with Dave and Alex. They had already been fooling around with drugs. By the next summer Dave had dropped out of Peabody and Alex was holed up in his attic painting terrifying, beautiful nightmarish scapes that nobody understood. What he called *The Life of the World to Come.* Two years later he was dead, and Dave a career junky. I was a freshman at Duquesne.

Cannibals. The word popped into my mind. Sterling's friends out there naked in the snow and smoke, devouring the entire world. Like those beauties on the Gateway Clipper holding up their fingers in fixed tallies of exactly what I and my friends were worth.

Though I couldn't have borne to have anyone see her, I nevertheless said to Sterling, "You can take your clothes off if you'd like."

"I know I can, but I'd prefer not to." She kissed me deeply.

I closed my eyes and felt engulfing me the green sticky deadly Allegheny. I squeezed Sterling until she cried out. I wanted desperately to be alone with her, to be sober, very sober. For her to listen carefully to every word I had to say about the way things were going to be forever with us.

Suddenly Bill, without a stitch, breached from beneath the water Sterling and I huddled in, huffed out two lungs of smoke, and planted himself like Atlas before us, the entire pool cascading off him in silver bullets.

"What are you doing with your clothes still on?" he asked.

Neither of us answered. Bill towered in the white smoky light. His smile frozen. The tips of his hair frosted. Tiny icicles dangled from his eyelashes. I couldn't take my eyes off him–so beautiful, so impervious.

"At least topless, Ster. It's been a while. How about you, *Paesano?* Let's see what a real hot-blooded *pene* looks like."

I assured myself that I hadn't been bothered by Bill's cracks. Everyone was wasted. Bill was merely an apparition, gaping out of the water. I had never been a fighter. No Felix. No Dave Mazzotti or Alex Caprio. Eugene always declared violence a chump's game. He knew guys on the avenue that would never stop. You had to kill them.

"If you're not prepared to kill a guy, then book. You'd have to kill Felix."

"Felix is an animal," Connie would say.

"That's what makes him invincible. Honor's another chump's game. I'll tell you what honor is, Cuz. Nine to five, and a little moonlighting. Wife and kids. Supper at the same table every night."

Connie nodded. "You listen to Eugene, Georgie. You're not like the rest of those losers."

Men of real substance smiled and walked away, made their peace over time, deliberately and with impunity. Snow mantled Bill's shoulders. He stood before us as if awaiting an answer to his inquiries. People flopped out of the pool, wrapped themselves in blankets and staggered toward the house.

I decided I liked Bill. I laughed, and held out my hand as if he and I had just concluded a business deal. Bill extended his hand toward mine. His smile faded and was replaced with empathy, sympathy, the kind of doleful recognition of God's mercy chiseled into the faces of plaster saints.

It made Bill look kind, and even wise, like doctors and lawyers, priests and shrinks. He became in turn an instrument of that mercy. It was as if Bill was whispering, *It's okay. I understand. Poor Giorgio.* Absolving me of my inferiority. The kind of man my parents would be at the mercy of when my father developed asbestosis from all his flame-proof years at the mill, or when my mother tripped in Sears and broke a hip or was simply too sad to scrape herself out of bed in the morning, when all day long they sat on their thirty-one year old slip-covered wedding furniture dozing and watching TV until at the very end they had to call the parish house for the final handout: the Last Rites.

Above all Bill looked relieved. He had been right all along about me. With this hierarchy established, we could now be friends. His hand still waited to grip mine. Sterling had not uttered a word. She sounded like she was crying, but it was the cold forcing her shivers. I laughed again. *Pene.* There was an Italian word with which I was familiar. I could barely speak a word of the old country, but like any good East Liberty boy I had mastered its profanity: *shit* and *piss* and *fuck* and *ass.* That's what I knew.

I punched Bill full in the face, then my hand metamorphosed into a knife and then a hammer in turns. I chopped and pounded at Bill, slashing mostly water, but catching Bill who foundered back, bleeding from his nose. Sterling shrieked. A few guys still in the water hurried over to help. Bill tried to swim off, but I collared him, clamped his ears and clubbed his head against the side of the pool.

I stabbed repeatedly, knifing Bill, but also my fist repeatedly against the concrete. I grabbed Bill's long hair and forced his head underwater with one hand—I felt Bill's fear, felt him breaking apart in my hand—while punching with the other until Bill's friends—Sterling screaming, "Stop, George, please stop," and crying—finally pulled me off.

Bill gouted up out of pool, blowing water, sucking air, coughing and weeping. "You're crazy," he screamed as I shook off the others and backed away. "You tried to kill me. You're a fucking maniac." Blood from his nose trickled into his mouth. His lips and around his eyes gleamed green in the misty light, the gnarl of snow.

"What kind of an animal are you?" Jamie shouted. "Get out of here. Go back where you came from."

For a moment, jubilant, I saw myself transformed. A tough guy, after all, and Bill had had it coming. *Paesano.* The living bloody hell with all of them. I'd fight each one. But when I glanced into their faces and saw not awe, but disgust, I knew what I was and what I had done.

"I'm sorry," I said. "I'm so sorry."

"Fuck you," Bill said. "Get out of here. Just get the fuck out of here."

The rest of them too. They told me to get out, go home, cross the river and get back to my cave. Fucking animal. They huddled off toward the house—Jamie with both arms around Bill—casting back looks in my direction.

Just Sterling and I standing in the pool, a blizzard muting everything. Suddenly ferociously cold, I was fatigued beyond death.

"Sterling," I said. I turned and barely recognized her. So small, neurasthenic, covered in goose flesh. Her hair hung dank like kelp; the blades of her hipbones shot out above her suit bottom. She looked used, complicit, like one of those East Liberty thug-broads after too many years wived to a foul-tempered three-time loser. Our Lady of Sorrowful Pimps, iconographic and cheap at once, her face greenish and misshapen like Bill's—as if she'd just been worked over too.

"Come on," she whimpered, taking my hand, leading me out of the pool, and across the yard where we mounted a side flight of steps to the carriage house apartment.

She wrangled me into the shower and bathed me. When she removed her bathing suit to shower herself, I closed my eyes and leaned against the shower wall. My right hand, swollen and blue, bled at the knuckles. She kissed it, toweled me off, bandaged me, then disappeared into the next room. I sat on the toilet in a towel and gazed at the palm of my hand. Yeasty, still leavening, its lifeline had disappeared. I listened to her beyond the wall: the hair dryer, the clatter of jewelry, the shimmy of cloth sliding over flesh, struck matches. I got to my feet, stumbled into the wall, rocking toiletries off the shelf.

"George," Sterling called.

I walked into the room. The candle flames, on either side of the bed, lapped at their wicks, spraying the ceiling with twin balls of light.

"Giorgio," Sterling whispered from beneath the comforts, her arms and shoulders, the tops of her breasts, uncovered. She had shed that stringy lank switchblade look and now bore the immovable lacquered beauty of a sarcophagus. More makeup than I remembered: eye shadow, powder, the lipstick looked black, but it was just the deceit of candlelight. Earrings. In her long brushed hair, white flowers. Gardenias. Garish strong. Maybe it was perfume.

Or maybe I was sniffing aftermath. She must have been out of her mind, this snowy night having folded her up inside itself, and she did not care one little bit now about holding back. She didn't care at all, and this not caring—this painted spirit in the bed—nearly brought me up sober. She could match me extreme for extreme, threshold for threshold. She held the secret. To the better life. But like her, I was too gone to be sober, so when she threw aside the covers and beckoned with her flat palm on the white sheet, enough that I saw down to where she cleft, I whispered a prayer and fell in beside her.

I had never even seen, much less been in, a waterbed. At first I felt like I was being swallowed, the movement of it too much like drowning. I thrashed and treaded, my head going under like in the foul Allegheny where the muck dropped off and I'd plunge a fathom, green water trickling into my mouth.

I had never really been with a woman. Never really. Sterling helped me with everything: the space where her neck joined her shoulders, her shoulders, under her arms, her forearms, above her navel, the hinges of each thigh, her calves, behind her knees, her feet. She insisted I look into her eyes the entire time. Made sure I saw everything: the long warm mitering of our bodies, the altar of water we spread ourselves upon.

I memorized her, that downward spiraling dive, the warm water of her body, fathom after fathom, and then I forgot. The last thing I remembered was her shivering, the locket I had given her bouncing off her sternum. Weeping perhaps.

During the night I started up in dream—drowning with Dave and Alex, mammoth carp gnawing on us—and the suddenness made me sick. Only when I tripped back from the bathroom did I realize Sterling was gone. My hand throbbed. I was naked, freezing, no idea where my clothes were.

When I woke the next morning, Sterling sat across the room wrapped in an afghan, filing her nails. Shot through with dazzling morning light—the sun shone outside and the snow refracted each prismatic bead of it—she was impossible to look at. There was hot tea, juice and toast. But I couldn't eat. Shame bloated me with nausea. My hand hurt terribly. Blood had prized through the gauze dressing. I was too sick to shower. Sterling said she'd help me, she'd like to. She called me *sweetheart.* I felt mindlessly cruel. I didn't need help. I took my clothes from her and slipped on my pants. I willed her to look away and she did.

"I'm sorry I'm being so snappy."

"It's okay," she said. "Look at your poor hand."

"I'm sorry."

"It's okay. I'm worried about that hand."

Right after waking, she had called Phil and JoAnn and told them we hadn't wanted to risk driving home the night before in such treacherous weather. She had asked them to call my parents so they wouldn't worry any more than they had already.

"My mother'll be like a maniac," I said.

"She'll think the very worst of me."

"No, she won't," I lied. "She'll just be pissed at me."

I looked for Bill to apologize, but he was gone. Sterling said it didn't matter. They had all gone too far. The whole thing had been a bad idea. What whole thing? I wondered. Sterling was sorry too. She drove—two hands on the wheel, pumped the brakes, used her turn signals, tuned the radio to classical music—through the country, into the suburbs, into the city and to the emergency room at Pittsburgh Hospital in East Liberty where I had been born.

Two broken knuckles. No stitches. Not even a cast. Just gauze, an ace bandage and a heavy whorl of adhesive. Sterling hovered over me for the three hours we spent at the hospital, filled out my paperwork—it was my right hand—helped me fabricate my story to the doctor and nurses: I had smashed my hand against the swimming pool wall while playing volleyball. She was cheerful, capable and faithful. I glimpsed the stellar, pious wife she would be. Every secret safe with her, a queen-like capacity for silent noble suffering. A bank of fortitude to rival the Blessed Mother. She would forgive her husband everything and triumphantly outlive him. Inexplicably, I felt myself resenting her. More than anything because we had finally made love, and it lay now not before, but behind, us. Love I was already fighting so hard to recollect and much much too ashamed of myself to talk about.

Chapter 20

Only after I run several blocks do I realize that Crow is no longer with me, that I've somehow left her behind. In front of one of the porno joints on Liberty, I gaze back in the direction I've come. There are a few stragglers ambling through the murky flurries, but no sign of Crow in her big black coat and black beret. A couple of skin freaks bust out the blacked-out door of one of the porno stores: sad and furtive, oozing shame. God's confused prodigals. Sunday and they have no place to worship, but a syphilitic glory hole. You can read it on their faces, mimeographed like varicose veins, that they know they'll burn for whatever they've seen, whatever they've done, so mortified by their lust for an imagined perfection of flesh, that they cannot even confess.

"Crow," I yell, then gallop back the way I've come, yelling her name over and over. The city cries back at me in a hollow steel voice, hemming me in with its impervious verticality. Real crows swoop from a thousand stories up, calling along with me for my disappeared girl. Their cries lift up and are swallowed by the whipping wind. Wearing only a thrift windbreaker, I am suddenly frozen.

"Crow," I scream as loudly as I can, and stop running. She is gone and there, on the Sabbath, in my home town, the place of my nativity, I am impossibly lost.

"Crow," I scream again. Then the idea of the river and its myriad bridges flashes into my head—as if the last act of mercy God might grace me with. For some reason, it seems important that I not cry, that I grant myself the last dignity a stupid man consoles himself with: that he did not cry or cry out at the moment of his comeuppance.

I turn down Sixth Street. In the distance looms the massive burnished bright yellow suspension of the Sixth Street Bridge: cables and girders, its splendid collusion with passage and eternity. I walk along Sixth, past the theatres and restaurants, past Heinz Hall, where I once, lifetimes ago, squired Sterling to the ballet. At the end of Sixth, I cross the street and mount the bridge deck, begin walking toward its jutting belly shrouded in fog and flurry, its apex invisible, its parapets seductive. Three hundred feet below, the Allegheny whispers beneath coal barges and tugs headed upriver from West Virginia. When I get to the bridge's exact middle, I see someone standing at the rail. A kid with hair past his shoulders.

"Alex," I say.

He turns, but of course it's not Alex. He wears a Steelers parka two sizes too big. He can't be more than ten. "Fuck you," he says, then sprints past me in the direction I came. I walk to the rail and look out over the river, scarves of fog deviling its surface, jets from the humming black barges fanning out behind them, lapping against the bulkheads, and over the wharf. I attempt to reckon the future through the sheet-iron face of the river, but it remains impassive, protective of the angels singing the Kyrie on its floor.

I walk back up Sixth toward Liberty, no idea what I'll do. "Crow," I say, but only so I can hear. People suddenly throng the streets. In fine clothes, what my father calls *glad rags.* Church has concluded. These blessed, unlike me, have destinations.

I see Crow, huddled on a bench, her feet propped on the valise, for all the world looking like a crow in her black raiment, black hair, though the milkiness of her face in the snow gives her away. She is crying and feeding bits of bread to the pigeons congregated at her feet.

She throws her arms around me and kisses me. "I thought I lost you. I was scared to death. In this place. This big awful place crawling with barbaric Yankees." She smiles.

I hold her against me, so slight she'll be ripped away by the wind whipping among the skyscrapers.

"C'mon." I grab the valise, take her hand and race toward a cab stand.

"What are you doing? We'll miss our train."

"1410 Saint Marie," I bark at the cabbie, push Crow in ahead of me, then scoot into the back beside her.

"Where are we going?" Crow whispers.

I slide my bad hand symbolically a few inches left to right—to say that I must at this moment observe silence. Crow, almost in my lap, holds my other hand in both of hers. I peer into the cabbie's eyes through the rearview as he eyes me suspiciously, as if there's something about me that seems familiar.

"You from East Liberty?" he asks.

"No," I say.

"The address you gave me. I'm from East Liberty."

"No, man, I'm just visiting."

He's checking me out in the rearview. Like he knows I'm bullshitting. Crow and I look like fugitives. Her hundred pounds of quivering alabaster in that mountain of a coat. The red lipstick. The beret. Then me: whatever I am. A matted hoary prophet-gone-wrong. I've aged twenty years since crossing the Fort Pitt tunnels all those months ago. Crow looks like she's eleven.

"I grew up on Shetland Avenue," says the cabbie.

He's still looking at me in the mirror. I say nothing, look out the window as we come up to the light at Penn and Highland, the crosshairs of East Liberty. The steeples of Saints Peter and Paul zoom above the skyline, the crosses at their tips invisible in the low-slung stony clouds. I want this guy to drop it, to shut his mouth and make it through the light.

"How long since you been back?"

"Look, man, I'm just visiting. That's it. The total story."

The light turns red and we're snared right there out in the open, next to a crowded bus island, columns of slouched Italians and blacks hurrying through the crosswalk to catch the light. Among them is Felix. I can nearly feel him, and it's all I can do to not barge out of the cab and run. Crow, reading my mind, squeezes my hand.

The light changes. The cabbie idles through the intersection and up Highland. The sidewalks are jammed with people. Beat cops amble along, walking German Shepherds. My hand is over my face. I want to throw myself to the floorboard.

"What's your name—if you don't mind me asking?" asks the cabbie.

"Listen. Just drop us off here."

"This isn't Saint Marie."

"No, I know. This is cool. Here's fine."

"Hey, man, I meant no offense. You just look familiar." He's studying me in the mirror. "I'll take you where you need to go."

I throw open my door.

"What are you doing?" he yells.

"Romeo," shrieks Crow.

"Stop your fucking cab, asshole," I shout, half out the door.

He slams on the brakes. I throw two twenties over the seat and drag Crow out of the car.

"You're the asshole," screams the cabbie, then screeches off.

We stand directly in front of The Pittsburgh Theological Seminary. Across the street is Peabody High School, and Peabody Field where as a kid I spent my days playing baseball. My parents both went to Peabody.

"Jesus Christ, Romeo. What was that all about?" Crow demands.

"I was just getting nervous. I felt too exposed."

"So you thought jumping out of a moving car would be less conspicuous?"

"Hey, Crow."

"Hey what?" Hands on her hips, ready to throw down.

"And don't call me by name, any name, no name," I bark. "No name. Okay?"

"Okay, I'm sorry. It just startled me a little that you were jumping out of a moving car. I just feel a little fucking startled, period, Mr. Fucking X. Is that so hard for you to understand?" She starts to cry. "I don't even know where I am or why I'm here. I don't even know who you are. I want to go home." She plops down on the curb.

People going by in cars stare at us. A police car angles our way after making the turn at East Liberty Boulevard, what used to be Hoeveler Street before the mayor and his cronies destroyed the neighborhood with their doomed scheme for urban renewal. I can't remember the way things used to be. The shawl of amnesia is settling over me—like the snow suddenly beginning to pelt down. Like Crow, I don't know where I am or why I'm here. Nor am I sure who I am either. But the cops bearing down on me are another story.

"Get up," I snarl at Crow. "Right now. The Cops."

She jumps up. I pull her to me, bend her back theatrically, and kiss her deeply and passionately, interminably—just as the cop car cruises by. I squint open an eye. Both cops look, but they're smiling.

"Okay," I say when I release Crow and the taillights of the squad car are in the distance. "I'm sorry. Really really sorry."

"Nice kiss, Romeo. Just keep me in the fucking loop. Please."

I take her hand and hurry her through the seminary's enormous wrought iron gates just as its bells chime. The tower is nearly invisible for the snow, but I make out the clock's Roman numerals: one o'clock. Still plenty of time to make the train. We veer off the flagstone walkway path and cut over the lawn, where I played football as a kid; through the apple trees, where we stole apples, the withered fruit at our feet flaked with snow; then across a side yard, squeeze through the skinny opening of another set of iron gates chained and padlocked. We're on Saint Marie, a little above Sheridan Avenue, two and half blocks from my house.

At the corner of Saint Marie and Sheridan crouches Chookie's Store, observing the Sabbath by closing down for the day, its entire façade barred and battened with rusted armored gates. From inside the door comes choked snarling. Tacked to the steel front door, a warning on cardboard states in crude dripping letters: *Attack Dog Inside Waiting to Kill You.* The sign across the storefront had lost one of the Os in *Chookie's.* In its place a hubcap with the Shroud of Turin painted on it had been nailed. Littering the curb and sidewalk are the hoods, the junkies, the fallen angels—whatever they might be. They are walking, but often barely, case-study cautionary tales about how—should you disobey God, the president, especially your mother and father—you can fuck up your life. Chookie's Corner, like a Station of the Cross (*Jesus Falls the Third Time*), is foreboding: where everything goes to hell for East Liberty boys. To my parents, it was the literal lair of Beelzebub, mysteriously laced with Satanic properties that weighted good boys down with anathema, where they learned to cut throats to cop the poison they punctured their veins with.

I was forbidden to so much as walk the same side of the street as Chookie's. But we lived but a few blocks down Saint Marie from it, and I knew all those kids. We had attended Saints Peter and Paul together, queued at the church altar rail for the sacraments. I played Little League with them. Their parents had stood sweating next to mine over boiling grease at the church fish fries every Friday, worked chuck-a-luck and ski-ball at the church bazaars, festooned their kids with scapulars, and rosaries, holy cards, and ashes, fed them pasta every Sunday, herded them to the cemetery at the Proper of the Seasons. Had them vaccinated and inoculated and loved them as they did the Christ Child. Alex Caprio and Dave Mazzotti. Plenty of others. Most of them dead or in jail or on the lam like me. Except for Dave, now the scarred acolyte of redemption. The last time I was on this corner I had been packing enough pharmaceuticals to waste the entire neighborhood and fetch me some serious federal time.

What had gone wrong? And when? What had turned bad in me? All those years, I never fell prey to the corner. I kept my nose clean, made all the right moves: college, Brooks Brothers shirts, admission to Georgetown and Yale Law. I had even crossed over—out of the neighborhood to rub elbows in the elite precincts of Highland Park, Shadyside, Squirrel Hill. I mixed with the wealthy. I spoke their language. I seduced their girls. I was the neighborhood Messiah.

But I never really was, but rather the scapegoat of my own self-mythologizing. Too good to labor on the open hearth like my father, or lay brick and cut stones like my uncles, I sold my soul for easy money, then thieved and ran away, disgraced my mother and father and broke their hearts. As if someone had put the eyes on me, the *malochio.* If only it had been something as romantic as a curse or black magic. All along it was my dark blood that sabotaged me, some twisted recessive gene that crawled out of the ancestral sump and lodged in my heart. Is crime any better than junk? I had been protected, and now I am no longer. I ache for that protection to be restored, but I don't know if protection is God or a gun.

Now, contemplating crossing a few feet in front of those villains, especially with Crow, I wish I had a gun. Dangerous, vicious Smack freaks, their souls already hanging on the side of Satan's smokehouse—just like those snake heads back in Saint Joan's County—they'll make a move on us guaranteed. They're already checking us out as we walk toward them.

"Dammit," I say to myself.

"What?" asks Crow. She's got hold of my bad hand.

"These boys down here. Rough crew. Junkies. Watch your step."

"Have you looked at yourself lately? Have you looked at me? Shit, Romeo, we look like we just tunneled out of the psych ward. I'm not afraid of them."

"Yeah, well I am. Hang on to your purse. You want me to take it?"

"Uh-uh. It'll spoil your image."

Crow understands every bit of it. She carved the epic poem about it on her brow. There is nothing about suffering that she doesn't understand. She leads me through them with dignity and witness. They stare openly as we approach, about them little clouds of cigarette smoke like vapor from the souls of un-baptized babies. Two of them, sitting in the gutter passing a bottle, get to their feet and stand as we cross Sheridan. As I put my boot on Chookie's curb, I remove my lethal hand from Crow's, ready for whatever hell is about to break loose.

Up close, they're just babies, the next generation of addicts, apprenticing at self-immolation, bundled into their cruddy shaggy coats and the first tufts of hair to sprout from their faces. Cigarettes in their lips, butts all over the sidewalk. The wind howls. They shiver, not leering at all, but like mendicants struck dumb at our passage. A great tenderness overtakes me for these children, marooned, as they are here, in expiation of my sins and Crow's—for everyone's, as I see it. Here in the snow storm, so ravenous for love, they suffer for all of us, spooning dope into their souls. How could I have not seen the pity of it before? These *stracchiones,* these poor little ravaged priests. Their crazy hats, their cigarettes. Their outlandish copulation. They've even read a few books and it hasn't helped: Kerouac, Rimbaud, Tolkien. Brilliant, they still want Heroin, so steadfast in their toil—like lilies of the field.

They look at me as if I am Isaiah, my minotaur head, my stricken hand I lift to them as they ripple toward us, widening as does water around a broken surface on the river, in awe. Of course, it's the junk, the shattered glass they walk upon, their parents wondering if they'll ever come home. They crowd against Crow and me, as if we are wholly remarkable. Up close, they appear even younger, some of them not more than ten or eleven. They hold out their hands—to touch our coats. Crow removes her gloves and grasps their hands. They reach toward her face and hair. Their eyes big as grapes and zombie black, impenetrable, as if they've already crossed over, yet there is that pinprick votive flicker in them, the pilot of their souls still running on its last few volts. Crow, like a saint in a leper colony, touches their wild hair and sooty faces.

They've got me hemmed against a wall of Chookie's, rubbing their hands all over me. Some of them are girls—denatured, hirsute, yet made up in the eyes and mouth like junked kewpies.

"Okay," I say. "That's enough."

Crow yells: "Romeo."

One of them grabs Crow's beret, and runs off; then two try to strip her of her coat, another running his hands across her chest, down her torso, grappling with the belt on her dress. She flails at them, cracking one squarely in the face with her fist, but then another wrangles at her purse.

"Get away from her," I scream. But they keep swarming, and I can't unpin myself, fingers running inside my jacket, beneath my shirt. Two girls fall to their knees and wrap around my legs. Crow is being dragged off. The front of her dress is slashed. There's blood sprouting across her bodice. They're biting her. With my good hand, I swing the valise at those still coming at me, and with my bad club the biggest boy in front of me across the head. I grab one of the girls on my legs by her tangled hair and lift her literally off the ground by it, whip her over the concrete, into another waif, who comes on as though possessed, head shaved to the nub and polished with rime, a lone blond brow across his eyes.

I make my way to Crow, dragging with me the girl fixed to my other leg, trying to chew through my pants. Crow won't let go of the purse. She's punching kids in the face. Three of them drag her by the legs around the corner, skidding her over the icy sidewalk into Andy Costanzo's boarded up barber shop. She's screaming for me, trying to sit up as she's dragged, kicking, still fighting to hang onto her purse, but beginning to lapse into narcosis—whatever had been stamped into her that night in Sprague's Field, whatever it was about Saint Joan's County and her family. The goddam secrets, the lies—what leads kids toward the vocation of junk and suicide—all inextricably wrought up in my own lore.

Crow is spirited away from me, out of my life, through the portals of Costanzo's where I got my first hair cut, and I don't even think to bash the kid eating my leg. I just yell *No* again and again because *No* is the synonym for every ugly thing since Genesis I wish eradicated. *Basta!* My God, they have my girl. Have kicked in Costanzo's door. As I turn the corner, her head flops over the moldered threshold. I reach for faces and eyes. I swing the valise. I fling my leg with the girl on it against the graffiti-splattered brick soldier mitering the corner of Chookie's: *Too much pretty boy, not enough gritty boy.* She slides off into grimy slush pooling at the drainpipe. I slip to one knee in the runoff. A kid barring my way into Costanzo's pulls a switchblade with a jade handle. A snowflake lands on the pearl button. The blade appears with a remorseless snick—an icy hypodermic. I catch a glimpse of Crow being dragged across Costanzo's floor by her purse straps. I kick at the kid. Under his nose crawls a dirty black mustache, his cheeks and forehead pocked orange with acne. He stirs the air in front of him with the blade. "Come on," he says, not giving an inch.

Somebody jumps me piggy-back, forces a finger into my eye, digs his nails into my windpipe. The switchblade lunges. I pivot 180. The kid on my back screams. Tiny bones crack. Then he and the switchblade, sudden intimates, crash to the pavement. I pop the kid, divested of his blade, twice in the face with my bad hand. His nose rumples, then gushes blood. When he brings both hands to it, I cuff him in the same place again, bash him with the valise, then trample him as I lurch into the barber shop.

It's the way I remember it. Three maroon upholstered gothic chairs, tissue gummed to the headrests, long prosthetic levers next to the footrests to crank and swivel the chairs, slick razor strops hanging to the floor. The twenty foot scrolled tin ceiling with its dangling rattan fans. The row of chairs facing a coffee table strewn with vintage copies of *Sports Illustrated, Boys' Life, Playboy.* The elevated shine stand, up on its altar, where Junior, the silent black barber shined shoes too and scraped you down with a whisk broom after you slid out of the barber's chair. His wooden box of polish and brushes, his pink chamois buffing rag at the foot of the chair where he crouched.

The shelves: once lined with electric clippers that had so scared me as a kid, before my feet reached the footrest, when Andy had to anchor the booster for me in the chair lap so I wouldn't leak out of it while my hair was being cut—back when my dad, Big George, stood next to me holding my hand while Andy hit the switch and the buzzing clippers threshed my scalp. Scissors and combs, jars of pomade, the white incubator where the towels were steamed, the shaving cream dispenser.

I half expect Andy, eating a fried pepper sandwich, to hobble through the curtain out of the back where he's been writing numbers in the bathroom, and ask me if I want a *Regular Boy's,* or kid me about the Princeton I graduated to once I learned about girls and wanted sideburns, the hot shaving cream puttied around my ears, his straight razor at my neck.

But here also, in this mausoleum, abides the sepulchral dust and despair of forgetfulness. Clots of my ancestors' ancient hair drift across the yellowed checkerboard linoleum. I see myself in the mammoth mirror: one entire wall fronting the barber chairs. There is the little boy at the rite of his first shearing, a hand hidden in his father's battered millwright's hand, in his other a package of Bazooka Andy's just handed him. There are no photographs, no journal entries. There is only *time was,* and what remains is *time was* and everyone forgets and it no longer matters when *time was.* Except for the living and their blurred dear versions of what might have happened. But there remains that little boy, now nullified by the man he mysteriously became who stands beside him: hulking in his scurvy salvaged clothes, dark and filthy, bleeding from his eyes and nose, his head a Levitical bust of long matted mane and beard, gray as mortar. Someone I don't know, whom I can't remember.

All this in the interstice between barging into Costanzo's and seeing Crow on the floor writhing in the grip of two boys, the front of her dress ripped open. Not blood on her breast at all, but the red primroses stitched across her camisole. One of the boys is at her head, punching her face, yet still she clings to the purse. I hurl the valise at him, then grab Junior's shine kit and bust him across the temple. He lets go of the purse and goes over like a tackling dummy. Crow reaches into it and pulls out her pistol, aims it into the face of the other boy. He scrambles away from her, his back to the cabinet along the floor—a beast, his hands before him, mewling and pleading like a baby child.

"You piece of trash," chokes Crow, nearly hyperventilating with her own tears. "You sorry piece of trash. Don't you dare cry while I'm crying. Don't you even dare try to suffer while I'm suffering."

"Crow," I say. "Baby."

"Please," croaks the boy. He swipes off his hat, revealing a miraculous head of curls.

"How old are you?" Crow demands, now on her feet, convulsing, barely choking out the syllables, her finger trembling on the trigger, a shoe gone, her dress near shredded, one of her bra straps severed and dangling.

"I don't know."

"Goddam, boy, you're old enough to explain to the devil how you landed in hell. Or maybe your mama can explain."

She cocks the pistol. When she puts the gun to his head, I scream *No,* and I'm not sure if it's that or the police sirens that get her to lower and uncock the pistol.

She turns to me. It's as if there is less of her every moment, as if her source is dimming, that she will simply deliquesce. "I just have just one more thing to do," she says, hovering over the beautiful boy, his tears streaming silently over his innocent face. She raises the gun, stuffs it in her purse, then bends and kisses his forehead. "Bless your heart," she says. Then to me: "Where's my fucking beret?"

I grab the valise, tug her out of Costanzo's, turn the corner onto Saint Marie. A few of the neighbors peek out through cracks in their doors. The street is dark. All the streetlights have been smashed. It's snowing hard. I can't tell where the cop cars are. We run down Saint Marie, cross Collins, up which a paddy wagon hurtles, lights and siren. When we get within fifty feet of my house, I see the ghostly interminable hulk of the Meadow Street Bridge, the bridge Alex flew off of. Across it, from the wasteland of Larimer Avenue, storm two police cars, mad hazards churning in the blowing snow.

I cut down Moga, Crow soughing, weeping, trying to keep up with just one shoe. A quick left and we are in the alley behind my house, the grotto with the Blessed Mother in her dry alcove, her hands extended to welcome us. The cops blow by Moga. Whirling lights strobe the bricks of Dilworth School where I attended kindergarten. The backboards have been torn from the wall in the schoolyard.

I lift the latch of the little gate and we walk the brick path my father laid through our tiny yard, the clothesline still up, my dad's garden patch fallow, the fig tree bent and interred to hibernate until Easter Sunday. The sirens double in volume, the various vehicles bearing down on Chookie's. Beneath the porch where my dad keeps the lawn mower and hedge clippers is a jelly jar with a key to the back door.

Chapter 21

My mom and dad were asleep in front of the noon news when I walked into the house.

My mother woke, saw my bandaged hand, shrieked, "Oh, my God," and started to cry. "What did you do?" she asked tearily.

"Just broke a couple knuckles. It's fine. I've been to the hospital."

My dad seemed only half awake. He gaped at me, then at my mother, until his eyes lit back to the TV. The newswoman reported an off-duty policeman had been shot in a drive-by on Paulson Avenue—not far at all from our house.

"See!" my mother exclaimed as if the shooting and my hand were connected. "You see the way crazy things happen?"

My father rubbed a hand across his face and licked his lips, then as if hearing gunfire bolted up straight in his chair.

"Old man Rosechild didn't tell me a thing about your hand when he called," said my mother. "Why would he keep something like that from me?"

"Mom, he didn't know about it."

"What about your girlfriend?" The way she said *girlfriend.*

"What about her?"

"Where's she? Here you are with broken bones and she couldn't walk up the steps with you?"

"I don't have broken bones. Actually, she insisted on coming in. She wanted to visit for a few minutes. I made her go home because I knew you'd be like this."

"Like what? Concerned? Worried? Half crazy after staying up all night wondering whether you were alive or dead?"

My father, still licking his lips and swallowing, harbored a look of utter incredulity.

My mother turned to him: "George, what the hell is the matter with you?"

"Nothing," he said, his speech slightly gummy. "My mouth is dry."

"Get a cough drop or something. Do you see your son's hand? Wake up."

"How'd you get hurt?" my dad asked.

I fed them the volleyball story.

"I don't believe it," my mother asserted.

"What do you mean you don't believe it?"

"I mean you've been telling one lie after another lately. Just like those cookies."

"You still harping about that?"

"You're up to something. All night long me and your father sat here in these chairs thinking you were laying in a ditch somewhere. Not a wink of sleep. The things that went through my mind. I wanted to kill myself. Your father. He won't say it. He thinks everything you do is cute. But I want to tell you: I had more respect than this for my mother and father. You took a knife and twisted it in my heart last night."

The slain policeman had left behind a wife and two small children. The widow was being interviewed. She just couldn't believe it. It just hadn't sunk in yet. She figured she was in shock. Her hair was shorter than a man's and she occasionally brought a cigarette to her lips. An older woman sat next to her on a couch and held the hand without the cigarette in both of hers.

"Turn that goddam thing off," my mother commanded. "We have enough misery here in our own house."

My dad hurried over to the TV and snapped it off.

"Mom, I'm sorry. I really am."

"Half the time you're never here, always shoved up the asses of those *ga-vone* Jews."

"Mom, what are you talking about? I said I'm sorry. Can we drop it?"

"And what's with this girl you're mixed up with?"

"'This girl?' Her name is Sterling."

"What kind of a name is that? All the refinement, but she can't show a little respect and stick her nose in the door."

"You're being ridiculous."

"And you're a little bastard."

"So what's that make you?"

From where he stood in front of the now silent TV, my father let out a low, throat-clearing roar: the sound of his displeasure rising in his craw, involuntary, bilious. I hadn't heard it in years. It was the alarm, like a pressure valve blowing, that went off in my father when things had gone too far and he had finally been goaded to action.

"You watch your mouth," he said. "You watch your goddam mouth. You're still not too much for me, boy. I guarantee you."

My mother lowered her face to her hands and sobbed.

My dad and I gazed at each other. I moved toward my mother, but when I got within a foot of her she put up her hand to ward me off.

"Don't come near me. You stink like garbage. Like vomit. Take your filthy clothes and leave them in the cellar. God only knows what you brought home. Look at you. *Ubriacone.* I smelled the booze on you the minute you walked in."

She raised her red, wet face and stared at me. I began to speak. She closed her hand into a fist, its forefinger splayed out like a knife toward the ceiling. "Don't deny it."

"Sylvia," my dad said. "Look how worked up you're getting yourself."

She turned on my father: "I did not raise a drunkard. I refuse to put up with it. You were a drinker when I met you. Always so quick with the bottle. I had to break you of it. Your son gets that from your side."

"You have rocks in your head, woman," said my father indignantly. "Calling me a drinker."

"What would you call it?"

"I wouldn't call it anything."

With a great huff she winched herself up from the chair, grabbed her cane and stubbed across the carpet. When she reached the stairs, she turned, lifted the cane and poked it toward us.

"Both of you stay away from me," she said in a brittle voice. "I'm going to lie down." She mounted the stairs, one foot, then the other, on each tread, slowly, agonizingly, aspirating like a bellows, whimpering and talking profanely to herself, until she disappeared and we heard the bedroom door clap.

I turned to my father. "I'm really sorry, Dad."

He sunk into his chair. "Thirty-one years with a strong woman."

My dad had tiled our tiny bathroom himself. Pink with turquoise trim. A long time ago. Some of the grout had wormed out. Around the bathtub fixtures the caulking flaked. Pink carpet, pink towels and a pink toilet seat cover. An extra roll of toilet paper, disguised as a poodle in a pink knit sheath, sat on the back of the toilet. On the sink counter was a row of my mother's prescription bottles, each one filled with pills that my father had razored in half so my mom, who had trouble swallowing medicine, could get them down with ginger ale.

I propped my hurt hand on the ledge of the pink bathtub, sunk down to my neck in the hot water and closed my eyes. I tried to imagine the telephone conversation between my mother and Phil. Phil would have laughed about Sterling and I getting stranded; he would have passed the whole thing off. Complimented my mother on what a fine son she and her husband had raised. How he and JoAnn admired me, were terribly fond of me. How his daughter, Sterling, their only child—I too am an only child—was quite taken with her handsome son.

Fond would have given my mother pause. *Taken* too. Old Man Rosechild held himself a little too high for what he was. She wouldn't have appreciated the familiarity. Who the hell, exactly, did he think he was? She would have been polite, but curt, not paying out any line to him whatsoever, remaining immovably unimpressed, responding with, *Yes, he is* and *We think so,* when Phil praised me, maybe as an afterthought remarking that Sterling *seemed* like a nice girl. She would have met his cheery *Good night, Mrs. Dolce, I hope we have the opportunity to chat face to face soon* with *Bye.* I doubted that she would have even thanked him for the call. There were no second chances with Sylvia Dolce. She would have hated Phil.

I tried to think of Sterling, but I couldn't fix on the right picture of her. It was as if she was still gnarled in smoke and snow. I simply couldn't sharpen the focus. Making love had been a mistake. I couldn't even remember it—like a poorly spliced film, strobing off the walls in my head. I still heard the sound of her crying, her insisting: *yes, no, yes, no, yes.* Like a child's game. Had I hurt her? Blood and snow is what I remembered. And Bill. Not Sterling's face nor her body sinking into the water bed under mine nor a single kiss or endearment. I was already asleep.

Game day checked in brilliant and deadly cold. Two above zero, mountains of snow, sun slicing blindingly into them. My mother was still not speaking to my dad and me. The weather had prevented her from going to church, putting her in an even fouler mood, though my father had insisted he'd accompany her. She limped about the kitchen making the sauce, frying meatballs. My dad sat in the living room reading the paper.

When I first awoke, I was still thrashing in the Ledges' pool. I carried with me that vague, yet pervasive, feeling of tragedy. When I had called Sterling the night before, Phil had informed me that she had gone to a poetry reading with JoAnn, then dinner, and they would not be home until very late. In fact, Phil had been about to pick up the phone and ring me about my banged-up hand when my call came in. Terrible. He was so sorry. JoAnn too. Sterling had been so upset about it. The hand was fine, I assured him, supremely relieved that Sterling hadn't spilled the entire fiasco—though I'd known she wouldn't. A stupid accident. I could be a real klutz in a swimming pool.

Sterling hadn't mentioned any poetry reading to me, and I couldn't help feeling, though it was merely my own guilt and insecurity, that Phil had been put up to the story. But that couldn't have been so. Mother and daughter were out for sure because Phil didn't hold back about the game: Ten thousand bucks. The Steelers couldn't miss. What's more, I had a little commission coming. Five hundred dollars of that ten grand Phil was sure to snag would go to me. Had it not been for me, for my trust in Phil—"and I mean this very sincerely, my boy, you know how I feel about you," Phil had interrupted himself—my willingness to have faith, true religious faith, in someone I didn't really know, then an awful lot of very fine things—"very fine things, indeed"—would have never transpired.

I cautioned Phil that there were no sure things. That I couldn't possibly accept the five hundred dollars. But Phil wouldn't hear of any of it. He was wrought up with sentiment and munificence. His voice cracked a few times. He invited me over for a drink. I was tempted by the offer. Get out of that crazy house I lived in: stand in front of the aquarium and gape at the fish with Phil in his patch-madras pants and navy pullover with the polo player swinging his mallet on his pouchy left breast. Ira curled up on the sofa. The étagère twinkling with the fragile Italian glass the Rosechilds had collected on their trips to Carrara. Ice clicking in the gin, the fragrance of limes wending through the house, the wealth and good cheer.

"I'm toasting you, George. What say you join me?"

Through the phone, I heard Phil pull from his drink. I took a swig myself—of something deep down and inescapable: three fingers of bile—and swallowed.

"Thanks, Phil. I better sit tight. I haven't been home much lately."

Lately. My evening at Hidden Valley rolled back over me. My smashed hand. Bill's face. Sterling slipping in, slipping out, her sweater on the floor, how the abandoned taste in my mouth rebuked me the next morning when I awoke drowning, alone in that carriage house waterbed without even remembering how Sterling had looked or felt. The one clearly beautiful, uncomplicated thing that God had dropped in front of me blacked out.

"George, I'm not patronizing you when I say this, but you're a good boy. A fine son, and I respect the fact that you still like to spend time with your mother and father. I had a nice chat with your mother last night. She is so proud of you, and rightly so. I really look forward to spending some time with your parents."

Poor Phil. *A nice chat with your mother.* What had my mother called Phil? *Old man Rosechild.* The *gavone Jew.* Phil really didn't know shit. He had no idea who the Dolces were. I wanted the conversation to end. I wanted this job over. Twenty-four more hours and I was cutting loose my partnership with Phil, finishing out my business in Pittsburgh, and launching the new life I'd dreamed of for so long. With Sterling, dammit, with Sterling, though she seemed at that moment so remote, wrapped in the riddle of poetry.

"What are you doing for the game tomorrow, George? Usual crowd here. They'd miss you. You've become indispensable to these gatherings."

I was empty. Couldn't remember what lies I'd told to whom. Without thinking, because I couldn't think, I said, "I'd love to come."

"Terrific. Here's an idea. Can your folks come? Maybe I should call myself and extend an invitation."

"You know, Phil, that's really nice of you to include them, but my mother's arthritis is so bad that she rarely goes out, especially in this kind of weather."

"Of course, of course. I understand. But soon, we're going to all get together. I'm going to make that a priority."

"Absolutely." You fool, I mused. How money has entitled you to be a fool. To trust people like my mother.

"Then we'll see you tomorrow, Son. Take good care of that hand. And you know where to get free prescriptions."

"Thanks, Phil."

"Thanks, nothing. Thank you."

There was a long pause. I heard the glass tip up, the melting ice tumbling into Phil's crooked teeth as he drained it. Then: "I want you to know that I love you, George."

"Phil," I said plaintively. I just couldn't say it. It wouldn't come out of my mouth. Not that it wouldn't have been true.

After a little bit, Phil said, "Then I'll see you tomorrow."

When it was time to get ready to go the Rosechilds, I couldn't make myself get showered and dressed. I watched a little of the pre-game with my father, then wandered upstairs and called Sterling. I didn't know what I would say, but I wanted to hear her voice, tell her I'd probably show up by half-time. The line was busy. I sat on the edge of my parents' bed, the heart of their wedding trousseau, and dialed the number a dozen more times without getting through.

At four o'clock, the Oakland Raiders kicked off into the balmy blue sky of California. I sprawled on the couch and watched the Steelers, outfitted in white jerseys, wedge and trap ineffectually. Turgid. Like Sumo wrestlers. Up the gut, Franco and Rocky diving at the three, five and seven holes. But Oakland was equally ineffectual. The first quarter ended with Oakland ahead 3–0 on a George Blanda field goal.

"For crying out loud, look at those donkeys," exclaimed my dad.

My mother dragged through the living room occasionally. Still snubbing me and my father—she hadn't even asked how my injured hand was—she peppered us with asides. *Look at them. Like apes*—when the camera cut to the Steelers' defensive front four. *Showoff*—whenever Bradshaw's puzzled expression flashed.

I wanted to get off the couch and lay eyes on Sterling, but an inertia—I tried not to think of it as despair—kept me pinned there mindlessly watching the two teams bash each other. I didn't want to be around Phil. I couldn't have stood his shiny, innocent face, all that hope and jingoism he conjured every Sunday at the thought of free money. On this particular Sunday I wasn't so sure I could tolerate the Rosechilds' charming friends who had been so kind to me: the roiling fire and cocktails, the smell of sterno, chafing dishes, the bubbling aquarium, their untroubled, tinkling optimism. I couldn't conjure a smile, a witticism, not one clever rejoinder. I didn't even feel capable of knotting my tie. At that moment, my parents' 1945 slip-covered couch from the May Stern Company in East Liberty—purchased after my dad got back from the war—and the aroma of my mother's sauce cooking in the kitchen were enough.

"Look at him, grinning like a monkey," my mother quipped. Jack Tatum, the Raider safety, stood over a Steeler he had just bushwhacked. She twirled a wooden spoon in her hand. A bitter smile swayed on her face. My father snored from his chair. Pittsburgh's Gerela booted a field goal to tie the game.

I closed my eyes for a moment and saw the $21,000 that belonged to me slipping away as the game clock ticked and the inept Steelers slogged into the Oakland defense. There was no way they'd cover the spread. All my life, I'd been lectured about the price of eggs and milk. *A disgrace, what's happening to the working people.* Harangued about turning off lights. *You think I work for Duquesne Light?* As a child, I had shivered in the few inches of water allotted for my nightly bath. Aluminum foil was washed along with the dishes and stored in drawers to be reused. Not a bean, not a grain of rice, ever thrown away. My family was without *two nickels to rub together, without a pot to piss in.*

My mother had grown up during the Depression: *pasta e fagioli* every meal weeks on end, brothers and sisters sleeping three, four, to a bed, selling anything that wasn't nailed down to the ragman who loped the streets once a week in a rickety wagon pulled by a blind mare. *Plenty of people shoveled shit for a living. To feed their kids. You think I'm kidding?* My parents had had thirteen cents between them the day they walked out of the lawyer's office after buying the house on Saint Marie. *Thirteen cents.* Poor, yes; threadbare, yes; but immaculate. *No filth. No bugs. No roaches.*

My entire childhood I had been repeatedly reminded of my privileged status. Their sacrifice and self-denial had secured for me the comfort and opportunity they never had. *Thank God.* But I had never felt privileged. Not until the instant Sterling walked into my life.

Suddenly I was frantic for her, to have her in front of me, the fact of her life running through me like an irrevocable signature on a black line. I jumped up just as the half ended, 3–3.

"What are you doing?" my mother asked. It was the first time she had spoken to me since I'd arrived home the morning before.

"I'm going to take a shower."

"With that hand?"

"It'll be fine. I'll cover it with plastic."

"If you get it wet, it'll get infected."

"Mom, I'll cover it."

"Your father'll help you get cleaned up."

"Mom, I don't . . ."

"George, wake up."

"What?" sputtered my dad, coming to. "What's the matter?"

"Georgie needs help getting his shower. With that hand."

"Okay." He didn't know what my mother was talking about.

"Thank you, but I don't need any help," I said, climbing the stairs.

"Yes, you do. Go up there with him, George."

My dad got to his feet.

"I'll take a bath instead of a shower."

"You still need help," my mother insisted. "That hand'll get infected and then what?"

"I'll get a hook."

"Yeah, go ahead. Laugh. Then you'll be like . . . What was that kid's name from Auburn Street?" She looked at my dad. "George, I'm talking to you."

"I don't know who you mean, Syl."

"Oh, Jesus. Go back to sleep. He lived upstairs from the Amorosos. The retarded kid."

"O'Toole," my dad guessed.

"No, not O'Toole."

"Then I don't know who the hell you mean."

"Whatever his name was, he got a splinter in his thumb and then went swimming up in Highland Park with all the you-know-whats, and little by little they had to chop his arm off."

"How come?" I asked, laughing. "Because he went swimming?"

"Because it got infected, smart-ass. Go ahead and laugh."

Twenty minutes later, in a coat and tie, I walked back down the stairs and stood in front of my parents.

"Where do you think you're going?" my mother asked.

"To the Rosechilds to watch the rest of the game. What's the score, Dad?"

"10–3 Oakland. Third quarter's almost over. I don't know what's the matter with the Steelers today."

"I hope they lose," my mother said.

I turned quickly from her to the TV. I couldn't look at her: the Dr. Scholl's footpads, Brach's hard candy she habitually sucked on from the orange glass candy dish, the cane leaning against the coffee table with the green glossy electrical tape my dad had wrapped around the handle for her.

The Steelers were going to blow this game, and ruin my epic gamble, the only shot my parents had of escaping the mess they were in shot to hell. And my mother was cursing them. The thought of her death flashed through my mind: the pathetic ineffable love I bore her, my quiet father trying to go back to sleep until her next oath. More than anything, I hated myself. I had to get out of there.

Oakland's slick quarterback, Ken Stabler, took a short drop and looked in the flat for Charlie Smith. Jack Ham, the Steelers' outside linebacker, darted out of nowhere and picked it off in Oakland territory just as the quarter ended.

"I have to go," I said. "I'm going to take the car. Okay, Dad?"

"Sure."

"What do you mean 'sure?'" my mother yelled. "He can stay home with you. Your father's not good enough to watch the game with? Things aren't fancy enough for you at home anymore? You can't be a bigshot here?"

"Listen, Mother, I'm not going to get into this."

"Boy, she's got her claws in you. That whole family."

"Mother."

"Syl, why don't you drop it."

"Drop it, my ass. I want to know what you're up to, Georgie. You're up to something."

"I'm leaving."

"All day I cook, everything you like, the bigshot, and now you're leaving."

"You haven't spoken to me, or Dad, for over twenty-four hours. I did not know my presence at dinner was so important to you."

"I guess you like that Jew food better."

"I guess I do," I said, then walked out the door. I stood on the porch for a minute and let the bitter evening cold wash over me. Through the brick wall I heard my mother's grinding tirade, my father's shushing, then nothing as I stepped off the porch away from them.

Sterling gleamed like the Blessed Sacrament. She kissed me twice, long and deep, lifted my hurt hand and kissed it too, then led me by the other hand into the living room where the Rosechilds and their guests hovered about the TV. The Steelers, in the time it took me to navigate the icy street from my home to the Rosechilds, had somehow gone ahead by a touchdown and were pounding away inside the Raiders' ten.

The guests all fussed over me. My hand. What happened? How sorry they were. My acceptance to Georgetown. How wonderful. Had I heard from Yale and Columbia yet? Happy Holidays. How good to see me. Phil and JoAnn jumped up from their seats to hug me. JoAnn and I exchanged kisses. Phil hauled me off and placed a big glass of gin with a lime slice in my hand.

"Boy, this is something," Phil said under his breath. "I think we still have a fighting chance." He was flushed and rumpled, his tie undone, one of his shirttails hanging beneath his sweater vest. "I'm so glad you got here."

A collective cheer rose up from around the TV. The Steelers had scored again. 24–10 with over eight minutes left to play. If it ended like that, I'd be flush. I took a big sip of my drink. A great rush of love for these people welled up in me. Eight lousy minutes. Everything was going to be alright.

"Jesus, what do we need?" Phil mumbled to me. Sweat on his brow, bluish broken blood vessels in his nose, bags under his eyes, his glasses dangling on his chest by their chain. Still he smiled, though the ice in his drink peeled from his shaking hand.

We. Poor Phil thought that he and I had bet the same nag. And all along, Sabbath upon Sabbath, I had been duping him.

"Another touchdown and an extra point and we got them," I heard myself say.

"They're sure to score again. Look at them. Swann and Bradshaw are geniuses. We can't miss," said Phil.

Another roar. A Steeler interception by J.T. Thomas. With a little less than four minutes to go. Phil slapped his hands under his armpits and leaned over the TV like a bird getting smaller and smaller. He still expected the Steelers to score again when all they'd do now is trap and trap until the clock died, putting $21,000 in my pocket, $11,000 of which Phil would have to kick in. Poor Phil, yes; but arrogant Phil. He thought he could master the sport without ever getting to know it. Football wasn't a slot machine, and it wasn't a whore house. It was danger and brains and, above all, brutality. Each time the TV camera panned to the dwindling game clock, I felt the weight lifting from me.

I grabbed Sterling and kissed her boldly. I told her I loved her. I walked to the bar. Sterling followed me and, from behind, wrapped her arms around my waist as I mixed another drink. The fish stared at us through the aquarium glass. Everyone in the living room took to their feet. Franco and Rocky hitting scrimmage between the giant tackles, two and three yards a pop, chewing that clock, moving the sticks. Phil had collapsed into an armchair, his lips moving almost imperceptibly as if praying.

"Let's get married," I said to Sterling.

She looked up at me, not exactly smiling, but as if she were going to ask me to repeat the question, as if she had not heard correctly. Then the Steelers fumbled, and the Raiders recovered. Stabler, like a magician, throwing little sideline bullets to conserve the clock, marched them seventy yards, for a touchdown, making it 24–17.

It was over for me. The Steelers recovered the Raiders' on-side kick and just sat on it for the remaining seconds until the gun. They threw their helmets up in the air, and hoisted Chuck Noll, their coach, to their shoulders. For the first time in their history they were going to the Super Bowl.

The Rosechilds' living room erupted. Kisses, hugs, dancing, toasts. Sterling still querulously gazed up at me until JoAnn flitted over and engaged her in a little jig. Phil positioned his glasses on his nose, smiled, hoisted himself from his chair, and walked very deliberately to me.

"Well, Son," he said. "One must be a gentleman about these things. There's always next week. Let's have a drink."

So we had another drink, and then another, and Phil and I patted each other on the back. For the moment, there was no longer any need to talk about money or worry about the outcome of a game. We were back to being men consoling and admiring each other. Phil was an extraordinary man. He had taken the hit—eleven damn grand—without whining, and still he had an appetite. The eleven grand that would pay my tab with Eugene. We had canceled each other. In many ways, I was relieved. I was through with Phil: no more bets. I wanted a break from it myself. *Basta.*

As the guests left, couple by couple, the Rosechilds and I drew closer together. Sterling kicked off her shoes, tucked her feet beneath her and crowded against me on the striped loveseat. Ira crawled up in Phil's lap. After everyone else was gone, JoAnn disappeared, returning in a nightgown and bathrobe. She made coffee, dimmed the lights and put Vivaldi on the stereo. We talked about our plans for the Super Bowl. Had I ever been to New Orleans? Our hotel was on Canal Street, easy walking distance of the French Quarter. Maybe we'd stay an extra day, maybe two, if it didn't interfere with the kids', my and Sterling's, classes.

I saw myself with the Rosechilds in every romantic city of the world: the practiced care of a loving family without bitter secrets, without a history of resentment and vendetta. They actually liked being together. Not like my family. Not like those East Liberty families I had known, growing up, who sat on their porches in either stone silence or shrieked at one another. Who kept at their fingertips an up-to-date account of one another's trespasses so that the day they were finally pushed to eke out their revenge because they had been eating shit for so long—they had had it up to here—they would have the proof, the law, the sacred writ to burn down a hundred years with one remark.

As I sat there sipping coffee, Sterling's hand resting on the back of my neck, I realized again I never wanted to part with this life, these gentle, generous people. Yet I was nagged by the oppressive sense that things were wrong: using Phil, what I had done at the party in Hidden Valley, the fortune I had been literally twenty-nine seconds away from snaring. And there were my parents to contend with. I hadn't even mentioned to them my trip to New Orleans. Suddenly I felt keenest my betrayal of my mother and father.

"I better get going," I said. "Thanks for everything."

"Oh, stay a little longer," JoAnn said. "It's still so early."

"I really have to go. Thanks."

"I'll be sad," said Sterling, wrapping both arms around me.

"How about a nightcap, my boy," Phil piped up. "A little fortification against the wicked north wind."

I was on my feet. "I have a clock to punch first thing in the morning."

"You have connections with the boss," quipped Phil.

My key in the door woke my parents, so my mom had no time to recollect our last interaction and fix her face into a mask of wounded retribution. Her surprised countenance registered only undisguised pleasure at the sight of her only child. The TV was tuned to *M*A*S*H.* Wounded on stretchers were being unloaded from choppers and rushed through the rain by shambling soldiers across the quagmire, the rotors beating their baggy fatigues about them.

"You scared me to death," my mother admonished.

"You glad to see me?"

"I'm always glad to see you."

I strode quickly to her and kissed her.

"You're home early," my dad said.

"Thought I'd catch up on sleep. Work day tomorrow."

"Attaboy."

"Did you see the end of the game, Dad?"

"Boy, they did everything but lose it. That Bradshaw's something."

"Showoff," pronounced my mother.

"You have any macaroni left, Mom?"

"My God, yes. I made a ton and then you disappeared. I don't know how to cook for just two people."

She roused herself, fell back in the chair with a groan, then heaved forward again and staked herself up with her cane. Hawkeye and Trapper, in scrubs, sat on their bunks, passing a magnum, drinking from champagne glasses.

"Real doctors don't act like that," my mother said.

"Where you going?" asked my dad.

"To put some food on the table."

"Let me help you."

"I don't need any help. Sit still. Turn off the television."

My dad got up, switched off TV and followed her into the kitchen.

She called over her shoulder to me: "What's the matter? Didn't your friends feed you?"

My mother laid the table with ziti, meatballs and sausage, bread, and insisted on fixing me a fresh salad. I ate everything she put in front of me. I told her no one could cook like my mama. I gave her the business about her weight.

"Go ahead and talk while you can," she said. "You better watch. You'll end up looking like your father."

"Eat all you want, son," said my dad. "At your age, you burn it right off."

"Who wants dessert and coffee?" she asked.

I didn't want any, but said I'd have some anyway. I was working up to telling her about the trip to New Orleans with the Rosechilds.

She returned with a tray of cookies and coffee. And a letter-sized envelope she dropped in front of me. Its return address was New Haven. Yale Law School. It had been opened.

"When did this come?" I asked.

"Yesterday," my mother replied.

"Who opened it?"

"I did," she said.

"We both did," amended my dad.

"I opened it," my mother confessed. "Your father told me not to, but I couldn't stand it, Georgie. I apologize. But I just couldn't stand it."

"What couldn't you stand?" I asked. She had begun crying. I looked down at the envelope with my name on it. The word *YALE* stood out like braille. Taking out the letter, I read *On behalf of,* then *congratulations,* refolded it and returned it to the envelope.

"Why didn't you give it to me?"

"Georgie, I'm so sorry. I just couldn't stand it."

"I'll tell you. She was pretty upset, Son. I thought she was going to take a stroke." My father held up his thumb and forefinger. "I was this far from rushing her to the Emergency."

"That other school, Georgetown. It's not so far away. Your father and me, maybe some weekend, we can drive up and see you or even take a bus. Your father can't drive long distances. But this one. It's the one you really want. It's almost in Canada. We'll never see you again. Duquesne. Pitt. They have law schools. Why do you have to go clear to the end of the world?"

"Mom, it's not that far."

"That's what I told her. And you'll come back for visits. And holidays."

"Of course I'll come home to visit as often as I can."

"I was being spiteful not giving it to you. God'll punish me. He's already punishing me. This crippled body. Your father out of work. Now you're leaving."

"Mom, I don't even graduate for another semester."

"Son, we're happy for you. Both of us. Your mother understands. It's just hard for her."

"I do understand," she said. "We want you to better yourself. Your father and me, we're two old *mezza-mortos.* What is there here for you? What do we have to give you? I should be happy. But how it feels, in here"—she clutched the bodice of her housed-dress in her fist—"is like I'm losing you."

"I'll come back to Pittsburgh and open a practice. I'll spoil you with expensive gifts."

"I'll be dead," she predicted. She mopped her eyes with kleenex.

"Don't talk like that, honey," said my dad, taking her hand.

My mother was right. She would be dead. I would never return to Pittsburgh. There were but a few chapters left in that book. My father was sixty-four, a year until he could retire from the mill with full pension. His gray hair had begun to whiten over the winter. All he wanted to do was sleep. My mother, sixty-four too, went to bed every night with swollen ankles. Her hair had turned pink. In another year she'd trade in the cane for a walker. She'd grow increasingly morose, my dad unconscious in his chair, as Lawrence Welk conducted his timeless orchestra and champagne music spilled into the living room, bubbles exploding on the scrubbed surfaces of my parents' sparkling house.

I would write them letters. We'd talk by telephone, the television in the background, like a Greek chorus alerting them of their approaching deaths. I'd leave them behind, inevitably, like any child leaves infirm parents. Like memories. Tableaux. Photographs of my wife and me—she'd never forgive me for marrying Sterling, a Jew—our children, framed in Easter palm, all throughout the Saint Marie house. My mother's reliquary of icons, along with the holy cards of her deceased friends and family. There at the end, she'd grow zealous, fanatical. When her eyes failed, Jesus would thread her needles. Shut in, she'd watch televised masses on Saturday night and Sunday morning. She'd dose herself with homemade Eucharist: little coins of bread, the body and blood of the Savior. *God understands,* she'd attest.

My father would stop talking, unable after a decade to square it in his snowy head that the mill had never started back up. As his wife got fatter and fatter, food would no longer appeal to him. He'd swear privately that he didn't believe in God. Never had. *Six feet,* he'd say and nod at his shoes, taking long, long walks until his wife hyperventilated with panic at his absence and said rosary after rosary.

As we ate, the portraits of Jesus and Mary on the dining room wall chided us. My parents had never seemed seduced by the glory of the Blessed Mother and her champion Son. All that blood and risk. That mumbo-jumbo. They favored the opposite wall: the picture gaping at me every night during supper. An old white-haired, long-bearded man in a green flannel shirt, head bowed in Grace over his bread. Thankful for every blessing. That old man scared me as a child. He wasn't piety, but enervation, that pig-headed blue-collar reflex for gratitude that your suffering is just a little less than your neighbors'.

More than anything, my parents had taught me never to take chances, to be grateful for my allotted portion of anguish, and just be glad it wasn't worse. That's what grace was: dogged, jackass acceptance. Now, there they were, my mom and dad, holding hands on the table draped with a thirty year old faded oilcloth they had bought with their wedding money.

That old snapshot of them mere minutes after the priest had consecrated their union: my smiling father smoking, as if he had just won the Academy Award; my mother looking straight ahead, intent on remembering nothing; while around them the families in a blizzard of rice mingled, little newsreel faces, the faces of the dead, fading into the cracked print. Going to sleep. That's what my mother called death. *Going to sleep.* The honeymoon sedan they had driven to Washington hulking at the Meadow Street curb. What remained of the honeymoon was a series of fuzzy off-center homages to The White House and the Lincoln Memorial. Even the photographs seemed complicit in revealing nothing. I've never known a thing about my parents: what they were like as children, what dreams they might have had, how they had met. Nine years after they married, I was born. There had been a miscarriage in the intervening years, a matter-of-fact bad break—they refused to call anything tragic—then silence.

I heard my father exclaim *fuck* once when a careless driver nearly careened into the two of us. On another day, by accident, I stumbled across my mother's sanitary napkins at the bottom of my parents' bedroom closet. That was the sum lot of intimacy: cadged secrets. Amnesia. In that wedding photograph, it was in their faces: my mother ill at ease, self-conscious, nauseous at her gardenia bouquet; my father comprehending perfectly that there is no such thing as perfection. His cigarette burning down to his knuckles. He and his bride about to catch fire, both of them so modest they'd rather go up in flames together, without uttering a word, than step into the world waiting at the bottom of the church steps.

"Don't think we forgot about the money we owe you," squeaked my mom.

"You don't owe me any money."

"Right is right, Son. We're keeping track. Every penny," seconded my dad.

"C'mon, Dad. I don't care about that money."

"So help me, God, Georgie, if I have to wait tables at Eat'n'Park on these goddam crippled stubs of mine we'll pay you back."

She was crying again. My father patted her hand.

"Why am I crying?" she sobbed. "I should be happy."

Chapter 22

As soon as I unlock the back door, and Crow and I step inside, I smell the sauce; and there is my mother, Sylvia Dolce, at the stove, in her immaculate gleaming kitchen—not a speck of lint, crumb, mote of dust; the pristine perfection of a magazine ad—stirring the big silver pot with a wooden spoon. My life returns to me in blinding radiance. She turns to greet us: glasses, red gingham apron, pearls, sweatpants, old-fashioned ladies white tennis shoes. On her face is unbridled euphoria at our appearance.

"Oh my God! Look who's here," she exclaims.

At her side, my father grates the *Pecorino.* He wears a Steelers sweat shirt and khakis, a pair of white Adidas, not a scuff upon them. He smiles broadly. "Oh," he says, like adoration, like *Selah* or *Behold*—the ineffable—as if he's seen an apparition, like he feels impelled to lay down alms, to die for us. From the stereo, Connie Francis sings *Al Di La.* The next life.

My mother and my father take each of us in turn, engulf us in embrace, then the kisses.

"You kids look so good," my mother says when she comes away. "Don't they, George?"

"They sure do."

"Mom, you look like a million bucks—like Gina Lollobrigida."

"Oh, you're so full of you-know-what."

"Hey, Dad, whatta you think? Isn't Mom a beauty?"

"You better believe it. Thirty-one years with a strong woman."

"You're another one," she says to my dad. "What an operator. I don't know how I've put up with you that long."

"No, it's true. You two look great," Crow says. "You always do. You never age."

"Thank you, Lydia. But the old gray mare . . . You know what I mean? You're the one who looks good. You have a cute new haircut. You kids must be hungry after your trip. Take off your coats and sit. I'm just getting ready to throw the pasta in. Fresh *tagliatelle.* Your father and I made them early this morning." On the counter rests a marble slab. She lifts the cloth covering it and there is the *tagliatelle,* long soft yellow strips of egg and semolina, salt and water. Then she motions toward the kitchen table. "Have a little something. Then we'll sit down and eat."

I look into the sauce. It bubbles ever so slightly, a measured pulse. Meatballs, sausage and spare ribs simmer in it. I break off a small chunk of Italian bread, dip it into the sauce, and eat it. I kiss my mother. "Perfection," I whisper.

"Oh my God. So dramatic all the time."

"What else you got, Mom, in case the Marines show up?"

"Artichokes, chicken cacciatore, baked mushrooms, a nice salad."

"Is that all?"

"Hey, smart-mouth, sit down with your wife and father and have a little something."

"You gonna sit down?"

"I have things to do."

My father, Crow and I take chairs at the little kitchen table: a platter spread with provolone, fontinella, *finocchio,* roasted red peppers, green and black olives, cipollini, lupi beans, salami, pepperoni, bread sticks. I peek into the dining room: long still-warm loaves of *Siciliano;* china stationed at each place for *primi, secondo,* the unhurried, comforting rite of the table; the flat winter light, as day latens, flaring in pitchers of purple chianti. My mother dumps the *tagliatelle* into the silver pot we have worshipped all our lives. Water with the pasta turning in it bubbles like an oracle. Stirring with the wooden spoon, my mother peers into it as if seeing the future.

My father pours a shot of Black Velvet for himself, then one for me. He pulls two cans of Iron City from the refrigerator. To Crow: "What for you, Honey?"

"Nothing, thanks. Maybe a glass of water."

"How about a nice glass of wine?"

"Oh, no thanks, really. Water's fine."

"Hey, Mom," I interject, "you ready for your shot and beer?"

"How about it, Sylvia?" my father says, laughing.

"Yeah, any old day," she cracks.

"We have some news," I say.

My mother turns to us, prophetically elevates the wooden spoon.

"I'm going to have a baby," Crow says.

My mother glows like pictures of The Blessed Virgin taking in the news from Gabriel at The Annunciation. "I prayed so hard for this," she sighs.

She weeps softly, rapidly—a lovely elegant cry—draping her mouth with a handkerchief she pulls from her apron pockets. Then she is kissing and hugging us. My father stands and follows suit. Then he kisses my mother's mouth, and she kisses his mouth. My father raises his shot glass. The amber light packed into it reflects the kitchen, all of us, the blessed prism of our lives.

"*Saluto,*" he says.

"*Saluto,*" the three of us respond.

My father and I down our shots, then chase them with Iron City.

"Honey, did you ever get your water?" my mother asks Crow.

My dad scrambles to the sink. "Oh, Honey, I'm sorry."

"*Stonare,*" laughs my mother, and points to her temple. "George, take their coats. Honey, have something. God love you. You're eating for two now." She hugs us again, holds our faces against her breast and kisses our foreheads and cheeks. Begins to cry again.

"Don't cry, Mom," I say.

Crow, crying too, stands and holds her.

My father beams. "She's just happy."

Torchy Connie Francis sings: *Ci sei tu.* There you are.

"Next year this time we'll have a little one," my mother says, then smiles. Behind her, columns of steam ascend to roost like little statues in her white hair.

The stage blackens. My parents disappear. Fabrication sustains us—its cloying falsity notwithstanding. *Next year* has always been an illusion: what is invoked, out of pain, for respite. Even when we know there is no next year, no baby, no heir. Next year, however, is a prayer—another time, not a real time. *Al Di La.* Yet are we not those shades in the vision: Crow and I, my mother and father? Yet ourselves as well—my parents in my mother's hospital room, Crow and I standing, at this very moment, in the abandoned forlorn kitchen on Saint Marie Street, sirens and surreal lights whirling through the cold black night—somehow perfected in the sentimental reflex of memory, the breathtaking way it serves and fails when needed most.

We were there with my parents; weren't we? In the kitchen for that instant of perfection, when there was *no fear in perfect love*? That endearing display at the announcement that their only child would supply them with a grandchild is surely what would have happened; and perhaps it did occur in some twilit astral seam that parallels ours, that specter home next door that we glimpse occasionally in dreams and delirium, the one prayed for, the one crayoned by children into primer pages. We reside in imagined epiphanies, hybrids of rehearsed longing and prayer: the illusion that someday, in this temporal place, all will be well, and we can finally lie down and rest.

The first thing I see when I enter my parents' kitchen with Crow and flip on the lights—snow, wind and sirens tailing us—is a near empty bottle of Jacquin's Rock and Rye on the table. Dirty dishes stack in the sink. Half an apple, browning on its plate, on the counter. Crumbs on the floor. The garbage hasn't been emptied. The heat is abominable. I walk through the dining room, into the living room, switching on lamps and overheads. The thermostat is set on 82. I turn it down to 68, then climb the stairs, Crow behind me. Sirens blare. The bathroom mats are crumpled, the shower curtain thrown back, soaked washcloths wadded in the corners of the pink tub, scurf ringing the drain. My dad's shaving gear is scattered across the vanity, the pink sink peppered with his stubble.

My parents' bedroom faces the street. The cop lights strobe red and blue severed arteries across the walls at exact intervals, the big crucifix above the bed hemorrhaging at each flash, the kingdom beneath it a welter of kaleidoscopic relics. The bed is unmade, a quarter-fifth of Black Velvet on the floor of my dad's side.

Dust bides over the dresser and nightstand and my mother's vanity. Stationed on it are a suite of ornate combs and brushes, a jeweled mirror—remnants of her fragmented trousseau—she's never used. An upholstered jewelry box. Easter palm. A bottle of Este Lauder perfume and dusting powder I bought her years ago for Christmas. A statue of the Virgin Mary, arms extended in supplication, the serpent entwined about her bare foot, utter weariness infiltrating her dwindling smile. So long she has stood this way. Like a proscenium behind Our Lady is a framed photograph of my mother as a bride—rosaries draping either corner—beautiful in all the ways a bride wishes to be: the snowy unending veil and gown, the mountainous bouquet of gardenias, asters and cymbidium, stephanotis, gardenias and baby's breath, white upon white. Pearl necklace.

My mother's white untouched body drifts in satin. Long black hair, guileless brown eyes, a smile cued by the photographer who counted to three and then committed to history this moment of what? Certainty? Happiness?

Fortitude? The parabola connecting this photograph to my mother in Saint Francis, thirty-one years later, is dizzying. But not more so than the disparity between the terrifying reflection of me in her vanity mirror and the photo on the vanity itself of me taken just before my exodus: what was to have been my college graduation portrait—had I graduated. A handsome clean-cut young man: chiseled determined Mediterranean features, white shirt, navy blue suit, maroon and silver striped tie, resolve in his dark eyes and jaw, a young man of infinite promise. Then pictures of me stationed across the room: from birth through infancy, kindergarten, grade school, high school; birthday parties; the sacraments of Baptism, Holy Eucharist, Confirmation.

Crow runs her hand across the headboard of my parents' bed, carefully fingering the intricate beadwork carved into the rich cherry, then up the inlaid scrolls flourishing the high four posts. She gazes about the room at the matching furniture that complete the suite.

"I could be standing in my parents' bedroom," she says. "It's the exact same furniture."

"I told you."

"But how can that be? How could they have the exact same furniture? Five hundred miles apart? It's impossible."

"And our mothers have the same birthday," I remind her.

"It's too much of a freaker, Romeo. I don't know if I like it."

"There's a lot not to like, Miss Crow."

"Maybe we're brother and sister."

"By furniture."

"Exactly."

We laugh. Then I spy fastened in a corner of my mother's vanity mirror a holy card: Jesus with the long brown hair and beard, hazel eyes of the misunderstood poet with a fugitive warrant dogging him. His left hand is raised in benediction. His right points to the flaming barbed heart painted on his cloak that yokes him to the fortunes of man. His power is awful: the sacrifice of the Mass. He must suffer and die hideously again and again, then come back to life. He wants shed of that entire Messiah persona, its Manichean funk, like he'll bust out of his red cape with its icon insignia—like a superhero slipping into his street identity, and incognito sneak back to his dad's shop in Nazareth. The holy card is emblazoned: *In loving memory of Giorgio Michele Dolce, Died January 31, 1975. And may Perpetual Light Shine on Him.* At its bottom: *DeRosa Funeral Home.* I turn the card over: The *Pater Noster*—in Latin.

I sink to my father's side of the bed. "Oh, no," I say. "Oh, no."

Crow hurries to me and sits. "What is it, Baby?"

"My grandfather. He died—the same month I left—and I never even knew about it. I'm named after him."

Crow takes the holy card and studies it. She puts her arms around me, brings my head to her throat, her ripped dress. Kisses my head. "I'm so sorry."

"Dear God, what have I done?"

She says nothing, rocks me against her until I stand and begin to make the bed.

My bedroom has been maintained by my parents as a shrine. It looks precisely as it did the last time I entered it. It's dusted, vacuumed. The sheers over the windows glisten. The pillows are plumped. My books queue in alphabetical order from the shelves my father and I built for them. My desk sits at attention: its blotter and compliment of pens and pencils, a slide rule, compass. Even the calendar on it is keyed hauntingly to the exact day upon which I stand and stare at it.

Above my bed is the requisite crucifix, a golden plastic Christ on a garish beige cross much too large for Him. My father won it throwing baseballs at milk bottles at Saints Peter and Paul's bazaar. Jesus's eyes are open. Real nails plow through his hands and feet. A smear of red where the spear pierced him. My mother said it was too gruesome to fasten over my bed, but I begged. Much of the gold veneer has chipped away, leaving Jesus now the color of iron.

The portrait of my 1962 Little League team, the Yanks, in our heavy flannels, taken at Larimer Field. My father—already fifty-one, team coach, in plaid shirt, wingtips, a Yanks hat clamped on his head, heavy glasses—looms over the rest of us. Fourteen kids: five black, nine white—two of them murdered; one a suicide; one in prison; one, a junkie, Kevin Bond, gunned down in a Frankstown Avenue honky tonk, remanded for life to a motorized wheelchair. And me—whatever I am.

Another portrait, seven years later, of my JV football team at Saint Sebastian's: at the back entrance of the high school, facing the invisible quadrangle and the statue of the Sacred Heart. We wear the blue and gold hand-me-down jerseys of the legendary '64 team. A sign on the wall adjacent to us joins three isosceles triangles in the Civil Defense logo, beneath which is printed *Fallout Shelter.*

Every ribbon, plaque, award, citation. The inventory of plastic saints and angels spread across my dresser. Scapulars and rosaries. Easter palm everywhere, in the drawers and closets. My *Saint Joseph Daily Missel.* A bottle of holy water.

In the midst of all of it a framed photograph of Sterling that arrests me with such longing, such utter displacement, and unacknowledged loss, that I cannot avoid staring at it, though Crow is at my elbow. My dear heart, Sterling, standing on a beach, three large old wooden homes uptide of her hulking on the bare horizon, a cauldron of purplish-white cottony clouds bunched over the houses, above her head. So angelically beautiful, she pales the icons thronging her. In a long pink dress, black hair spilling beneath a wide-brim straw hat, her face shadowed and querulous, unsmiling, almost lost, amnesiac. Her right hand lifted—a bit like Jesus's in the holy card—but more in warning, or perhaps farewell—as if she wants it all to stop, to be released from this reliquary of my past.

When I turn away, Crow picks up the photograph. "She has pretty hands. I've never seen such long fingers." Then she returns it to the dresser. "You can't stop looking at her. Can you?"

"I'm not looking at her."

"You know what I mean. You love her more than me."

"That's not true."

"But we don't love each other at all. Remember?" Crow responds.

"I don't remember." And this is true. I don't remember not loving Crow.

Bees wake and rev in her eyes. "I don't want to talk about it." She walks out of the room.

I catch myself in the mirror over the desk: some derelict from the Old Testament. I follow her and close the door.

My parents have always been models of thrift. In truth, over the years, they've deprived themselves, though never me, their only child. Largesse when it comes to food, however, has always been their signature indulgence, their way of holding their heads up. They didn't have things—cars, houses, clothes—but they held onto the conviction that eating as well and as bountifully as anyone anywhere made their hardship and the hardships of their ancestors worth it. My ancestors: who lurched into Ellis Island, nothing but ocean in their amnesiac skulls and a swart, black-maned brood of babies. The only warmth, the only wealth, they harbored were the embers burning in their sockets, evident in every crude photo that's survived. They abandoned poor-mouth to the jagged hills of Italy, huddling feverish weeks in steerage on the beating Atlantic—then the Depression: *not a crust of bread, not even two nickels to rub together.* Polenta and macaroni. Period. Seven kids on each side, eight if you counted the dead, but they made do and they stayed together.

Today, however, when I open the refrigerator, I'm shocked. There's so little in it: a few yogurts, cottage cheese, milk, juice, the door lined with condiments, two eggs, a stick of butter. A chunk of Romano, not even wrapped entirely in its Saran wrap; a corner of it is gray and hard. No salami or capicola, chipped ham, four kinds of cheeses. No cokes and ginger ale, no beer, just a single can of Iron City I remove and set on the kitchen table. No tempting leftovers—eggplant parmesan, stuffed peppers, lasagna—carefully stored and labeled. I clean out what's spoiled, the fruit gone bad on the counters, the moldy bread in the bread box—though I salvage half a hardening loaf from Stagno's. Things didn't simply go all to hell since the very day my mother entered the hospital. My poor mom and dad have obviously been treading water for a while, just hanging on. And now, my dad, unraveling with my mother on the eighth floor of Saint Francis, her busted hip to boot, is raiding the liquor cabinet.

The freezer is almost bare, but I find a container of my mother's sauce, set it on the stove in a pot. The cupboards are no better. Only one pound of rigatoni. I put the water on to boil, take out the garbage, and do the dishes. Crow sets the table and salvages enough lettuce from the browning head of Romaine to make a salad. We lay a fresh table cloth on the dining table. I pour two shots of Rock and Rye, pour the rest down the sink, pitch the bottle, then crack open the Iron and wait for my father.

When my father walks in, he is overjoyed to see us. He holds us and kisses us. Crow helps him out of his coat. There is none of the bitterness from earlier in the afternoon. There is even a spring in his step, though he's carrying a cane, what he calls a *bastone.* It's as if he expected us to be there.

"Smell's good, kids."

"Mom's sauce," I say. "You hungry, Dad?"

"Oh yeah. I'm hungry."

"You eating okay?"

"I eat all the time, Georgie." He sits at the table and motions for me to sit across from him. Crow pulls dishes and silverware out of the cabinets and walks into the other room to set the table. He takes off his fedora and places it on the table, runs his fingers over the crease, around the band, raises the shot glass in my direction, pauses for a moment, as if there's something to toast. "*Saluto,*" he says.

We throw down the shots. I swig some beer to chase its cloying, then pass the can across the table. My father holds up his hand—*No*—in that timeless Italian gesture. He looks so much like my grandfather: the silvering flint complexion, twelve hours of beard coating his face in thick white stubble, magnificent ears, the crazy shock of hair, thoroughly white now, whipped up on his crown. Old now, but still looks like you could bust a brick over his head and he wouldn't flinch. His big brown hands are whorled and gnarled, outsized, the knuckles like vertebrae, blunt fingers, blackened nails. I have one hand like that, but its history is disgrace.

"I don't buy much beer any more," he says. Then: "Lot of commotion down on the corner."

"Yeah, I don't know what's going on."

"It gets worse every day. You see what it looks like up and down the street? I don't know what we're going to do, your mother and me."

I get up and reach in the fridge for the Romano, dip into the cabinet for the grater, drop the pasta into the water. "Rigatoni okay, Dad?"

"Yeah, rigatoni's fine. You want some wine with dinner? There's wine."

My father eats heartily. Heavily peppers his macaroni, a fork in one hand, bread in the other. We hardly speak. He has said more today to me, and with more pain, more labor, more candor than any other day that I've known him. I have forced him to string together words he thought he would never have to say. For today, perhaps forever, he is at the end of words, and the fatigue deviling his face is the strain of knowing there is more to say. He is lost without my mother.

"When do you kids have to leave?" he asks.

"I don't know, Dad. We have train tickets for tomorrow."

Crow finally looks at me. She has not said a word about the train we'll never catch, that pulled out of the station one hour ago, the tickets still in her purse. She knows now, as do I, that we have no destination, no plan whatsoever, that when we left Queen just two days ago, we made a pact with random, stepped into the blind, that now more than ever we don't know who we are or how we fit together, but we are very much on the run.

She has showered and changed into a green dress patterned with big moon flowers, lace at the V-dipped collar and cuffs, a rawhide necklace and Dave's communion rosary around her neck, red lipstick. Nothing else on her face. Ebony hair cowls her starkly white face. She sits next to my father, occasionally rubbing his back, refilling his water glass, asking him what else she can get him, assuring him that the food will restore him, then a good night's sleep. Everything will be alright.

He accepts her solicitude with gravity, but appreciation, as if he's known her all his life, that accepting her kindness is a matter of routine. He visibly softens at her touch as she does what I cannot do. “Thanks, Honey,” he says again and again, though he cannot forge a smile nor will he say her name.

When he has finished eating, she guides him along with me upstairs, lays out fresh pajamas for him, sets water on the nightstand.

“Good night, Mr. Dolce,” she says, tears in her eyes, then throws herself into his arms. He holds her a long moment. Then she kisses him.

“Thanks for everything, Honey,” he says. “I feel bad about the way things turned out. Another time, I hope.” Then he smiles.

Crow smiles. Tears roll down her cheeks. She kisses him again. To me: “I'm going to bed.”

“Sit,” my father says, motioning to the bed, as soon as Crow leaves. “I wish I had money to give you, Georgie.”

“Dad, I wish you'd take that five hundred.”

“No more about that five hundred. You'll need it anyhow. What are you going to do?”

“I don't know, Dad.”

“The police were here, after you disappeared and the pharmacy was robbed and the car stolen. More than once. You know, they put two and two together.” Stuck in a nightmare, he shakes his head. “We couldn't accept that you would do something like that. The drugs. Stealing. The whole thing.” He wags a finger before my face. “But don't think for a minute that your mother's stupid. She knew the score on this one.”

“Dad, I'm so sorry.”

He lifts the hand, my grandfather's hand. “I already said as much as I'm going to say on the subject. It's just a good thing your mother's not in her right mind, that they have her so out of it with all this medicine. I don't know what she would have done today when you walked in that room. I guess if she hadn't already had a nervous breakdown, she would've taken one right there.”

My father sits next to me, unlaces each shoe, stands and slides them under the nightstand. He takes off his pants, change ringing in the pockets and drapes them over the vanity chair, where he has placed them every day since he and my mother married in 1945. He takes off his shirt and hangs it in the closet, stands there for a moment in his white boxers, white T-shirt, each skeletal ridge and knob exaggerated. He's thirty pounds lighter than the last time I saw him. He slips into his pajamas, an exuberant flannel Scotch plaid—my mother has always bought his clothes—and sits again next to me.

“What I wanted to tell you is that this pharmacist did not press charges. Did not accuse you of anything. Like you disappearing and all this trouble at his drug store are two different things. No connection.”

"So, there are no warrants? No nothing? I don't have to worry about the cops?"

"Not unless you've done something else."

I want to be pissed off now—at my dad. For talking to me like this. But I must be still and listen without flinching. I have studied Saint James on Crow's couch in Queen: . . . *he is like unto a man beholding his natural face in a glass: For he beholdeth himself, and goeth his way, and straightway forgetteth what manner of man he was.* Here in my parents' bedroom, in the home in which I was loved so passionately—here in East Liberty, of course—I cannot run from what I am. Back here on Saint Marie Street—where just a few hours ago, I was in a terrible fight. That kid sliding off my back with a switchblade in his spine. I catch myself sidelong in my mother's vanity mirror. There it is. Incontrovertible: *the perfect law of liberty.* I can only hang my head.

"Anyhow," my dad continues, "he didn't give you up. Which means he was up to something too. Right?"

I turn to him and start to lie, but his look heads me off. "Yeah," I say.

"Let me tell you a little something about your old man, Georgie. I been around the block a couple times. I grew up in this neighborhood. I've seen some guys. I know what's what. Just because your mother and I are two simple people who came by everything the hard way—by working for it and eating plenty of shit in the bargain—that doesn't make us stupid. I'm not ashamed of anything."

He's ashamed of me though. He won't say it. But I hear shame in every molecule of this house—the conversations my parents have had over me still wafting in the cornices, whispering: *Ignominioso. Disgrazia.*

"What I want to tell you is that Eugene came over one night after you left, and explained what happened. About Felix Costa and the jackpot you landed yourself in. He felt real bad about it, Georgie. You know we all go way back."

"Eugene shouldn't feel bad. He didn't do anything wrong."

"Jesus Christ, boy, everybody feels bad. Anyhow, Eugene told me there was a third party involved. That's gotta be Rosechild, right?"

Again I suppress the reflex toward falsehood. "Yeah."

"Okay, the good thing is he didn't turn you in. He's got insurance. The car and break-in. It's nothing to him and, without you, they have nothing on him. Besides, what he did, the gambling and so forth: small potatoes next to what you did. So he played it smart. Your mother and I notified the police and filed a missing persons report. They came here and talked to us. They would've put two and two together with the pharmacy; but, like I said, Rosechild didn't press charges. He called here every day for two weeks to see if we had heard from you, cried like a baby on the telephone, just couldn't get over you were gone, what a good boy you were. Your mother wouldn't talk to him. Jew this and Jew that. She blames him and his daughter for everything. I talked to him. I finally told him we'd let him know if we heard from you. Maybe he was just covering his ass, but there was something about him when I talked to him that wasn't just bullshit—like he meant what he said. I don't know. I guess, now, after over a year figuring you're gone for good, he's stopped shitting little green apples."

"I am gone for good."

"What's that supposed to mean? We don't have the money to help you out of this. We barely have a pot to piss in. I'm done at the mill. They'll never call me back. Your mother and I, we both know it, but we never bring it up. We sit around and talk like when we first got married—like a couple of dreamers—that maybe things'll straighten out. All those years, I should have listened to your mother when she told me to get out of the mill, look for something else. The wildcats, the strikes, laid off half the time. But I believed in the Union. I wanted to stick it out. For her. For you. Now I see I was a fool. I'll end up with only half my pension. But who can see the future? Now all we want is for you to come home. We don't even know where you live, and I guess it's better if we don't know. Isn't that a hell of a thing? Every time the phone rings, a knock on the door, your mother thinks it's you. She gets up in the middle of the night because she says she hears you. 'That's Georgie down there in the kitchen.' The novenas and the rosaries. 'How about if I give some money to the church? Maybe God'll send Georgie home.'"

"Maybe I can get the eleven grand," I say.

"This Costa. He won't listen to reason and he's charging you interest—compounded monthly."

"Says who?"

"This is what Eugene told me."

"What if I talk to Eugene?"

"You better leave him out of this. Connie took the kids and left him."

"Why?"

"I don't know what all happened, but a lot happens over the course of a year—especially when you're my age. I do know that he got in Dutch with Felix."

"Over me?"

"That I don't know. I haven't seen Eugene since the day he showed up here, not long after you left, to explain things to your mother and me."

Eugene and Connie loved each other; they were in it for the long haul, happy in their five room house. They were making a go of it—with little Eugene and Michelle—on Eugene's electrician wages and whatever extra he made on side-jobs and knocking down a little book for Felix. Connie baked and had a garden. She made all the kids' clothes.

"Maybe I can get the money," I repeat vacantly.

"You got rocks in your head, Georgie? How the hell you gonna get the money?"

The telephone rings, the same old phone that's been on the night stand forever, the one I spent so many hours talking to Sterling on.

My father picks it up, says hello, then hangs up. "Wrong number," he says. "I miss your mother. She's a great lady, Georgie. You don't even know. And she's tough. That phone used to ring and, your mother, she'd be on the phone all night with one of her girlfriends. I'd watch television. Maybe I'd watch a ball game and fall asleep and she'd come in after she got off the phone—two solid hours sometimes—and give me a little hell about snoring, and then we'd have a little something and watch the news together and pretty soon I was waking her up because she was snoring and we went to bed. That was our life, and I miss it. Now she's in the hospital and then to that other place for rehab. And whatever's going on inside her mind. Look in the closet." He nods his head toward the closet. "You'll see a wheelchair and diapers. These were supposed to be the golden years." He manages a smile, then puts his arm around me. "I'm sorry for opening up on you like that in the hospital."

"You have nothing to be sorry for, Dad."

"I spoke harshly. But I gotta ask you, Georgie, just for myself . You'll have to forgive me. Between me and you. Your mother'll never know. It was you. Wasn't it? You broke into the pharmacy. Robbed the cash register, stole the drugs and the car?"

More words have issued from my father tonight than I thought were in him. Because he's never been one to cast his feelings into words, to tip ever to anyone how he feels, what he's thinking, I have in my arrogance misapprehended him. In my juvenile heart, I thought his silence meant that he couldn't be penetrated by sorrow. He was too strong for it; he'd never allow it to have its way with him. His entire company, save him and few others, were massacred at Normandy. I saw him as merely sacrificial—simply making way for me, the promised one. Clearly he is the promised one. But none of the promises have been kept.

Nor has he committed words to paper. A few syllables here and there: my name on my lunch bag in his hieroglyphic scrawl, hacked like I-beams, scraps from grocery bags clipped to dollar bills, then fives, then tens and twenties, with *Drive Slow, Lots Love, Dad.* Nothing much to leave a trail.

But, tonight, my father, the sudden nihilist, his world in charred flinders about him, has recorded his cached words in blazing tapes that will play in my head unbidden for the rest of my life. They shall burn across my blood like a curse: the sound of my beloved father's voice pounding in my veins evermore in perfect chiseled iambs: *defeat, disgrace, deceit, erase.*

Yet he still loves me. This is what I cannot bear.

"Yes, Dad," I finally answer.

"I guess I knew that. Of course, I knew. But . . . And was that stolen money you left in that envelope for your mother and me?"

"The money I left for you and Mom was what I had left in my savings account. I know I've been a worthless son, but I wouldn't have implicated you and Mom like that."

"I thank you for that, Georgie. I really do. And I'm ashamed to say that your mother and I ended up spending it. We hung onto it as long as we could manage, waiting for you to come home, so we could hand it back to you, but then things got so bad."

He looks down at his hands, hanging in his lap like mammoth ancient spiders. The room is dark. He gets to his feet, and opens his dresser drawer. In it are his handful of neckties, immaculate white ironed handkerchiefs, dress socks, gifts he's been given that he's never used—cuff links, tie tacks, collar bars, scarves, a bottle of English Leather. He rummages around and pulls out a cigar box, turns and hands it to me.

Inside is a pistol—not at all like Crow's tidy .22. Bigger, with more heft, and longish, the grainy butt scored with ground-in filth, slippery, a band of electrical tape at its base, its sight filed away, rust at the bore where bullets have passed into the night with the report of death and ill will, blood and lament—an engine that thrums with bad news.

"Dad, what are you doing with this?"

"A fella at the mill gave it to me. Back during the riots. When they shot King."

Martin Luther King in April, Robert Kennedy in May. The photograph of the motel balcony in Memphis, Jesse Jackson and Ralph Abernathy, looking deeply into the bluest black night, its "lips dripping with interposition," the promised land a mirage fading across the molten Delta, Dr. King sprawled at their feet.

What haunted me more was the image of Kennedy cruciform splashed across the front page of the *Press,* his eyes—clearly he'd departed, his soul peering out through the gashes in his sockets—attempting to narrate the passage between here and there. His look of unearthly astonishment. As if trying to describe what had happened himself: what it was like to be shot in the head, whatever abbreviated intentions he had had at that moment being escorted by Rafer Johnson through the Beverly Hills Wilshire kitchen, to have those thoughts displaced by an inconsequential spall of molded alloy dedicated from its inception to be his last notion. He wanted to say something. That was apparent. But that part of him had been eviscerated. Someone held his head up. He was handsome. There was still the blaze in his cornea guttering up, the prelude to the cathodes on his irises dwindling into disillumination—for that instant, snared in the bulb-flash, the black puddle of blood nimbusing his blasted skull.

They always shoot them in the head, in the face, in the throat. Now I can shoot someone with that kind of exquisite resolve. But who? Felix? Phil Rosechild? Myself?

"Your mother never knew I had this thing." My mother—who went to bed and cried for Bobby Kennedy. Not for King, but for Kennedy. "Take it." The gun in its casket sits in his hands.

"I don't want it, Dad. You hang on to it."

And just like that, he makes a face like *okay,* flips the lid of the cigar box closed and tucks it back in his drawer, returns to the bed and sinks down next to me. "Now I'm tired," he says. "Tomorrow's another day."

Through the gossamer sheers, beyond the panes, the raging snow throws its ghostly pall of light.

"I'm sorry, Dad. I'm so sorry I did this to you and Mom."

He takes me against him. I lay my head on his shoulder. He kisses my head. He kisses each cheek in turn, holds my face between his hands and gazes at me. "I wish I could give you something, Son."

I kiss his cheek. I hang onto him for a little bit, then get up to leave. He stands and extends his right hand. I proffer my bad. He takes my sorrowful hand and simply holds it, studying it as if it harbors the answer to how we have arrived at this unfathomable pass.

"Your poor hand," he says. "My boy. My boy's poor hand." His voice breaks.

"Squeeze it, Dad."

He smiles. His hand tightens over mine. And I feel it: the might of my father—like when I was a kid. There in my parents' bedroom, where I was conceived, we shake hands. Then I turn and walk away, fastening the door behind me.

The hall is black. A faint seam of light leaks out from under my bedroom door. The cedar chest rests, there along the wall, in its cloistered alcove. Above it hangs the daguerreotype in its heavy brass frame of my father's mother, Maria Cristina Bocchiccio, sprigs of brass laurel crossed at its base with the scripted legend: *Memorare.* The mother my father can't recollect. Gone before he knew her: dark, expressionlessly beautiful, resigned, an Adriatic woman who birthed her eighth child, then bled to death on Carver Street on The Feast of the Assumption, 1920.

I open the chest, inhale the archive of our family: christening gowns and bonnets, bronzed baby shoes, my mother's wedding gown, my parents' wedding portraits, birth and baptismal certificates, my grandfather Giorgio's delicate parchment *Certificate of Naturalization,* 1911. On it, my father, six months old, is listed along with one of my aunts and an uncle. Five more babies would follow. The marriage certificate of my mother's parents, Giovanna and Alphonso, 1915, also parchment, falling apart at the creases, ornate script and outdated gorgeous penmanship.

My parents' marriage certificate.

My father's Purple Heart and *Honorable Discharge from the Army of the United States* as a PFC in the 101st Radio Intelligence Company. My letter from the Selective Service listing me 1H.

A lush Della Robbia zippered velvet purse. Within a dozen rosaries. One I remember from my childhood somehow: crystal prismatic beads, silver crucifix stamped on its back with *Italia,* the Christ that hangs from it ivory. My mother owns rosaries the way seamstresses own thimbles. She let me pray on this one when I was first navigating the chaplets and mysteries and decades as a little boy. It was so enormous, I could step through it.

A pin with a likeness of Saint Dominic Savio, and the legend: *Saint Dominic Savio Club*—to which my mother belonged. Saint Dominic, an especially pure boy, I'd read about in Butler's *Lives of the Saints.* The entry referred to the "all but bloody fields of teenage purity." I hadn't known then what that meant, but tonight I stand in that field, in the wake of that squandered purity.

My mother's class ring: *Peabody High School, 1937.* A tie bar with the United States Steel escutcheon: *40 years.* My mother's engagement ring: six little diamonds, and at their center elevated a large diamond. Delicate, so indescribably beautiful I can't imagine it on her finger. Nor have I ever seen it there. A sprig of ubiquitous Easter palm, creased, brittle.

The life insurance policies, my mother and father's executed will—everything to me, the beneficiary, the heir—their only child. *Beloved*—in the vernacular.

And lastly, along with the receipts for their monthly payments, the sales agreement from the Catholic Cemeteries Association of the Diocese of Pittsburgh, for their final resting place in Mount Carmel Cemetery—finalized on Christmas Eve, 1969, without even the vaguest inkling on my part.

I lower the lid of the cedar chest, sit on the trove of my birthright and cry bitterly for perhaps a minute—with neither sound nor tears nor tremor. Then I rise and walk into my bedroom.

Crow's back is to me. She stares at the photograph of Sterling. Candles flicker throughout the room. She is completely naked. In the candlelight, she gleams like a glow-in-the-dark statue, made of magic aggregate that stores light and, once the light extinguishes, glows incandescently like those that still line my dresser: Saint Joseph, Saint Anthony, the Blessed Mother, the Infant of Prague. Night after night, as I hunkered in my child's bed, fighting off the onset of nightmare, trying to remember my prayers, as the windows blackened, they gazed down on me in benediction

"How's your father?" she asks without turning.

"I don't know. I guess more than anything he's exhausted."

She turns. There's a bit of the harlequin to her. It's the light, the pallor of the candles, the snow blanketing down now in quasars of white. And her skin, glowing as if from within—like mother's milk, bluish, deliquescent. Her hair is moonless black, pinned at the sides with silver barrettes, revealing the coded glyphs across her forehead, the *time* tattoo a watery blue just beneath her navel. Like an invitation. Like an injunction.

"Romeo," she whispers, holds her arms out like a child. Then, again with more volume. Sexy teeth, coming together, the generous mouth, red red her lipstick. A woman who will chew through flesh if so-minded. She smiles. Her eyes blush. The bees bat shut their long-lashed lids. I take her, slight, tensile, against me. She yanks my shirt out of my pants, runs her hands under it. Over her shoulder, Sterling stands at earth's apogee, the Atlantic at her feet, beatified, iconic, so far beyond my ken that I close my eyes to forget her and squeeze Crow until a tiny *oh* escapes her—as if something long concealed has revealed itself.

I disappear into the abyss of Crow's long kiss, and when I surface I am spread in my old bed, my clothes on the floor, she hovering above me with a basin of warm water and a wash cloth, swabbing every inch of me, wringing ceremoniously the water from the soiled rag, the water darkening. She dips down to kiss me, breathing into my mouth the occultation of her eyes. Then she lies atop me, pours into the topography of my body, assumes me into her, warm, but like dry ice, smoking, whispering, her mouth against my ear, in the language scarred into her brow: *the negation of George Dolce.* Against me hammers *time time time,* Crow's dancing shadow beating across the ceiling like Joan of Arc swooning at the stake, the tarriance of flame in the folds of her execution frock.

Chapter 23

We'd been flying down Fifth Avenue in Sterling's Mercedes. When she asked me to slow down, I increased my speed, traffic lights like ellipses, and drove more recklessly. The mansions lining the street were big as mausoleums.

"Why are you doing this?" she screamed.

"What was with that guy from Haverford? The one your father told me about?"

"Not true love, Giorgio."

"What then?"

"Stop the car."

I pulled into Mellon Park and parked next to the tennis courts. Despite the fierce cold, the court lights were on. The nets danced in the wind. A few bundled people walked their leashed dogs. We got out and stood next to the car.

"What was it then, Sterling?"

"There is no *what,* Giorgio."

"What's that supposed to mean?"

Little clouds sprung out of our mouths. Sirens split the night.

"It means what I said to you the first night we met," said Sterling. *"Improvisation.* Not *preoccupation.* I don't walk around with my guard up at all times. I met this guy. I fell for him. He treated me like shit. My heart broke. I took to my bed. Stopped eating. Stopped shaving all the places women shave on their bodies. Ignored personal hygiene. Didn't go to class. Said I would take my life, but never tried. I reread my Salinger books. I wept, returned home to Pittsburgh for a while, got some help, and then I was alright. Basically I just improvised for a while."

"What about Bill?"

"Bill is all in your mind. He never meant a thing to me. The one great act of improvisation I've seen from you is when you attacked Bill. I was aghast, but thrilled."

"A gold-plated, spoiled little debutante like yourself thrilled at cheap hoodlum violence?"

"I can't really help what thrills me, Giorgio."

I gathered her in my arms and kissed her. She threw up her hand to keep her beret from falling off.

When we came apart, she smiled and said, "It was still inexcusable."

"The kiss?"

"You know what I'm talking about. At Jamie's."

"I know and I'm sorry."

"But you've not said a single word about it. Those people are my friends."

"I'm sorry."

"And you're feeding my father the very thing that will destroy my family."

"What are you talking about?"

"Come on, Giorgio. What do you think? That you're smarter than everybody else? You know what I'm talking about. The gambling. The goddam gambling."

"How do you know?"

"I can read your mind. It's why you love me. And I can read my father's as well. Please do not insult me further by denying it."

"Does your mother know?"

"Everything."

"You know, Sterling, He's not a child. He knows what he's doing, and what's more he can afford it."

"He has no idea what he's doing, George. He's a sick sick man. And you've been taking unholy advantage of him. He loves you like a son."

"You snap your fingers and whatever you want appears. You don't know what the other side is like."

"You are not the only person that's ever had a childhood." I said nothing. "Why don't you face your sense of inferiority?"

"That's bullshit."

"Really? You're at heart a mama's boy. No, wait. You hate your mother. Which is it, Giorgio?"

A police car slowed as it passed.

"I asked you to marry me yesterday, and you never answered," I said.

"I'm still thinking about it."

"I want you to marry me."

"Marriage is my father's idea. We can't get married. We're kids. We've known each other three weeks. Not even."

"You say you love me."

"I do love you."

"Prove it."

Button by button, she undid her long black coat and swung it open like a gunfighter. She wore a black leotard, a pleated red plaid skirt and tights. A streetlight threw down its frozen light on her. The police cruiser had come to a halt.

"Did you like making love to me?" she asked.

"Yes." I moved toward her. The sirens seemed interested. They moved closer. Louder.

"With your smashed hand and lacerated ego?"

"Yes."

"We could make love right here on the icy earth. Have you ever done that, Giorgio?"

I snaked my arms inside her coat and gripped her nylon waist. Smooth as opal. Black like the night cold.

"Have you ever been that careless?" she goaded.

The last time I had seen Alex had been at Dave Mazzotti's little brother's high school graduation party. Alex sat on the back porch floor with the sketch pad he carried everywhere. It was all he had left. He showed me extraordinary drawings of a syringe, bent spoons, a zippo, works, little waxed baggie corners with the shit in it tied off with jute. *Tools,* he called them. *Sistine Chapel. Have you ever seen Leonardo's drawings*? He laughed. That dilapidated doper laugh. One of his front teeth gone. His hair long and greasy.

Alex believed that by rendering the images of his desire, drawing them so lifelike, that he could reach into the borders and grasp them—*authentic* was the word he had used—that he could manifest them. They would appear. *Like the Transubstantiation. These are my sacraments. My sacrifice.* He had studied it somewhere. He had books on it. Used to have books on it. He leaked that broken-down laugh. *But don't worry. It's all up here.* He tapped his temple. *Everything memorized. Dewey Decimal down to the Dewey, Georgie.* Death rattle laugh. *My body. My blood.*

I laughed too. *Okay, Alex,* I said.

Toward the end, Alex hunched down to Pitt and pimped his plasma for dope, sold off his paintings for chaff so he could cop, finally took to kicking in storefronts in broad daylight and simply reaching in for what he thought he could sell. *Manifesting. The Life of the World to Come.* Alex had *careless* down pat.

"Does this little skirt remind you of those Catholic girls you plundered under the consecrated bleachers, Giorgio?"

"Stop calling me Giorgio?"

"Is it too much for you? Sweet Giorgio. Shall I lie back now? Is this a wager? Double or nothing? Odds? That you'll get the girl to strip?"

It wasn't fair: how in this script such dialogue had been forced on Sterling. Making her some kind of witch. But she wouldn't hush. She had hijacked my vision.

"You just can't believe that a bum like you has a girl like me. Happiness is an inch away, but you have to blow it."

"I'm sorry," I said. "When I'm sorry, I break things. I set things on fire."

She took a step back, her hands held out in front of her. I grabbed her wrists, cleaved her to me and kissed her. She didn't struggle, but her lips tasted of *No.* Her arms had fallen to her sides. The policeman was out of his car. He had a flashlight in his hand. He switched it on and beamed the light in my face. I let go of Sterling, and turned to face the cop.

It was a just a dream, but I aimed to make a scene, prove to Sterling how much I loved her. Like *I love you so much I'll fight this cop.* But the officer gave me neither the chance to attack nor explain. He came straight down with the flashlight on my scalp, sending me to my knees. My hands went to my head. The policeman grabbed a handful of my hair, bowed me back with a knee to my back, forced me face down in the snow, dropped the flashlight and handcuffed me. In the bar of light the flashlight leaked over the snow I saw my blood.

I'm okay, I told myself once I was fully awake. I didn't put much stock in dreams. It had been a dream after all, yes, and people didn't tell the truth in dreams. I was merely upset about having come so close to the really big payoff, about my parents, how helpless they suddenly seemed, how no one ever told the truth. I had not even been able to tell them about my Super Bowl trip to New Orleans. But I had been admitted into Yale—more than a tolerable barter.

I had to talk to Sterling. I'd see her that evening when I drove her to the airport. She was going to Bryn Mawr for a New Year's Eve party the next night, and would be back the day after New Year's. We'd get things resolved. I was through with her father as a gambling associate. I'd work for Phil, finish up at Duquesne, and strike out for New Haven in August.

In the meantime, I'd fall in with Eugene and Felix, wager modestly myself, and replenish what I'd lost. My dad would begin collecting unemployment in a little over a month. We weren't in such bad shape. *Just sit tight, keep cool and gut it out.* I'd settle things with Phil later in the morning. March in, collect Phil's loss—Monday instead of Tuesday was payday because of the way the holidays fell—drop the money at Eugene's during my deliveries, and see if the lines had changed for the college Bowl games. Then finesse things with Sterling. Tricky, maybe. But I loved her. No question. And I wasn't about to let anything jeopardize that.

At ten o'clock, I clipped into the pharmacy, triggering the bell that tinkled when someone entered. Phil stood behind the counter meting out pills to their little cylindrical bottles. He glanced up and smiled.

"Top of the morning to you, George."

"Morning, Phil."

"How's the hand?"

Not bad. Coming along."

"Very good. Very Good." He glanced for a minute at my bandaged aching hand. It had the weight of iron. "The end of the year, my boy. Time for new initiatives, new plans, better plans, to be hatched. Also, a classic morbid time for regret. But let's have none of that. What say, let's have a drink? It's not too early for you, is it?"

"Thanks, Phil. But if I drink anything now, I'll be useless for the rest of the day."

The bottle of gin sat on the shelf behind Phil. He had already been drinking.

"What a precarious balance," Phil went on. He held up a pill. "The correct amount of these little devils will save a life, yet maybe a grain or more over what must remain exact, even an infinitesimal amount, will kill you. Exactitude, George. It's what we all long for."

Maybe Phil was drunk. He had a moony penchant for eloquence and melodrama when he drank. *Exactitude* indeed. This was a man I was getting ready to hit up for the eleven thousand dollars I owed Eugene.

"Do you believe in God, George?"

"I don't know."

"It's the shank end of the year, my boy. If ever there was a time to believe in God, it's now. There's still time to make a killing."

"Phil, I need to settle up with my guy today."

"It's not Tuesday, George. Tuesday is pay day."

"I know. I forgot to mention it. That was an oversight on my part. But he's not going to be around tomorrow because of the holiday, so today's the day."

"But I want to bet the Bowl games."

"That'll be next week's tab. I still have to pay him today. Protocol."

Phil smiled. "Of course. Protocol." He turned and pulled down the bottle. "I don't have the money, George."

Phil: the pleasant, baggy florid face, his white polo shirt collar lying outside the collar of his maroon sweater, the glasses like a scaffold depending from his neck. Still smiling, Phil lifted his hand off the bottle and raked it through his sparse brown hair. Phil was exactly my father's age. I had never seen my father cry. I realized, with profound disgust, that Phil was fighting tears.

"What do you mean you don't have the money, Phil?"

"I just don't have it." Phil's eyes welled up and bulged.

"You can give it to me tomorrow then."

"I don't have it to give you. I don't have it."

I trembled, fighting myself now, attempting to remain cool, smart. *Eleven thousand dollars.*

"Okay, Phil. When will you have it?"

"I don't have it. I never had it. I never will have it."

Phil sunk to the stool behind the counter and wept. Phlegmy, guttural, his face bowed in both hands. The pleated hairless skin at his crown gleamed in the overhead fluorescence.

I couldn't help but feel sorry for him. This was Phil. Mr. Rosechild. A man I had come to admire. A man who had really come to mean something to me. Sterling's dad. But not having the money? Of course he had the money.

"I gotta have the money, Phil."

"There is no money, George," Phil blubbered, an all-out desperate child's heaving. "I'm sorry."

With my left hand, I picked up the bottle to throw, then set it back down. I looked again at the translucent dome of Phil's head, the skin like cellophane.

"Jesus Christ, Phil. I owe the bookie eleven thousand dollars. How can you not have the money? How much do you have?"

"I'm broke. I don't have any of it. A few hundred, maybe."

"What in the goddam hell were you thinking betting all that money if you didn't have it? Huh? Jesus Christ. What do you think my guy's going to say when I show up without his money? What do you think is going to happen to me? I can't believe you'd hang me out to dry like this. What about all that bullshit that I'm just like family?"

Phil looked up. Like a picture of one of those pitiful UNICEF kids on TV. Every trace of sympathy flooded out of me; I was in real trouble. Panicky, can't-think-straight electric trouble. I swept the loose pills and packed prescription bottles off the counter to the floor where they bounced and clattered.

Phil jumped and backed up a pace. He tried to smile again. "There. It's better now," he said. "We'll figure something out." He took out a handkerchief, mopped his face, then blew his nose. "We'll work this damn thing out."

"Just tell me one thing, Phil. Do you have eleven thousand dollars to hand me?"

For a moment Phil attempted to grind out an answer that might please me, then merely shook his head *No* and sunk to the chair again, now dry-eyed, catatonic, ancient.

"How the hell can you not have the money, Phil? The cars, the house, the business, club memberships, tuition at Bryn Mawr, everything? You think I'm stupid? You live like a king. I want the goddam money." I picked up the gin bottle again and shook it in Phil's face. "How about if I bash your fucking head in? That's what's going to happen to me when I walk in and tell the bookie I don't have his money, that I put up ten grand I never had in the first place. I just can't believe you'd do this to me."

"Do whatever you want to me, George. But I don't have the money."

"You are fucking loaded, Phil. How can you not have the money?"

"It's an illusion."

"Please. Just speak English.

"I'm in hock, mortgaged, overextended to my neck. I haven't paid taxes in years. This entire operation, absolutely everything, is about to crumble. I'm always no more than a minute from putting a bullet through my head."

"Borrow the money. Then put a bullet through your head."

"No one would lend it to me. My creditors are about to lynch me. You don't understand."

"No, you don't understand. You don't know what kind of trouble I'm in." I brandished the bottle again, and this time Phil cowered. "You better come up with that money. I'm not holding the bag on this."

"I just thought everything would work out," Phil quaked.

"Well," I said, returning the bottle back to the counter, "you thought wrong. I'm going to take a walk around the block, Phil. And when I come back. I don't know what when I come back. But you better have a plan. Does Sterling, or JoAnn, know anything about this?"

"No, no, no," Phil said shaking his head, not looking up. "Absolutely not."

I walked up Highland Avenue to the reservoir. No one else was out. I stood at the railing and stared at the frozen water, the wind cutting me until I shook. A flock of pigeons scuffed over the ice. I cried out and they flung up gray into the gray sky and wound out of sight. The air was so frigidly sterile that the world had lost its smell. Phil had asked me if I believed in God. I still couldn't say, though I knew that people in my position prayed for help. Hesitant to squander my paltry store of indulgence, I wasn't quite ready yet to plead. So far nothing irrevocable had happened between Phil and me. Under the circumstances, my response had been measured. Judicious. No one could blame me for anything.

When I returned to the pharmacy, the lights were doused, the door locked and the CLOSED sign mounted in the window. Phil's Audi was gone. The Vega squatted under a mound of snow. I broke into a run toward the Rosechilds' home. Seven blocks, falling twice on the ice, once on my bad hand, until I stood in front of their house, winded, tasting blood, torrents of smoke filing out of my lungs. The last two fingers on the hand were blue. I couldn't feel a thing below my wrist. The Audi queued in the driveway behind Sterling's car and JoAnn's station wagon. I considered kicking in the door and dragging Phil's sorry ass into the street. Jack him up in front of his wife and daughter. I walked home.

A feather duster poked out of my father's back pocket as he vacuumed.

"You're home for lunch," he said when I walked through the front door.

"Nah, I'm done for the day. We closed early for the holiday weekend."

"You hungry?"

"Nah, I'm fine. I was hoping I could borrow the car for a little while. Where's Mom?"

"Upstairs in bed."

"What's the matter?"

"One of her bad days. She had a little spell."

"What kind of spell?"

"She fainted. One of the pipes in the cellar busted. The plumber was here all morning. What a mess. She got herself good and worked up—the money, the mess, the cold, the whole shooting match—and *bing.* Good thing I was standing there. I wanted to call the paramedics, but then she started carrying on about that, so I shut my mouth and made her a cup of tea. She's asleep."

My father switched attachments on the vacuum, got down on his hands and knees, and snaked the hose under the couch. He got to his feet gingerly, switched off the machine and began dusting.

"Is that why you're doing all this?" I asked. "Because Mom's sick?"

"Where you been, Georgie? Except for the cooking—she won't let me in the kitchen—I been doing all the housework since I been laid off. Your mother's not a well woman. I'm worried about her. Sam DeLucia can get me a few hours at the Kennilworth washing dishes. He'll pay me under the table. Until my unemployment kicks in. But I'm afraid to leave her by herself. She's driving me crazy."

My father, after a life of hard knocks, sixty-four damn years old, washing dishes, laid off, waiting for the Union to settle. Doing housework for his sickly wife, moaning about money in her sleep as her ankles swelled. While Phil just walked away from an eleven grand tab and cruised home to eat lunch in his townhouse.

"I don't want you to worry, Son. No matter what, you go on with your life. Everybody gets a shot, and you got a good one. This is a sinking ship, Georgie. Swim away."

On the way to Eugene's, I swung by the Rosechilds. I needed to corner Phil before I picked up Sterling later to drive her to the airport. It had to be bullshit that he didn't have the money. Yet there was not a doubt in my mind that Phil had been telling me the truth. The three cars were still there. The way things were, I didn't trust myself—nor how Phil might react—to drop in on them. I noticed someone pass in front of the upstairs window. I cruised by, stopped at a pay phone and called. JoAnn answered. I hung up. Then I dropped by the bank, closed out my checking account, $286, and withdrew in twenties the rest of my savings: $1800.00.

"You got to be kidding me, Georgie," Eugene said. He smiled the way people betrayed by someone close to them smile. We sat in Eugene's cellar office. From upstairs, the sound of the television and EJ motoring through the house on his new Christmas Big Wheels filtered down to us. The naked pipes over our heads vibrated.

"It wasn't my bet, Eug."

"I know. You told me that."

"Can you give me a little time?"

"Till tomorrow, maybe the next day."

"How about longer?

"I can't float you for eleven grand, Cuz. It's too much. You see this house. Go up and explain this to my wife. Look at my kids. You think your good intentions will feed them? Or the fact that we go way back? I got Christmas bills coming out my ass. I live beyond my means already. Connie's mom's in a nursing home. I got responsibilities. I'm a man. This ain't no game, Georgie. College boy. It's time to make like a grownup."

"I'm sorry, Eugene."

"The real kicker, my man, is that you dumped me in the soup big time. With Felix, the professional maniac. You got in on this in the first place because of my say-so. We were about to cut you in on the action, make you a junior partner. Remember? I trusted you because of who you are, who your mother and father are. And you put me and my family in jeopardy. Making me look like a jagoff. It comes back on me when one of my customers reneges. What the hell do you think Felix'll say when I tell him my figure is light eleven big ones? This is business, Cuz. Big business—this kind of money. We're not a lending institution. He's going to cuss me out berserk and then he's going to come after you."

I had heard stories about gamblers who stiffed bookies. Sometimes they made you their stooge till you worked it off: paint their house, mow their grass or drive them around; make you their houseboy. Cut your balls off with menial shit-eating chores. Until they decided the debt was paid. You might also end up a bagman, running around town collecting illegal cash. Or standing on a corner hawking hot cameras, smuggled cigarettes. You could end up a dope courier, crossing the state line with a trunk full of weed.

I knew a guy from the old neighborhood who had to lam it out of town. Word was they were looking to lay some real damage on him. Could never come back. Even when his dad died, this guy wouldn't risk sneaking back in to town. Then there was Billy Palmieri, a small potatoes grifter and tinhorn man about town. Always into something, dibbing and dabbing. He'd take action on a baby's first word, how many Buicks would cross Larimer and Meadow in the next ten minutes. He had the disease big time. One weekend, he dangled out there too far—too boneheaded to lay off—and ended up having to split. A few months later the *Post-Gazette* gave him an inch in the obits: found dead in a Columbus hotel of natural causes, age forty-seven.

"What do you mean come after me?"

"I don't know what I mean. I know he won't let it slide."

Eugene reached into his fridge and pulled out two little High Lifes, opened one and slapped the other in front of me.

"Can you help me with this, Eug?"

"Whatta you want me to do? Here. See this beer. I can help you with this. Drink all you want. Get *stonare.* I can tell you to take care of that hand. But I can't help you with eleven grand. I'll advise Felix to be lenient. Once he stops throwing shit after I tell him about this."

I unscrewed the cap and drained the beer in one swallow. "If I tell you who it is, maybe you can help me."

"You want me to muscle this guy? No way. I'm not Luca Brasi, Georgie. I'm an electrician working a side job so I can knock down a little extra for my family. I'm no different than your old man. The danger shit does not interest me at all. That's Felix's department. And we don't want to know nothing about some third party. Your name is on this package, Cuz. Even if we knew who it was, it wouldn't matter. It's up to you, not us, to turn up the heat on whoever screwed you."

"What about my parents?"

"Nobody's gonna bother them. You got my guarantee on that."

"Eug, honest to God, what's going to happen? What's Felix liable to do?"

"You know, Georgie, I wouldn't want to set the line on that one. Felix is unpredictable. He likes you, but he has this thing about anyone getting over on him. No matter who it is. His own mother even. And he's nuts. We're talking about a hill of money here. I'm not saying something bad's going to happen. No *Godfather* shit, though it does happen. Whatever he comes up with, act like you love it. If the deal is you have to swab out his damn toilet, cut his toenails, you give him a big cheery *Amen.* Do not cross him. Do not mouth off. I'll do what I can. I can tell you one thing for absolute Mount Carmel tombstone sure: he will get compensation. No matter what. And with interest—for every minute it's late."

I looped by the Rosechilds again. Phil's car was no longer there. Obviously, he had just shot home for lunch. To get away for a couple hours. But, when I reached the pharmacy, it was still closed, and no sign of Phil.

I drove back to the Rosechilds and knocked on the door. Sterling answered, still in her nightgown and robe. Her hair was twisted up on top of her head. She held a butter knife.

"Giorgio," she sang and threw herself on me.

Something cracked in me, a tiny fault out of which things began to leak. Above all, I was scared nearly witless, and this fact terrified me more than my fear. I didn't know what to do. My first impulse was to cry—I wanted Sterling to hold me like she might a baby—yet something even more insistent had me by the throat: I wanted to punish Phil. Make him suffer.

"Is everything okay, George? You look a little stunned."

"I'm always stunned at the sight of you. I was just cruising by and decided to say hello."

"I'm glad you did. Come in and sit. I'll make you some toast. Is your hand better?"

"It's fine."

"Let me see it. It looks painful."

"It's fine. Where is everybody?"

"Mother and Daddy took off on some mysterious interlude. Daddy closed the store early, wonder of wonders, and announced that he was whisking Mother off for a romantic New Year's holiday. He said he told you all about it."

"Yeah, he told me," I lied. "I just didn't know they were leaving immediately."

"He was so cute. He wouldn't even stop for lunch. He made Mother drop everything and pack. They hustled out of here about a half hour ago."

"Where to?"

"Don't know. Ligonier, San Juan, Paris. It's impossible to say with him. Some later-to-be-disclosed destination. He wouldn't even say how long they'd be gone. They'll call me at Bryn Mawr. You haven't listened to a word I've said. Have you?"

"I gotta go, Sterling."

"You just got here. What's the matter?"

"Nothing. Really. I need to talk to you."

"Fine. Come on in the house and we'll talk." She took my left hand. "I'm right here."

"I can't now. I gotta go."

"Okay, George. I don't know what this is all about, but whatever it is, I can handle it. I assure you. So please don't spare me." She pulled her robe tight around her.

"Now's no good. Just promise me we'll talk. When I see you again?"

"Tonight then. Whenever you'd like. I can still count on a lift to the airport, can't I?" She smiled, but only halfheartedly.

I pulled her against me and held her for long time, my face in her hair, the bad hand throbbing, my mouth open as I swallowed the air surrounding her.

Chapter 24

When Crow is fast asleep, I slip out of bed, open my closet and inspect my former wardrobe: herringboned sports jackets, suede patches at the elbows; rack of neckties; and a row of monogrammed Brooks Brothers shirts my mother had washed by hand, on crippled legs, hung to dry even in the winter sun, then ironed and starched in the cellar: yellow, blue, pink, charcoal and burgundy pin-stripe, tattersall, blinding ecclesiastical white—shirts sharp enough to bring blood. My mother and father loved them as much as I did: my immaculate patrician destiny. Their dream was that I'd never raise a callous earning my daily bread. They busted their asses, did without, so I might dress like the heir of plenty.

I put on a blue oxford cloth shirt and a pair of khakis my mother had ironed and hung over cloth hangers for me over a year ago. The pants are way too tight. I pull up the zipper, but don't bother buttoning them. I get a pair of clean socks from my dresser and put on a pair of high top black Converse All-Stars from the back of the closet. Then I pad down the hall to look in on my dad: curled on his half of the bed, bedclothes pulled to his chin. His mouth is open, a slight buzzing snore, almost a *tick-tick-tick* as if secreted within him—among the sprung, mis-spliced wires, capped sockets, taped frays—has all along resided the mysterious circuitry of detonation. Losing his job, his son, his father, now his wife—the disintegration of East Liberty, the vertigo he fought dangling stories high from cranes on the open hearth at Edgar Thomson all those years.

I was seventeen—the age he was when he first punched in there—before I saw the steel mill where he broke his back and ate shit for every nickel he and my mother put by for my comfort. The occasion of my visit was anything but curiosity. I needed his car, a '64 two-toned rose and beige used Rambler, for the senior after-prom picnic. Still in the tuxedo my parents had rented for me, having never slept, hung-over, doped with lust, I dropped him off that foggy May morning at 7 A.M. in Braddock, named for General Edward Braddock, the commander of the British forces during The Seven Years War. Braddock had trekked there to engage in The Battle of the Monongahela on July 9, 1755. He was sixty years old, three years younger than my father the morning I left him to his forgettable toil. During the battle, General Braddock took a ball through the arm that entered his chest. He was carried, purportedly, to a spring where his grievous wounds were bathed—the site upon which the Edgar Thomson Works, the first steel mill robber baron Andrew Carnegie built in America, was erected in 1873. Four days later, Braddock died. With him was a twenty-three year old volunteer aide-de-camp, George Washington, who read from the Bible over the general's grave.

My father and I came into Braddock that morning over the long dizzying Rankin Bridge. Across the Monongahela was Kennywood, the legendary amusement park, where my mother, father and I went once a year for my school picnic. The wooden tracks of its roller coasters looped up over the dank horizon like entrails. Braddock was a depressed dying mill town, three bars in every block, streetlights turned on in the afternoon so the school kids could see their ways home through the ore dust. No one walked the streets. We passed Hotel Puhala, Local 1219, Good Shepherd Church, an Isaly's, the Greater Immanuel Apostolic Temple, a crude sign stenciled above its entrance: *You must be born again of water and spirit.*

Then the mill, rising in story after story of mizzly dank that corrugated the gray sky, long slender stacks spitting murk and intermittent jets of flame. It fumed along the river for what seemed miles—like a medieval city-sized forge, mist and smoke cloaking it, water slurrying down shafts of giant cooling towers: a pell-mell bric-a-brac of catwalks, gantries, parapets, bridges, cogs, pipes, armatures. Patched and soldered, its angles askew like a deranged child's play set. An occasional flair rose up from within, a radioactive glow and gray cloud weltering up as each ladled heat decanted on the open hearth and the slab casters keened. Snaking through the mill was an entire railroad.

Coal barges docked along the wharf. The river was green. Orange life preservers hung from the gunwales. Employee parking lots stretched upriver: thousand of cars, monuments to the product, desiccating in the caustic fallout. Lording over it all, like a teed gargantuan sooty golf ball, loomed an oval tower tattooed with the corporate logo: *USS.* Not a soul visible, neither outside nor within, around the compound a high rusty cyclone fence, then jagged frets of barbed wire.

Parts of the mill had been forgotten, abandoned. Shanties of rusted sheet metal where ghosts roamed. The mill was haunted. My dad had told me about the train yard where Joe Wolf still cried out for his severed legs, and the shrill weep of Little Annie who had fallen into a melt, and was subsumed in the molten spew, back when children labored chained to blast furnaces,

When I was a little boy, and declared I wanted to work in a steel mill like my father, he was adamant: I would never work in a mill. I was going to college. Period. I had been three months away from entering my freshmen year at Duquesne University that first and only time I glimpsed Edgar Thompson Steel Works, and witnessed my father pin on his millwright's badge and queue into the smoke through the big gates with the others stiffs. Working in a steel mill was the last thing I wanted to do. I hope back then that I knew enough to love my dear father, but I was certain he didn't know a blessed thing about what it meant to really be alive.

I sped away from him that morning without an ounce of regret, the fresh twenty he had just handed me wadded in my rented pants pocket, the radio blaring, the dial on the speedometer moving clockwise, faster and faster, dangerously so, as I hurtled away from him along the potholed road stretched in front of me and the mill train whistle moaned.

It's snowing hard. I see it from my parents' bedroom window beating in the halo around the streetlight at the mouth of Meadow Street Bridge. Snow falls over East Liberty like the weight of ancestry. It's as if my father never had a country, nor the words in any tongue to describe his anguish. I take the quilt folded at the bottom of the bed and lay it over him. Today has been a little too much for him. Yet, tomorrow, like Lazarus, he will rise at dawn, and by rote perform his offices and ablutions: the coffee, shave, scrape and shovel the Newport out of its snow bank, then drive to Saint Francis to spend the day with my mother, dragging with him that ever-ticking bomb, counting off the seconds until its ultimate revelation.

I throw on my dad's big mill parka, one of his tossle caps, and walk out the front door. Six inches of snow on the ground. It whips down, beautiful, soothing, around each snowflake an octave of light. I head back up Saint Marie toward Chookie's corner, past boarded and burnt-out houses, insane dogs flogging their chains to get at me. A car on blocks hulks at the curb in front of the Pezzulos' house. The DeLashes, the Raddis, Montes, Donatos, Taburrinos. All gone, the houses in ruins. Not a soul out, not a light on. Costanzo's is boarded, bright yellow crime scene tape Xed across its front door.

I trudge purposefully by it all until Saint Marie dead-ends at Highland, then make a right, and walk the abandoned avenue until I reach the Rosechild townhouse, quiet and dark, discreetly elegant in the picturesque snow. I creep around back to the patio doors and peer within. Phil, in his bath robe and pajamas, half-glasses clamped at the tip of his nose, in a little cone of light thrown by his reading lamp, a book on his blanket-covered knees, a shimmering tumbler of what can only be Beefeater's on the rocks, one of his hands floating through the air to *Tosca,* simpering in affirmation from the stereo. A perfect fire rolls in the hearth.

He's not changed a bit since last I saw him: standing behind the counter at his pharmacy, confessing he didn't have the $11,000 he owed me, the $11,000 that would have canceled out my own debt, the $11,000 that I stiffed the maniac, the Big Mustache, Felix Costa for—that sent me lamming out of Pittsburgh, crossed over in an instant to the underworld.

What should I do to Phil? Is it enough to kick the shit out of a meek aging pharmacist? Wreck his house? Burn it down? And then the pharmacy? I realize that I have come to exact revenge—which is precisely what men in my position do.

I stride to the door, turn the knob and walk in on Phil.

"George," he says, smiling, as if expecting me. "George. My God, I was hoping that was you. How very lovely to see you." On his feet, without hesitation, taking me in his arms. "George," he says again. "How very good to see you."

Despite everything, I find solace in his embrace, and it is only when he lets me go that I'm able to say, "Hello, Phil."

"Please sit, Son. What can I get you? Your usual?"

"Why not?" I want to be angry at him—I've come after all for reprisal—but when he totters to the bar in his worn-out backless leather slippers, smiling because I have appeared like a beloved son he figured never to see again, save in dream, my fondness for him overwhelms me. There is a great comfort seeing him reach for the glass, scoop a few cubes from the sterling ice bucket, pour the Beefeater, splash it with tonic, squeeze the lime, and drop it in—just the way he used to do it for me.

Out of nowhere springs Ira. He pads daintily across the bar, stops when he gets to me, and stares balefully. I won't be surprised if, in this vision, he'll speak, chide me for my absence. I pet his head, gently squeeze his ears. "Ira," I say. He meows that he's glad to see me and insists that I take him in my arms.

Phil hands me the glass. "How's that hand?"

"It's okay."

"I know a terrific hand man at Shadyside, and a hell of a plastic surgeon too. You let me know."

I stroke Ira. He stretches his head up under my chin.

"Ira isn't the only one who's missed you, George."

"I'm not George anymore." I take a gulp of the gin. I haven't tasted gin since the last time I stood in this living room where nothing's changed. The oriental carpets, leather sofas and love seats, the étagère with the Hummels and Italian glass, the leather bound Knight Shakespeares, Tiffany lamps, the plants and compotes of fresh flowers, exotic fish swimming in the aquarium, the Franz Kline above the mantle—the practiced opulence of the well-to-do. I think of my mother on the eighth floor of Saint Francis, my father swallowed by his lonesome bedclothes, that wedge of graying Romano in my parents' refrigerator. I begin to hate Phil all over again.

"Not George anymore?" he asks with concern. "What do you mean? Who are you?"

"I have an alias now, Phil. I'm on the run. Remember?"

"Sit." He sits down and motions to a chair on the other side of a little table where he's laid his big red book, *The Stories of John Cheever.*

I sit, sip my drink, and pet Ira.

"The extra weight becomes you," Phil says. "And the hair and the beard. You look so manly, like a lumberjack, a longshoreman."

"It's my working class blood, Phil. It finally bubbled to the surface. Besides, I wanted to look the part of a fugitive."

Phil peers at me querulously, as if he has no idea what I'm talking about. As if he's forgotten his epic betrayal. I feel myself fading away. I take a long swig of gin. Ira jumps from my lap, saunters to the hearth and lies on it, flickering in the flame-glow, as if playing out his part in the script.

"George, I still think there's a way to make this right."

"How's that, Phil? You wrecked my life. You devastated my parents."

"Am I the one who did that? Was it me?" Phil asks this as if he truly can't piece together what happened between us. Or perhaps he's merely being Socratic. I clench my fists. The bad hand twists into a paralytic claw.

"You fucking Judas," I say, trying not to scream.

"Please, George. You'll wake JoAnn."

"I don't give a shit. Get her down here. I have a few things to tell her."

"I could have pressed charges, George."

"Yeah, you could've. But you were protecting your own sorry ass. You weren't doing me any favors."

"I didn't want to hurt you. I felt—I still feel, I'll always feel—terrible about what happened." Tears well up in Phil's rheumy eyes. He sits forward in his chair, looking at me. He ages ten years in that moment and, again, I feel sorry for him.

"Jesus Christ, Phil. I thought we had something. I thought you cared about me."

"You broke Sterling's heart, George."

JoAnn suddenly calls from upstairs: "It's awfully loud down there, Phil."

"It's just the TV, Sweetheart. I'll turn it down." Phil gets up, flicks off Puccini, and turns on the television. Johhny Carson talking to Don Rickles. They're laughing hysterically.

"Don't you dare say that to me," I hiss, shooting to my feet.

"She waited and waited for you that night, New Year's Eve, to take her to the airport. She cried her eyes out."

"What did you tell her?"

"She planned to marry you."

"What the fuck did you tell her?"

"I told her absolutely nothing, nor JoAnn. They know what any nitwit might infer. You left an ample trail of circumstantial evidence. JoAnn and Sterling were devastated. I didn't have to fabricate. I didn't have to masquerade. I was befuddled and heartbroken myself. I huddled with JoAnn and Sterling and wept. Truly. I loved you. I thought of you as a son."

"I'm not your fucking son, Phil. Don't you dare insult my father, you fucking Judas, you wheedling weasly jagoff."

"Keep your voice down, George. Just calm down. Please."

I loom over Phil. "I want the fucking money, Phil. And I want the interest on top of it."

"I'm sure we can work it out. Please sit. Let me get us another drink."

I back off, but I do not sit. Phil shuffles by me, the glasses on his nose. The belt of his terrycloth robe trails him. His back is to me as he fixes the drinks. Through the French doors, leading to the Rosechild garden, the snow keeps coming, obscuring the angel poised in the middle of the frozen fountain.

"Where's Sterling?" I ask.

Phil turns, very deliberately walks to me, and hands me my drink. "She went to pieces."

"I don't want to hear about that. Where is she?"

"She had to be hospitalized."

"What are you talking about?"

He sits. "Please," motioning to the chair.

I sit.

"She had a breakdown. She's always been fragile in that regard. I know I mentioned that disastrous fling she had with that boy from Haverford. And then you disappeared, and the subsequent fallout: the robbery, the car."

"Where is she?"

"I can't tell you that. What I will tell you is that she dropped out of school, and is trying to get better."

"I want to know where she is."

"George, as you say, I'm a Judas, a wheedling jagoff. Correct? I accept that judgment. But what are you? Who are you are to march in here and expect a full accounting of Sterling after how you, not I, treated her. What's more, her image of you is rather tarnished, to say the least. Not only did you stand her up that night, causing her to miss her flight, but you turned out to be a criminal. A criminal, George. Crimes against her father, endangering her wellbeing, traumatizing her mother, sending her into a psychological tailspin she's yet to recover from. Crimes I covered up for you. What's more, she ended up telling us about what happened at the Ledges that night—the real story about how you injured your hand. So count yourself blessed. You've gotten off easy. I owe you nothing. Now get the hell out of here or I'll pick up this phone and call the police. Like I probably should have done the first time around."

"Because you were too much of a fucking coward."

"You're exactly right, my boy. A fucking coward. But, again, what does that make you?"

"You owed me eleven thousand dollars that some homicidal gangster was waiting for me to deliver to him. My ass was on the line."

"I remember well that afternoon in the pharmacy on December 31st when you shook that bottle in my face and threatened me. You seemed to me that day the homicidal gangster."

"I was doing you a favor placing those bets, allowing you into my confidence. And then you fucked me, left me in the shit and blew town. What did you suppose was going to happen when I showed up on payday eleven grand light? How did you expect me to react?"

"I will always be sorry for that. But I'd say I did plenty of favors for you as well. Plenty. I opened up a number of doors, formerly closed to you, with even more ready to swing open at my behest. JoAnn and I were truly delighted at the prospect of you as a son-in-law. As an heir. So, in the vocabulary of the wager—in which you so expertly schooled me—I think we're looking at a push."

I'm dizzy, maybe from the two glasses of gin. But in truth from the narrative Phil has laid out. My powers of rationalization are so profound, it's been so easy to brand him the villain. His epic betrayal: leaving me owing thousands of dollars to the bookies. But what I have done? Stolen and pillaged, destroyed my parents and Sterling, threw away the better life that I had worked so hard for, had so narcissistically mythologized. I ran. I am a coward, no better than Phil.

Greed. Greed all along, my tragic flaw, that doomed me. My rapacious lust for fame and fortune, the ultimate condescension I bore for my ancestry, for the people who whelped and nurtured me, who traded their futures for mine. Greed that made me dupe Phil in the first place, moving those lines around so I could make a killing at his expense. In truth, he has no idea what a lowlife I am. Hoisted by my own petard. Shakespearean tragedy East Liberty style.

"Right now, George, you don't have a leg to stand on. My story is air tight. I'm an elderly effeminate man, George. You scared me. I hurried home, and spirited off my wife to the airport. We were in West Palm Beach by nightfall. Not the first time I had surprised her on a whim with such a junket. When we returned, I discovered that the store had been broken into and robbed, the pharmacy vehicle stolen, and you disappeared. Thank you, by the way, for disappearing. You did all the work for me. A year ago, perhaps, people might have listened to your side of the story—the handsome, thoroughly groomed, charming soon-to-be-Yalie. That cachet, however, has evaporated. You're nothing but cheap East Liberty dago trash—what you were all along—and you very much look the part. I am sorry, morbidly so, for my part in this, but I'd say our business has once and for all concluded. Your disappearance will forever remain a mystery—just one of those things. It doesn't take long for the police to close the file on the likes of you."

"I have to see Sterling." Framed photographs of her perch all over the room.

"That can't happen, George. That simply can't happen."

I'm afraid I might begin to cry, and beg Phil to forgive me, to *please please* welcome me back to the graces of the Rosechild family and its burnished life. It's as if I'm hurtling at unfathomable speed down the shaft of a reversed telescope, my future, my past, collapsing into the vanishing point of regret, Phil growing smaller and smaller, more remote, as I dwindle and finally evanesce into the snowstorm behind me.

"Godammit, I am going to see her, and you're going to tell me where she is."

"Phil," JoAnn calls from upstairs.

Phil smiles at me and shakes his head, then walks to the bar, picks up the phone and dials seven digits: the cops. He's looking at the TV, at Rickles and Carson laughing their asses off. He drinks from his glass as if I'm not there.

My bad hand snakes out, and clamps his throat just as he is about to speak into the receiver. His face transmogrifies, as if for the first time he recognizes that he has trifled with the wrong person, that privilege will not save him from vendetta. He wants to beg me for mercy, charm his way out this, but my mutant fingers embed like fangs into his windpipe, and all he can do is gasp. He wraps both his hands around my hand and wrist. His tongue lolls out, his eyes mute as doorknobs, his spectacles miraculously in place, his vision pristine. I shove him back against the bar and bow him over it, pin his head against the zinc bar-top, and squeeze.

His back is breaking. I feel through his jugular its tensile yield. His vertebrae pop like buttons stretched across a fat belly. But, in a feat of gymnastics, he swings his legs up off the carpet and twines them like a lover around my waist. He's lost his slippers. His feet are tiny, sheathed in black silk socks motifed with jolly gold whales. He still holds the receiver, through which I hear the dispatcher saying, *Hello, hello.* There's no way now to read his mind. The portals to his soul are fogged over. He wants to crack that black phone across my skull. Yet he doesn't have the wind for it. *Hello, hello.* He can speak to the law only in the Morse code of his last clicking breaths.

Surely used to prank calls, the line suddenly goes dead. Maybe I'll wrap the phone cord around his neck and bash out his brains with the phone, but this strikes me as too derivative, too cliché. My old inquisitor, the helmed beefeater, clutching his halberd, occupies in jaunty arabesque his label on the gin bottle stationed at Phil's head. His idiotic outfit, in motley, the crinkled sash, the fey beard. He's the perfect companion for Phil—two pretentious fops tethered to the jug.

With my left hand I grab the fifth and funnel it into Phil's purple mouth, pour a farewell nightcap down his throat, drowning him in the hair of the dog. Poetic justice. Irony at every turn.

"*Saluto,* Phil," I whisper. "*Cento anni.*" A hundred years.

His little feet fall limp and he slides off the slab, lies there on the gorgeous Oriental in his PJs, still holding the phone. Carson and Rickles crack up. They just can't get over how dead the pharmacist is. *Jesus Christ, a dead pharmacist,* Rickles blubbers. It's the funniest thing they've ever seen. They slap each other on the back. They weep. They howl.

When I reach the Rosechilds', it's late. A golden wreath hangs on the front door. Snow garlands the threshold. The townhouse is dark, not the faintest glimmer of a light. Phil and JoAnn have gone to bed. I gaze up at their bedroom window, then to the one on the other side of the second story—Sterling's room. The panes are black. She's gone. Graduated. Perhaps in New York, acting. My life with Sterling is beyond remote—as if in my yearning I have dreamed her, and in the bargain dreamed myself worthy of someone like her. The ache as I stare at the Rosechild house, realizing that I'm still irreconcilably in love with Sterling, a figment of my longing, makes me remember why I'm here: to make Phil Rosechild pay. But it seems the only vengeance I'm capable of exacting is against myself. I pack a snowball to fling at the house, but in my bad hand it crumbles and disappears in the endless white thrall floating down from Heaven.

Chapter 25

I eased the Newport up to the wall of frozen gray slush at the curb in front of my parents' house. Big flakes whipped in the headlights. I switched off the ignition and looked around the street, dim and muted by the snow. Porchlights and lit windows here and there, the Dolce house among them. A house

I would have to forget. Maybe that had been my plan all along. It was only the ninth day of winter. Monday night. An eternity till spring.

I left the $1800.00 in an envelope, sealed it, scrawled *Mom and Dad* across it with a yellow *U.S. Steel* pencil I found in the glove compartment. In there also was a small two-paneled brass Saint Christopher icon, a cross between the panels. The first panel had gone green over the face of the Christ Child who sat on the shoulders of Christopher as the saint navigated them across a roiling stream. The second panel was a compass, the four directions emblazoned with circled capital letters: *N, E, S, W;* and in its middle the prayer: *Behold Christopher, then go your way in safety.*

I closed my eyes, spun my forefinger around the outer rim of the compass and let it stop: *South.* "Okay," I whispered. I placed the Christopher back in the glove compartment. I left my keys on the seat beside the envelope, got out, locked the car, and trudged up the street into the rushing snow.

It was black night and snowing hard when I reached the pharmacy and opened the front door with the set of keys Phil had given me. I flicked on the lights. Pills still littered the floor. The tipped gin bottle lay on the counter. The beafeater, on his back, leered up at me. I grabbed the flashlight behind the counter, doused the lights, and opened the register. There were six twenties, five tens, five fives, and seventeen ones. I stashed the bills in my shirt. Also, in the register, was a key on a Mercedes-Benz fob. It opened a cabinet that housed narcotics and other lethal drugs.

I dragged the light across the shelves behind the counter, found nothing that interested me, then hurried into the back room. I opened the cabinet: Morphine, Demerol, Dilautid, Cocaine. I placed each jar into an empty packing carton. From the open shelves, I scooped up what I recognized as barbiturates, amphetamines, various painkillers and dumped them in on top of the others. For a minute I stood there, shaking, resisting the urge to bust up the place. But my hand hurt too much, and I felt pushed to get this business done.

I dropped the flashlight, locked the pharmacy behind me, set the carton on the sidewalk, unlocked the Vega and began hacking the car out of its frozen caul. I placed the box in the front seat, then edged in beside it. The ignition wheezed again and again, fluttered, then shuddered to life as the gas finally ferreted through the line and sniffed the spark.

Down on the corner, a flaming trash drum—my dad called them salamanders—spat its bewildering light across the shaggy coats of Dave Mazzotti, two other guys, and a girl. A curtain of steel draped and padlocked Chookie's front door and windows. I noticed for the first time that a few of the houses in the block were vacant, *FOR SALE* signs staggering in the snowy front yards. One house, the Umbertinos', had been gutted by fire, its brick face scarred and blackened.

I pulled the driver's side up to the salamander and cranked down the window. The barrel's heat hit me in the face. The people around it looked up.

"Dave," I called.

"Who's there?" Dave called back.

"George Dolce."

"Hey, Georgie boy," Dave laughed, tripping to the curb. "What happened to you, driving this punk car? Careful. You'll get fingered for a working slob. Bandaged hand too. Where's the princess?"

"Get in."

Dave stepped around the car and got in. "Holy shit," he said when he saw what was in the carton. "The prodigal has returned."

"I have to unload this stuff, Dave. How much will you give me for it?"

Dave ripped through the box. He lit his lighter and read each label. "This is a righteous load of contraband, Georgie boy."

"How much?"

Dave smiled. "I'll give you twenty bucks for the box."

"C'mon, Dave. It's worth a fortune."

"Maybe you can't tell by looking at me, but I don't have a fortune. I got twenty bucks and maybe with my associates"—he nodded toward the salamander—"I can pull together a little more. Why don't you drive across the bridge and sell it to the spoons?"

"That's what I'll do."

"Yeah, do that. They'll be reading about you in the morning paper: East Liberty Messiah martyred on Larimer Avenue."

"Alex was the messiah," I said.

"Yep. You remember the time the three of us busted the taillights out of those junkers parked in the lot behind the Esso station? We thought all that colored glass were jewels. And here you are with jewels again. If I thought I could scrape myself back up off the sidewalk, I would fall to my knees, and hail your bad ass."

Dave stared straight ahead at the plummeting snow. The windshield wipers creaked. Steam rose off the hood. Dave stunk: days and days of the same clothes, his unbathed body, ratty hair and beard, his spirit secreted so far under the compost that it had begun to rot too. Scarred puffy face, nose running, lips blue.

He turned to me: "You know me and Alex were as smart as you any day. Maybe not me, but Alex was. He idolized you. Always said Georgie's gonna be somebody some day. Well, that's enough sentiment for now. I got to get back to wasting my existence. Time is precious. There's not much in the way of life expectancy for young men of my pedigree. Alex understood that perfectly. Sure you don't want to part with a little of this? For old time's sake?"

"Take it."

"Huh?"

"Take what you want."

"I got twenty lousy bucks, Georgie."

"Forget the money. Think of it as a belated Christmas present."

Dave flicked the lighter, dipped in and filled his pockets with Morphine and Dilautid. "I was never much for speed and tranks. Housewife shit." He looked at me for a long time. "What kind of mess you got yourself into, Georgie?"

"A big one."

"I'm sorry. We could have been better friends. I always cared about you."

Dave wrapped me up in his arms and held me for a few seconds, then he lumbered out of the car.

"Here," I said. "Take this too." I yanked out the envelope with the plane ride and Super Bowl ticket in it, and handed it to Dave.

"What's this?"

"A little surprise. Something to remember me by."

"I don't need anything special to remember you, Georgie-boy." He smiled. "But thanks. Happy New Year."

"Happy New Year, Dave."

"This isn't really the dark side, Georgie, like the nuns used to say. It's just before the light. The blinding light."

I drove over the Meadow Street Bridge, the bridge from which Alex had leapt into the Hollow, and turned left at Larimer Avenue. Not a soul was out. The wind had picked up, rifling the traffic lights and street signs. Snow roared across the avenue.

I turned at Joseph Street. Still no sign of anyone. If I could find Kevin Bond, I'd give him something from the box. Then I spied him, angling out between two houses, breaking into a run, a big coat flapping about him. I sped up, skidded into the curb. The figure disappeared. Probably just a ghost, homeless, freezing.

It couldn't have been Kevin anyway. His legs hadn't worked in years. Several of the houses on Joseph were boarded up, the Bonds' among them. Isaac had died a few years back, my dad one of the pallbearers.

Kevin. My mother, when she'd heard he'd been shot, that he was a junky, said he'd be better off dead. They hadn't expected him to live. Ever since I could remember, she had predicted her own early death. *I'll be dead,* she'd declare, as if all she wanted was to have it over with, get all the bullshit behind her since there was always so much of it ahead. She just wanted to go to sleep. Like Alex. Like Dave. For the first time, I knew what she meant.

I turned the Vega around and retraced my route, scattering out my open window as I went the contents of the carton beside me. Like an angel, a small God, I left in my wake a trail of painkillers, blessed little pills and powders dropped in the snow, taking flight in the wind, coating Larimer Avenue with numbness and euthanasia and finally sleep. Until it was all gone. All over.

With one hand, I nosed the Vega south through the last streets of my deserted childhood—the snow flinging itself against the impervious earth—then on into downtown Pittsburgh where skyscrapers mooned above massive bridges levitating over the three freezing rivers commingling into ice. Across the Fort Pitt Bridge, through the Fort Pitt Tunnels. Inside the southbound tunnel, it was suddenly dry and white. The future whispered. Behind me the past had already built its wall of indifference.

On the other side of the tunnels, I hit a blizzard. One passable lane. Ten to fifteen miles per hour. Cars littered the highway, more and more at each milepost. I knew to pull over. My hand was bleeding. I could barely see the road. Instead I accelerated, the Vega fishtailing, tires lathing ice, hissing, the road skidding ever south: where there existed a sun of thaw and everlasting, poinsettias burning wild red on its green breast, Sterling flaming miraculously among them like Saint Mary, assuring me that I had been forgiven a thousand times. It was safe to come back: every dream bled out of me would be returned. In the life of the world to come.

About the Author

JOSEPH BATHANTI, born and raised in Pittsburgh, is a professor of creative writing at Appalachian State University, as well as the former poet laureate of North Carolina. He is the author of eight books of poetry and two novels, among other works. His novel *Coventry* won the 2006 Novello Literary Award, and his 2014 collection of personal essays, *Half of What I Say Is Meaningless,* earned the 2012 Will D. Campbell Award for Creative Nonfiction.